INVADERS!

Where the altar had been was rubble. On top of the rubble was the abbot. His nose was seared off and his belly provided the home for a Saxon spear. Other spears, axes, and crossbow bolts jutted at various angles from the corpses lying amid the debris.

"Why?" Christopher asked. "Why?"

Baines held him by the shoulders. "They want the land. They want what is ours." He picked up the sword. "Today we are *both* knights."

Christopher held up the battle-ax until it touched Baines's sword. "And may we send the animals who

SQUIRE

BOOK ONE OF THE
SQUIRE TRILOGY

PETER TELEP

HarperPrism
An Imprint of HarperPaperbacks

This is a work of fiction. The characters, incidents, and
dialogues are products of the author's imagination and are
not to be construed as real. Any resemblance to actual events
or persons, living or dead, is entirely coincidental.

HarperPaperbacks *A Division of* HarperCollins*Publishers*
10 East 53rd Street, New York, N.Y. 10022

Cover art by Tim White

First printing: May 1995

Printed in the United States of America

HarperPrism is an imprint of HarperPaperbacks.
HarperPaperbacks, HarperPrism, and colophon are trade-
marks of HarperCollins*Publishers*

❖ 10 9 8 7 6 5 4 3 2 1

SQUIRE
is for Christopher Schelling

ACKNOWLEDGMENTS

My friend, best man, and agent Robert Drake provided criticism and encouragement, guiding me from outline to final draft. I know of no other agent who is as talented, timely, and hardworking. I am a better writer because of him.

I am indebted to my editor, the eponymous Christopher Schelling, for not only purchasing the Squire trilogy, but for his tenacity, his patience, his kindness, and support. Christopher boosted my confidence and made my first experience with a professional editor a memorable one.

David Hamilton and Joan Vander Putten workshopped the manuscript, each offering critiques that were extremely helpful. David gave me many suggestions on how to solve plot problems. Joan provided grammatical help, a fresh point of view, and listened to my long-distance lamenting without hanging up. For all their help, I am grateful.

Vince Clemente, Harlan Ellison, George Lucas, Joel Rosenberg, Lucius Shepard, Sandra Watt, and Timothy Zahn all inspired me through their work or words.

Mom and Dad. Thanks for the obvious. And the obscure. And everything that lies between. I love you both.

Lastly, to Nancy, who, on August 21, 1993, made me the happiest man this side of Camelot.

AUTHOR'S NOTE

The Arthurian legend contains many anachronisms and contradictions that are maddening to writers who wish to be technically and historically accurate. While the military strategy, accouterments, and politics were carefully researched, some were borrowed from other time periods for dramatic effect. Indeed, the description of King Arthur as "a knight in shining armor" is a misnomer. In the 6th century, the time Arthur supposedly lived, he would have worn leather plates. Yet if one settles a suit of 14th-century armor on the son of Pendragon he is restored to his venerable image. That aside, lean back, quibble if you must, but most of all, I hope you enjoy the story.

PETER TELEP

SQUIRE

PROLOGUE

Cornelia's cry of labor was carried on a breeze which swept down Leatherdressers' Row in the village of Shores, South Cadbury, England. It floated over the cobbled street past the densely built, gable-roofed houses with their backyard gardens. Inside one of these workshop tofts, Cornelia lay on a coarse woolen blanket spread out over a trestle bed. The stench of saddles from the nearby bench was tight in her nostrils, and one of the midwives hovering over her signaled for another of the unglazed windows to be thrown open, the last.

Sanborn, Cornelia's husband, wiped perspiration from his hands onto his woad blue tunic, then complied.

Cornelia arched her back and moaned, this time louder and much longer.

Sanborn turned from the open window and stroked his beard with a hand as rough as the leather with which he worked. "Is she dying?" he demanded.

The midwives, in their somber workaday kirtles, their hands covered with the ointment they rubbed on Cornelia's belly to ease her travail, ignored him. Finally, one answered, "No." The hag was curt and kept her eyes focused on her task.

Sanborn was supposed to be excluded from the room, but insisted on being present, and this had annoyed the midwives; their rudeness was expected.

Another contraction made Cornelia call out, "Sanborn!"

He craned his head as his name escaped their house and village and floated on the wind toward the river Cam.

Not far from Shores, a group of knights stood before a moss-covered rock. Embedded in this rock was the perfect sword Excalibur. The legend was known throughout the land: *Whosoever shall draw this sword from the stone is rightwise king of England.*

Lord Uryens of Gore, surrounded by a feeble, wiry abbot and the other kings of this Easter day tournament, locked his hands onto the hilt of Excalibur and heaved, murmuring for St. Michael and St. George to give him the potence to pull this sword into the open air, where all might see and recognize him as king, wielder of Excalibur, of power. Tremors developed in Uryens's arms, then woke into violent shakes. A bellow formed at the back of his throat; it exploded from his lips with such force it startled the abbot, who fell backward onto the damp grass. The cry weaved its way through bark and gorse shrubs toward the calm waters of the Cam.

Uryens released his grip on Excalibur, stood back, and drew in a deep breath.

"Enough of this game, Uryens!" shouted Lot of Lowthean as he stepped up before the rock. "Behold the true king of England."

Lot was much younger than Uryens, his beard sparse, his hazel eyes wide and determined. What escaped his lips were not murmurous prayers to saints, but a growing bawl, which evolved to a great crescendo as he tugged.

The abbot was back on his feet and asking God to grant them a king for this divided, dying land.

A final roar blew out of Lot as he fell away in failure.

Disillusioned, the lords halfheartedly continued

their tournament for the right at another chance to pull Excalibur from the stone.

Nearby, a young squire searched in vain for his brother's sword, but discovered it stolen. There was no time to find another. Innocently enough, he approached Excalibur. The squire's hands were drawn to the hilt. There was a force unknown to the natural world between his flesh and the metal. His fingers touched the sword, and a surge, as if from the core of the earth, rose through Excalibur and into the squire.

One of the midwives cried, "The child is coming."

Sanborn stepped closer, cast his shadow over his wife and the soaked blanket. The nearest hag pushed him away as a broken sigh came forth from Cornelia's lips.

The squire tightened his grip on the sword with only the simple notion to withdraw it to supply his need. He lifted, and as he did, the head of Cornelia's baby freed itself from her womb. Then, as easily as the sword slipped from its stone prison, the rest of the child's body entered the world. The newborn took his first breath and exhaled a cry.

Those near the knoll turned to see the squire with the sword impossibly raised in his hands, and they too cried out—in disbelief. The abbot approached, then fell to his knees. Lot followed, ripping off his helmet as his jaw went slack. Uryens, accompanied by others, stared on, astonished.

Inside the workshop, the heavier of the midwives tied the baby's umbilical cord and cut it at four fingers' length. She washed the boy and rubbed him all over with salt, then gently cleansed his palate and gums with honey, to give him an appetite. She dried him in fine linen and wrapped him tightly in swaddling bands.

The pain gone, Cornelia's expression was soft as she received her son. For a newborn he was strangely peaceful in her arms, entering his new world with certainty, and imminence.

PART ONE

CHRISTOPHER OF SHORES

1 Sir Hasdale, lord of the castle of Shores, rode down Leatherdressers' Row under sunbeams flickering with dust motes, some of the beams playing off his short, golden locks and olive-tinged armor. He stopped before the toft of Sanborn and Cornelia. From within the small house, Sanborn heard the lord's approach and came out to greet the knight as he dismounted from his courser. Their embrace was long, nurtured by a lifetime of business and friendship.

Hasdale pulled back. "The abbot tells me you have a son." Sanborn nodded proudly. Hasdale continued, "I have another saddle order for you, and if the work is fine, I'll pay you double."

Sanborn grinned. "Lord, you know the work is always fine."

"Yes," Hasdale said, "I do."

"Thank you." Sanborn knew the money was for the newborn. Hasdale would not make an open donation, for Sanborn would have rejected it. Thus was the little game Hasdale played. Sanborn felt better about taking the money this way. He gestured to the doorway. "Cornelia has warm pottage and beer."

"I can't. More orders to place. And as my sister begs, a wife to find."

The men chuckled. Hasdale climbed back up on his war-horse, adjusted his feet in the stirrups. "My regards to Cornelia and your son. Have you named him?"

"Christopher," Sanborn answered.

"The patron saint of travelers. I could use him." Hasdale waved as he trotted off.

The smell of Cornelia's mud oven at the back of the house beckoned to Sanborn. He went inside, walked through the hall, and put a loving hand on his wife's shoulder. She turned from her stove and kissed him. The pottage was not yet ready, so he moved into the yard behind the house. He checked the garden, then the pegged-out tanned hides from which he made his saddlery. He fed the chickens and the sow, then returned inside. Christopher lay quiet in the crib Sanborn had made for him.

"I tell you, Cornelia, that child is a watcher."

"He'll be a great craftsman someday. An apprentice is a watcher, yes?" Cornelia asked.

"I feel like he's studying me already."

After breakfast Sanborn took off his tunic and settled down at his bench with a hammer. He smoothed the leather covering of a saddle peak over its wooden frame, which was held firm in a vise. He grumbled a bit about the shape of the frame that the joiner had made for him. Though Sanborn called himself a saddler, and was a member of the saddler's guild, he did not make the complete article from start to finish at his own bench. It would be a serious breach of the municipal bylaws, as well as a crime shocking to all right-thinking persons, for a craftsman to stray beyond his own craft. *With the poor work this joiner does, I've mind to,* Sanborn thought.

A completely furnished jousting saddle, such as the one Sir Hasdale had ordered from Sanborn, called for the cooperation of four different crafts. First the joiner made the wooden frame. Then Sanborn would cover it with leather and do all the tooling and stamping called for by the design. A painter would display the personal arms of the customer on the saddle. Finally, a loriner would provide anything made from steel that went with the saddle, such as the bit and stirrups. Sanborn had had many a shouting match with sloppy painters and loriners, although the joiner was the headache this morning.

Silently, Christopher watched as his father mumbled to himself and worked.

2 By the time he was in his fifth year, Christopher had examined every inch of the workshop, explored every mousehole, leather scrap, and window corner. Next he covered the backyard, occasionally trampling the vegetable garden and hearing his father cry out in that voice which sounded as if it came from the sky. That voice struck fear in him, but he was forever lured to the garden—forever lasting about a month.

On one particular sun-soaked afternoon, Christopher stood in the road.

The road! What a place. Visions of silvery men, visiting with great animals whose feet were as big as he. Sounds of hawkers and laughs, compliments, and arguments. Smells of fresh-killed rabbit hung over the backs of horses. Things happened in the road. Different every day. He had to be out there. Had to.

"Christopher! Get out of the road!" he heard his mother shout as she came through the front door to fetch him. As always, she pulled him inside by the shirtsleeve. When his mother returned to spinning with her distaff, Christopher slipped outside again.

In the distance he heard the clomping of a horse, and the shouts of people as they hustled out of the way. It was a black mare running wild through the streets, saddleless, its origin a mystery. The steed was well up the road and Christopher moved over the stone to the middle for a better look at her. The animal was perfect as she came toward him. He was the only one in the road, squaring off with the horse, small, feeble, in his little tunic and breeches, smiling innocently at the fiery eyes of the dark charger. He heard his front door open, turned to see his mother cry out to him, then he looked back at the steed.

The horse was less than fifty yards away, thirty, twenty, ten. In his mind's eye Christopher saw the animal leap high in the sky, blocking out the sun as it passed over him. He remained in the road, thinking it would happen.

But the animal stopped dead in the street before him as voices around Christopher hushed. It was as if the horse had somehow known that it was not Christopher's time to die and could not trample him.

He saw his mother bite her lip as she came, scooped him up in her arms. The horse drifted on, and Christopher kept his gaze locked on it as long as he could before Cornelia shut the door, and they were inside.

Christopher didn't know why, but after his mother wiped away her tears, she gazed upon him a long time, an odd look clouding her face.

Later, he ambled into the backyard garden, sat down, and yanked out some turnips.

3

The old Roman fortress stood, waiting for Christopher.

A great banquet was to be held at the castle of Sir Hasdale, a celebration of his marriage to Madam Fiona, daughter of Conway, a great knight banneret in Hasdale's army. All inhabitants of the village were invited to attend. The thought of visiting the castle for the first time struck Christopher like lightning, causing his eyes to gleam like sunlit gems.

The great castle climbed into the sky, as if providing a stone-piled path to the heavens. Christopher had only seen the wide gray walls from a distance, had only heard the wondrous tales of what was behind the stone, what magic, what miracles, what excitement.

Five years had passed since the idea of visiting the castle had first taken root in him. Now that Christopher was ten, the dream fruited into reality.

As he pulled on his finest tunic, he heard the voices of his father and mother from downstairs. Cornelia asked Sanborn how she looked. Sanborn only grunted his approval and Cornelia became agitated. Christopher hustled from the loft and down the stairs to meet them.

"I'm ready. Come on. Let's go. Let's go!" Christopher had trouble remaining in one spot.

"You will behave yourself today," his mother warned.

"You represent a young, future member of the saddler's guild, son. And you must act accordingly."

"Can we go now?" Christopher pleaded.

They all left the house and were joined by the other leatherdressers, who were also donning their brightest, most ornate clothes. Knots of craftsmen talked and laughed in anticipation of the great feast. Christopher could already smell what must be pig cooking on a spit, its sweet scent luring him forward ahead of his parents and the others. He forgot about his feet, not feeling the ground under him as his eyes and nose seemed to lift him.

"Christopher. Don't run!" Cornelia ordered.

Christopher didn't see the large stone that cropped out from the road, waiting for his sandal.

And down he went.

Cornelia hurried through her friends and neighbors to her son.

Christopher rolled over on his side. There was a

stinging sensation in his arm; he looked up at it. He'd ripped his tunic and scraped the skin beneath. It was not a serious injury, but the tunic . . .

Cornelia was flustered. "I told you not to run!"

"I'm sorry. My tunic. Look at it."

"Let's go back. I'll patch that arm and see what we can find for you to wear."

Christopher felt relieved that the scolding would not continue, and a few moments later they were approaching the moat around the castle, Christopher feeling the itchy wool of his second-best tunic.

Everyone else from Shores was inside, which to Christopher was good. It was as if he would be making some kind of entrance. The notion made him hold his head higher. As he gripped his mother's hand and they set foot onto the large, worn timbers of the drawbridge, he studied the exterior of the castle close up for the first time.

The curtain walls were immensely thick, with four round corner turrets and small windows which, on the lower levels near him, were no more than slits for defense. Christopher thought he could see eyes blinking behind those slits but he couldn't be sure. They passed under the two D-shaped towers that made up the gatehouse and emerged into the outer bailey, a wide, open courtyard. Here was a stone path which would lead them to the keep, that massive square tower in the rear of the castle, where the festivities were to be held. On their way toward the keep, Christopher watched knights practicing with wooden swords in the exercise yard, the scene causing splinters of awe to work their way under his skin. *Throw me a sword and I'll join you!* he thought. He saw pigs and goats milling in the stables, saw an armorer outside his stone hut cleaning some rusted link-mail with sand and vinegar as two apprentices fitted a knight with a mended helmet and newly sharpened spatha. He watched as two old men dug weeds out of a long, narrow herb garden that was only a few yards away from the lord's precious beehives. The men sang a song above the buzzing of bees, a tune that could also be heard escaping from the open windows of the keep ahead. Minstrels played along, and the anticipation reached a breaking point within Christopher. They drew closer to another, smaller moat which surrounded the keep, and mounted the drawbridge which would take them over it. He looked up. This was the tower he'd seen numerous times from his own backyard. But now it was very close. He nearly fell onto his back, dizzy with its ominous, overbearing presence. He shifted his gaze down as they passed through the stone tunnel that opened into the inner bailey. Here were the kitchen, granary, and a few other storerooms. For defense, the entrance to the keep was by a stone staircase leading to the second floor of a forebuilding on the side of the great tower. If an enemy entered the forebuilding, he would be assailed by warriors from above and below. Christopher played out a siege on the keep in his head, imagined himself leaping down on the barbarian attackers and drawing the blood of victory. Another image shattered the daydream.

The welcoming arms of a pear-shaped abbot stretched out toward Christopher and Cornelia as they reached the entrance to the forebuilding. The red-nosed churchman hugged Cornelia and then Christopher. The abbot reeked of something. A second and Christopher knew what it was. Ale.

As they moved into the relative darkness of the alcove, Christopher whispered to his mother, "The abbot is drinking ale."

Cornelia put her index finger to her lips. "Shush."

They stepped into the sparsely furnished garrison quarters, smiled at a small group of fighters who were removing their link-mail, then moved quickly

toward another staircase, which would take them up
to the great hall.

When they came from the shadows of the stairwell
Christopher could not believe his eyes. All of it hit
him at once—and it was almost too much to take.
The great hall. He had never been inside a room this
large, with so many great wooden beams and rafters.
The chapel he had considered big, but it was nothing
compared to this. The great hall: the center of all
domestic life in the castle. He moved forward with
his mother, breathing in the place.

On each side were trestle tables whose benches
were filled with villagers Christopher recognized.
Roasted duck and pig, steamed vegetables, and
freshly brewed ale were abundant, and many hands
lifted to many mouths, making the food vanish
quickly. The music blared, the minstrels danced and
played around the stone-circled cookfires in the center of the floor, and the melodies and smoke
escaped through a rectangular hole in the ceiling.
Directly ahead, upon a high dais, a long, white-
clothed table provided a place for Lord Hasdale;
Fiona, who had not appeared yet; the steward; and
the other banner and bachelor knights of the castle.
Pages dodged people in order to refill elaborately
decorated drinking jugs and restock plates around
the high table. Up above, standards draped down
the walls, and a large escutcheon displaying
Hasdale's coat of arms hung centered among the
flags. Christopher admired the many colors of the
standards as a tug on his arm from Cornelia sent his
gaze off in another direction.

"There's your father," Cornelia said.

From the very first trestle table, Sanborn waved
them over. Christopher and his mother threaded their
way through the crowd and were seated. A portly, gray-
bearded man, his soft-faced wife, and their son, who
looked about Christopher's age, soon joined them.

"Cornelia, Christopher, this is Lord Heath, brother of the steward, his wife Neala, and their son Baines."

Christopher and his mother bowed their heads politely, then smiled.

The boy, Baines, tugged on the veil covering his mother's hair. "I'm off to the garderobe."

Neala understood. "Hurry back. You don't want to miss the toast."

Baines nodded, then looked at Christopher. "Want to come?"

Christopher looked to his mother for approval. The expression he desired appeared on Cornelia's face. But she added a warning to the look. "Don't make me come and find you."

The two boys hurried off as the adults exchanged smiles.

Christopher and Baines weaved their way through the merry villagers and ducked down a hall which quickly gave way to a side room that was the garderobe. Three men sat, elbows on their bare thighs, lined up on a long, benchlike seat, under which was a hollow stone base that resembled a rectangular well. If it had not been for the open window above the men, the stench would have been unbearable. As it was, Christopher and Baines held their noses. Relieving oneself would not be a very pleasant occasion today with all the villagers here.

"I can wait," Baines said, grimacing. "Come on."

"Where are we going?"

Baines was already on his way out, not answering Christopher's question.

When they came back into the great hall, Baines asked, "Have you ever been here before?"

"No."

"Then I have something to show you."

"But the toast . . . "

Baines smiled. "You'll be glad you missed the toast for this." Baines gestured with his head toward a tunnel exit guarded by two sentries on the opposite side of the great hall.

Christopher became anxious. Baines was a trouble-maker and Christopher was about to let himself be lured into trouble not of his own making. But no one would believe that after they were caught. If he followed Baines now, it would have to be of his own accord.

"What great wonder are you going to show me?" Christopher needed to know, needed to make the decision easier.

"One such as you have never seen. I vow you'll be pleased." Baines's words, wink, and smile convinced Christopher to go.

"It better be."

And they strolled their way across the hall, snatching up bits of meat from the plates of pages making their rounds. They chewed hungrily over the rising din as more people drew into the hall. Baines stepped up to the first sentry.

"I was told by my uncle, Steward Farrel, that both you men must report to the garderobe at once. There is a disturbance there."

The sentries shared concerned looks, and the one near Baines said, "On our way." The men abandoned their posts.

Baines's grin was dripping with self-satisfaction.

Christopher was impressed.

The two slipped down the narrow tunnel, ascended a short staircase, and shadow-hugged the walls as they neared another room, the lord's solar. This was Hasdale's bedroom, warmer and more comfortable than any other room in the castle. They heard women talking and giggling inside. The boys found another staircase leading to a balcony overlooking the solar. They went up, crept to the edge of the wooden railing, and slowly, furtively, peered over.

Christopher's jaw dropped. "Ohhhhhh . . . "

Hasdale's pregnant sister Alina sat in a window alcove, using the good light for her embroidery. But it was not she at whom Christopher looked.

Directly below him, two other damsels were preparing a bath for Fiona, filling a wooden vat with buckets of water. They laughed over a joke Christopher could not quite hear. Again, they were not the object of Christopher's fascination.

It was Fiona, standing near the vat, disrobing. Her skin shone milky white and her body possessed curves and muscles that Christopher never knew existed. He had never seen a woman as beautiful or as naked as she.

Baines looked at Christopher, then whispered, "They always bathe before a banquet."

"My mother has told me that nakedness is ugly. We must always keep covered," Christopher said.

Baines pointed down to the luscious Fiona with an index finger. "Do you still believe that?"

Unsuspecting, Alina talked to Fiona, her eyes fixed on her work. "With Jennifer gone, I'm not sure I want to use another midwife. Perhaps the lord can do it."

Fiona snickered. "That's insane. What does a knight know about childbirth? Butchering they know, birthing they don't. Jennifer is gone now. You have to accept that. Your baby will be delivered by another and will be strong and healthy."

Alina put her embroidery down on her lap and massaged her bulging belly. "I wish I was as sure as you, madam."

Their conversation was lost on Christopher. He watched as Fiona slowly slid into the vat, her pendulous breasts shrouded by the water. The damsels began to wash her shoulders and neck with soap made of animal fat and wood ash.

Suddenly it dawned on Christopher what he and Baines were doing, where they actually were—and the consequences if they were caught. He turned his head, about to tell Baines he wanted to leave. He saw the first sentry coming from the stairwell with vengeance scrolled all over his face.

"Baines!" Christopher yelled.

The women down below looked up, then screamed.

Baines turned his head and saw the sentry, shadowed by his partner in the wings. The two boys shot up and fell back toward the rear of the balcony. Baines looked down. Along the railing hung a series of ornamental drapes. He climbed over the front of the railing.

"Where are you going?" Christopher shouted.

But Baines's escape route became apparent. He lowered himself and clung onto the thin, colorful fabric. The damsels hurried to fetch Fiona's robe as Baines swung precariously over the vat.

The first sentry was on Christopher, grabbing him sharply by the shoulders. Christopher conceded defeat without a struggle.

The second sentry went to the railing, tried to reach down and snag Baines's arm.

The drapes tore under Baines's weight. Baines let out a cry as he plunged downward, landing squarely in the tub of water with the naked Fiona.

It was amusing, sure enough, but fear shoved its way into Christopher and wiped the grin from his face. He was in deep trouble not of his making. But, of course, who was going to believe that?

The sentries led the soaking Baines and trembling Christopher to Lord Hasdale's table and reported the incident.

"I should severely punish you both. But it is a day of celebration. And forgiveness is the order here." Hasdale directed his next words to Baines. "You, young man, desire to be a squire. To be *my* squire your father tells me. You'd better remember that the next time you consider spying on my wife."

"Yes, lord," Baines answered.

But Christopher did not hear Baines's reply. His mind had singled out and locked onto a few simple words: to be the lord's squire. He became lost in that idea. He saw himself gripping a spatha, slamming it home into Hasdale's hand as the lord met an attacker head-on. Being there on the battlefield, sharing in it all, feeling the rumble of horses, and hearing the sounds, the wonderful sounds of metal and man and victory. *That* was a future.

Christopher did not like the look on his father's face as he filed back to their table; he knew it meant punishment.

4 Lord Garrett, a man seeking greater things than his Celtic blood could grant him, marched through Sussex, Dorset, and Devon, in search of a land to rule for himself and the Saxon army of two hundred he had recruited. Celtic fortresses had been taken and lost, and his men had become weary and disgruntled. With false promises, Garrett kept his warriors forging onward. Now they were in Cadbury, where, in the south, the castle of Shores rose out of the wasteland, an inviting stone-walled oasis. According to Garrett's spies, Hasdale's men would be tired and full from a day of celebrating the lord's wedding. Most of the townsfolk had gone home to their tofts, and so there would be no peasant levy behind the walls to help defend them. The time for an attack could not have been better.

When night fell, they daubed paint on their faces, finger-combed their fierce beards for luck, and attacked Sir Hasdale's castle, first swimming the moat and reaching the berm, then slapping their ladders against the perimeter walls. Crossbow bolts split the air and found the sentries in the drum towers; garrison men poured Greek fire over the wall's edge, setting many of the Saxon attackers ablaze; blood splattered the old Roman walls and streets; howls of dying and injured men echoed over the clatter.

Garrett feinted and riposted his way through Hasdale's defenses and groped up a crumbling ladder, climbed through a window, and found himself in maid's quarters. The torchlit decor was drab and boring. He burst outside the room into a hallway, then found and clanked up a spiral staircase. He was on the ready, knowing he was at a disadvantage climbing the stairs. An attacker could easily swing around the center post and deliver a death blow. But now, no such attempt was made. He emerged outside onto the rear wall-walk. Some of his men had made it this far and were engaging the Celts. One-handing his broadsword, he hacked the left arm off an attacker; a blood mist caught his cheek. Two Celts drove forward, one seizing Garrett's sword hand, the other driving a blade forward. Garrett grabbed the blade driver's wrist and pulled the Celt past him. He tugged his sword arm free from the other Celt and, in one fluid motion, slipped his blade into the man's Adam's apple. The Celt fell, gurgling. Garrett pivoted away, came face-to-face with a man he recognized through the red crow on his shield as lord of the castle.

"You are a sight, Garrett," Hasdale said.

Garrett sneered. "Let me gouge out your eyes and spare you this vision of pain on your wedding day."

"Lot warned me of you. The man of two tongues, raised by Celts only to become ruler of heathens. Are you proud?"

Without answer, Garrett struck Hasdale across the breastplate with his sword. The blow sent the armored knight backward, but the blade did not pierce link-mail. "You were once a Celt. Now you're no more than an animal. What happened?"

Garrett's sword met Hasdale's, and the gritty metal-on-metal sounds reverberated in their ears. Garrett answered, "I grew tired of being the second son, second to lands, second to rule. Never again."

Among the flickering shadows of firelight, one of Garrett's warriors held a pregnant woman from behind and struggled to push her down the staircase Garrett had ascended. Garrett watched Hasdale's expression flip from rage to fear as the Celt spotted the woman.

"Alina! Alina!" Hasdale cried.

Garrett seized the moment, broke free of the struggle, and beat Hasdale to Alina. He looked into her pleading eyes, concentrated on those blue, tearful orbs as he savored the million-year second. He tensed, felt chills spidering about his groin as his sword pierced Alina's bulging belly. He plunged the blade deep, then ripped it upward as she shrieked her last, blood-choked breath. He buried his face in her neck as she fell back, pulled on her soft flesh with his teeth.

She was lovely. She was dead.

Garrett cocked his head and saw Hasdale wailing like a wounded beast, his blade raised, about to come down on him. Garrett withdrew his sword from the dead infant in Alina's belly and ducked out of the way. The warrior clutching Alina caught the blow; it cracked the Saxon's skull open and sent blood and brain matter seeping up where hair met blade. As Hasdale tugged his sword out of the dead Saxon's head, Garrett looked to the outer bailey and saw the Celts getting the upper hand. He struggled toward the front wall, where a ladder waited. Hasdale pursued him, but was intercepted by two more Saxons, whose wild blows kept him at bay.

On the ground, Garrett called for retreat. The night wind dried and crusted the blood on his cheek as he and his men fell back into the misty wood.

5

The next morning, Airell, Sir Hasdale's most stalwart and revered knight, staggered down Leatherdressers' Row like a drunkard. He had followed the invaders into the wood and battled them once more.

Inside his house, Christopher slept on a trestle bed in the loft. A *ka-kank* echoed from somewhere. The boy's eyes snapped open.

Christopher rolled on his straw-filled mattress and brought his small frame to the window under the gable. He surveyed the street below. A man was in the road. Not just any man—a knight! His neck and one of his metallic arms were covered with blood, but Christopher could see his chest rising. Gingerly, Christopher toed his way down the wooden steps and creaked open the front door. The sun was arcing higher, and he squinted to get a better look at this strangely wonderful sight in front of his home.

Airell's face was slashed by branches and stained with dirt. His bascinet sat on the stone near him, dented and reflecting the sun. His bloodied arm shook occasionally and soft moans escaped his lips. There was an awful stench about him that Christopher could not identify. He moved closer, crouched, and leaned over the man. Without warning the knight's good hand rose and locked around Christopher's throat, pulled him down close to the man's face. Christopher shivered and tears built in his eyes as he gasped for breath. The knight's eyes opened. The hand on Christopher's throat fell slack.

"Boy," Airell managed, trying to cut through the backed-up bile and blood in his throat, "I need—" Airell could speak no more.

Christopher's pulse raced like a shrew's. He ran toward his house, scuffled past the front door, and rushed toward the stairs. "A knight!" he shouted.

When he arrived in the loft, Sanborn and Cornelia stirred, then awakened. Sanborn let his wool pillow fall to the floor as he climbed out of bed. He stumbled to the window at which Christopher pointed. The boy felt his heart trip-hammer in his chest.

"He's right, Cornelia. It's one of the lord's men."

"I'll get my fire started," Cornelia said.

Christopher watched his father pull on his breeches and shirt, then followed him barefoot downstairs and outside into the road.

Airell was still. Even his twitching arm was frozen now. Christopher helped his father remove the knight's armor, then link-mail, pulling the latter slowly over the man's head. As Sanborn removed Airell's belt, Christopher yanked one of the knight's boots off, then another. Sanborn pulled Airell into a sitting position, leaned down, and hoisted the man over his shoulder. Christopher was surprised at his father's strength, but knew from the small grunts he made that the feat wouldn't last long.

"Get the door!" Sanborn shouted, shambling with his load, knees buckling. Christopher ran ahead and held it open for his father.

Airell was set down on a small pile of dry straw in the rear corner of the house. Cornelia removed his shirt and cleansed his wounds with warm, damp rags. With some fine threads of leather from Sanborn's bench, she stitched a deep gash on the side of his neck, then a long cut which snaked down his forearm. Another more severe puncture in his chest she managed to close, but what lay beneath made everyone fear the worst. She applied cool mud to the wounds, then covered them with damp linen rags. Airell slept.

Outside, Christopher gathered some of Airell's armor. He reached down and picked up the bascinet, unable to resist the temptation to place it on his head. He belched out a warrior's cry and struck an invisible invader with his air sword. Helmet still on, he entered the house.

"Take that off!" his father commanded.

Startled, Christopher quickly did, then moved to the corner where Airell was and set his first load down. The armor was heavy!

"Come here, Christopher," his father said. Solemnly, Sanborn noted for his son's benefit, "The spoils of a knight."

The cuts on Airell's face gave him a twisted, maniacal look. His head hung down at his shoulder and saliva drooled from his mouth onto his chest. His arm jittered again, and his eyelids fluttered. In this state, Christopher thought him a vision from black sleep—fearful, haunting.

During the day, Christopher did chores, then visited the church with his mother. They prayed for Airell, and heard the abbot's telling of the attack on Sir Hasdale's castle. Afterward, Christopher studied the strange carvings of beasts on the chapel's outer walls. As always, he got lost in the pictures and Cornelia had to pull him away. When they returned, Sanborn reported that Airell had not stirred all day, despite Sanborn's hammering.

While his parents talked of the siege, Christopher sat watch over Airell. The knight fought a nightmare battle in his head, and murmurs of commands escaped from him as his head jerked from side to side. Christopher was so rapt by this sudden display that he did not inform his parents, but continued to watch, drawing what he could out of whisper and thrust of hand.

"Garrett," Airell repeated, "Garrett."

Who is Garrett? Christopher wondered.

Airell's eyes opened, and his face mirrored some great agony. "*AHHHHHHHHHH!*"

Sanborn and Cornelia were silenced by Airell's call. They hurried to his side.

Out of breath, the knight was conscious, eyeing his sanctuary. "I-I apologize for my outburst. I am Airell."

"You fought a battle," Christopher said. "Did you win?"

Cornelia shot her son a fierce look. Christopher lowered his head.

"We drove them out. But . . . we took great losses. Sir Hasdale's sister . . . she's dead."

Cornelia and Sanborn, knowing this, nodded reverently. Christopher, on the other hand, wanted to know more of the battle, every cry, every rise of shield. He could feel that desire tingling in his fingers, but knew he had to repress it. Maybe later he could speak to Airell alone.

"You need a meal," Cornelia said, then moved to her mud oven.

Sanborn leaned close to Airell's ear to let the knight in on a secret. "You'll find my wife's cooking rivals that of the castle's cooks. She'll not disappoint." Sanborn winked.

Airell tried to sit up, but the effort was futile.

By nightfall, their houseguest was back into a troubled sleep. Christopher rolled over repeatedly in his bed. How could he rest with a great knight just below him? His desire to sneak downstairs increased, kept him tossing, thinking, considering his next move. But while doing that he still remained in bed, thought not translating into action, but into anticipation and fear.

Sometime later it began to rain. Droplets tinkled off the roof; large streams poured off the edges and splattered on the street below, almost loud enough to cover his father's snoring. Christopher listened. Somewhere in the distance a horse cantered along, then was gone. The rooster cried a false alarm from the yard. The din became heavier. More rain. More restlessness.

There was a dream that came and went. Christopher could hardly remember the details. It woke him, though, and chills drove their points home along his spine. He sat up, rubbed sleep grit from his eyes, yawned, then padded his way downstairs in darkness. As timbers below protested his weight, Christopher made his way to the sleeping knight. Airell's face was in shadow as Christopher approached. He reached down and stroked the knight's bascinet, conquering the desire to put it on once more. He drew closer to Airell, and through the dusty, static-filled air saw the knight's eyes were locked open. Airell was breathless, still. Christopher put a hand on Airell's shoulder, nudged him. Nothing.

Christopher drew in a breath, stepped back. His shock dissolved into sorrow. He could not take his gaze off Airell's eyes. Those eyes would forge future time and thought, darken forever the skies of his mind with carnage.

6

Many tents dotted the green slopes of the Mendip hills, and above them, the smoke from cook-fires billowed into a sky thick with gray, ominous clouds. Lord Garrett and his party of four galloped toward their camp, returning from a journey to Gloucester, down the waters of the Severn, which emptied into the Bristol channel. The morning air knifed their cheeks and steam shot from the nostrils of their coursers. Garrett felt hunger knot his stomach and was relieved they were almost home. Home, a questionable diversion for now. He dug in with his spurs and his horse responded, kicking up more muddy grass in its wake.

Upon his arrival, his men were red-eyed and agitated. There was a Celt who, under truce, demanded to see Garrett, and had ferreted through the camp all last night.

"So where is this man who believes me a hiding coward and my men to be liars?" Garrett removed his bascinet, set it down at his feet. He took a heaping spoon of pottage from a bowl handed him by one of his men and gobbled it down.

From a nearby tent, a figure glistened into sight. He was a knight banneret, and even in the darkly cast day, he shone brilliantly. His armor was freshly forged, and his bejeweled chest plates bore the blue ox of Lot of Lowthean. He was not the lord, though. A deep scar rivered from the corner of his left eye and ended midcheek, the only mar on an otherwise clear, angular face. As he strode toward Garrett, his expression blackened. Garrett choked on his pottage, coughed hard, bent over, and felt the torch in his throat finally cool. When he looked up, it was into the near-black eyes of the Celt.

Garrett cleared his throat once more, then spoke. "Have you come to rescue me again from the earthen claws of the barbarians?"

"No," the Celt answered. "I come under orders of my lord to kill you." The knight swallowed, and his voice cracked. "God help me."

At the mention of his true mission, Garrett's men were upon the Celt, circling him with sword tips and baring their teeth like wild dogs. One of the Saxons yelled, "He's the liar! Let us take his head!"

"No!" Garrett shouted. "Leave us. Now!"

Disgusted, the Saxons withdrew and dispersed. Garrett could hear their murmurs of his "being in bed with the enemy." He would deal with that problem later. He gestured for the Celt to walk with him down a gradually descending slope which rolled into the lingering mist. They began, and Garrett looked at the Celt's face, now pale. "Haven't the stomach for it, have you,

Quinn? We're to hold court here in my camp. Is that it? You're a man on the ground with no weapons."

The Celt stopped, reached down, and grabbed a gloveful of grass and wet earth. "Each day you proclaimed yourself a Saxon, another handful of this was dumped on Father's head."

"I love you, brother," Garrett said, "and I hate you. I desire your cunning, your strength, but I despise your allegiance to a dead man whose misguided Celtic ways drove me out."

"Don't blame Father for your dank condition."

Garrett clenched his fists. "You don't know how I felt in the castle with him. You, in the north, not caring. In his eyes, I would never cast a shadow of my own, and the land would never be mine. How many nights did I sit with the tip of an anlace under my chin, or buried my nose in a mug until ill?" Garrett raised a balled hand before Quinn. "You weren't there."

"But I am here now to see your rage, and how your petty jealousy has continued to oppress you," Quinn countered.

Garrett shook his head, gritted his teeth. "You're so wrong. I'm astride this Saxon army carrying a standard of joy. For the first time in my life, men turn to me, *die* for me. And in time, I will possess a land. The hands of our father are no longer on my neck."

Quinn took his index finger and traced the scar on his face. "Remember this?"

Garrett did. He thought of the tournament, how his inadequacy as a squire had caused Quinn to lose a decisive joust. The lance he had handed his brother had a hairline crack. He had not checked it as he had been taught. Garrett's father had known of his carelessness and had been about to beat him severely for it. Quinn had interceded, had defended Garrett by saying he had checked the lance himself and it had cracked *during* the joust. Garrett's father had not believed a word of it, and had continued toward him. Garrett remembered the tremble of impending pain as his father had reared back with the whip. Then Quinn had sprung forward and snatched the weapon from his father. The man had roared and snatched the whip back, turning it on Quinn. Garrett considered how his brother had stood, slowly closing his eyes as the thin tongue of leather had licked a bloody line across his face.

Garrett answered his brother. "I would not have done it for you."

"I know. And I tell myself that should make my duty easy, clear, without pain or guilt. But I lie. To myself. My callous heart is lost and I cannot find it. All I know is we are the last. We're all we have in this world. As I look at you, the task is too great."

Garrett smiled and urged his brother, "Then come. Let us not weep, but join ranks to end this tearing of hearts between us."

Quinn's brow raised. "You will leave the Saxons?"

"You will join them?"

The two brothers stared at each other, then laughed heartily for the first time in many years. The air had turned so light between them it made Garrett want to step up and hug his brother, tell him how he had never stopped loving nor admiring him, how much he had missed him. It was so good to see Quinn, so good to share this perfect moment of disagreement as they had so many times before.

"What can we do?" Garrett asked.

"Ride very north and join the Picts!" Quinn joked.

Garrett chuckled again, but something over Quinn's shoulder caught his attention. Four Saxons on rounseys rose over the slope and galloped down toward them, their swords swinging high above their heads.

Quinn barely had time to turn around.

"Noooooo!" Garrett wailed with every decibel of sound his vocal cords could supply.

The blade of the first attacker skimmed horizontally through the air and missed Quinn's neck by inches as he shifted and ducked out of the way. But there were four of them, and as Quinn's gaze was taken by the first man, the second brought his sword down and took Quinn's ear off. Quinn's agony echoed throughout the hills.

Garrett slammed his arm under the leg of the third rider and dismounted him from his steed. Growling, he found the fallen Saxon's broadsword and slashed an artery in the traitor's neck. A crimson flower blossomed over the man as he spun to his death.

Quinn staggered on his feet, held his bloody head, tried in vain to stop the fourth horseman, whose blow to Quinn's chest sent him flat on his back. The three remaining Saxons climbed down and teamed up on the fallen knight, ramming their swords into the seams of Quinn's armor, penetrating link-mail and tender flesh beneath as Garrett hustled toward them.

Intent on his killing, the first Saxon did not see Garrett's blade rise and behead him. The two others fell away from Quinn and steadied their weapons. One, out of breath, said, "We . . . we have no quarrel with you, lord."

Everything that was Garrett pumped, throbbed, pounded, beat, echoed, thundered, rolled, and cried to God as he stood facing the butchers. One sound: the rhythm of his breathing; one smell: perspiration; one taste: blood; one feeling: excruciation; one vision: death.

Garrett lowered his head to his brother, turned, and did not feel the sword drop from his grip as he fell to his knees. He cocked his head back, moaned to the rain clouds, "He was my brother!"

The two Saxons were shocked at this revelation, exchanged frightened looks, found and leapt on their rounseys, and galloped away from the camp.

As the thunder had clapped within him, so did it above Garrett as he threw himself across his brother's chest. He remained there, even after a spate swallowed the land.

Elgar, an aging loyal warrior, came down to Garrett and pulled his soaking lord off Quinn. Elgar slung Quinn's body over another war-horse that followed. The corpses of the Saxons were left to the rain.

Sitting behind Elgar on the courser, Garrett slowly closed his eyes and felt the anguish of his lost family cut an indelible wound across his soul.

He bled all the way back to camp.

7

Christopher had finished the saddle, but thought the pommel made by Ames much too large; it seemed to ruin all of his work. His temper grew, and he picked up the saddle and threw it against the wall of the workshop. Had Sanborn been there and not at church, Christopher knew he would've been scolded for that action. Thirteen years old, and this was what he had to look forward to. Life behind a bench, hands rough, his body reeking of leather. His father already told him he could make a saddle as well as any experienced craftsman—and he wasn't officially an apprentice yet. Seven years of learning how to do something he had already mastered in seven moons excited Christopher about as much as cold cabbage.

The sound of a horse outside sent Christopher scrambling toward the door. He knew who it was. "Baines! You're late today."

Baines was astride a beautifully groomed black rounsey that could only belong to Sir Hasdale. Indeed, it was Sir Hasdale's, and Baines, brushing wisps of brown hair out of his eyes, had become one of the lord's three squires.

Baines winked. "What'll it be today? Swords? Halberds? Lances?"

Christopher climbed on the rounsey behind Baines. "Anything—"

"But saddle making," Baines finished.

They trotted down Leatherdressers' Row, then once beyond the village galloped through a narrow path in the wood, dodging branches, laughing, and scattering rooks and starlings, which flew from leaf cover and wheeled overhead. They broke into a moss-covered clearing, and Baines reined in his steed.

"Today," Christopher said, thumping on the ground from the rounsey, "I will be your squire—*Sir* Baines."

Baines's lips curled into a grin at his sudden knighthood. "That Saxon over there," Baines pointed to a tree, "has challenged me to a test of arms. Are we ready to meet the challenge?"

"We are, lord," Christopher said. "Your lance." Christopher handed Baines the imaginary weapon.

Baines examined the lance, then tossed it to the ground. "Cracked."

Christopher's eyes widened. "Forgive me. Here's another—one I have studied thoroughly myself." Christopher genuflected as he handed Baines the second air lance.

"In what direction is the attacker, squire?" Baines asked.

"North, lord."

"And as we pass *I* will be north and *he* will be south."

"Correct, lord."

Baines shouted. "Then why are you not running ahead of me, getting behind the Saxon, for if he knocks me off, I will be weaponless on the moss and you will be standing idle on the enemy's side of the battlefield."

Christopher thought about it a minute. "Yes, lord!" He took off for the attacking Saxon tree, arrived, and moved behind it. "Spatha ready, lord!"

Baines brought his rounsey around in a wide circle, moving back to get up enough speed. Christopher watched him shout at the horse, dig heels in the animal's ribs as boy and steed drove forward.

In midclearing, Baines moaned in agony and fell back off the rounsey, his spine meeting earth with a wind-knocking *thock*. He lay dazed as Christopher released his grip on the shadow spatha in his hand and rushed to his side. Baines's eyes were closed and he wasn't breathing. Christopher pulled open the squire's tunic and shirt, put his ear to his friend's chest, heard a heartbeat. Baines's eyes opened.

Christopher smiled. "You frightened me. I thought—"

"You thought I was dead. You're partially right. We're both dead."

Christopher was nonplussed. "How? Why?"

"The Saxon knocked me off. You saw I was down, without arms. What did you do?"

"I ran to your aid."

"Then why are you not pulling me to my feet and handing me my spatha?"

Christopher looked away, ashamed. He knew when he saw Baines fall he had forgotten everything, dropped the imaginary sword by the Saxon tree. "The spatha is not with me."

"I know," Baines answered, then sat up. "I did the same thing when my lord tested me. Thank St. Michael it was only practice."

"Then—"

"I fell intentionally." Baines pulled himself up, brushed his tunic and breeches off. "I've taught you to ride a rounsey, carrying sword and shield—not an easy skill. I've heard lords say if a boy cannot ride by thirteen, he will never learn properly. But can you fall?"

"I have. Twice," Christopher answered. "Both

times I walked with the pain for days." Christopher remembered the early evening he was allowed to ride a loriner's hackney. He had started forward near the wood, lost his balance, and come crashing down on a thicket that cut lines in his back through his shirt.

"You have seconds to decide which way to adjust your body. One wrong move and you may break your neck. A proper motion will deny you walking pain. Mount my horse."

Christopher did so and moved the steed around and back to the edge of the clearing. He shouted and dug his heels in as Baines had done. He felt the wind rush over his face and the muscular rhythm of the horse. He reached the halfway point. Time to throw himself off. Icicles of fear pierced his nerves. He tried, couldn't, kept going, reined in at the other side. He rode back to where Baines was, feeling dejected, a failure.

"Your memory of pain is too clear. It will take time to conquer the fear—but you will."

"Maybe." Baines's confidence in him made Christopher's spirits rise one level in the darkness.

"Why do you wish to become a squire?" Baines asked. "Besides the fact you loathe saddle making."

Christopher considered the question for a long moment. It was a feeling coiled around his heart, one he could not describe. "I'm drawn."

Baines nodded his understanding, then gestured that they leave. As they slipped back into the wood, Baines said, "We're going to the Cam. I have something I want to show you."

Those words were too familiar to Christopher.

8

Garrett gazed at Quinn's funeral pyre all afternoon. Only embers now, a thin wandering line of smoke trailed up and was dispersed by winds, which also swept the sky azure, giving way to the sun. Within Garrett's head a black, motionless sea with reflective waters drowned his thoughts, choking hope, memory, future. A cyst of violence grew in him, tensed every muscle. A hand touched his shoulder, and he jerked his head around.

"Lord," Elgar said, his voice smooth and whispery, "The tents are packed. The cookfires are doused."

Garrett turned back to the pyre. "You were the filth of the land when I found you. What every Celt imagined a Saxon would be. Blackened, wearing arm rings, and riding short horses with no saddles. You were stupid and vulnerable."

Elgar did not answer, let his hand drop off Garrett's shoulder.

"I made you who you are," Garrett continued. "*I* brought you the great war-horses from the north; *I* showed you how to ride, to fight, to win." Garrett swallowed, rubbed his forehead, then spit into the pyre. "And this is how—"

"Not me," Elgar interjected. "A few who would take our campaign into their own hands. We are not responsible. Only them."

"Why didn't you stop them?"

"We didn't know."

"I have lost faith in my men. I do not trust them now. Maybe I don't trust you, Elgar."

Elgar moved in front of Garrett and hunkered down, blocking Garrett's view of the pyre. "I have taken what you have done for us and buried it here." Elgar smacked his chest. "I will always be loyal. You have to believe in that."

Garrett stood, and Elgar followed. Garrett stared

into the man's eyes, tried to read what he could from those flecked irises. "Do not betray me, Elgar. It is a plea. And a threat."

Elgar nodded. "What is our destination now?"

"Shores."

"We lost many men there," Elgar reminded. "And Hasdale has reinforced the towers with a larger, better-equipped army."

"We won't have to attack the castle. I want the village burned to the ground. If all goes well, I plan to have Hasdale's baby son in my arms when he turns his lands over to me."

Garrett pivoted away and marched toward his waiting courser. Was it Quinn's death that sparked this sudden attack on Shores? The thought had floated in his head since his first defeat there, though the odds of victory seemed slimmer as the years had gone by. Now it was all or nothing. Was he just being reckless, trying to prove to himself that the words he spoke to Quinn were truth? Garrett felt a nerve in his eyelid flutter as his foot slid into the stirrup. *My life will not be in vain,* Garrett thought. *As it seems my brother's was. God help him.*

Garrett and Elgar led the long line that was the Saxon army down from the hills toward the quiet nest of Shores.

9

Their reflections were perfect in the water.

As his rounsey drank from the Cam, Baines led Christopher through the marshy, mysterious shoreline. Their sandals became encased in mud, but Christopher didn't mind. The cool sensation was good and took away the occasional itch he got in the warmer months. The humidity was high, and by the time they reached Baines's destination both boys had sweat dripping from their brows. Christopher wiped his forehead, then eyed the landscape. They were standing in tall grass near the water. In the distance, trees were sparse, and cattle grazed, their heads low and their bellies full. Above the cows, crows circled and swooped down on unseen prey.

So what wonder was Baines to show Christopher now? In the past it had been naked women, dismembered corpses, stolen jewels, and, perhaps the most dangerous of all, with a captured Saxon, who hung shackled to a wall deep in the belly of the keep. "Want to see a real Saxon up close?" Baines had asked. Christopher remembered the feeling of the Saxon's spittle as it ran down his cheek. The man did not want to be taunted by two boys, and his only defense had been his mouth.

But what now? How would Baines top himself, Christopher wondered, here in the middle of nowhere? Sanborn and Cornelia would be home soon from the chapel, so Baines had better make haste.

Christopher's friend dug around in the grass, close to the earth. This Christopher found even more odd. "What are you doing?" he asked.

Baines became more frustrated as he pushed tall blades of grass and reeds aside, finding only mud below. He kept his gaze fixed on his search as he answered, "I know it has to be here—wait!"

Baines leaned down and came up with a package wrapped tightly in brown wool and tied with leather string. It was long, rectangular, and Christopher guessed right away it must be a weapon.

"Let's go back," Baines said, tucking the package under his arm.

"What is it? A mace, javelin, sword?"

"Patience, Chris."

"The heat has taken mine away."

"I'll show it to you and then we'll go for a swim."

"Good!" Then Christopher remembered he was supposed to be back at the toft working on more saddles, making the asses of knights comfortable as they paraded into battle. *I comfort the asses of men!* he thought. *Where is the glory in it?* "Maybe we'll have to skip the swim. I have to get back," he told Baines, not happy or comfortable with a word he uttered.

"If you must."

They returned to the spot where they had left the rounsey. Baines got on his haunches near the horse and unwrapped the package. The object that emerged from within the wool reflected the sun with even more intensity than the Cam. It was a weapon, all right. A broadsword. The most ornate and intricately detailed blade Christopher had ever set eyes on.

"Where did you get it?" he asked Baines.

"You would not be happy if I told you. Suffice it to say I have it now and it is mine. I've hidden it here for a while but I fear someone will come upon it." Baines rose with the sword, gripping the hilt with both hands. "I want you to have it. It will be yours— but best you hide it, perhaps in your yard, or your loft. Never show it to anyone."

"Tell me how you got it—or I won't take it." If possessing the sword was dangerous, Christopher needed to know why.

Baines was apprehensive. He sighed, twirled around, and struck a patch of grass with the blade, mowing it down instantly. "You must take it. It's too great a prize to toss away."

"How did you get it." Christopher held firm.

"I stole it from the lord. Satisfied?"

Christopher stared at Baines, as if he suddenly did not recognize him. How could his friend do such a thing? Steal one of his own lord's swords? "Why did you do it?"

Baines's gaze would not meet Christopher's. "He

has over a dozen spathas. It is such a waste. He never uses it. All the smith's work has been wasted."

"Why didn't you just ask the lord for it?"

"He would never let me have it. I'm not worthy of a sword such as this."

"You have to give it back. I won't take it from you." Christopher considered how much fun they could have practicing with the sword, how much trouble Baines would be in if he confessed to Hasdale what he had done, how great the punishment would be. Right and wrong were very clear, but right meant punishment and wrong meant fun. Baines had always opted for fun.

Christopher continued, "I know you're thinking you will be in a lot of trouble if you give the sword back. But you are a squire. You told me a squire must be true and loyal to his knight, yet you are not true."

"Perhaps I can replace the sword without Hasdale knowing. He has yet to notice its absence." Baines's eyes were wide with the idea.

"Is that being true and loyal?"

Christopher watched as Baines's gaze dropped to the earth. He had struck a chord in his friend, the same one he had struck times before.

Baines looked up, his face full of guilt. "You are my conscience, Christopher," he said. "And maybe that is why you are such a good friend. Would you like to try it out before I return it to Hasdale and confess my crime?"

Christopher slowly smiled, first for Baines's compliance with right, second for the opportunity to wield a great broadsword. He had played with the simple, functional spathas down Armorers' Row, those used by the garrison and villagers alike, but never a true fighting sword, one that was almost mystical in its proportions, as if it had been forged by the hands of some greater force, perhaps even God. As

Christopher took the blade in his hands, he felt something on the order of love, not for the object, but for the moment to be physically linked to a life which was only a dream. The sword represented *that* world, *that* existence which worked on a higher level than saddle making. He held the blade up close to his face, studied the metal, saw his own eyes, reflected by the blade, deepen with intensity. He felt as if he could stand here in the mud, gripping the hilt of the sword, forever, for to let the sword go would be to let the dream go. His mind created greater symbols than truly existed.

"It looks good in your hands," Baines said. "Why don't you attack the Saxon grass. Show it your power."

Christopher's trance was broken by Baines's words. "What?"

"Try it out," Baines suggested.

Christopher turned from Baines and struck a mighty blow to the barbaric, waving grass, chopping off the advancing blades with the single stroke.

"I see fear in their eyes, those Saxons. They will return to their camps in the hills with stories of the mighty Christopher, who, with his unstoppable blade, cut hordes of them down in a single afternoon."

Christopher laughed as he lowered the sword. "Those days will never come for me. I'm next in line to become a member of the saddler's guild, remember?"

Baines shrugged. "There must be a way out."

"There is no way out of bad blood. There is only fate."

"Why? Why must you bow down to something you despise?"

"I must obey my parents."

"Yes, you must. But must *they* control your future?"

"I'm helpless."

"This is a problem we will work on," Baines said. "Now how about that swim?"

All this questioning of his future and the dismal direction in which it was heading made Christopher rebellious. Why must he obey his parents? Why couldn't he ask Hasdale if he could become a squire? Would it truly kill his father and mother if he did so? Why must he return now to sit in the thick air of the workshop and labor over a saddle when he could enjoy a cool swim?

Christopher pulled down his breeches. "A swim it is."

A moment later the two boys were naked and splashing about in the Cam, the only disturbance on otherwise tranquil waters.

Christopher went under the water and held himself there. He enjoyed the refreshment and absolute solitude the Cam provided. He closed his eyes and pictured himself coming home that very afternoon and breaking the news to Sanborn and Cornelia that he wanted to become a squire.

Sanborn would be screwed into his workbench, as always, as if it were a part of his own body. Cornelia would be at the mud oven cooking lunch, or gathering vegetables in the backyard as was her wont in the afternoons. When he entered, Christopher knew it would go thusly:

"The saddle for Steward Farrel has been waiting for you all morning. Where have you been?"

"Out with Baines."

Sanborn would rise and fire off that look, the one that tore Christopher's soul apart and promised a whipping afterward. "Out with Baines? Again? And why do I find the Tressel's saddle on the floor? Why do I come home and find your bench abandoned and you out taking in joys? Why must you make me whip you? I love you, Christopher. You are my son. Make me proud—not ashamed."

His father had another talent besides saddle making. He knew how to combine love with guilt, deriving from the mixture a substance as potent and lethal to Christopher's dreams and aspirations as a battle-ax to the heart.

Now, how would he break the news?

Cornelia would come in and provide more fuel to the dream-burning fire. "Your father works day and night to provide a good home and a good future for you, Christopher. You owe him your honor and your respect. How quickly you forget that when you gallop off with Baines."

The poisonous mixture would take effect, and Christopher would swallow back his words, bury his notions to become more than a simple saddle maker because he owed it to his parents to become one.

But did he?

Did he have to sacrifice his life for them just because they were his parents? By giving birth to him, did his own mother actually curse him to a life of leather and hammers and foul smells? Why did she have to marry a saddle maker? Why not a knight? Damned fate! Damned fate!

None of this would solve the problem. He needed a plan of attack, one which would shield him from the guilt.

Christopher exploded out of the water, inhaling deeply. He raked his hair off his face and rubbed his eyes with the backs of his index fingers. He looked around. Baines was gone.

"Baines!" The rounsey was still watering on the shoreline, so his friend could not be far.

Then Christopher saw it.

Smoke.

Clouds of blackness rose from the distant tree line. Not some traveling band's cookfires, but a tremendous fire blazing from the direction of Shores. But how had it started so fast? He had only been under the water for a minute.

Baines broke through the tall grass. He was deeply worried and his eyes never left the smoke. "Let's go!"

Christopher's future was suddenly very petty in the

shadow of the smoke. Here he was in the water worrying about how to tell his parents the truth, and in the meantime his past flamed away.

Christopher mustered all his force and drudged his way through the water and onto the shoreline. He tugged on his breeches and tunic, then hopped onto the rounsey with Baines.

"The sword!" Baines pointed at the blade lying on top of the wool wrapping.

"Forget it!"

"No," Baines said. "We may need it."

Baines's words sent fear rushing through Christopher's veins. *Please let it be only a fire,* he prayed silently as he climbed back down from the horse and fetched the blade. He swung himself up behind Baines, clutching the weapon in a trembling hand.

They started off, and once beyond the marshy area around the Cam, they were at full gallop over a path cutting between two open fields of low-lying grass, an emerald sea whipping by them. Muscles in their steed's legs flexed, and hooves pounded the dirt.

Christopher's eyes went repeatedly to the sword as they traveled. Could he use it if he had to? Should Baines use it? Should he *let* Baines use it? He had never killed a man before. In fact, he had never struck a man with an actual blade before. He had never even seen a real battle before. Should they hide if Shores were under siege? They didn't stand a chance if they engaged the enemy, did they? *Perhaps all this worrying is for nothing and it's only a fire. Yes, that's it. Only a fire.*

When they reached the end of the path and the beginnings of the forest that would open up into the village of Shores, they found a dead man lying in the dirt, a mace buried in his skull, the hilt sticking out like some odd handle with which to carry him around.

Baines reined in the rounsey, and the two boys

stared at the corpse. The man was not more than twenty, his face contorted in terror.

"That's Ames," Christopher said. "I spoke to him about a pommel only a few days ago."

"Saxon bastards!" Baines cried. He dug his boots into the horse and they lurched forward.

Christopher gulped down saliva and repressed a shudder as they entered the forest and made a serpentine path around trunks and brush. The shouts of unseen men and the terrified cries of women drew closer. Tears began to well in Christopher's eyes. *My home*, he thought. *My home.*

10

Garrett's spy stood on the forward wall-walk of Hasdale's castle, gazing at the tremendous mushrooms of death sprouting above the nearby Shores.

Garrett had trained the spy well. He passed perfectly now. He spoke, drank, fought, and even loved like a Celt. But underneath his civilized mask was the mind of a barbarian, a Saxon true to soul. He took the name Kenneth, for he was the most comely of his Saxon brothers. And so it was he had come to the castle of Lord Hasdale bearing a message and gift for the lord from the imaginary Sir Lincoln of Lowthean. Lord Hasdale and Lady Fiona fell easily under his charm, and for the past moon he had been able to move freely within the castle.

Garrett had had misgivings about sending him, suspecting faults in Kenneth's loyalty. But Garrett had no other choice. Besides his natural Celtic looks, Kenneth had practiced the language until he had mastered it. He was perfect for the mission.

Kenneth hustled inside the connecting tower, tak-

ing a spiral staircase down to the outer bailey. He
ran by the armorer's hut, which teemed with garrison men being fitted with arms by squires who
scrambled to meet the clamorous orders of their
masters. Stone-throwing mangonels were being lined
up along the perimeter walls, as were the trebuchets,
their slings pulled taut, ready to fire a rock at a
moment's notice. All was chaos and excitement and
anxiety.

The drawbridge in front of the keep was rising and
Kenneth caught it just in time. He staggered down
the planks as the floor behind him moved up. He
made it to the stairs of the forebuilding in seconds
and took them two at a time.

As he entered the stone housing, Hasdale's men
readied the murder holes in the floor and ceiling,
pointing crossbows into them to shoot up or down at
the attackers.

Kenneth found his way to the great hall and rushed
across it toward the lord's solar, knowing it was there
that Fiona—and her child—would be.

It was too easy. No one stopped him. They
assumed he sought refuge in the keep. He was a simple messenger, but his death would not sit well with
Sir Lincoln—the ghost, ha!—and so he would be
amply protected. He belonged in the keep, close to
the child. As Kenneth set foot on the stairs leading
to the solar, he chided his leader Garrett. *You
thought I would betray your plans—well I haven't
thus far!*

A gray-haired maid huddled over the child's crib in
the solar. Fiona was at the window, staring at the
long string of men pushing out of the bailey onto the
drawbridge. Horns blew, filling the air and the spirits
of those around the castle with a sense of strength,
the ability to meet the challenge and return *holding*
one's shield, not *on* it.

Kenneth heard the horns, but his spirit was already

filled with something else. He felt his back for the dagger tucked behind the waist string of his breeches.

The heads of the women turned as Kenneth stepped fully into the room.

"Kenneth? I thought you'd be with the steward," Fiona said.

The maid gave Kenneth a passing nod, then returned to feeding the child.

"Are we the only ones here?" he asked.

"My other maids have fled to the cellar."

Kenneth visibly shivered. "My lady, I . . . I fear for my life."

Fiona stepped from the window and put a comforting arm around Kenneth. "My husband would not allow anything to happen to you. Besides, we're safe here. Stay with me. I enjoy the company of a man from a distant land. Tell me a story to take my mind off of death."

Kenneth pulled slowly away from Fiona and went up behind the maid. "I'm afraid I can't," he said, and in one fluid stroke withdrew the dagger, brought it around the maid, and buried it in her heart. The maid's head fell back on Kenneth's shoulder as Fiona screamed. Kenneth saw the maid's eyes roll back in her head and couldn't believe how warm and wet the woman's blood was as a wave of it broke over his hand. Then Kenneth cocked his head. Fiona started for the door.

Kenneth let the old woman drop to the floor. The child began crying. Kenneth seized Fiona by the arm and threw her deeper inside the solar. Then he went to the iron-studded double doors and pulled them closed, just as sentries tried to pry them back open. He hefted one of the drawbars in place, securing Fiona and himself inside. He turned his attention back on Hasdale's wife.

"Shut that child up!" he ordered.

Fiona went to the baby, a boy with azure eyes that were now full of tears. She tried to shush the infant. Her hands shook so much that she could not touch the baby, could only whisper softly to him, "There now, easy, go back to sleep, there . . . " Her voice cracked.

For the past moon Kenneth had lusted for Fiona, but the timing had not been right. He wanted her more than ever. But now? He was to escape—somehow—with the child. Or perhaps not escape and hold wife and child hostage in the castle. Either way, raping Fiona was not in the plan.

But what reward would Garrett give him for delivering the child? A pat on the back?

Fiona would be his reward and he would enjoy her now.

Kenneth pulled the dagger out of the dead maid and set it on the floor near him. He slipped off his boots as Fiona regarded him with eyes that spoke her dread. She knew what would come, and that was all right with Kenneth. Better she conceded to the inevitable. He removed his shirt, then breeches. He picked up the dagger and stood naked before her. His erection beckoned for attention—and would get it. He padded toward Fiona. She fell away from the crib and toward the wall behind her. Kenneth followed, never letting the prey out of his sight. Fiona's eyes darted from possible escape route to possible escape route. Finally, her back to the wall, she pushed along the cold stone until she reached a corner of the room. She slid down and tucked her knees into her chest.

Kenneth leaned down and grabbed Fiona by her thick, black mane, pulling her head up. Her frightened gaze met his. He held the dagger firmly under her throat, then pushed his erection toward her lips. She cried as she took him in her mouth. Kenneth felt the warmth and wetness of her. He drifted into a soft moan which gradually became full, guttural, and throaty, ringing from his Saxon vocal cords like a battle cry. Her tongue sent minute bolts of lightning through his inner thighs, and the muscles in his stomach and feet tensed. He went up on his toes as the exquisite moment approached, and when it did he felt his erection pulse as if his heart had left his chest and found a new home there.

11

Black sleep was a place of comfort compared to this.

Death littered the landscape. In fact, it *was* the landscape. Christopher and Baines stared into the eyes of a dead armorer, whose body was charred from the neck down and whose face was also blackened but somewhat intact. The man was in front of his burning toft, and it appeared he had been rolling in the stone-covered street trying to extinguish himself. Trying.

Armorers' Row was a series of funeral pyres, the burning gables of house after house caving in and sending flurries of sparks twirling up into the smoky sky. There were villagers still inside many of the homes, men and women who had hidden from Garrett's men only to die in their dark mouseholes. Their muted cries barely escaped through burning timbers.

Christopher's eyes were teary from more than the smoke. He knew that by nightfall the entire street would be leveled. "Take me home," he said tersely.

The Saxons were at the far end of Shores, finishing their job as Baines and Christopher forged onward toward Christopher's toft, turning down a side road which would intersect Leatherdressers' Row.

It was hard to find a toft which was not on fire. Christopher wanted badly to find one, perhaps small proof that some would be spared—perhaps, dear God, his.

They still had not seen a single Saxon, though they heard them in the distance. Strangely, their shouts reminded Christopher of his own father; the days when Sanborn simply could not get a saddle right and would scream out in rage, take the saddle, and throw it out into the street, then march into the backyard, sit down near the garden, and bury his face in his knees. Those cries, of frustration in one case and battle in the other, seemed oddly similar. Both tapped into the darkness and trepidation inside Christopher, both made him want to rush to his loft, jump into bed, and bury his head underneath the pillow.

Christopher's mouth opened and he took in air quickly as their mount rounded the corner and came onto Leatherdressers' Row. Then he closed his burning eyes and coughed. He composed himself and slowly, almost not wanting to, took in the view.

Something in his stomach gave way, as if he had been punched.

Where was home? It couldn't be here, in these flames, in these two rows of fire flickering and attenuating, then roaring as the tofts that were their fuel fell in on themselves.

Who were these people lying in the road, these black people with thin trails of smoke wafting from their scorched bodies? They were not the residents of Shores. Those people were healthy, vibrant craftsmen, shrewd businessmen who could get double for leatherwork when the need called. They were not black statues strewn about on stone with arms that groped for nothingness.

"Take me home," Christopher said once more.

"We're here," Baines shouted back. "Dear St. Michael, we're here."

"No." The tears fell freely now, lumbered over Christopher's cheeks and dropped into his lap. His grip on the sword's hilt tightened, his knuckles became white, and his arm stiffened, ready to deliver blows of retribution.

Where had the fear gone? Oh, it was still there, in his throat now, the terrible lump that wanted to escape past Christopher's lips.

They cantered down the Row, eyeing the whole horrible scene before them. Besides being burned, some leatherdressers had met their fates by sword, or by the sharpened hook of a halberd, or by battle-ax, or, as they had seen, by mace.

When they reached Christopher's house, they found it burning furiously. Angry snakes of smoke poured out of the broken and blackened windows.

Christopher handed the sword to Baines, hopped down from the rounsey, and rushed to the front door. He found the iron handle hot to the touch and swore as he withdrew his hand and nursed the tingling skin.

Baines dismounted and followed Christopher around to the back of the house where they found the rear door open and burning. There was a battle-ax sunk deeply into the wood of the door and Christopher eyed it with hatred. Baines pulled out the ax as he followed Christopher inside.

"Mother! Father!" Christopher shouted.

No answer came through the smoke-laden air, that in a moment had the boys coughing.

"We have to get out!" Baines shouted.

"No!"

Baines moved back toward the door as Christopher lingered. If Sanborn and Cornelia were in the loft, they were surely dead. He couldn't see much through the smoke, but it seemed they were not down here. He knew if he stayed longer he would pass out, and then reminded himself they had been at the chapel. Yes! The chapel. Christopher followed Baines outside.

They took in precious air and coughed hard; their stomachs heaved and their mouths drooled.

When he felt somewhat recovered, Christopher managed, "They were at the chapel."

Baines shot Christopher a downcast look and shook his head. "The chapel is the first place they burn. Attack their souls first and then their hearts. If your parents were there . . . "

"We're going." Christopher turned away from the house as a section of roof succumbed to the flames and fell with a loud *cha-chump*. More flames rose from the opening in the roof and Christopher felt their heat on the back of his neck.

"Christopher," Baines called.

Christopher turned around. Baines tossed him the battle-ax, which Christopher deftly caught. Had he not been charged with so much anger he might have dropped the heavy weapon, but now, at the ripe old age of thirteen, he hoisted the ax and rested it over his shoulder, knowing he would return the weapon to its owner—blade first.

12

Fiona was nude and strapped to the four-poster bed. Kenneth had torn his tunic and used the pieces to tie her arms and legs to the heavy oak posts. She was spread out for the taking. He stood there, still gripping the dagger, his eyes filled with all that was Fiona: her pert nipples, her long lithe legs, her tiny stomach, which had shrunk to near-perfect flatness after pregnancy. Her hair was wild, and she reminded Kenneth of a woman he had taken in Sussex, a woman whose voice he would never forget. Something feline about it. She had purred and cooed at him and he wanted the same thing now.

"Have you ever had cats about the castle, my lady?"

Fiona regarded Kenneth with a look that said he was truly mad.

"Have you?" he asked again.

Fiona cleared her throat. "No. The lord does not find cats pleasing."

"The lord is a fool!" Kenneth shot back.

Fiona struggled with her cloth bonds; they were tight—Kenneth had made sure of that.

"Do you know the sound a cat makes? The purring? The rolling of the tongue that is so agreeable?"

Fiona rolled her eyes. "Yes."

"Make that sound."

"Why?"

Kenneth charged the bed and put the knife back home under Fiona's throat. "No questions."

Fiona's throat worked under the edge of the blade, barely missing its razor-sharp edge. A deep swallow would draw blood. She opened her mouth and the sound came: "*Purrrrrrrrrrrrr . . .* "

Kenneth pulled the blade back slightly to give her more breathing room. "Again," he ordered.

"*Purrrrrrrrrrrrr . . .*"

The throbbing in his groin increased, and Kenneth climbed onto the bed, carefully balancing the dagger over Fiona's throat. He positioned himself above her, then reached down with his free hand to guide himself into her.

A sound at the window alcove alerted him. He cocked his head in time to see a burly sentry swing from a rope into the alcove.

Kenneth pulled away from Fiona.

The lady of the castle fought her bonds as violently as ever and shrieked, "Kill him! Kill him!"

Kenneth turned and kneed himself off the bed, then sprang to face the sentry. The fat man was armed with a short spatha and smiled a yellow-toothed smile under a thick beard and moustache. Kenneth knew his own death would please this loyal servant, but pleasure would only be granted to himself in this room.

The sentry tore off his bascinet, revealing a quilted hood covering his head, ears, and the back of his neck. He looked a little like the dead maid to Kenneth, with that headgear. He'd join her in a minute.

It was strange, fighting a man naked. It felt like the days when Kenneth was a boy, wearing arm rings and loincloths, learning how to dance the battle dances and spear food from the trees. There was something distant and natural and fierce about it.

The sentry jutted his blade forward, taking a few aggressive steps toward him. This amused Kenneth, for it was in this second that he grabbed the man's spatha by its blade end and quickly yanked it from him.

Kenneth's palm went crimson, but the wound was not deep. He tossed the spatha to the other side of the room and chuckled. The fat man was caught completely off guard by this maneuver, and suddenly found his hand empty. He fumbled about his waist belt for a short spatha, but Kenneth was upon him with the dagger. He drove the blade into the sentry's ear and pushed it in all the way to the hilt, hearing an odd, crackling noise like tiny leaves rustling inside the man's head. The loyal servant crumpled.

The sentry's partner drifted into the alcove, released his grip on the rope, and hit the floor with a *ka-chunk*. Kenneth slipped the dagger out of the fat guard's ear. He kept himself low, drove forward, and buried his dagger in the other sentry's groin before the young man had time to react. Kenneth pushed the sentry to the window ledge and then beyond, let the man drop to the berm below, a metal erection protruding from the guard's breeches. After watching the man fall, Kenneth looked up, saw no other sentries advancing down the rope. He yanked his head inside, crossed the room, and fetched his breeches. He slipped them on, and then his boots. Bare chested, he picked up the tiny, cloth-wrapped baby from its crib and started for the window. The child squalled louder than ever, and Kenneth had to repress the desire to muffle the infant—muffle it for good.

"Don't take my baby!" Fiona was a woman possessed; she arched her back, rolled her head from side to side, growled, and squealed again. She was a mother caught in a trap, watching as her young was taken from her. Fiona's animal instincts visibly pulsed with life.

But so did Kenneth's. "We'll make a fine Saxon of him, my lady," he said.

"Damn you to hell. To hell! Do you hear me?"

Kenneth gripped the rope with his good hand, the child with his bleeding one, then wrapped his boot around the rope for more support. "I hear you, my lady. I hear you."

Kenneth drew in a deep breath, then started down the rope.

As the heat built up on his hand, a curious thought occurred to him. What was the real pleasure in doing what he had done? Yes, the sexual gratification was there, but that wasn't entirely it. There was something else he couldn't put his finger on at the moment, but he knew it had something to do with power. Power and control. He didn't mind being hated as long as he had power and control. With power he could find those who would love him, and then control them. That *feeling* he got when others pleaded to him, begged him. It put him closer to what the Celts called God. He had heard of the evils of power, but it felt good to hear her plead with him, so good to hear her purr under his command, so good to be there and be the center of her universe, the axle of all she would say and do. To be in control. Of spirit. Of mind. Of body. That was larger than life.

13 The outer walls of the chapel, the ones Christopher had studied many times before, the ones with their wondrously strange carvings of beasts, had collapsed and were nothing more than black wood filled with glowing embers.

With every glance, all that Christopher had known in his life, all of the familiar surroundings and familiar faces were disappearing. It was like a chess game, he the pawn and some great force removing all his friends from the board, and then the board itself, leaving him in a void. He felt as if he were dragging his heart behind him as he circled around the chapel with Baines. The two boys stepped over a portion of the fallen entrance and stepped into the still-hot remains. Immediately, their hands went to their faces as they were assaulted by the stench of burning flesh.

Where the altar had been was rubble. On top of the rubble was the abbot, that jolly, red-nosed man, whose baritone voice would fill Christopher's ears every Sunday. The abbot's nose was seared off. His belly provided the home for a Saxon spear. He died before the fire and was left to burn with the rest of the congregation, they, too, having been killed before the flames.

Spears, axes like the one Christopher was holding, maces, and bolts from crossbows jutted at various angles from the dark corpses lying amid the debris. Christopher began turning over bodies, looking for Sanborn and Cornelia, relieved and yet horrified when he turned over the face of a woman, saw it was not Cornelia, thank God, but that it was, in fact, Ula, their next-door neighbor. He gagged, but forced himself to continue as Baines stood by watching with blighted eyes.

Finally, Baines took his sword out of the ash-covered earth where he had stabbed it. "Enough. Let's go. Before we're caught."

Christopher ignored Baines; a force drove through him that was unstoppable: the need to know.

Baines stepped out of the church, leaving Christopher inside.

Christopher made it to the front of the chapel, where two more bodies waited for inspection. The larger one had a spear in the head that had entered from the base of the neck and sprouted from the mouth. The smaller had a battle-ax buried in the middle of its back and had fallen forward, obscuring its face.

Christopher came upon the bodies from behind, standing closer to the larger one. As the face came into view, he fell to his knees and lowered his head. His eyelids shut. He couldn't look anymore. The larger body was Sanborn. Christopher didn't need to see the smaller one to know it was his mother. Here they were, sitting innocently in church, praying to God, praying for salvation. His stomach boiled over and the bile burst from his mouth. He coughed hard and felt his guts turning inside out. The smoke had taken its toll on him. The smoke, and the Saxons.

He saw Baines waiting for him by the rounsey as he came from the chapel. His friend peered nervously over the horse, hunting for potential attackers.

Baines regarded him. Christopher's face reflected it all. Baines grabbed him and held him. Christopher felt so alone now, but such small comfort was an oasis amid the flames.

"Why?" Christopher asked. "Why?"

Baines pulled back from Christopher and held him by the shoulders. "They invade. They lay waste to our lands, our families—our lives. They want the land. They want what is ours."

"We can't let them have it."

Baines stepped back and picked up the sword. "Today we are *both* knights."

Christopher held up the battle-ax until it touched

Baines's sword. "And may we send the animals who did this to their graves!"

Baines mounted the rounsey, Christopher following close behind. They hurried off toward the far end of Shores, where the Saxons waged their battle.

It was foolish, yes. But the feelings were so strong that they made it right. The vision of his father's speared head, blackened but still familiar, floated in his mind's eye. Christopher wanted the single man who had thrown that spear. He wanted him alone for thirty seconds. No matter how great a warrior, how large or muscled or mean—he wanted him. Vengeance was like a potion inside him, tensing his limbs and igniting within his heart. It made him kick the rounsey along with Baines, caused his vision to tighten, to blur at times, then to refocus on the mental image of putting his ax into the heathen who had taken his parents from him. It was a powerful image, a controlling one, one so overwhelming that Christopher could not fully perceive its effect on him. He knew only how he felt.

Five Saxons, flaming torches in their hands, surrounded a farmer's supply hut. They did not look like the Saxons described to Christopher by the abbot moons ago, but more like Celts in battle armor, their coursers waiting in the road for them. Baines pulled on the reins and directed the rounsey around the smoldering remains of another hut a hundred yards away. Obscured by a pillar of smoke, Christopher and Baines dismounted and grabbed their weapons.

Five against two. Make that five men against two boys. Make that five Saxon animals against two inexperienced children.

"An ambush is our only hope," Baines said, waving the smoke from his face.

"We have to get them now, while they're on the ground." Christopher held the Saxon battle-ax with two hands, preparing himself to storm the attackers.

"Agreed," Baines said. "But we have to get closer."

They used the smoke and whatever standing walls were left of the surrounding huts for cover. They moved rapidly and secretly, weaving in and out of the rubble until they were only twenty yards away, crouched behind the round, mossy wall of a well.

Christopher's pulse was a steady drummer; it beat a loud, quick rhythm in his ears. He felt his breath race, and the nerves in his legs quake. The closer they got, the larger the Saxons became. If he was going to do it, something inside him would have to snap.

Baines's own anxiety snapped first, and without warning, Christopher's friend charged the Saxons.

And it was that action that caused Christopher to leap from his nest behind the well and drive forward alongside his friend.

Christopher had never felt like this before. His body had a mind of its own; it flexed and moved and readied the battle-ax as if a demon had taken hold of it. But it was him. *He* ran head-on with his friend toward the Saxons.

The attackers turned from the hut they had fired and dropped their torches. They ran toward the spathas hanging from their coursers and *sringed!* them from their scabbards.

Could he do it? Could he engage a Saxon, man against man, he against another in a battle for their lives?

Christopher ran out of time to wonder. He brought his ax up and slammed it home into the first Saxon he came upon, knocking the soot-faced barbarian onto his back. But the Saxon managed to swing at Christopher with his blade; the riposte cut a thin line across Christopher's breeches and nicked his calf.

Baines thrust his sword forward, trying to wedge it in the crease of another Saxon's armor, near the man's shoulder. But the Saxon took a free arm and, utilizing his metal protection, pushed the blade aside and out of Baines's grasp. The sword tumbled to the ground and the Saxon chuckled with delight.

Baines went for his lost sword, but found the tip of the Saxon's spatha poised before his nose.

Christopher turned his attention away from his bleeding calf and saw Baines's dilemma. He rushed forward to help his friend.

The seconds ticked away. Too many of them.

I can't make it! I can't stop him!

The Saxon drove his blade into Baines's mouth, jerked it abruptly forward until it sprouted in a crimson *pop* from the back of the boy's head.

The Saxon released his spatha, and Baines fell backward into the dirt, the tip of the blade pinning him to the earth. His arms and legs jerked, guided by runaway nerves and reflexes, and his bowels emptied themselves into his breeches. His eyes were open and very still. Very still.

The Saxon freed his blade from Baines as Christopher arrived.

"Baines! Baines!" For a moment, Christopher forgot about the Saxons around him, feeling only the death of his friend, as if the spatha had dug a hole in his own head and sent ripples of pain through his own body. All of it was even more unreal now: his parents in the church, the villagers he'd known, and now Baines. It *was* black sleep, it *was.* He shook his head, no, not able to accept any more. It was too much, too much in one day. He felt the world tumble around him, the ground spin up and smack him in the head, the sky rush in circles around him. Something wanted to escape inside him, an animal whose bite was lethal and whose roar would shatter eardrums.

Christopher fell to his knees and let out a cry such as he had never sounded before. Even the Saxons were taken aback by it as they stood over him with their spathas trained on his back.

The cry was followed by other cries, these from behind Christopher. The Saxons cocked their heads. Christopher looked up from Baines.

A dozen of Hasdale's mounted men galloped toward them, the two lead men armed with crossbows. A pair of bolts found two of the Saxons and the men fell in twin heaps to the ground.

The other three Saxons stood ready with their blades. A Celtic horseman drew near to one of the barbarians and engaged the man with a mace. The Saxon struck a futile blow to the Celt's chest and the Celt answered the blow with a riposte to the side of the Saxon's skull. Bone collapsed and hair sank deep into the head, swallowed by blood. The man fell with a strangled moan.

Two left. The Saxons knew better than to play such odds and beat a hasty retreat toward their coursers. Christopher rose and darted after one of the Saxons, the battle-ax vised in his hand. He pulled his ax arm back and brought the weapon high in the air. He was on the heels of the man when he brought the ax down.

CRACK!

Christopher was both glad and repulsed as the man dropped, and he tripped over the Saxon, sailed through the air, and rolled onto the ground. The dust cleared, gave way to the enemy soldier, whose head leaked blood around the ax buried in it.

At thirteen, he'd killed a man.

Christopher sat up and pulled his knees into his chest. He stared at the dead Saxon a moment as Hasdale's men put the last of the attackers to death behind him. The gurgling sounds of the men they were killing didn't bother Christopher. Numbness set in, a retreat from reality that had begun with Baines's death. He felt the warm wetness around his calf, but ignored it. Images again. His father. His mother. Baines. Another one, distant, cloudy, but there. The knight. Airell. His eyes. All of it was the same. Death.

Someone called him, called him "boy," said it over and over again. He didn't move. He was afraid to do anything. He sat in the road.

14

It was a sight: Kenneth marched toward Garrett with the child in his arms. Garrett could not contain the emotions rolling inside him. "Look, Elgar," he said to his old companion. "Behold Hasdale's child—as promised. Kenneth did not fail me."

They had made camp in a wide expanse of grass a mile outside Shores, and now stood, reeling in victory, their gazes captured by the soft skin and tiny hands of the baby before them. Garrett took the baby from Kenneth and nestled it in his vambraced arms. A sight it was, he in all his metallic power, holding this frail, helpless boy.

"You don't realize how much power you possess," Garrett said to the baby. "You can do something that no man in this army—including myself—can do."

Kenneth and Elgar smiled. They knew Garrett referred to Hasdale's love for the child, his willingness to turn over his castle for the return of his son. They bargained on love—and knew they would win.

"Was there much trouble?" Garrett asked Kenneth.

"None," Kenneth answered, his voice full of self-satisfaction.

Garrett nodded. "Indeed." He turned to Elgar. "Send off the messenger."

Elgar lowered his head in obedience and stepped away from the men. He marched toward the tent which housed the messenger.

Garrett brimmed with joy. "Tonight we'll feast in Hasdale's great hall! A castle at last. Dear St. George, a castle."

Kenneth regarded his mastĕr with disdain. "Lord, must you always refer to your Celtic gods in the fields of victory?"

"Each man owes his debts," Garrett shot back. "Yours are to me. Remember that."

Kenneth nodded, and Garrett watched his spy bite back something further. It would be better if Kenneth did not challenge Garrett. He would hate to kill the man, but if he continued to question orders as he had in the past and continued to scrutinize every word Garrett uttered, enough would be enough. A great loss, yes. But if so, a necessary one.

By dusk a small party of Celts cantered their way across the field toward the Saxon camp, torches casting elongated shadows in their wake. Garrett and Elgar watched as the party approached, saw it was led by knight banneret Wells, Hasdale's champion, a lean, gray-haired man whose body was as fit as any young man's, and whose fighting skills had earned him the title he wore boldly.

At this point, perfection made Garrett nervous. Somewhere along the trail something had to go wrong. Garrett knew his plan was not perfect, but so far it had proved him wrong.

What could happen now? The party was small, surely his army outnumbered them twenty to one. Perhaps Hasdale had something else brewing in his mind. But what? He would have to wait and find out.

The Celts paused fifty yards away and four of them dismounted. Wells led the way, three others marching behind him. Garrett recognized two of them as Sloan and Condon. He had engaged both men in combat and respected their hand-to-hand fighting skills. The third was unfamiliar, clean-shaven, looking far too young to be associated with the others.

Elgar leaned close to him. "Our men stand ready."

"Good."

There was something wrong. Garrett could feel it. The men stepped closer, narrowing the distance between them. Then they were face-to-face. What was it?

Wells spoke first, his voice flat, steady. "We must see the child."

"Hello, Wells." Garrett felt his nerves relax. They were going to bargain, and now he would toy with them, fill himself with the heavy wine of domination. He had them. "Can we share a jug first?"

Wells's sharp face was set, and if the man had any fears, he did not betray them to Garrett. "We must see the child," he repeated curtly.

Garrett frowned. "Very well." He saw the resentment in all their faces, knew it was driven by their defeat, and their defeat made him feel even more alive. He gestured for Elgar to fetch the child.

He took a step closer to Wells, his own pair of guards drawing closer with him. "You are well, I trust?"

Wells remained silent. There was something missing from the man Garrett had known, as if he were without a soul, just a mound of flesh before him acting out the will of another without question. But he had known another Wells, a man who desired to be a lord himself, who, before serving Hasdale, had served his own father. All was not right. The change in Wells edged around Garrett's mind. Where was the man? He needed to bring the answer closer— but it lingered on the fringes, gnawing at Garrett.

Elgar came forth with the child and stood next to Garrett. Wells leaned in to view the baby.

The horror came from a man who had intentionally turned off his emotions, and when it did, everything clicked inside Garrett's mind. In that second he recognized the pure brilliance of it.

There was a flash. A tiny knife appeared in Wells's hand and he thrust it into the child's head.

Elgar's mouth hung open as he pulled back from the Celts, the dying infant jittering and gurgling in his trembling arms.

Wells stepped back. "The castle of Shores is Hasdale's!" Then he turned and stormed with the other three knights back toward their coursers. The Saxon guards snapped into pursuit.

Garrett stood in awe. Hasdale had ordered his own son put to death in order to save his castle. What kind of a man could make that decision? The beauty of it. Garrett did not know if he could do that himself. Then, slowly, his own defeat began to take hold, giving way to anger. He turned toward the tents, shouting, "We lay siege to the castle. Now!" Then he paused.

The taller of Garrett's guards caught the youngest Celt in the back of the neck with his javelin. The Celt stumbled forward, then collapsed with a *fromp* into the grass. The other three Celts vaulted onto their horses as the other guard split the air with his javelin; the spear landed between man and courser, impaling the earth.

The Celts galloped off as the guards stood. Behind them, Saxons mounted and prepared to charge after the party. The taller guard withdrew the javelin from the Celt he had slain, then marched away.

Inside his tent, Garrett was in a frenzy, slipping on his gambeson and then his hauberk, smoothing out the shirt of link-mail over his chest.

Kenneth entered; his face bore his concern. "Lord. We make a grave error."

Garrett studied his spy, considered what means of death he would use on the man. The anger was a wild boar, impaling his head with its sharp tusks. He was about to find his spatha and do it quickly, simply. But as he studied Kenneth, he wondered if the spy's concern was genuine, perhaps not born of jealousy or ambition. He softened a little. "Why do you say that?"

"I remind you, lord, I was sent to take Hasdale's child so we *would not* have to attack the castle. Hasdale continues to add men to his garrison. I believe an assault now would be futile."

Was he right? Was Garrett being rash, planning with his heart and not his head? And if he was, was his ability to lead becoming frayed, the tight coils of his spirit unwinding into a shapeless, powerless lump? Garrett considered Kenneth's words, and with regret, began to see the truth in them.

Garrett placed a hand on Kenneth's shoulder. "I have doubted you in the past, and feared your own ambition. But now I listen."

"I only seek the same things you do, lord. A castle to rule, a victory to celebrate."

Garrett turned away from Kenneth, his eyes running idly over the seams that bound the tent together. "Call our men back."

"Yes, lord."

Garrett heard Kenneth leave. He remained still, thinking. His adversary had revealed unexpected strength to him. Hasdale was strong, much too strong. It was a new challenge he would have to meet, but by the blood of his brother and the curse of his father he would do it.

15 "See there, boy, the beams of light? Those shafts that wedge through the clouds and strike the earth? They carry souls to Heaven. Did you know that?"

The survivors of Shores had been brought back to the castle: Christopher; a short old man and his shorter wife, whom Christopher recognized as farmers, having seen them on Sundays at the chapel; and a plump, vociferous merchant, whose leg had been badly burned. The others' wounds were being tended to inside the keep, while Christopher sat on a stone bench in the outer bailey listening to Orvin, Hasdale's father, a man he had heard much about but had never met. Orvin refused to let the women of the keep attend to Christopher—he demanded to do so himself; the reasoning behind his insistence was a mystery to Christopher.

And so they were together, the wizened man with the shock of long, snow-white hair that whipped like ivory flames in the stray breeze, and Christopher. Orvin was good with the needle, despite the condition of his hands. He had only pinched Christopher twice, and now applied cool mud over the stitches running across Christopher's calf. When he was done, Orvin pulled back to admire his work.

Christopher studied the rays of light filtering through the cloud cover in the west. He tried to see the specterlike forms of his mother, father, and Baines floating slowly, gracefully, through the light and vanishing into the clouds. But there was only the light.

"It's all up there. All of it. In the sky. I can see it. Can you?"

Christopher faced Orvin. The old knight's gaze was upon the azure wash, and his nostrils flared as he inhaled deeply, obtaining an almost unnatural satisfaction, savoring the breath as though it were to be his last. "See what?" Christopher asked.

Orvin directed his attention to Christopher, and the boy noted the light in the man's soft, gray eyes. It was a strange light, one which sprang from within the old man, one which Christopher found both odd and interesting. "What will be," Orvin said simply, then repeated for effect, "What will be."

It was becoming clear why Orvin wanted to attend to Christopher himself. Who else but a boy would be willing to sit and listen to a stoop-shouldered prophet of fancy? Once a great knight, he was now reduced to telling stories of magic to Christopher. But there was something comforting about Orvin, as if indeed he did possess some bit of magic over the hearts of men, and if it gave pleasure to him, Christopher didn't mind being the man's audience. "If you are a soothsayer, what is the future then?"

Orvin bowed his head, closed his eyes. A moment went by, and Christopher watched for something to happen, a puff of smoke like that he'd seen come from a performer at a festival, something that would indicate magic working.

But there was nothing. Christopher wondered if Orvin had fallen asleep, and so he nudged the ancient man. Abruptly, Orvin snapped his neck back and his eyelids flung open like shutters that had been pushed too hard.

"Sorry," Christopher said.

"I see nothing yet," Orvin said. "But the past is vivid." Orvin shifted his body closer and put an arm around Christopher. He held the boy and Christopher felt a little awkward at this—but he understood. The memories of his parents and Baines were fresh, the sounds of their voices still echoing in his ears, their smells, their touches, all of his senses still aware, still experiencing the details of them. The sympathy from Orvin, a man he had just met, was good. He needed a shoulder and had found one.

A shadow passed over old man and boy. Christopher looked up, and the urgent desire to stand passed from his head and into his legs. He began the maneuver, but a strong hand rested on his shoulder and eased him back down.

Lord Hasdale stood before them, framed by the tableau they had stared at and the monolithic gray walls of the keep below. "How is your leg?"

Christopher had never spoken directly to the lord before, had only listened to him, and though his vocal cords worked, he suddenly forgot how to use them, in the face of such an important man. He nodded, swallowed, swallowed again, then finally managed, "Better." The word came through a parched mouth, one that only seconds before had been moist.

Hasdale hunkered down so that his eyes were level with Christopher's. "Tonight we hold a mass in the chapel for those lost. Your father was a fine craftsman and friend. And your mother was a strong woman, one whom Fiona admired. I share deeply in your loss." The lord turned his gaze to Orvin. "If you haven't already heard, Baines met his fate."

Orvin shook his head and pursed his lips. "He was the best squire I ever trained. He would've been a great knight banneret."

Hasdale rose. "His body will be burned as a knight's."

Orvin brought a hand to his head, massaged his temples with his fingers. "Where is the importance of life, when it is so fragile and regarded with such frivolity?"

Christopher was struck by those words. It was their world, and everyone knew violence was the way, but no one liked it. Yet no one did anything to change it. Killing was a means, it was an act to demonstrate power, to communicate something to another. But there was such finality, such pain attached to it. His parents were gone forever; his friend was gone forever.

"Here I am under the sun," Hasdale said. "And it is the darkest day of my life. I have seen my village lost, some of my best fighters lost, one of my squires lost, and my son . . . my son killed."

Christopher had heard of the birth of Hasdale's son, but news of the child's death was a surprise. He wanted to know—but was afraid to ask.

Tears slipped in short spurts from Orvin's eyes. The old man bit his thumbnail and his head shook no, ever so slightly. His gaze was nowhere and Christopher watched, becoming more melancholy himself. If he stayed where he was any longer, he, too, would break down. He didn't want to do that in front of the lord. He wanted to be in control, be as much a man as he was capable of being.

Christopher stood, shifting his weight to his good leg. He addressed the lord, though Hasdale's back was to him. "May I rest inside now, lord?"

Hasdale turned around, studied Christopher for a long time. Christopher was unsure what Hasdale thought, and felt unnerved under his gaze. There was desire in the lord's expression, longing, something. "I'm sorry. I see things in you that make me happy— but also give me great pain."

Christopher was at a loss. All he could think of to say was, "I'm sorry, my lord. I wish only to serve you."

Hasdale stepped close to Christopher, gazed directly into the youth's eyes, and his voice came as a soft whisper. "We will all live through this."

From behind them, Orvin hauled up his creaky frame, releasing a soft moan in the process. He brushed the tears from leathery cheeks, the wrinkles out of his long tunic, then came unsteadily over to his son and Christopher. "What's to become of the young patron saint of travelers? His future is unseen by my watery eyes."

"His father told me on more than one occasion that he is already a master craftsman, an expert saddle maker."

"At thirteen?" Orvin challenged.

"That's what he said."

No, this wasn't happening. Christopher could not remain silent and let the lord sentence him to the bench for the rest of his life. He had to say something. He had to open his heart to these men and speak the truth. But in speaking the truth, wouldn't he betray the memory of his parents? His father wanted him to become a saddler, and his mother had stood like stone behind Sanborn. Christopher would be abandoning the family trade. But wouldn't they want him to be happy? That had to be most important. *Forgive me Father and Mother, and please try to understand.*

"We'll have to put him to the test," Orvin said.

Say it! Tell them you want to be a squire!

"True," Hasdale replied, "but you know, the men who found him told me he and Baines attacked five

Saxons on their own, and Christopher here downed one himself. Great courage from a boy."

Orvin's eyes drifted over Christopher, as if trying to see the capability of such an act somewhere within a saddler's lean son. Christopher almost felt Orvin's probe, but concerned himself more with the positive direction in which Hasdale took the conversation. "It it is true, lord. And I need . . . I beg of you not to place me at the saddler's bench."

"But isn't that where your talents lie?"

"You said yourself, lord, that-that I showed great courage. I-I wish to become a squire and serve a knight, lord. I've wished it since the very first time I set eyes on one of your men."

Hasdale's face filled with consideration. He looked at his father, who shrugged. The lord rubbed a thoughtful hand over his chin.

Christopher's stomach fluttered and chills climbed a winding staircase up his back.

The lord stretched out his arm and pointed his index finger at Christopher. "You have your chance."

Dream and reality met in Christopher's mind. *Yes!*

"But—" Hasdale added, "if you fail, you will serve me with the skill you were born with. Now go. Sleep. When your leg has healed you will join my other trainees on the practice field."

Christopher limped past the men, looking over his right shoulder at the knights, who seemed to be forever practicing on the exercise field. He'd seen them many times before, since his first visit to the castle, but now the image of himself on that field was clear, reflected as if by the Cam, undistorted by the fleeting waves of past desires. He would be trained. The words had come from the lord himself. He kept rolling the idea, for the meaning of those words still did not completely register within him.

I am going to become a squire? Yes!

" . . . and this is my squire, Christopher," he said out

loud as he set foot on the drawbridge of the keep. The sound was sweet, like the call of morning birds opening his sleepy eyes. He could listen to it over and over and never become tired of it, never become numb or absent to it. He was on the threshold of a new life, leaving the burning remnants behind, but taking all the memories and all the pain with him, for it was those that would fill him with the desire to succeed.

PART TWO

THE TRUE SERVANT

1

Twilight washed down the skies above the castle, and as the shadows grew, so did Lord Hasdale's fear. Indeed, it had been a dark day; only one small light in a young boy's face to carry him through.

He was filled with dread as he strode down the torchlit hall. He walked swiftly, and the breeze he created lifted the tapestry hanging on the wall to his right. Before the cloth settled, Hasdale turned down another dim corridor.

The door to Wells's chamber was slightly ajar, and light wedged through the crack and illuminated Hasdale's fist as the side of it made contact with the warped oak, pushing the door inward.

His knight was living well. One could have mistaken the chamber for the solar, though there were no windows. Wells had two open chests at the foot of his poster bed, one for clothes, one for documents, silver plates, and gold coins. Wells's torches were mounted in ornate stands, and a hooded fireplace warmed the stone floors.

Hasdale's champion was living too well.

Two heads popped out from under the silk covers on the poster bed; one was Wells, the other a dusky-skinned woman not his wife.

"Out of bed," Hasdale ordered, the muscles in his jaw flaring.

Startled, Wells climbed from the bed and stood. He wore his shirt, but was naked from the waist down.

The nude damsel rushed to a chair across the chamber to retrieve her clothing. She dressed nervously as Hasdale scrutinized her.

Wells slid his breeches over his knees and asked, "What is it, lord?"

"Sloan and Condon searched their hearts and found where their loyalties lie. I have spared them."

Wells tied his waist string and backed away from the bed, his body tensing, his eyes searching through the shifting light of the room for something.

Hasdale found the object of Wells's desire: his broadsword. The blade was in its scabbard and rested across the arms of a chair near the door. Hasdale looked to the damsel. "Leave us."

Like a scared doe, the young woman bolted out of the room, the torch flames leaning in her direction as she turned down the hall.

Hasdale picked up the sword, pulled it from its steel covering, and let it lead the way toward Wells. Each step he took was measured, drawing out more fear in the man before him. "I sent you to bargain with Garrett."

"Search your heart, lord," Wells shot back, his voice uneven. "You could not have made the decision yourself—but it was the right one. One life sacrificed for all we have here."

Hasdale stepped closer to his knight, looked over the tip of the blade, saw the man shudder, and felt the familiar and comfortable power he held over Wells, a power that had once been impregnable, but now was breached by Wells's faltering loyalty. "Perhaps I would have made the decision—but it was mine to make. Mine to make."

"Lord, forgive me, but I know you. We would have sacrificed half the garrison in order to rescue the child. And if we failed, you might have succumbed to Garrett's wishes and turned the castle over to him. There was doubt among your best, and we three agreed it was the only way. It was a show of strength—of your strength—not an act of betrayal. We offered you succor. See now how Garrett's forces are already heading north. We have won."

All the words in the world would not take the feeling of loss away. Hasdale kept replaying the look on Fiona's face when he told her the child was dead, how her eyes narrowed and her cheeks rose and her mouth formed a grimace. He went over all of it in his mind as he stood before Wells, hearing words that formed simple, logical sentences, courses of action which fulfilled the desires of the many, yet left him cold and empty. Was it the curse of being a lord? Was it his own attachment to his emotions, to the love of family and fellow man that made him a weak leader? Could he have made the decision to put his own son to death in order to preserve the castle? There were no answers, only anger.

Wells fell to his knees. "No more bloodshed. Please, lord. I ask for your forgiveness and for your mercy."

Hasdale touched Wells's breast with the blade tip. He could never forgive the man for what he had done. Never. He could kill Wells right now, but killing him wouldn't bring back his son. Wells had been exceedingly loyal over the years, and this was his first and only betrayal; in that fact Hasdale found mercy and lowered the sword. "I divest you of your knightly services to this castle, and ban you from this land." Hasdale could not bear the sight of Wells anymore, for looking at the man would always remind him of his dead child.

"I will not argue, lord. But do know I did it for you. As terrible as you may think it was, when we are both gray and near death you will thank me."

Hasdale threw Wells's sword at his feet, the *klang* as shrill to his ears as the dialogue in which he was engaged. "Never. Now make haste and begone before sunrise."

Hasdale stepped into the hall, closing Wells's door behind him. He fell back against the thick oak and sighed, his throat tight and his eyes heavy with tears. *My men doubt me. I've lost their confidence.*

A young, dirty-faced page hurried down the hall, regarding the lord with curiosity, then, recognizing his master, scurried even faster until he rounded a corner and was gone, a field mouse into his hole.

Hasdale pushed himself off the door and started for his solar.

2   After staring at the pig turning round and round on the spit for several moments, Christopher began to dream about slicing a large portion of the meat off and chomping on it, letting the juice roll down his chin and onto his neck, enjoying the feeling and the taste, the utter barbarism of it all. Warriors ate hard and mean, and he would learn to dig in with his hands and his teeth, wipe his chin on his sleeve, and belch as they did. The glory of it . . .

Around him, the kitchen was a flurry of activity. At a low wooden table, a side of beef was sliced and placed in an iron cauldron by two gaunt-faced men who wore white aprons over their faded shirts. Near the beef was a pair of plucked geese, which would be placed on the spit when the pig was done. At another table, a cook with the features of a cherub made pastries while a young boy at his side received a bag of spice from the wardrober. An old woman in white bonnet and red robe, her movements somewhat bird-like, drew water from the square well sunk inside the stone walls. She brought the bucket over to the baker, a man built like the loaves he lined up, then returned to the cook's table to help with the beef.

"Boy!"

Christopher turned from the fire toward the voice.

One of the lanky cooks at the table looked at him with disgust. "Keep the faggots going into that fire. Don't stare at it! If you can't do this job—then it's off to the scullery with you."

The other cook chipped in to his partner, "I don't believe the boy was staring at the fire."

The cook who had yelled at Christopher turned to his helper. "Who asked you, Lloyd? Always putting your nose in other people's business and not minding your job. Look at how sloppy your cuts are. I've a mind to report you to the lord himself. You'll be washing plates with the boy there."

As the two cooks continued their banter, Christopher limped through the open kitchen door and emerged into the sunlight filling the inner bailey.

He had volunteered to help where he could, his leg permitting, and Hasdale had suggested helping the overworked cooks in the kitchen. Though Christopher appreciated the wonderful sights and smells, the people were a bit harsh, though nothing compared to his own father. He had kept their fires hot all morning, but now simply wished to rest. He found one of the stone benches and lowered himself onto it.

A moment later, he spotted Orvin slipping from the kitchen doorway, a confiscated loaf of bread in one hand, the other bringing a piece to his mouth. The old man saw Christopher and raised the loaf in recognition, then shambled over. Christopher made room on the bench, and Orvin sat down with an *umpff* and a crack of his spine. This, of course, made the self-appointed prophet let out a moan.

"Hello, sir."

"Tired of the kitchen, are you?"

Christopher shook his head, no. "Just resting."

Orvin proffered a piece of bread to him. Christopher

took the piece and nibbled on it tentatively, then, finding it to his liking, pushed the rest of the bread into his mouth and chewed.

"I'm glad we have a chance to chat today," Orvin said. "We can even begin your training."

"Now?" Christopher asked, though the word barely escaped through all the bread in his mouth.

Orvin handed Christopher another hunk of the loaf. "You will listen—and you will not interrupt. You will not ask questions, for in what I tell you all answers will be apparent, and if they are not, you will look harder for the implications of answers. Do you understand?"

Again, Christopher's mouth was full of bread, but between chews he managed, "I think so."

"What is a squire?" Orvin asked.

Christopher began to answer, but found another shard of bread pushed in front of his mouth.

Orvin continued, "He is a boy who desires to become a knight. And so he must learn to serve a knight before he can become one. It is a job that leads to a greater job. True?"

Christopher thought about answering, but knew his words would not be recognizable. Indeed, a mouthful of bread taught one how to be a good listener.

Orvin swatted a fly from his face, then forged on. "Obtaining greatness can only be done by mastering humility. To realize that every man is a servant. He is a servant to his heart, his mind, and to God. A squire is a servant—but so is a knight."

Christopher had never thought about it that way. He never pictured a knight as a servant, though he knew all knights served their lords and all lords served their kings. A servant was a serf, a page, a leatherdresser. Not a knight wielding a broadsword. These were mental images he would have to cast away.

"A true servant's spirit is not sullied and acts as

one with mind and heart. This servant has found his place in the world, has acted to the best of his ability and employed his true talents."

This started to sound like Orvin's way of talking him out of becoming a squire. "True talents" meant making saddles.

I have to say something! Damned bread!

"You will discover within yourself what is fated for you, and when you know and accept that, you will truly be at peace. Now, I know you are at war within yourself, worried about the training, about being alone, about many things I also agonized over at your age. But put your fears aside and stand tall in the air of a new future for yourself."

Big words, important words; they took on a scope that was so far removed from his workshop bench, the toft, Shores, that Christopher felt guilty about his new future, a future bought with the blood of his parents.

But he would never forget them, always love them.

Christopher finished chewing the bread, swallowed, rubbed his tongue around to dislodge any stubborn bits from his teeth, then cleared his throat. "May I speak?"

Orvin chuckled, and as he did he didn't see the loaf on his knee slip off to the grassy yard. "You already have, boy." Then the weathered man looked down. "Oh, clumsy, Orvin."

"I need your help," Christopher said.

"Of course you do," Orvin said, retrieving the loaf, then brushing a bit of dirt off it; he continued to inspect it for more particles.

"I need you to help me build a pyre for my parents."

Orvin looked at Christopher, and he saw the old man's lips tighten as a sympathetic look that eased Christopher's pain washed over Orvin's face. Orvin nodded, then slid an arm around Christopher's shoulder.

3 Christopher stared with a fierce sorrow at the pyre. It was a great conflagration, filling the desolate street that was once Leatherdressers' Row with golden light. Orvin's hand rested on his shoulder as both watched the fire turn the bodies of Sanborn and Cornelia darker than they already were, and then finally into ash and bones. The smell of burning flesh was thankfully masked by the thick, almost-sweet smoke of the blazing beech; Orvin had chosen the wood wisely.

The tongues of fire were hypnotic, licking at the air, dancing, and sending Christopher's mind off in a dozen directions. He pondered what Orvin had told him earlier. He considered what the actual training would be like. He remembered killing the Saxon, how that had reminded him of the knight Airell. His head was filled with so many ideas, so many emotions, he wanted to let them all out and ride each free course for as far as it would take him. But the dominant thought, the dominant feeling, was sorrow. Saying good-bye. Forever. To hold Mother and Father in mind's eye, never in true eye. To remember would be to keep them alive in himself, but they would never be alive to others—unless he shared the stories of them with those he knew.

"My father was very strong," Christopher told Orvin. "His hands were like tools themselves. And he used them so much that sometimes my mother would have to soak them in oil for him. She liked to do that, and I know he liked the way it felt. She used to play with his hair when she soaked his hands because she knew he couldn't fight her off." Christopher nodded wistfully. "I remember that."

"I myself have ridden in a saddle your father made. I have never felt one as comfortable."

"You must ride a mule. An easy saddle job."

"Not for this body," Orvin mused.

"Perhaps I will make you another in exchange for the training."

Christopher suddenly realized he had assigned himself time to the bench. So be it. The training was worth a lot more than a single saddle and some lost time.

His gaze wandered from the flames to the street beyond. He had been right about the Saxon devastation. Every house was in rubble. It was odd being able to see so many backyards where once there had been gables blocking all view and casting long shadows over the road. Shores seemed much larger now, its charred flatlands broken only by the surviving stone chimneys that rose out of the ashes like soiled grave markers. It would be some time before the village of his childhood was populated again.

Two horsemen of the garrison trotted by, acknowledging Orvin and Christopher, as they set out to patrol the outskirts of Shores, and to see how the half dozen serfs salvaging what they could from Armorers' Row were progressing. Normally the steward would be with them, but with yesterday's attack, extra precautions were taken. Christopher could feel the tension within himself and see it in others.

Orvin's attention had been on the fire a long time. He gestured hello with a wave to the soldiers, but never turned his head.

Christopher studied his profile, wondering what the man saw as he stared at the pyre. "You look hard into the flames." It wasn't exactly a question, but Christopher knew it would spark something within Orvin.

"Yes," the old one said softly, gaze still locked on the pyre.

Perhaps he sees my future—and all he says is "yes."

"See anything? I mean, do you *see* anything?"

"I sensed the first time we met that you doubted me," Orvin said. "And now you ask if I *see* anything in the pyre? I see flames."

"You look at them the same way you look at the sky," Christopher observed.

"Indeed, I use the same eyes."

Whether Orvin was a necromancer or not, he certainly had a natural talent to frustrate. And he had cast a spell on Christopher, one which made him need to be around the man—even though at the moment he wanted to choke an answer out of him. "Do you see anything else in the pyre, anything that is not there—but there?"

"Oh, I like that kind of talk," Orvin said. His head turned away from the blazing mound and his gaze lowered to Christopher. "'Anything that is not there—but there.' Oh, yes, that *is* good. You're getting the idea now." Orvin closed his eyes. There was no odd look that crossed his face, no twisting or writhing of his body, no smoke or lightening or darkening of the sky, simply an old man who, after a moment of silence punctuated by the crackling of burning wood, said, "There will be many more fires like these."

That didn't seem like much to Christopher. He wanted to know if he would become a great knight, loyal and true to his lord, winning many tournaments and achieving many victories on the battlefield. All he had received was the promise of more fires.

But not just any fires. Funeral pyres. And then Orvin's words saddled themselves on Christopher's mind. They meant death, more of it.

He had befriended the prophet of doom.

"Do you know who is going to die?" Christopher asked.

Orvin opened his eyes. He raised his eyebrows and bands of wrinkles rose on his forehead. The hint of a grin was on his lips as he revealed, "Yes."

"Tell me," Christopher said, dreading what he was about to hear. It was probably someone he knew, probably someone he liked. Maybe the lord. Maybe even Orvin; the lord's father was beyond even middle age.

Orvin turned around and set his sandals in motion away from the pyre. Christopher followed. As the old knight led Christopher up Leatherdressers' Row he said, "We're all going to die, Christopher. All of us."

Christopher shook his head as a smile curled his lips, then nudged Orvin in the ribs with his elbow. The old man let out a soft groan, then a dramatic fit of coughing. "You really are a prophet, Orvin."

Gentle zephyrs tugged at their shoulders and blew the hair from their foreheads as they continued. Christopher considered Orvin's words once more. Yes, we are all going to die, but Orvin had promised many more funeral pyres. How much more death would lie in the course ahead? Hadn't there been enough already?

Slaying the enemy was not a part of the death Christopher considered. That was the function of a knight, and killing a Saxon was just that, killing a Saxon. Death meant pain; it meant losing someone close to you, someone you loved. Who was to burn on the pyres? Loved ones or enemies?

"Life is the journey," Orvin said, "for I have already told you the destination."

"Death," Christopher noted sadly.

"Heaven is a better place."

"So the abbot told me."

"You doubt him?"

"If I had a glimpse of that place . . . "

"But you already have," Orvin said with surprise.

"I know I've seen Hell," Christopher said, pointing with his thumb over his shoulder in the direction of Shores, "but Heaven? Where?"

"You have seen it, and will see it again. The next time you will know."

It was hard to become angry with Orvin; he was, after all, being Orvin. He wasn't going to simply tell Christopher, and Christopher released his clenched fists and the anxiety from his heart. "If you're with me, will you let me know when I am looking at it?"

"I will," Orvin promised. "Indeed, I will."

4 Christopher's sleeping chamber was on the fourth floor of the keep. He stretched out on his wool-stuffed mattress and stared at the rafters; his eyes traced the cobwebs that spanned between them. He heard the footsteps of sentries on the wall-walk above, the only sound filling the lonely, dark room. Christopher had requested to sleep in the squires' chambers in the outer bailey, but Hasdale insisted on this quieter, more comfortable room for recuperation. Christopher had heard the serving women gossiping about the special treatment he received. After all, he was only the son of a simple craftsman. Why was Hasdale regarding him with such importance, putting him up in a private chamber in the keep? Christopher knew the lord had taken a liking to him. But deep down he knew there was something else, revealed by the lord himself. Christopher brought him happiness and pain. Christopher had become a son without a father—and on the same day the lord had become a father without a son. There was the link, and Christopher hoped to add another bond to it, that of squire to knight.

The steady pace of footsteps was a beating heart, putting Christopher slowly and surely to sleep. He rolled over on his side, dug his head deeper into the goose-feather pillow, then glanced at the torch mounted on the wall near the door. He closed his eyes and was swallowed into the freckled darkness. Millions of minute points of light flashed over and over: the echoing image of the flame he had lingered on seconds before.

More footsteps. The sounds of his own breathing. The vague smell of incense from somewhere. And then . . . utter darkness.

"You—a mere boy—challenge me?"

Garrett sneered at Christopher, and Christopher tried to repel the Saxon leader's cockiness from his thoughts. They stood in the middle of the great hall, surrounded by all the inhabitants of the castle, Lord Hasdale himself standing on top of the long dais table.

The armor hung heavily on Christopher's shoulders. Relief would come only with victory. He held his broadsword, the one Baines had given him at the Cam, steadying the great blade with both hands and shifting his weight from right foot to left foot, trying to hold himself back from lunging recklessly at his opponent. He was frightened, but the desire to kill grew, nurtured by the horror caused by this beast—this Garrett.

"For the deaths of my parents and the death of my friend, and for all the pain you have caused those of Shores, by God, draw your sword and give me the chance to avenge what you have done."

Garrett unsheathed the spatha bound at his waist. He gestured with his sword to the crowd around them. "So many witnesses to your death. Do you not wish to do this privately? I am a sporting man and will spare you the embarrassment of such a public display, such a public death."

Christopher felt alone. Baines could not help him now. He had to tap farther into the anger, let it pulse not only through his legs, but through his head and heart. Yes, the desire to kill had grown, and he could feel it now in his jaw as the muscles tightened and his teeth ground into each other. Then his head throbbed and his heart threatened to rip through his chest and melt through his breastplate.

He sprang toward Garrett.

The Saxon deftly parried Christopher's sword as the bejeweled blade came down toward Garrett's head. Garrett then struck a hard riposte to Christopher's shoulder. The impact rang like a church bell.

Pain shot through Christopher's arm. He spun around as Garrett one-handed his sword and swiped horizontally, making contact with the steel protecting Christopher's ribs. The armor sang; Christopher echoed it with a moan. He felt the desire to fall to his knees but fought it hard, biting back the bolt in his side.

"I offer you another chance for privacy, young one," Garrett said.

Christopher sent a black look Garrett's way, then straightened himself, gripped his sword with both hands, and drove forward. Garrett deflected the first blow, but Christopher kept going. Blow after blow his sword fought the Saxon steel that blocked it, and finally a single strike slipped through Garrett's defense and made contact with the Saxon's exposed Adam's apple. Christopher pulled his blade back and saw blood spew onto the gorget that protected Garrett's collarbone. One of the Saxon's hands went to his throat and his gaze swept the room for someone to help him.

He had injured his opponent badly. Triumph was a hot meal filling his belly, bloating him with serenity and the promise of a good night's rest afterward. Smiles were as abundant as cheers from the crowd, and Christopher drew them in, the fine wine of victory. He lowered his sword and stood, his breath slowing and his muscles loosening.

His gaze fell on a young maid, her deep, brown eyes as shiny as her long ebony hair. Her skin was clear and full of color, and white robes over an even whiter shift hid what Christopher knew must be a perfect figure. It was this whole image of beauty that controlled him, made him stand, rapt; the essence of this girl was a new reality.

He didn't see Garrett charge toward him, a bleeding animal shrieking and screaming and howling, his spatha held high over his head.

Christopher's stare shifted from the girl in time to see the point of Garrett's blade razor toward his head, come straight between his eyes—and suddenly he was lying awake in the chamber, clutching his head with both hands. The sweat poured off him even though the room was comfortably cool.

The nightmare had torn apart his system. He tried to find all of the pieces that were himself and put them together. He sat up in the bed, gulped back the lump in his throat, and wiped the dampness from his face. The footsteps above were good to hear, protective, reassuring. He remained there until his breath came slowly, and then he climbed out of the bed. Christopher got on his haunches, lifted the mattress, and pulled out a package wrapped in wool. He placed the package on the bed, untied the leather bindings, and folded back the wool to reveal the sword.

It was all he had left of Baines. After he had explained to Hasdale how he had acquired the blade, the lord let him keep it. The blade had not failed him in the dream. He had failed. Christopher picked up the broadsword, stood, then held it out into the shadows of the sleeping chamber. Abruptly, he pivoted and swung the blade through the air; steel whistled, the nearby torch flames rustled in the sudden gust. How could he stand there in the face of someone as dangerous and malignant as Garrett and fix his eyes on a girl? How could he let a blade be thrust through his head and do nothing? The thought of it brought chills to his spine.

He sat back down on the bed with the sword, let a finger trace the hilt and then the blade. He wasn't ready yet. He wasn't a knight. He wasn't even a squire. He had to learn. He needed the training, the practice. And then he'd be ready—as the broadsword would always be.

Sunlight filtered through his window and paved a golden road on his bed by the time Christopher finally got back to sleep.

5
The leatherdressers' hut was the smallest of all huts in the outer bailey. Though the craft was as important as any, save for the armorers', the saddlers were relegated to a small, dank corner just beyond the shores of a small, foul-smelling pond.

Orvin stood near the water with his mule. The animal didn't mind the smell of the pond and drank the water with steady movements of its tongue. Christopher came from the hut with his leather measuring tape and winked at the senior as he gestured with a finger for Orvin to turn around, back to him. The old man complied, and Christopher measured Orvin's buttocks with professional flair.

"No man has ever measured me for a saddle," Orvin noted, his voice carrying the tone of a man who was impressed.

"It is customary to measure only the horse. Make the saddle fit the horse and let the man adjust to the saddle. My father always measured both."

"That's very good."

Christopher went to the mule, and not disturbing it, placed his tape over the coarse gray hairs, taking width and length of the animal's back. He made mental note of the measurements and repeated them twice in his head. "Your backside is in good hands," Christopher joked, then turned toward the door of the hut. "I have work to do."

Orvin nodded, then started for the mule. "Come on now, Cara."

Christopher looked over his shoulder. The mule continued to drink, and though stubbornness was common in such a creature, Christopher could see by the look on Orvin's face that he had long since abandoned his patience and eyed the beast with complete contempt.

"Fine, then. You stay here all day drinking from this filthy hole. And if you fall ill—do not seek comforts from me." Orvin stiffened and marched off.

The mule's eyes did not leave the pond.

Christopher grinned, then slipped inside the hut.

March and Torrey, the two leatherdressers who worked there and men with whom Christopher had dealt on many occasions, were out delivering saddles to a party of archers who had assembled in a practice field near the Cam. March and Torrey were not freemen as Christopher and his father were. They were serfs who resided in the castle and paid their rent in leather services. At least Hasdale was a fair man and regarded the saddles March and Torrey made as equal in worth to the ones he commissioned by those on Leatherdressers' Row. But Christopher had twice come across the careless work the men tried to pass off as quality. He smiled inwardly as he examined some of the finished saddles hanging from the rear wall of the hut. *I could teach them a lesson or two,* he thought.

Christopher cleared himself a spot on the long bench that made up most of the small box around him, left the door open to lessen the stench, then sat down to work. He spread out a large piece of tanned leather over the table, but was interrupted by the sound of laughter from outside. Christopher looked up, and through the open doorway could see, on the

opposite side of the pond, three young girls who
stared at him, whispered secrets in each others' ears,
and giggled. One of them looked vaguely familiar,
but Christopher could not place her. He rose from
the bench and went outside the hut. Even though he
had just started, it was good to get out for a moment.
The hut warmed up as the midday sun beat down
with a steady, inaudible rhythm on the wooden timbers of the roof. The air carried the scent of the girls,
a pleasant, almost soaplike smell that wafted and
drowned out the rotting fumes of the pond.

They were all about thirteen, more or less, and
Christopher wondered why they were not at work in
the keep, sewing, mending, receiving instruction from
their mothers. Their brightly dyed livery glowed with
more color than Christopher had ever seen on anyone.
The girls of Shores wore plain, workaday clothes that
were uninteresting to his eyes. But these were castle
girls, and Christopher was completely attracted to
them.

One of the girls wore a headband woven of dark
leather, the color matching her hair. She was the one
that he seemed to recognize, but again, her smile and
the flicker in her eyes set off no triggers in his mind. Her
dress was the brightest of all, a green that was deeper
and held more secrets than the hills of Somerset.

She spoke to him. "Is that your mule?"

Christopher glanced at Cara, the tired old animal
that Orvin so loved and so hated, then returned his
attention to the girl. "No."

Christopher detected his own reticence building;
he wondered if words were going to continue.

She's beautiful.

"Oh," she said.

Christopher smiled. He felt his stomach edge a bit
toward his knees. Words were no longer a luxury he
possessed.

The two other girls were much more timid; they

kept to themselves and found the boldness of their friend entertaining and lived vicariously through it. Christopher sensed *she* would be the only one talking.

"What is your name?" she asked.

You have to answer her. Now think! Say it slowly, play it over a few times. My name is Christopher. I'm Christopher. Christopher. Chris.

"Uh . . ." He had to swallow. And then, finally, "It's Christopher."

"Are you from Shores?" She continued her examination of him, and he could see how comfortable she was conversing with him and suddenly he was very jealous of her. How dare she *not* be nervous.

If she's not nervous than neither am I.

"Yes, I'm from Shores."

"I'm sorry," she said in earnest.

"It's all right now," he said, feeling like the greatest conversation wielder that ever stepped foot in the bailey. "I've found a new home here."

She left her friends and crossed very slowly around the pond until she stood a mere three feet from him. She did smell very much like soap, a long bath most certainly in her recent past. A quick image of Fiona slipping into her tub passed through Christopher's mind and then dissolved, only *she* had taken the place of Fiona. He couldn't believe the clarity of her complexion, how smooth and fair it was, and how full and deep her lips were. There was such a sharp juxtaposition between her and the surroundings, Christopher felt the strange desire to take her someplace else to talk, as if she did not belong here, as if she would somehow be spoiled by the muddy ground, the pond, and the steamy, stench-filled hut behind him.

"I'm Brenna. It means raven maid. My hair is much the same color as my mother's—and the bird's, as you can see." She pulled a thick strand of her dark mane and twirled a finger through it, as if to prove the fact to Christopher.

"You've been to Shores before, haven't you?" he asked.

"Never."

"I'm sorry. I thought I knew you from somewhere."

Brenna shook her head. A giggle from her friends caught her attention and she glanced quickly over her shoulder and widened her eyes, eyes that said, "Quiet! I'm talking to him!" Brenna turned back to him, apologetic. "They want to meet you."

Saddle making was a lost art in the face of these three girls. Christopher was so entranced by their faces, their smell that he forced himself to walk without a limp, bearing the pain for the sake of presenting the girls with an image he hoped would live up to their expectations. He made it to the other side of the pond without passing out and greeted the other two girls.

"This is Mavis, and Wynne," Brenna said.

Mavis was the tallest of the three girls, with blond hair plaited in a neat pattern and topped with a white coif. She nodded politely, and when Christopher took her hand he felt her tremble. As he had seen his father do, he kissed Mavis's hand, and the girl's cheeks went crimson. He repeated the greeting on Wynne, whose thin brown hair was parted in the middle and ran like so many ribbons down the sides of her head. She, too, shook and blushed under his touch.

But he had forgotten to greet Brenna with such a hand kiss. It wasn't too late. He turned to her, reached out, and took her hand. "I beg your forgiveness. My absentmindedness was terrible." The back of her hand was soft, and, as his lips met her skin, he lingered a moment longer than he had on the other girls, saw himself in his mind's eye kiss not her hand but her lips. When he pulled back and his gaze was on her again, he could see he had affected her. A rose glow gently bloomed on her face.

Here he was, a poor craftsman's son surrounded by the great curtain walls of the castle of Shores, standing in the presence of three of the most lovely girls he had ever seen, wooing them with his simple though honest chivalry.

The future was not paved completely in death.

6   In the silvery light sliced by the deep shadows of the curtain walls, Christopher made his way back to the keep and took a seat at one of the trestle tables of the great hall for dinner. Orvin sat next to him, tearing into a pork rib with his few remaining teeth. The sound of the old man's eating was not a pleasant one, but Christopher knew he would grow accustomed to it; there would be hundreds of meals in which to listen to the horrible music of Orvin's mouth.

Brenna sat with her parents on the other side of the room, looking up at him occasionally. His gaze never left her table, food going into his mouth like faggots into a fire: just piling in without regard to content. Meat, some kind of vegetable, some unimportant liquid to wash it all down. Her smile meant much more than the hunger that struck his body.

Orvin licked his fingers, and then his lips. "You should enjoy your food, not shovel it down like pottage."

Christopher saw Brenna look at Orvin, then her gaze suddenly dropped to her plate as the old man's eyes met hers.

It was an ugly grin that cracked open his leathery face. "Fenella's daughter has eyes for the young patron saint next to me."

Christopher turned away from Orvin and stuffed a large chunk of boiled carrot into his mouth. He chewed hard, burying his true feelings in the act. He wasn't sure if he could tell Orvin, if it would even be proper to converse with the daughter of serfs. If he ever decided to marry Brenna, it would only be by the permission of Lord Hasdale. She was, in effect, a piece of the lord's property, and Christopher had never dealt with a serf on this level.

Who am I kidding? I have never dealt with any girl on this level.

"Oh, come on now, boy. Tell me about her. Have you met her?"

There was a knot in the wood of the trestle table that seemed to stare back at Christopher. He shifted his gaze to his plate.

"A life of leatherdressing. Sounds lonely. You could have been trained as a squire, but you refuse to open your thoughts to your master."

"That's not fair," Christopher blurted out.

Orvin leaned in close to Christopher. "Come now. Tell me of young Brenna. Hold out the olive branch to an old man and let him relive the days of his youth."

"Otherwise you refuse to train me."

"Knowledge has its privileges."

Christopher sighed deeply for effect. He tossed a quick glance to Brenna's table and saw that she and her parents had risen to leave. No matter now; he was stuck telling Orvin all about it. "She says she likes the way my cheeks look when I smile. All right?"

Orvin moved his eyebrows up and down several times, the skin on his head and around his eyes rippling like waves across a brown, lackluster sea. "She is in love with you."

Christopher frowned, then shook his head. "No."

"Oh, yes."

"She enjoys my company."

"Trust your master on these things."

"I just met her today."

"She is in love."

"How do you know?"

"The ravens have told me."

Christopher remembered that Brenna's name meant "raven maid." Was she linked to the ravens other than by name, birds with which Orvin communicated? The whole thought was ridiculous. "You see the future in the sky and find out what love lies in the hearts of young girls by speaking to the ravens. I cannot—"

"Doubt is a fever that will forever strike you down, young patron saint. If you would clear your mind and let the open arms of fate embrace you, you would be a much happier lad."

"She is a serf. I'm not sure if—"

"She serves my son. And if she wishes to befriend you, to *love* you, then so be it. Those lines have been crossed many times before. But heed this warning, do not let love blind you—as it always does."

Christopher took a long swig of wine from his tankard, then wiped his mouth on his shirtsleeve. *Do not let love blind me—as it always does.* It made as much sense as everything else Orvin had tried to tell him; that is, it made no sense. "How can I avoid blindness when it is sure to come?"

"Do not look too deeply into her eyes. Let her make you happy. That is all." Orvin adjusted himself on the bench, a loud, ugly movement that disrupted the uninitiated.

"Tell me of your own experience with love, Orvin. Hold out the olive branch to this young man so *I* can learn from the mistakes you made."

Orvin squinted a little, staring deeper with his mind's eye into the suddenly beckoned past. He was years away from the table, the great hall, and Christopher could tell from the old man's silence that he had opened up many doors, some of the chambers beyond radiating with joy, others brimming with the shadows of death. He hoped he had not upset Orvin, for the empty reaction he was faced with made him uneasy.

The old man's parched face gave way to a smile,

and relief spilled over Christopher. "My son's mother was a great woman, a strong woman, a wise woman. She let common sense dictate her decisions and was always full of advice. I would not be the man I am if it were not for her."

"Why?"

Orvin patted his heart. "This old drum, which somehow continues to beat, has always been my guide." He tapped his head with a black-nailed index finger. "Never this."

Christopher furrowed his brow, thought very hard about Orvin's words, tried to piece some advice out of this puzzle from the past. "So a man must let his heart be his guide, is that it?"

"Not completely," Orvin said. "There must be a balance of mind and heart. And love can give you that—or take it all away."

Christopher stood. "If I try to consider this any more, I will go mad and run wild through the bailey like the dogs!"

"That's love."

Christopher trunked it all away. If love would drive him mad, then he'd rather not think about it and just let it happen—if it had to. And perhaps that would be the pattern. "Good evening, master."

"Sleep well, young patron saint. Dream."

Christopher slid from behind the bench and moved toward the tunnel exit that would take him up to his chamber. If he would do any dreaming at all, it had better be about Brenna.

7

Below the mist-shrouded castle, past the jagged ramparts that surrounded it, and beyond the thin forest that grew from the slopes, ten squire trainees were lined up in the middle of a rolling, open field. Ten boys of varying heights and builds and lengths of hair were shoulder to shoulder, a motley crew of pubescent plebes who stood under cloudy skies on wet grass with sleep grit still lodged in the corners of their eyes.

Four tall weapons racks behind the squires supported a wide array of lethal irons and were damp from the early-morning dew. Near the racks, two archers on horseback were paused, scouting for a pair of varlets to serve them. Not every boy would serve a knight, but attending an archer was no less honorable a task, and would turn a lad into an expert bowman.

Christopher pulled on the padded tunic Orvin had given him; it felt hot and sticky. He hated the humidity as much as getting up early in the morning. But, it was his first day on the practice field, his calf finally healed enough to support the rigors of the training, and he would miss it for nothing.

Orvin sat on top of Cara and watched the proceedings from some fifty yards away. Christopher winked at the old man, who acknowledged with a slight tip of his head.

As Christopher stood, anticipation of another kind filled his mind. Tonight was the rendezvous with Brenna. They had planned it all week and were going to meet in the empty prison cellar after dinner. Brenna's parents would think she was at the chapel with Mavis and Wynne. Christopher would slip out of the squires' quarters and arrive in her arms soon after midnight.

His heart ached for her as his sandaled feet sank into the mushy earth. He was sure the other boys felt as uncomfortable as he did, but their faces revealed nothing. Nine names had whipped past his ears in such a hurry he had barely caught the syllables of one. Later, when the session was over, he would have to meet them again. There was nothing exceptionally friendly about the other boys, for they all wore the same dark masks of determination, all standing very stiffly like statues as the gusts of thick, wet air split around them.

"If any of you do not know me, my name is Sloan, and I am one of Hasdale's battle lords." He paced before them in full armor, and Christopher could not help but admire his stout stature. He was immense, pure muscle and steel guided by a keen mind that took in information through near-black eyes, a stubby, rough nose, callused fingers, and a wide, thick-lipped mouth.

The boy next to Christopher turned his head slightly, and Christopher caught the motion on his periphery. Christopher looked at the boy. The pale, would-be squire with the stubble of hair growing below his lower lip crinkled his nose and bared his clenched teeth. Christopher looked away.

Sloan ran a hand over his bald head, pulling the perspiration from it before continuing. "Some of you may find today's session a bit simple, but it is a combination of endeavors that will turn you pages and scullery serfs into squires, and perhaps even knights."

Christopher liked Sloan. He spoke simply and truthfully and wasn't the austere trainer that he had expected to find.

"You there, what is your name?" Sloan spoke directly to him.

"Christopher."

"Step up here. You're to be our first victim."

Christopher was hesitant, looked to Orvin, who urged him on with a hand wave. He put his feet in motion. Christopher felt even colder as he came within a few feet of the battle lord. At this distance, he could see the scars embedded in the man's skin; one clean slash across his forehead, another jagged line through his eyebrow that skipped over his eye and cut down the top portion of his cheek, finishing near the earlobe. The hair of the brow had not grown back and gave it an odd moustachelike look.

"Arms identification. It's a simple game, and many of you think you've already mastered it." Christopher was close enough to smell the wine on the battle lord's breath, and twitched his nose several times as Sloan spoke to the boys behind him. "But you have not."

Sloan led Christopher by the arm over to the racks. Christopher studied the several-sized lances and glaives, the halberds to hook mounted men off their steeds, the picks and javelins and spiked maces. He glanced over the bills, spears with varying tips and side hooks, the deadly balls and chains, the cat-o'-nine-tails, and the battle-axes of differing designs. One rack held nothing but spathas, dozens of horn and brass-hilted types. Christopher knew he could identify each and every weapon on the racks, but as Sloan had said, "Many of you think you have already mastered it." There was a catch.

"The knight who chooses you as his squire has his own style of battle. He prefers certain weapons at certain times, and he wishes to be handed these arms in a particular manner that he alone is comfortable with. Speed, quick thinking, and sense of touch are most important."

The delivery of arms didn't seem much different than the delivery of saddles or the delivery of dinner plates; one need only know where the package was going and how to present it. Christopher's confidence jumped up another notch. It was a good chance to show the rest of the squires what he was made of. If he did well, every boy that followed would be measured against his performance. He had to set the standard.

"I will call for a weapon and Christopher will retrieve it for me. I will stand twenty yards away and he will hand the weapon to me in the manner in which I instruct him. Glaive! The shortest one!"

The burst from Sloan's mouth caught Christopher by surprise—but only for a millisecond. He darted for the rack and scanned the weapons, found the shortest glaive, grabbed it, turned around, and sprinted toward Sloan. The battle lord had taken his described position. Christopher handed him the weapon point up, and Sloan motioned with his index finger that he wanted the point down. Christopher spun the spear around and presented it to his instructor.

Sloan repeated the process with Christopher, who fetched some fifteen different weapons. The other squires scratched themselves or folded their arms or shifted their weight back and forth, watching with vapid eyes as the tedious and what seemed to be ultimately unchallenging process continued. When Christopher was done, his breath ragged and his face ruddy and damp, Sloan moved in front of all the squires to deliver his next dialogue. Christopher remained where he was, in front of the rack.

"The delivery of weapons must become second nature, and that only develops over time. But we have to speed up the process." Sloan stepped back over to Christopher and reached down into a small leather pouch belted at his side. In the battle lord's hand appeared a long, woolen rag.

"Turn around," Sloan ordered Christopher.

Christopher saw the world go to darkness as Sloan tied the blindfold tightly behind his head. Hoots and guffaws from the squires commenced.

Sure, retrieving the weapons seemed beyond simple. But now it was a different game.

"Problems invariably arise on the battlefield. Smoke, nightfall, the chaos of an ambush. You must be able to find and deliver the weapons to your master without your eyes. It seems impossible—but it's not."

Christopher concentrated on the last vision of the rack he had seen. He tried to pinpoint the location of each and every weapon he had returned there, but some of them were fuzzy, obscured by nerves, pressure, laughs from the squires, sweat, and his staggering heart.

"The long-handled mace!"

Christopher moved forward in the direction he felt was the rack. Raucous laughter erupted from his peers. He was in a realm of pain and darkness, searching blindly for his future, and was spat and chuckled at all the way. For a moment he thought of giving up, but he set his jaw and turned his body in another direction. After half a dozen steps he stumbled into a rack. He felt the weapons: spathas. Wrong rack. But he knew where the other rack was. He drifted sideways and came upon his destination. His hands fumbled over hilts and tips and spikes and long tongues of leather. More sickening laughter. He felt a mace, ran his fingers over the weapon; satisfied it was the long-handled one, he clutched it, pivoted around, and stepped gingerly back toward Sloan.

"Here, squire! Bring me my mace!"

Christopher followed the voice and drew nearer to Sloan. He slid his hand up on the weapon so that his fingers were just below the balled end of the club. He held the handle out for the knight to take. The weapon slipped from his fingers into Sloan's. Then light stabbed his pupils. The blindfold had been yanked off. Christopher rubbed his eyes with the heels of his hands and blinked back the sudden day.

"A bit slow, but for a first time, respectable. We'll work on it, Christopher. Return to your place in line."

Christopher balled his fists in pride as he rejoined the other trainees.

While the next boy ran through the weapons routine, Christopher observed that none of the trainees in line were laughing. Each watched the next victim intently, seeing themselves in that boy and wondering how they would do blindfolded.

The last boy to run through the routine was Doyle, the trainee next to Christopher who had shot him that ugly look. Doyle appeared to be the oldest of the crew, perhaps even sixteen, and slightly taller than the rest of the trainees. Christopher noticed that Doyle was faster than anyone he had seen thus far, and feared Doyle was swifter than himself.

When the time came for Doyle to run a weapon blindfolded, Sloan chose the middle-sized javelin, perhaps the hardest weapon to identify, considering there were three other javelins that were almost identical, varying in length by mere inches.

But Doyle proved his competence and ran the javelin back to Sloan with the precision of a sighted man. Christopher could not help but be envious. The other squires openly expressed their admiration by nudging Doyle with their fists as he found his place back in the formation.

"You run very well," Christopher said.

Doyle did not reply to the compliment, but remained cold and stoic next to Christopher. It was odd standing next to someone who really wasn't there, and as Sloan spoke more about what would follow in the days ahead, Christopher began to think of Doyle as an obstacle: there, something that must be stepped around, and something you do not talk to. Perhaps Doyle felt the same about him.

When the session was over, Christopher watched as Doyle marched back toward the castle alone. Christopher was accosted by the other boys and answered their questions about the burning of Shores, the story that had been passed around the castle about his slaying a Saxon, and the death of Baines. He answered these questions with an absence caused by the mysterious and abrupt boy named Doyle. Why was he so reserved?

After Christopher finished conversing with his new friends, he climbed on Cara's waiting back and let Orvin lead the mule back toward the castle. The mule's steps were measured and smooth, and it was good to take the weight off his throbbing and limp legs.

"The pressure was on you, being first," Orvin said.

"I thought about that for a moment. But then I just acted."

"As you should have. Do not be surprised if more rigors are placed in your arms than in any other's. It is by Hasdale's request."

"Then it was no accident that I was picked first."

"You held your pennon as high as any other."

"But not as high as one."

Orvin did not address Christopher's reference, but Christopher knew the old man understood. Doyle's flag had flown the highest.

The breeze was balmy, and the sun burned off the morning haze and opened up the clouds. The path took them through the thin, verdant stand of trees that broke into the base of the hill supporting the castle. As they started up the rise, Christopher's curiosity leaked to his lips: "Who is Doyle?"

The sonata of meadow pipits flitting from branch to branch and the thumping of Cara's hooves on the dirt filled Christopher's ears. He waited for an answer to join those sounds, but none came.

"Who is Doyle?" he repeated.

Orvin made a noise with his mouth that could have been the phrase, "I don't know," but Christopher was unsure. What he was sure of was that Orvin hid something. The lie was easy to read.

"You know everyone, Orvin. Tell me."

"He is Baines's brother."

Christopher was at once shocked—and then in total disbelief. "No he isn't. Baines had no brother."

"Doyle was taken by Weylin, a traveling jewelry merchant, when he was very young, and only returned to the castle when the merchant was killed while stopping briefly—but at the wrong time—at Shores."

"He was kidnapped and forced to serve the merchant?"

"At first, yes. But I believe he grew to love the man."

"So he's a lot like me," Christopher said. "Without parents."

"Oh, he has parents. But they do not know their son."

"Does he know I was Baines's friend?"

"He knows Baines was killed with you."

"I don't think he likes me," Christopher said, his voice full of resignation. "He probably blames me for his brother's death."

"His feelings cannot be that strong," Orvin answered. "Baines was a brother that Doyle barely knew."

"I hope you're right."

Orvin's reasoning carried truth, but the sneer on Doyle's face was a picture hanging firmly on a wall of Christopher's mind. He decided he would not cower in the presence of Doyle, despite the boy's aggressiveness. In fact, he would try to befriend Doyle. There was so much he could tell Doyle about Baines. Christopher and Baines had been like brothers for a brief time, and to rekindle that kind of friendship with Doyle might ignite a part of Christopher that had fallen into midnight, a part that Baines had lit so brilliantly.

8 Green mold covered the walls of the long, narrow hall that led to the prison cells. There was a particular scent to it, not the characteristic fetor that wafted from the pond outside the leatherdressers' hut, more a musty, tight stench that sneaked up on the nostrils. A leaky well created much of the dampness in this stone tomb, one that was never fixed, and perhaps just as well. Prisons were supposed to be cold, dark, damp, and this one would live up to every criminal's expectations right down to the mystic spiderwebs tracking its ceilings and the dark, cracked corners where wall met floor, the gatehouses of rat holes.

The door to the cellblock was open via a new leather sheath covering the snoring jailer's spatha on the far end of the hall. Bribery was a new talent of Christopher's, one he felt at once comfortable and at once nervous about. A double cross made him nervous, but old Regan had taken the new sheath in his paws, and his three chins pushed out as he leaned down and inspected the work. His beefy face reflected a smile back to Christopher, and the deal was sealed. The open door was Regan's end of the bargain. No double cross. Relief.

Christopher pulled the iron-barred door slowly toward him. There was no creaking noise that, from the looks of the rusted hinges, should have come. *Regan must have oiled them.* The jailer did not want his slumber disturbed. *Good.*

He passed into the cellblock, shifting his head from side to side, scanning the miserable interiors of cell after cell. Shackles hung from the walls, the floors, and the ceilings, all manners of binding a man evident in each of the quarters. A prisoner could hang from the ceiling and the wall, the wall and the floor, the floor and the ceiling. Christopher felt empathic pain flicker across his ankles and wrists as he imagined what serving time here would be like. *Unshackle me, damn you! I'm innocent! INNOCENT!* Groans of pain and the howling of the mad were sounds that seemed to echo still off the stone around him.

Christopher arrived at a cell near the end of the block, pushed in its iron door—which this time protested loudly—then stopped. He edged the barrier a few more inches so that his body could pass through.

He heard Regan shift his position in the high-backed chair, then continue his snoring, mumbling something about youth and the lieutenant and "no, don't tickle me like that."

Inside the cell, Christopher set down the woolen blanket and the two pillows he carried. He unfolded the blanket across the floor. Bound within the garment was a richly enameled drinking horn and a thin clay jug of ale plugged with a cork. He had sneaked the horn out of Orvin's chamber and figured on having it back before his master rose in the morning. He knew how important the horn was to Orvin; it was only to be used on the most special occasions: a victory celebration, a marriage, a birth, a death.

And, of course, a midnight rendezvous with a beautiful girl in a dungeon.

Christopher placed the ale and the horn to the side of the blanket, then positioned the pillows on the wool, leaned back, and tried out the makeshift bed. The stone floor was extremely hard, but he shrugged it off. It wasn't exactly a poster bed in the solar, but it was theirs. And it was private.

The sound of tentative footsteps rose above Regan's snoring. Christopher bolted up from the blanket and slid out into the hall. He turned his head to see Brenna walk toward him, her face betraying her trepidation, clearly born from the location of their meeting place.

She voiced her misgivings. "Are you sure this will be all right?"

Christopher nodded, put his index finger to his

lips, then gestured with his thumb to Regan behind him. Regan breathed like an armorer's bellows, a great bag of wind inhaling and exhaling and capable of keeping even the most stubborn of fires hot.

Christopher led Brenna back to their cell, where they both settled on the blanket. Brenna would not lean back on the pillow, but sat upright, her eyes still taking in the eerie decor of the prison.

The cork came easily from the jug, and Christopher filled the drinking horn with ale. He proffered the horn to Brenna, who took the ale and sipped on it twice before returning it to Christopher.

Christopher downed a huge gulp of the fresh brew, then smacked his lips, refilled the horn, then downed another swig.

"What do we do now?" Brenna asked.

What Christopher wanted to do, and what she would *let* him do, were two different things. What they both wanted to do was a third. He had started with a kiss on her hand, and graduated to a kiss on her cheek one evening as he said good-bye to her just outside the garderobe of the great hall. But now the stone walls and iron bars boxing them in had ironically opened up a world of private possibilities to him. No one would ever know or see what happened here except them. He had fantasized about her on more than one occasion. He saw them alone, in each other's arms, their bodies pressed tightly together as he buried his face in her neck.

"I don't know," Christopher said. "What do you want to do?"

Brenna shrugged. She twirled an idle finger through her ebony hair. Christopher had seen her do this before, and he took it as a sign of her boredom. He had to extract himself from her twirling.

He grabbed her hand and turned it over, palm up. "Did you know that I'm a chiromancer?"

Brenna smiled, shook her head, no. Keeping company with Orvin paid off in situations like this. Christopher had become an amateur storyteller with a keen sense for whimsical tales that always involved himself.

"Oh, yes," he continued, "I studied with two of the finest when they passed through Shores. I can tell you things you never knew about yourself, and things that will happen to you."

Christopher passed his finger slowly across Brenna's palm, pretending to see things in the skin that made his jaw drop and his vocal cords rustle with "ohs" and "ahs."

"What is it?" Brenna asked.

Christopher widened his eyes, then raised his eyebrows several times as Orvin was fond of doing. A sly smile nicked the corners of his mouth. "You really need to know this, but you have to unlock the messages within me first."

"How do I do that?"

By the way she asked, Christopher knew she was on to him. "With a kiss."

Christopher's desire was no visible surprise to her. She slid herself across the blanket, leaned forward, and closed her eyes.

The moment was here, and Christopher felt a sudden surge of panic quake within him. All the anticipation and expectation of kissing her fully and squarely was now at the forefront. And with the perfect moment upon him, the fear of success, of obtainment, wrestled with the desire to lick his lips and kiss her.

"You filthy swine! Get in there!"

Christopher turned his head so quickly that he felt a muscle lurch in his neck. Brenna shot to her feet. Christopher stood and peered slightly beyond the iron door.

Two armored sentries hauled in a drunken, barefoot young herald whose torn stockings and tunic, blackened left eye, and bleeding knuckles advertised either a brawl he had been in or the fist-happy work of the sentries. Probably both.

One of the sentries strong-armed the herald into a cell three doors down from theirs, then slammed the iron door after the man. "You'll not see the light of day this week," the sentry promised in a baritone voice that bounced off the walls.

Christopher turned back to Brenna, knowing his face did not reassure her. In fact, it terrified her. She was about to say something, but caught herself with a hand over her mouth. The sentries started down the hall toward Regan. They would have to pass their cell.

Christopher yanked up the blanket and pillows, threw them against the side wall closest to the approaching sentries. He pushed himself against that wall and stood with Brenna, gripped her hand tightly, and wished he could disappear into the cracks in the stone behind him. Their bodies stiffened as the sentries passed by on their left. A pair of long shadows glided across the floor of the cell.

As the sentries tried to wake Regan, Christopher and Brenna hustled up the blanket, ale, and horn, then moved to the opposite wall of the cell, pressing everything as tightly as they could against it.

Regan told Christopher that they hadn't had a prisoner in the dungeon in over two moons. It was Christopher's luck that business had suddenly improved in the cellblock.

But it was also Christopher's luck that the guards, having notified Regan of the recent inmate's arrival and location, slipped by them without incident. They let out their breaths.

Christopher looked to Brenna. She was striking in the dim light, parts of her face illuminated then cast in shadow, the total image of her face held back, teasing him with its completeness.

Both of them still fought for breath as Christopher

moved quickly toward her and let his lips find hers. It was wet and soft and nice. Their kiss.

And as if on cue: "You! I almost forgot about you!"

They turned their heads to see Regan standing in the hall, squinting at them and rubbing his stubble-laden jowls.

"Did they see you?" Regan was emphatic.

Christopher shook his head: they didn't.

"Thank St. George. I'd be finding a home instead of a job here. Now I've got company, Christopher. You have to go." Regan turned around and shuffled back toward his chair.

Christopher leaned down and folded up the blanket while Brenna returned the cork to the jug of ale. As he stacked the two pillows on top of the blanket, Christopher felt hands pull his head around. Suddenly, Brenna's lips smothered his. The kiss lasted nearly two minutes, and when it was done they both sighed deeply.

Quietly, they left the cell and trudged down the hall, stopping briefly to spy the herald lying supine and unconscious on the floor of his cell. The boy was a mess.

Moments later, a rat appeared from a gap between the stones in the corner of the cell Christopher and Brenna had vacated. The rodent scampered to the drinking horn lying on the other end of the cage, sniffed at the horn, then began to slowly lick its rim.

9

The hut that housed the squires-in-training sat along the rear curtain wall of the castle and was behind the armorer's workshop. By day, the armorer's incessant hammering was unbearable, but by night the hut was cool and quiet.

Christopher did not want to wake the others as he slipped under the posts that supported the loft where they slept. But in the darkness of the quarters he misjudged the distance and stumbled into one of the wide beams. The clay jug of ale he carried fell to the earth. The jug didn't break; it didn't make much noise at all. But any sound would be picked up by the fine-tuned young ears above.

"Christopher?"

Christopher bent over and picked up the ale, then answered in his own loud whisper, "Go back to sleep!"

"Did you kiss her?" another voice asked.

"What was it like?" still another wanted to know.

"Shush!" Christopher ordered as he mounted the wooden ladder that would take him to the loft. There was little chance of slipping quietly into bed now, and the whining of the timbers under his feet went ignored. He reached the top, set down his belongings, then palmed his way onto the dry, chipped floor.

A dozen low-lying, foldable cots were lined up on one side of the room. The opposite was obscured by rows and rows of neatly stacked grain bags, as these quarters also provided a backup supply room for the kitchen. The squires-in-training didn't mind the grain bags. They had fun in the late evenings tracking down the mice that darted in and out of the crevices formed by the bags. Mice hunting had become a competitive sport here in the squires' hut, and as Christopher moved toward the last cot tucked into the corner of the loft, he nearly tripped over Bryan, one of the long-haired pages. The trainee dug his hand under a grain sack, engaging the Saxon mouse with clenched teeth and stiff shoulders.

"Oh, I missed him!" Bryan whispered.

"Don't you ever sleep, Bryan?" Christopher stepped over the boy and dropped his blanket and pillows onto his cot. His eyes had adjusted to the darkness of the loft, and Christopher could see Doyle, three cots down from him, staring blankly at the ceiling. Christopher watched the boy a moment, considered talking with him, but decided it best he get some sleep. Sloan had promised them a grueling session for the next day. He arranged his pillows and fell back onto the thin mattress. He tossed and turned for what felt like two hours. Frustrated, he reached down and picked up the jug of ale on the floor to his right; he uncorked it and drank the remaining brew with deep, loud gulps. Finally, he fell into a numb slumber.

The familiar and irritating call of the roosters perched on the fence poles of the livestock pen woke the squires. Christopher rubbed the bloodshot orbs that were his eyes as he sat up in bed. Then he collapsed back onto his pillow, rolled over, and pulled the blanket over his head. He heard the voices of the other trainees as two of them decided to fetch a few buckets of water from the well and wash up. Their banter was the same every morning, and Christopher would usually participate in it, but he had returned late the previous night and the ale took its toll on his system. He could taste the brew lingering in his mouth, and the beats of his heart filled his head. Despite the creaky cot, the thin, straw-filled mattress, and the itchy woolen blanket, he felt absolutely wonderful just snuggled there. He convinced himself that it would be all right if he missed that day's session.

"Out of bed!" someone cried.

Christopher felt himself lifted and suddenly lightning struck his body in the form of a wave of cold water. His blood went icy and his teeth chattered. Through squinted eyes he saw Bryan the mouse catcher holding an empty well bucket, and behind him the rest of the squires were circled around and laughing. Christopher raked his fingers through his sopping hair, then went for the blanket to dry himself, but it, too, was soaked. He got quickly to his feet, shivered hard, then yelled, "That was not necessary! I was getting up!"

Bryan shook his head, not believing it.

Christopher stormed out of the loft and climbed down the ladder. When he got to the earth floor he spun around and collided with Doyle, who was on his way back up.

"Sorry," Christopher said, surprised.

"What happened to you?" Doyle asked.

"Little wake-up from Bryan."

"I guess it worked."

"Yes, it did."

"See you out there."

Doyle's last was spoken as a challenge, but Christopher wasn't particularly interested in that. As Doyle mounted the ladder behind him, it occurred to Christopher that he had actually conversed with Baines's brother. This was an excellent new start, and perhaps they could forget about yesterday and the darker past and focus on the future.

The shivers never seemed to leave his body, even after Christopher dried himself, donned his padded practice tunic, a clean pair of breeches, and leather riding boots. His eyes still burned from the lack of sleep and his stomach spoke the garbled words of a man hanging from a gallows tree.

Ham steaks and quail eggs answered the cries of his belly, and warm goat's milk replaced the taste of ale. The great hall was unusually quiet as most of the garrison had already eaten and gone. The lord's table was empty, as was Brenna's. Her family had not arrived yet, and Christopher expected that he and the rest of the trainees would be on the practice field by the time they did. Even Orvin had not appeared that morning. It felt like a Sunday.

Sloan arrived by the time most of the boys finished eating, and assembled the trainees into two lines. They all marched out of the keep, through the pair of gatehouses, and descended the slope, leaving home behind them.

Christopher walked closely behind the trainee in front of him. He didn't think about much as he marched, noticed the simple things: the weather was much more agreeable that day, the air drier, the sky clearer, the sun already cutting through the tree line and edging its way higher. The grass was still wet, but would dry off much more quickly than the day before. Sloan had told them that mud would become their friend, but perhaps they would not meet Sir Mud.

As they came from the wood and stepped into the beginnings of the field, Christopher noticed that the weapons racks from the day before were present, but were now joined by four targets, each about a hundred yards apart. Christopher recognized the targets as quintains, but they were designed differently than the ones he'd seen used at the tournament held outside Shores a year earlier. The target itself was a tanned leather hide, probably filled with straw, and stretched over a round, wooden back wall. The target was supported by iron legs, a tripod arrangement that was standard and secure. But a fourth leg rose up through the center of the tripod and extended beyond the tops of the other legs. Mounted on top of the fourth bar was an iron ring, and fastened to the iron ring was a chain as thick as one of Christopher's arms. On the end of this chain was what appeared to be another target, this one rectangular-shaped and wrapped with many more hides than the round target. Christopher imagined this swinging, baglike target in use, and suddenly knew that his notion to stay in the loft had probably been a good one.

They didn't say it was going to be easy.

Sloan led them to the same spot as before and they resumed the same formation. Christopher belched inwardly; breakfast wasn't agreeing with him. The sour taste of bile mixed with eggs made him want to spit. Instead, he grimaced as he swallowed.

A dozen saddled, bridled, and shod rounseys came forth from the forest and trotted onto the field. The steeds were led by the stable master, a man with a serious overbite and the sad expression of a monk. He slid down the red hood covering his head, then tapped his courser with his quirt. The horse quickened its pace.

The rounseys arrived before the trainees, and Sloan stepped up to address the man. "Good morning, Galvin."

The stable master was a sour serf. "If one of these boys hurts any of my ladies, I will take it up with the lord."

"What happened to our usual practice mounts?"

"They're in West Camel, I'm afraid. On loan."

"Rest assured, I'll make sure your ladies are treated with kindness and respect."

The stable master nodded, then reined his courser around and galloped off.

When the master was out of earshot, Sloan announced to everyone, "You will ride hard and to the best of your ability. A man who worries more about his horse than himself will find an early grave on the battlefield. Yes, they are loyal creatures, but they are tools. Never forget that. Attachments to them will lead to pain."

Sloan was honest, brutally honest. Christopher hadn't had the opportunity to become attached to a horse, but he had seen many knights who swore by the same steed, and when that animal died, they walked the land like lost souls for at least a moon. They wouldn't even use the same saddles, regardless that the device fitted the new animal perfectly. It was a superstition, and one of the reasons why Christopher's father had never run out of work.

Before they were allowed to pick out a rounsey, the trainees ran through the arms delivery routine once more, this time delivering weapons to a mounted Sloan. Christopher found his speed improved, despite the sick feelings daggering his head and stomach. Doyle's time was better as well. They both accelerated at the same pace, but Doyle seemed locked into that higher notch. Christopher would not let it bother him. What did bother him at the current moment was the idea that he would have to ride, put his belly on top of one of those steeds and charge a target.

As the others moved quickly through the horses, inspecting and choosing, Christopher absently picked the first beast he came upon. He got sicker as the idea grew into the reality. *I have to get up on this horse? Now? Ohhhhhh . . .*

It was amazing how the excitement of becoming a squire could be so easily blighted by a hangover. The desire to succeed never left Christopher, it was simply overcome by the desire to puke his guts out.

"Mount your horses!" Sloan ordered.

Christopher blinked hard as the sun finally cleared the tree line and was full in his face. He turned to his rounsey, a brown mare with eyes that were large and seemed full of sorrow. He checked the saddle, recognized the craftsmanship as March and Torrey's, and snickered. Besides feeling internally ill, he would have to endure perhaps four hours on this slapped-together piece of dung.

They didn't say it was going to be this *hard.*

Before climbing up, Christopher went over to face the horse. "Take me quickly but smoothly like a mule. Understand?" The animal's large, globular eyes stared through Christopher. He shook his head

resignedly, then stepped over and levered himself
onto the rounsey, praying under his breath.

Ten horses were poised in four lines some three
hundred yards behind the targets. Christopher noted
the arrival of four garrison men, simple sentries
recruited for target duty. Each of the men manned a
position behind a target, readying both hands on the
bag that hung from the chain.

Sloan would explain it, but Christopher already
had a good idea what would happen. They were supposed to charge the targets with weapons, javelins
probably, and the garrison men behind the targets
would try to stop them. In Christopher's mind, he
would glide gracefully toward the target, dodge the
swinging bag, center his javelin, then rein in his
horse, all while not throwing up. That was a best-
case scenario. He repressed the ugly images of a
worst-case scenario; they were too vivid, too real, too
close to what might really happen.

Sloan didn't disappoint. His explanation was clear,
save for the news that the swinging target was not
exactly a target and would be used in attempts to dismount the squires as they threw their javelins. If one
of the heavy hide bags made contact with
Christopher's torso, he knew that, besides falling,
he'd empty himself onto the grass.

Christopher purposefully waited on the back of
one of the longer, three-horse lines. He would watch
two other boys make their runs before he did. That
was helpful. He half expected to be forced into going
first. That notion sparked another and he looked
around for Orvin. The old man was nowhere in sight.

Sloan raised his arm, then lowered it, and the first
boy in every line was off. Christopher watched as
small, dry clumps of earth arced low in the air behind
the first horse in his line. The trainee approached the
target, drew back his javelin.

The garrison man feinted left with the bag, then

swung it right. The heavy, hard hide slammed into the trainee's shoulder as he released his javelin. The weapon fell short of the target, earthing itself about a yard from the tripod's base.

The weapon wasn't the only thing that fell. The rider's left foot slipped out of its stirrup at the moment of contact, and the boy dropped right, crashing hard onto the ground. But it wasn't over.

The trainee's right foot remained lodged in its stirrup. The mare dragged the boy. Christopher flinched as he saw the heavy hooves of the horse come down on the trainee's hand, and then his arm. Agonizing cries came from the boy as the target man hustled after the mare. The horse stopped on its own accord, and the target man freed the boy's leg. The trainee began to cry.

Runs at the target were held up while Sloan checked on the condition of the squire. The fallen boy's arm and hand were badly bruised, but he hadn't broken any bones. The trainee was lucky. He would sit out the rest of the day's session, but Christopher knew he would be back on the morrow.

Bryan was the boy ahead of Christopher in line. He turned back to face Christopher, and let out a long, leery sigh. "Want to go ahead of me?"

"No. But don't fret. That was a freak mishap."

"How can you say that? They're *trying* to dismount us."

"Grip your pommel, not your reins. Try it."

Bryan grabbed the pommel of his saddle, tested the strength of the wood, the support it would provide. "I will."

Doyle was in the line next to Christopher's, and would ride at the same time as Bryan. Seeing the almost familiar features of Baines's brother reminded Christopher of the squire practice he and Baines had shared only a short time ago. Baines had tried to teach him how to fall. If he had learned anything, he had better utilize it now. Walking pain was the alternative.

Arm down. Bryan and Doyle sprang forward.

Doyle dug his heels hard into his mare, and the animal leapt ahead of Bryan's. Doyle steadied his javelin.

The target man swung the bag at him.

Doyle blocked the leather hide with his forearm while he sent his javelin razoring through the air. He caught the target, though off-center. Above all, he had remained on his mount.

"Excellent, Doyle! Impressive, boy! Impressive!" Sloan shouted.

Bryan neared his target, but his bag man was more creative.

The man feinted right, feinted left—then came left, sending the bag whipping through the air.

Bryan gripped the pommel as Christopher had suggested and took the bag flatly in the face. His javelin fell from his hand as his body arced back under the impact. He was terribly shaken, but he didn't fall.

The right side of Bryan's face took on the deep shine of an apple as he trotted back toward Christopher. Blood trickled from the boy's nose. Bryan smiled, and raised a balled hand. "I remained in the saddle. Next run I hit the target."

Christopher returned his own clenched fist of strong will. He moved his rounsey to the starting position, took the javelin Bryan handed him. He paused, and the world took on different and strange dimensions. Height became fear, width heat, and depth spelled promised pain. Rivulets of sweat inched down the sides of his cheeks as he looked at the target and the ugly half grin on the garrison man shadowing it. He began to feel dizzy, a kind of spinning down and over through the horse that placed him upright again. *Ignore everything and ride!* he screamed in his head. His heart seemed to stop for a moment, then kick in again. His fingers rubbed the cold steel of the javelin while his right hand clamped the shoddy pommel March or Torrey had commissioned. He looked to Sloan for the start, and saw Orvin approach on Cara over the battle lord's shoulder. The old man spotted him and raised his head. In the foreground, Sloan's arm dropped.

His boots went to the mare's ribs. The animal dug its hooves into the dry grass. Christopher bounced up and down in the saddle. Breakfast flooded the back of his throat.

The garrison man stepped back with the swinging bag.

Christopher neared the target, drew back his arm, swallowed. The bag came for his head. He ducked, put his face down near the pommel. The bag passed over his head as he jabbed the target with his javelin, not throwing it, but stabbing it underarm. A direct hit, off-center, but a kill.

"Nice move, Christopher!" Sloan yelled.

Christopher heard the congratulatory remark, but could not acknowledge Sloan for it. He remained in his forward position on the rounsey, and when the horse drifted into a canter and then finally stopped behind the target, Christopher sat there breathing, feeling his cheeks draw in and his mouth fill with saliva.

Orvin trotted up as Christopher expelled his steaming, half-digested breakfast onto the grass. "A rough night, followed by a rough ride. Am I speaking the truth, young patron saint?"

The singsong tone of Orvin's voice made Christopher feel worse. The old man took great pleasure in seeing him suffer. Then Orvin's words registered: "rough night." He cleared the fire from his throat. "I couldn't sleep last night," Christopher tested.

"Or you didn't have the time to."

"What are you saying, Orvin?"

"I'm saying a squire trainee does not make deals with jailers. A squire trainee does not slip out into the night with a young serf girl and expect to perform his best on the practice field the next day. And most of all, a squire trainee does not borrow something without asking its owner first—especially something as cherished and sacred as my drinking horn!"

The horn. He'd forgotten to replace it. Where was it? He searched his memory, didn't recall seeing it in the loft. Did he forget it in the cell?

"Not only did you take my horn, but you carelessly left it in the dungeon to be gnawed at by the rats!"

At least he'd received his answer, if not his death sentence.

Christopher's head was already lowered, but now in shame as well as nausea. "Sorry," he uttered, then coughed.

"Do not look too deeply into her eyes," Orvin warned, then turned Cara around and trotted away.

Christopher resumed his place on the target line and watched his peers make further runs. Doyle completed another successful attack on the hide, and Bryan managed to get his javelin into the target, but it didn't penetrate deep enough and fell out.

He almost felt better as he prepared for his second run. Almost. The little demon of guilt was on his back. He had betrayed Orvin's trust. It wasn't a deep betrayal, but still, it smarted. He would narrow himself now, fix his mind on the training and the training alone.

Easier thought than done. In the face of Brenna's eyes, hair, lips, he wasn't sure what he'd do.

Orvin did not stay to watch, and that was part of the hurt. He would have been proud had he seen Christopher dodge the bag and opt to hit it with his javelin instead of the target. An even harder mark, but Christopher sent his rod needling into the heavy hide, surprising the life out of the garrison man. The bag swung back at the man, the javelin sticking out of it. The pole struck the sentry in the ribs, and though the link-mail of the man's hauberk muffled the serious pain, the force knocked him onto his backside. Those watching burst into laughter. Christopher turned his rounsey around and looked at Doyle. The boy pursed his lips and nodded, impressed. *Top that,* Christopher thought.

Unfortunately, Doyle did. Utilizing two javelins, the boy rode without holding the reins, hit both the main target and the bag while not so much as slipping in his saddle.

Dammit, he's good.

For the rest of the afternoon, the trainees attacked the quintains. Christopher fell only once, but it was a good fall and the pain evaporated quickly. Bryan continued to be battered, and returned with a new injury after every advance. Even the boy who had been trampled decided to give it a go, and with a fierce vengeance buried his javelin in the target.

By nightfall, the squires returned to the great hall for dinner. Many sat together while others joined their families or friends. Christopher noticed that Doyle ate alone, his parents on the opposite side of the hall shooting him worried and longing looks. Doyle ignored them.

Next to Christopher, Orvin was engrossed in his cut of well-done beef. God's greatest gift to Orvin was not the old man's knightly abilities, not the old man's knowledge or the old man's perception for truth; it was food. And Orvin loved it so. The time between meals Orvin spent dreaming about the next plate that would rest between his elbows. There was eating and not eating. And once in a while, something else.

Christopher chewed heartily on his own beef as he took in the view of Brenna. At first he tried to pretend she was not there. But he was weak in the face of her. Orvin could see the future. She blinded him, but if darkness promised her lips on his, then he would plummet into the void. He was torn between being a squire and being a lover. Couldn't he have both? Couldn't he create his own balance, mind and heart working in unison as Orvin said they must?

"Tell me, Orvin. How does a man create this balance of mind and heart you spoke of? I seek such a balance now."

Orvin was annoyed to be pulled away from his beef. The old man wiped his shriveled lips, took a sip of ale from his tankard, flared his jowls, rolled the liquid around inside his mouth, then swallowed. "The trick," he said, "is to be a man."

Christopher felt anchored by frustration. You had to watch every word you uttered around Orvin, for he always sought the small, sometimes literal interpretations of what you said, never reaching for the general meanings. "How does a *boy* do it?"

"A boy does not," he said.

It was a simple, perfect truth that Christopher refused to accept. "I want desperately to be a squire. But I also—"

"You must find your way. I have spoken all I can on the subject. Are you going to finish your meat?"

Not now, he wasn't. Christopher slid his plate over to Orvin, who did the rippling skin incantation with his eyebrows.

Christopher's gaze found Brenna once more. She twirled her hair with her index finger.

10

The dimensions of the castle of Uryens of Gore doubled those of Hasdale's fortress. Built high on a man-made mound, the castle was fortified by over a dozen towers that each supported stone parapets resting on stone corbels. The spaces between each corbel enabled defenders to drop rocks and fire arrows at the attackers while being shielded by the surrounding corbels. Hasdale admired this arrangement as his party crossed the open drawbridge and slipped into the fettered shadows drawn by the raised portcullis of the gatehouse. His own tower defenses were wooden hoardings, erected hastily in the event of an attack, and usually not at all. Trouble was, one catapult shot would take out a hoarding and render the soldiers inside vulnerable or already dead. Dropping rocks on an enemy was always an effective means of defense, especially against a battering ram, but protecting oneself while doing so was a problem that Uryens had solved here. He must talk more about defenses with the man, plan to reinforce his own towers the same way.

A ruby sun nicked the western horizon as they were heralded, then dismounted in the outer bailey. Hasdale took Sloan, Condon, and Malcolm, a boy barely eighteen whom he had just knighted. It was apparent from his weak jaw and bubbling eyes that Malcolm had never seen such a large castle. The boy's wonder bruised Hasdale's ego. He wished it were his castle the boy gaped at. But no matter. Petty jealousy was far from the order of the day.

They were welcomed by the humble and gracious steward, Blaine, a man so rawboned that Hasdale was afraid to breathe too close to him, for a sudden exhalation might cause considerable damage.

"Lord Uryens is out now, but will be back later in the evening. He will greet all on the morrow in the great hall," Blaine said. Then the spatha-shaped man led them into the keep, where they were shown to their quarters on the fifth floor.

Fires blazed in each of the chambers. Sloan and Condon would share quarters, while Hasdale and Malcolm would take another. They stripped out of their armor, hauberks, gambesons, shirts, and breeches, and dropped comfortably into each of their beds. They had ridden for five days, sleeping under thin tents on hard earth, waking up damp and stiff and hungry each morning. Hasdale had almost forgotten the comfort of a poster bed, but as his stiff back made contact with the wool-stuffed mattress, he was marvelously reminded.

Hasdale's palm grew red, and his armor became scuffed and dull from embracing the many lords here in the great hall. He knew as many as fourteen of the other knights, and felt a great sense of fellowship as he sat down at the longest trestle table he had ever seen, his three loyal men to his right.

Uryens's great hall wore the name much more fittingly than his own, even more so now with so many great knights drinking and eating, exchanging battle tales, and making toasts so rough that tankards occasionally broke and shards of clay dripping with ale fell to the table.

Banners and pennons displaying the coat of arms of each of the knights hung from the rear wall of the hall, and below them, at the head of the trestle table, the king took his place, attended by two pages.

The king. Hasdale had never met his lord, only exchanged messages with him. He looked as intelligent and as carefully measured as Hasdale had imagined. He had drawn a mental picture of the king via the communiqués, and it startled him to see how close the face in his head matched the face before him.

The crest of the helm sitting on the table next to Arthur's plate was a dragon, and the matching bronze-colored armor he wore was so polished that it caught the morning light and threw it up into the rafters in a fountain of shifting beams. The musculature of his body was apparent, and his face generated an aura that no man could not acknowledge. There was something magnetic about him, not because he was the king, not because he had pulled Excalibur from the stone when no other could, not because he had gathered them here to create a battle plan to defeat the invaders of their land, and not because his striking sea-green eyes, his long, soft hair, and trimmed beard reflected an almost religious image to them, but simply because he *knew*. And they trusted. Arthur knew how to defeat their enemies, he knew how to bring peace to the land. He would show them how to build a dream from nothing. What man could resist?

Uryens took a seat to the left of Arthur. Another knight whom Hasdale did not recognize sat to the king's right. Uryens rose, and the room fell silent. "Welcome, knights. You know why we are here, and you know what it is we all seek. Today we will clear a path that will lead us to our goal. The king will show us the way."

Arthur stood.

Everyone stood. Steel *ping*ed, link-mail shook, bench legs dragged across the stone floor. All eyes found one man.

The king gestured for all to be seated.

After the clatter, Arthur took a sip of deep red wine from an ornamented mug, set it down, then pulled on his beard thoughtfully. "How does a king unite a land? How does a land unite men?"

No one dared venture an answer. Hasdale assumed the questions were rhetorical, as he hoped the others did.

"Loyalty. Truth. Fellowship. We all stand together or not at all. The time has come to attack instead of defend. We must spread the word of peace throughout our land by driving out those who spread death.

"We have many enemies. Each of you, separate but linked by the common cause, must engage and conquer them. It is the vision that will strengthen us, drive us to victory. If we follow it, we follow a common path toward peace."

Cheers of approval filled the air and wafted up through the cookfire vents in the ceiling.

"This union," Arthur continued, "is only a first step. But it is an important one. And we all must swear allegiance to it—or ban ourselves now."

From the rear of the trestle table, Hasdale saw a lone knight rise. The simple action jarred him. How could one man actually address the king in such an abrupt fashion? He could not imagine himself standing. He could hardly bear the sight of another man doing it.

"I challenge your ideals," the knight said.

He was a half head taller than Hasdale, but about as broad across the shoulders. His armor was dark and unpolished, and his long, chestnut hair was pulled back in a ponytail. His headband bore a single jewel in the middle of it, and it was this jewel that caught Hasdale's attention as the rogue spoke. It was a blue gem of indeterminate type, a third shining eye that focused on Arthur.

"Go on," Arthur said, "speak your mind, Mallory, as I know reticence is not a problem of yours."

"This talk of truth and fellowship and vision. What do these ideals lead to? A man charging into battle with ideals in his heart comes back with an ax in his head! We must kill them! Force them out because it is our land! Ours! We should keep the faces of dead children in our minds, not these visions of a future peace. Anger, force, the setting of a jaw and the gripping of a blade, stiff, hard, might, will of iron, and fire in one's veins. Those things equal victory. Not these flights of fancy you peddle us."

The words, like glaives in his ears, made Arthur react. Hasdale saw the king's face become flushed, saw how he uttered his retort through gritted teeth.

"If it is revenge you seek, Mallory, then go. No knight here will follow that quest."

Those words woke guilt in Hasdale. He found some truth, some relation to Mallory's words. He did know he wanted Garrett and the spy Kenneth dead. He did know why. And did acknowledge it was out of revenge. The losses were still tangible, missing limbs throbbing with phantom pain. They were holes in his spirit, never to be filled, only to be dealt with, to come to terms with. Would Garrett's death make it easier? Maybe. Maybe not.

Mallory had gall. Gall up to his ears. He spun around and marched toward the tunnel exit, all eyes following the man as he left. Murmurs spilled low near the tabletop.

Arthur shook his head. "Any others to join him?" And then, screaming at the top of his lungs, venting the pain Mallory's challenge had caused him, Arthur repeated, "I SAID, ANY OTHERS TO JOIN HIM?"

The question, the challenge, hung, lifted from the air by no one. All knights secured their positions. Even Hasdale, whose mind continued to be sprinkled by a light rain of doubt, kept his mouth closed.

Arthur blew out a puff of air, let his lips tremble like a rounsey's. "Good. Now, I turn this gathering over to Lancelot." Arthur gestured to the flaxen-haired knight on his right, who stood. "He and I have designed battle plans for each of you. Listen carefully. And a dagger to the heart of the next man who interrupts this meeting."

11

"He's taken you, hasn't he?"

"Yes."

Christopher and Doyle sat together on the live-stock fence, watching four archers converse loudly as they examined a new courser one of them had just acquired and brought into the outer bailey.

The tallest of the bowmen was Varney, a beady-eyed, close-cropped young man whose rose-colored tunic and scaled shoulder armor set him apart from the other men who donned simple, more comfortable gambesons. Varney boasted he was the best marks-man among the group, and Doyle believed it.

"I hope I can attend him well. I expect him to be very demanding," Doyle added. "But no more so than the lord."

"The boy that Hasdale selects will be in for a rough time."

"You'll make it," Doyle said.

There it was. Christopher knew the rumors of Hasdale's affection for him would reach the trainees. He hadn't considered how to handle the situation, but knew jealousy and resentment would certainly arrow his way. He figured now he'd shrug off the truth, wall it up in the prison, let Regan guard it, and release it to no one, except by his approval. "The lord has not made his choice yet, and besides, there are many others as worthy as me."

"None of us has ever killed a man."

"What does that have to do with it?"

"I've heard Sloan say on more than one occasion that experience is the true training, that real battle prepares one for another. Practice is only practice. When blood is spilled, it must be a different thing."

"If I'm chosen, it will be because of my talents as a squire. Nothing more."

"You can believe that—if it makes you feel better."

"It's the truth."

"No, it's not."

Christopher pushed himself off the fence post, began to walk away from Doyle, then his pent-up rage turned him around. "I didn't ask for what happened. It just did. If it angers every boy that I'm chosen because I killed a Saxon, what can I do about it? What's done is done!"

"It angers no one," Doyle said. "All of us know that you are the one; you will serve Hasdale. You have been in battle. Everyone respects that. Everyone."

"But it's not the only reason, right?"

"Well . . . " Doyle smiled. "You're a fair squire—when you're not sick."

Doyle's grin was infectious. Christopher found himself smiling. "I don't know what to say."

He really didn't. Expectations had been replaced by comforting truths. The fact that everyone already accepted Christopher's place as Hasdale's squire was both unbelievable and wonderful. He felt taller than his height, broader than his medium build. A force took hold of him, and the most important thing he drew from it was courage. The courage to accept what was happening. He would not fear the success, but revel in it.

But a fact still ghosted him: the lord had not officially chosen.

Doyle closed his eyes. "Maybe it's about time you—" There was a catch in his voice. He frowned a moment, breathed deeply, then, "Why don't you tell me about my brother?"

Christopher stared at Doyle: the tightly shut eyes; the white-knuckled fists; the laborious rising and lowering of his chest; the twitching of a nerve in his neck. He seemed to be bracing himself for the impact of past and present.

Orvin was right about Doyle; the new varlet did not blame Christopher for Baines's death. But Orvin

was wrong when he said the feelings were not that
strong. Never knowing a brother, and then losing him
must unsheath some powerful emotion within a person. Guilt? Shame? Sorrow? Longing for the past,
for what was, what could never be? Dreams of a day
when brothers could reunite? Doyle's tension might
harbor all those things.

Christopher would tell Doyle all about Baines, but
the story of his friend would be a celebration of life,
not death. There were too many roads of *that* yet to
travel.

"I guess I could start by telling you about the time
he fell into Lady Fiona's bathing tub—while she was
still in it. . . . "

Doyle's eyelids snapped open.

12
Spittle flecked the old man's lips, and his
eyes were rolled up to heaven. "Revenge is a sin
against God, son. And the sky is not with us. You
mask the truth by telling me it is the king's will, but I
see through the forest of your heart."

Hasdale was at the window alcove of his solar,
absently watching a serf drive his grain wagon
through the bailey. The wagon stopped before the
squire's hut, the serf climbed down, called out, then
vanished through the doorway of the quarters.
Hasdale pivoted from the window and returned his
gaze to his father.

He studied the man who had raised him, the man
who had taught him everything, who knew everything. And for the first time in his life, he deafened
himself to Orvin. He knew his father would argue the
point long after the castle walls had crumbled into
the earth and the tide had come in and drowned the

land from horizon to horizon. In their graves, Orvin would roll over and argue the point. But his father's stalwart behavior made his own arguments no less credible. He had a wife who had become a recluse, shut herself up in one of the sentry towers. She would barely speak to him and would not sleep with him. The shame of Fiona's rape was too deep, and the loss of her child was a leech sucking the will to live from her. He had lost his sister, Alina. He had lost Wells, his best battle lord. He had lost Baines, his too-young squire. And the more he thought, the more the numbers grew. Family, friends, loyal knights, servants, those he knew and the relatives and friends of those he knew formed the links in a world-long chain of death that led back to Garrett.

It was revenge. It had to be.

"My scouts have picked them out in the Mendip hills. He likes to camp in that remote region. He expects no one to journey that far to attack him. I am mounting this campaign, Father, and as I will repeat for you, with the king's support."

"Your heart is not right for it. You go with the wrong intentions." Orvin thought a moment. "Why doesn't Uryens engage Garrett?"

Hasdale found his spot back at the window, let his father's question fade unanswered.

The squire trainees formed a line that began at the grain wagon and weaved into the hut. Sacks were passed from boy to boy, and they talked about the day's training and scolded each other for not keeping up the pace. Hasdale searched through the night mist for Sanborn's son, but could not see him. "I wish to take the boy, Christopher, with me. Is he ready?"

"He has mastered the skills shown to the group. Sloan rates him very highly."

"Then a day of practice with me and he'll be ready for the hills."

"In body, yes. But in mind . . . I need to work further with him."

"Philosophy is quickly silenced on the battlefield, Father. I have listened to your magic principles and your thoughts on combat for too long, and I will not subject the boy to them. If he knows the ways, and practices with me, that will be enough. His own heart will define what he experiences. He does not need you to do it for him."

The solar had become a conversational battlefield. But to Hasdale's surprise, it was his father who conceded first. "Perhaps you are right. I am old and my mind is too keen on rumors and dreams and other things. Let the boy accompany you and watch you die. I only wish to serve." Orvin put his heavily veined feet in motion and was out of the solar in a dozen steps.

Orvin had left the old trick of a father behind. Hasdale remained at the window watching the grain chain, feeling bleak and stormy at the same time. Orvin was a wizard at creating a war within Hasdale. His father told him he would die—not that he believed a word of that. What his father had really told him was, "I love you. I fear for you."

The squires finished unloading the wagon and filed back into their quarters. The bailey became silent, save for the footsteps of his men on the wall-walks. A faint breeze lifted the banners poled on the gatehouse, and Hasdale looked beyond them to the moon; it was veiled in clouds. He ran tense fingers through his hair as he traced the illuminated puffs of white with tired eyes. The desire to sleep came and went. He remained at the window, played out a million options out of guilt, but circled back to the same conclusion. They would attack.

13

Two mounted coursers galloped furiously over deceptive grass that concealed a freckling of shallow ditches. Hasdale and Christopher turned sharply, in perfect unison, coordination so keen they seemed two parts of one whole. The lord cracked his quirt on his mount, and the coal black steed leapt ahead of Christopher's, breaking the pair. Christopher followed suit, and his own like-colored courser galloped toward the lord, finally overtaking him.

"Who taught you to ride?" Hasdale asked, shouting over the rhythm of hooves.

"Baines."

"And a fine job he did!" With that, Hasdale heeled his courser forward.

It was a chase, and a haphazard one at that. This wasn't simple arms identification, or the more difficult target run, or even the incredibly frustrating archery practice that Christopher had been put through. This was a total disregard for safety and a mad run to explore something he did not understand. What did this prove? Riding skills, yes, but why over this part of the field? Hitting one ditch would end it all. He had done fine thus far, but he knew he couldn't sustain the effort.

Again, he goaded his courser after Hasdale. Again, all four hooves of his horse seemed to leave the ground. He felt his mouth grow cottony as he spotted a ditch under a thin fence of grass only a yard to his right. It was sheer luck he didn't drive his horse right into it. The ditch blurred past and he turned his attention forward in time to see the next ditch. He tried to bring his courser around the hole, but the momentum of the horse was too great and the steed's left leg folded into the soft cavity.

A sequence of things happened to Christopher before he hit the ground. He had seen the ditch, and,

of course, his mouth dropped in horror. The attempt
to round it was merely reflex; his eyes already told
him it was too late. He felt his body drop, then be
pushed left. He was arrested by the thought of getting his booted feet out of the stirrups, and began the
process as the left side of the courser made contact
with the ground. The animal's ribs pressed his left leg
into the grass, and then he reached out toward the
evil earth as it came up at him. His arm was
extended, but it caved in at the elbow under the force
of his own weight. The effort was not entirely futile,
for it was that arm that lessened the impact of his
head. A numbing ringing drummed through him a
second after his skull popped back up from the
ground.

There he was, lying on his side, still in the stirrups
of the fallen courser as the horse struggled to pull
itself up and he struggled to get free from it. The
hairs on his crushed leg took the form of pins and
needles, not growing from the skin, but burying
themselves into it. The feeling was good, though; no
heat or ice or extreme bite. It was a hidden, bloodless
feeling that unfortunately foretold future pain.

Through glazed vision, he saw Hasdale come
toward him. The lord's figure momentarily blocked
out the noon sun, then slipped under it as he dismounted and ran over.

For a moment, Christopher had felt deserted on
the field. Hasdale had bounced toward the dusty hills
in the distance while Christopher's world jolted
ninety degrees left. But the lord was here to help, and
he valued the relief of that more than anything.

Baines would have told him this was a bad fall. An
extremely bad fall. You only had seconds to decide
what to do. Seconds never seemed to be enough. If
he could have freed his boots . . . Ifs, ands, or buts
wouldn't spare him the walking pain, or the tide of
embarrassment that now rolled in under the relief.

Hasdale slipped Christopher's right foot from its stirrup. Feeling that action, the courser pulled itself to its feet, favoring its broken left leg. Christopher's left leg still hung from its stirrup, and Hasdale attended to it with skilled and immediate hands. The freed leg thumped to the ground, deadweight.

"I'm sorry, lord."

Hasdale reached down under Christopher's arms and pulled him up to his feet. "How do you feel?"

"Fine," he lied.

"Honest failure is one thing," Hasdale said, "concealed truth is another."

He turned away from the lord, brushing stray hair from his forehead, feeling rankled and caught and useless. "My head hurts, and my leg is numb."

Hasdale dropped to his knees and lifted Christopher's leg, put it through a combination of lifts and bends. "It's not broken. When the blood comes, so will the feeling." He stood. "As for your head, I've a root back home that'll cure it."

Christopher nodded, then he saw his courser over Hasdale's shoulder. He painted a mental picture of the horse as an old, lame serf beast begging for alms from the lady of the castle. Sunset was upon the mount. He tried to believe what Sloan had said: "They are tools," but he stung with the responsibility for this steed. The hostlers back at the castle would probably put the horse out of its misery. Christopher's own misery over the incident would linger. *Damn.*

"If her leg mends, she'll pull a cart. I won't slay her. I can see what that would do to you."

"She was only mine for a day, and I feel my poor riding caused her this."

"You lasted longer on this field than Baines. Poor riding. Ha!"

They gathered up Christopher's fallen belongings, tied the injured courser behind Hasdale's, and trotted back toward the stone walls pillaring the eastern sky.

It was a simple excuse: he needed to change into his gambeson before they ran through the weapons delivery. And so Christopher was inside the squire's hut, peeling himself out of his riding tunic, shirt, and then breeches. Bryan was the only other boy in the loft, the rest joining in a mock siege on the rear curtain wall. Christopher groaned loudly as his fingers touched the bruises blossoming over his left hip, buttock, and ankle. Pain screeched in his skin with the intensity of a wheelless axle across cobblestone. He had just wanted to see what the wounds looked like; now he was sorry.

Bryan pulled his head back at the sight of Christopher's leg. "Ouch," was his only comment.

"My feelings exactly," Christopher answered.

He climbed into the gambeson like an old man, struggled with his no-good limb, gasped, contorted, hopped on one leg. The points where bruise met leather felt worse. Nude, it was not so bad. But how would he explain arms delivery in the raw to Hasdale?

The climb down the ladder? An exercise in torture.

Garrison men who were off-duty gathered around in the exercise yard to watch their lord at practice. Nearly a dozen of them assembled near the keep's moat, sitting or standing near the shores of the opaque waters. Tankards of ale were passed around, and belches punctuated their grunts and baritone exchanges.

Christopher stopped dead when he saw the crowd. *Well that's perfect. That is just . . . oh, God, create a little sanctuary for me. Get me through this. Please!*

He put his feet back to work, every step toward the yard a mindful step closer to the pyre he would lie in after.

A pole arms rack, and shorter, club arms rack were

in place to the right, while a pair of quintains stood far off to the left, past the onlookers. Another knight stretched his body near the rack, a fighting partner for the lord. Hasdale stepped up to the man, who pulled up the faceplate on his bascinet to expose his scarred face. Those deep canyons could only belong to Sloan. The battle lord and Hasdale exchanged a few words, Sloan referring to the sword he held. Hasdale took the blade and examined its hilt.

This is getting even better. . . .

He would have to perform in front of his lord, and in front of the man who had trained him. Someone tapped his shoulder. He cocked his head.

"Listen to what I have to say and let it ring in your ears until the sun sets on your life." Orvin's words were hushed and came quickly.

Christopher wanted to turn around, but Orvin held him by the shoulders so that his eyes could not leave the practice field.

His master continued, "You cannot think why you are doing what you are doing—only that you are. Do not examine your feelings, but let them go. Imagine them sleeping in the loft or lost or forgotten. Think only of the demands of your master and reach for those needs with immediacy. Think *like* your master. Try to feel what he feels. Those are the experiences you must have. The emotions are not yours—but his. Join with him in body and mind and spirit. It is a marriage, a pyramid of power that rules you. Forget your own pain, your doubts, your fears. They will not help you now. Go."

Orvin shoved him forward. Christopher swiveled his head and saw the old man move briskly away.

"Christopher!" Hasdale called.

He decided to jog toward the yard, an obvious demonstration that he felt much better now. At least his head did. The root Hasdale had given him when they had returned was so bitter-tasting that he had tossed it away, but fortunately the ringing in his ears had subsided.

Christopher's eyes were sore with tears by the time he crossed the bailey and assumed his position in front of the pole arms rack. There would be no jousting this afternoon, so Christopher removed the six lances from the rack. He placed the poles behind the wooden support so they would not interfere with the javelins, glaives, bills, scythes, and halberds waiting there. This was not the crowded rack he had practiced from, and selection would be swift and free of accident. Yanking a halberd from a crowded rack was dangerous; the hooked blade of the weapon could catch on the halberd next to it or the shaft of another weapon, bringing two weapons toward you, the sharp head of one in your face. Sloan had fingered the scar across his eye as a visual reminder of what could happen. No trainee made that mistake, and every trainee was disappointed at the revelation that one of Sloan's mighty slashes had been acquired when he was only a squire trainee, and not as a knight on the battlefield. It was a letdown, but Sloan wasn't concerned with creating an image for himself, only with training squires. The trainees understood.

Sloan and Hasdale mounted their horses. Christopher went for a pair of javelins. He knew the one Sloan preferred, but had to guess at which one Hasdale would like. Maybe something Orvin had said could help. He tried to clear himself of the outside world, tried to imagine his head on top of Hasdale's body, flexing Hasdale's fingers, feeling what javelin would belong there. He right-handed the longest pole; he'd give it to Hasdale.

Sloan angled by and Christopher tossed the pole as he had been taught. Sloan's gauntleted fingers wrapped tightly around the weapon. The knight winked.

Hasdale circled around. Christopher readied the longest javelin. He fired a last-second glance back at the rack, his eyes taking in the other javelins there. He locked his hands around the weapon, shook it a little, as if to instill some kind of correctness into it, some kind of magic that made it the one Hasdale wanted. It was a guessing game, but Orvin knew something about tipping the odds in the squire's favor. This javelin *felt* right.

Christopher held the pole out to Hasdale, who quickly appraised the weapon, then over his smile of satisfaction ordered, "Javelin!"

He sent the weapon sideways into the air. His lord's metallic hand bit the pole, then slid into the correct hold, a forearm's length from the base.

Sloan and Hasdale charged their targets. Each defied the bag man who tried to dismount them; each centered his javelin as the crowd nodded and chatted their envy.

A weak connection birthed inside Christopher: a link to his master. It was the one he hoped for and felt was growing. There was some doubt, though. He wasn't sure how he had selected the right weapon. He had simply followed Orvin's instruction. But he also remembered another part of the lesson, the part which told him not to wonder why, not to examine his feelings, only to act. It was hard. It was letting yourself rest in the hands of something incomprehensible; you had to wonder if you were doing the right thing.

Three more target runs followed, and neither of the knights was dismounted. By the second run, some in the crowd already yawned, knowing Hasdale and Sloan were much too good for the target men. Hand-to-hand. That's what they wanted to see.

The knights raised themselves off their coursers. Christopher took the reins of each horse and guided them toward the stable master's right hand, who waited on the sidelines. The hostler was a stubby red-head with a plague of freckles across his cheeks, and a pinioned grin that flashed and was gone as he received the mounts from Christopher.

Hasdale and Sloan faced each other, ten yards apart. Christopher knew they wanted weapons, but which?

Help me, lords! Which is it?

Was he supposed to know? He'd watched tournaments but had certainly forgotten the order of weapons—if there was an order. Neither Sloan nor Orvin had covered such formalities in their lessons.

He shrugged and sighed, spun around and grabbed a pair of halberds, again, knowing the one Sloan preferred. The other was selected by way of Orvin. Christopher stepped carefully toward the lords, holding the poles in the pattern of an X across his chest. He stopped, pulled his arms apart, breaking the X into a pair of I's. Sloan took his halberd, barely looking at Christopher as he did so. Hasdale tilted his head slightly and Christopher saw his eyes track the form of the weapon. The lord nodded and received the halberd.

Another, what seemed to Christopher, lucky guess. He told himself it wasn't a lucky guess, that it was Orvin's instruction and the link he made with Hasdale. But how could he select the right one from so many? The fact chewed on his intellect. It grew harder just to act.

Sloan and Hasdale both two-handed their halberds as they bent their knees and swung their weapons back and forth, ferreting out openings in each other. Sloan moved first, an overhead swing at Hasdale's shoulder. The lord dodged the blow, and, as Sloan's arm came down, Hasdale saw a chance to riposte; he turned and slammed the butt of his halberd across Sloan's back. Sloan stumbled forward, his face creasing and his free hand going to the pain.

Hasdale decided to hook Sloan's legs. He brought his weapon around, and was about to center his blade and catch the right greave covering Sloan's kneecap. But Sloan jerked around and warded off the attack, utilizing the shaft of his halberd. The two weapons locked up in each other, hook caught on hook, and the men lifted the irons so that they pushed at each other's chest, trying to force the other back, groaning but smiling at each other.

It would have been a stalemate had Sloan not fallen back. Christopher thought it odd that his trainer suddenly slipped his hook free and retreated a half dozen steps. It probably had everything to do with the fact that Hasdale was the lord and Sloan was not. Or it had nothing to do with it. Sloan was either being polite or really had weakened. Christopher preferred the former.

The knights paused, their breathing loud and mechanical. Their faces were still split with grins almost menacing, diluted only by their loyalty and friendship. They dropped their halberds.

Christopher nearly missed his cue. He thought it most curious that they would engage without weapons now. Then logic, only a hairbreadth away, elbowed his head. *Maces! Now!*

He went over to the club arms rack, searched, looked, eyed, spied, trusted. He came up with two and brought them forth.

Hasdale's mace was too short.

It wasn't a big issue, and it shouldn't have bothered him that much. The problem was, at the moment Hasdale shook his head, no, you've the wrong one, Christopher saw the other squire trainees join the crowd in the background. His peers had missed all of the other correct choices and perfect moves he had made. Now they witnessed his blunder.

He staggered back to the weapons rack, his spirit hovering somewhere around his ankles. It was down-and-out horrible timing that the other trainees watched now. He could almost feel their taunting eyes on his shoulders, and though none did, he thought he heard one of them yell, "Fool!"

He trudged back to Hasdale. One mistake distanced him from the whole yard, filled his head with so much doubt that thoughts of reverting to saddle making invaded his mind. Defeat was as uncomfortable as any physical thing, and if it were physical, Christopher suspected it would be hot and wet and heavy and solid; it would burn, soak, and crush. Defeat would walk the lands, choke the air, and create a death silence in its wake.

He had made only one mistake.

"Two out of three," Hasdale said, accepting the replacement weapon, "are good odds for any squire of mine."

The drama in his mind climaxed, the curtains fell, and defeat was dead.

Christopher backhanded a band of sweat from his head, then blew out a heavy sigh as he walked back to the racks. When he turned around, he saw the trainees thrusting their fists in the air for him.

14

"You don't have to go, do you?"

"Yes, I do."

"Why?"

"Where the lord goes, I go."

"But you're not ready yet, are you?"

"He thinks I am."

"Do you think you are?"

"Sometimes. Most times."

Christopher studied Brenna's face, the gloom and worry clearly molded there. Then he looked away, part of him already ascending the Mendip hills.

Hasdale had told him about it matter-of-factly, as if commenting on the quality of an ale, or the feel of a saddle. Oh, by the way, you're riding with me to attack Garrett's army. Maybe it was the lord's way of downplaying it to Christopher. But since then, anticipation and abject fear had braided inside him, knotted up his system and driven him wild, made him want to do something physical, like run or leap or dive—or hide. But he had to tell Brenna, and, in a way, say good-bye to her. For now.

It had barely occurred to him that it could be their last good-bye.

It had definitely occurred to her.

They hadn't been able to find a good place to talk, and so it was they stood on the bottom of a staircase that led up to the maid's chamber. And it was here, listening to the diminuendoes of distant servants calling out to each other, and bathed in the reddish light of the hall, that Christopher realized how much he cared for her.

"If you're not ready . . ."

Christopher knew the end of that sentence. "I trust the lord. And you have to trust me, Brenna."

She bit her lip, and the tears came.

He touched her shoulder. She pulled away.

"Brenna."

"My mother told me being with you is wrong."

And this time he grabbed her shoulders, giving her no opportunity for escape. "It's not wrong. Just wait for me. Just wait."

She collapsed on him, nudging her head into his neck and shoulder. He stroked the raven maid's hair as she cried.

He had to come back. If only to stop her tears.

15

Through the night, they worked. Some said, "like dogs," others, "like mules," still others more poetically put it, "like slaves chained to the vengeful will of their master." It was no secret why Hasdale wanted to attack. They all knew. Some agreed with his motives, some not. But they all worked.

The armorer's bellows breathed life into the fires as the dirty-faced men with gnarled hands hammered last-minute corrections into a steady stream of new spathas. Bascinets, gorgets, shoulder-protecting pauldrons, breastplates, elbow-shielding couters, cuisses, poleyns, greaves, and sabatons were checked and fitted with all other parts of armor, while link-mail was mended and cleaned. Axes, glaives, spears, and halberds were honed on whetstones, as were the iron tips of arrows. Longbows, shortbows, and crossbows were waxed and tested, quivers filled, and weapons racks and tents folded and stowed on supply wagons.

In the stables, Galvin directed ten hostlers in the shodding of coursers, rounseys, and his beloved mares. The horses were fitted with the loriner's bits and stirrups, and recently delivered saddles from March and Torrey. A dozen lampblack coursers, which made up the lord's party, were behind the stables, leather plates strapped onto their faces and flanks by two of Galvin's most skilled men.

It was hard to believe, but the kitchen bustled even more than usual. Seniors, who usually loitered about the castle drinking ale, growing fat, and attending to children, were commandeered into the food preparation chain. They wrapped smoked pork, beef, and chicken in salted linens, and tucked the packages into wicker baskets. Dozens of clay flagons were filled with ale and wine, corked, then fitted into traveling trunks that would be loaded onto the flatbeds of the food carts. Vegetables, both cooked and raw, were packed, and the scent of hundreds of loaves of bread being rolled, baked, slid from the oven, and basketed, wrapped the castle air in heaven.

Under an ebony sky and a waxing crescent moon, the

members of the garrison who would travel to the Mendip hills came together in the outer bailey, forming first into lances, groups consisting of a knight, infantryman, two mounted archers, and the accompanying squires and varlets. Once these small parties were assembled, the fighters joined in a pair of lines which started at the gatehouse and stretched back to the keep's moat, bending around the body of water and weaving past the storerooms. The lines were led by the lances of Hasdale, Sloan, Condon, and Malcolm. Behind them were the other eight battle lords, including Fiona's father, Conway, and farther back, a peasant levy of archers and infantrymen armed with spears. In all, nearly five hundred souls would trek to the hills.

An overweight serf woman elbowed and bellied her way to Hasdale. "Lord!" she cried, in a voice too deep, too loud, "you take too many! You leave us with no protection here!"

Christopher, part of Hasdale's lance and one of three of the lord's squires, was astride a young brown rounsey, an even patch of white hair splitting the horse's eyes and reaching down to its nose. Christopher nudged his way between Hasdale's two senior squires, Collis and Murdock. He watched his lord's reaction carefully, seeing how his master would handle the panic maker.

"I leave you forty men-at-arms! And there is no other army within forty days of here."

"The invaders are sly, lord. Perhaps they—"

"Enough, woman!" Hasdale turned to Christopher and gestured with his thumb to lose this woman.

Christopher swung a leg over his saddle and hopped to the ground. He grabbed the woman by an arm and escorted her away from the battle lines.

The pudgy serf wrenched her arm free. "Unhand me, devil child! Going off to kill and only a boy!"

The woman made the job easier by pounding off toward the keep under her own power. Christopher wasn't used to being called "devil child," let alone a killer. He watched her merge into the crowd. It was a frenzied night.

Doyle trotted up the line and arrived next to Christopher, just as he remounted his horse. "Nervous?" he asked.

"I'm the veteran. I should be asking you that," Christopher chided.

"Well are you, anyway?"

"I will be in ten days."

"I already am." Doyle was rather on the pale side.

"Good."

"Why is that good?"

"At least you'll be alert."

"Don't worry about that." Doyle wheeled his rounsey around. "I hope it doesn't rain."

"It will."

"How do you know?"

"It's my luck. Trust me."

Doyle guided his horse back to his lance.

It was no easy task, assembling and readying twenty-five score of men; the eastern sky was a dim orange by the time preparations were complete.

While waiting for the order to leave, Christopher stared at the sunrise, trying to read signs of victory or defeat.

What will be?

The brightening sky reflected no reply.

Christopher lowered his gaze to Hasdale, watched as his lord stood in his stirrups, cocked his head back toward his men, and shouted, "Onward!"

As the lines passed over the drawbridge, Christopher repeatedly gazed over his shoulder, not believing how many horses and men were behind him. Every so often he would catch Doyle's eye and wave a hand to him. He knew Bryan the mouse catcher was with them as well, but cantered somewhere just ahead of the peasant levy. Doyle, Bryan, and he were the only trainees who were allowed to go. The others would stay home and attend the bare-bones garrison guarding the castle.

He took turns carrying Hasdale's banner with Collis and Murdock. The poles were thankfully lighter than they looked, and would be turned over to the official banner flyer during the battle. He felt awed as the flag ruffled with a little life and he saw the red crow spread before his eyes.

Hasdale's senior squires kept to themselves, making Christopher feel like a fifth wheel. Hasdale didn't really need him on this campaign but insisted he come; he could use the experience, and wanted to learn as much as he could. But, Christopher had found, the more questions he asked the senior squires, the more irritated they became, and so he decided he would learn for himself.

Bread and ale were passed around. They weren't stopping to cook breakfast this morning. They would push their hardest the first few days, the horses and the men being fresh.

As Christopher chewed on his loaf, he thought of Orvin. He wished the old man had come to see him off, but Hasdale had told him his father was ill and wished to remain in his chamber. It didn't bother him as much then as it did now. The thrill of leaving and the rush of preparing cleansed the small wound that Orvin's absence had opened. But now he had nothing to do but eat; eat and contemplate the under-current of sadness he had detected in Orvin's voice in the practice yard. Something had been wrong with the old man. Perhaps it had been the illness coming on. Or perhaps it had something to do with the battle. They did coincide.

If a mouthful of bread taught one how to become a good listener, then it also taught one to become a good thinker. Unfortunately his thoughts were laced with worry. *Orvin had better be all right.*

The first night was nearly like all the rest: a clouded, starless sky that seemed to be folding in on the land; a small portion of meat, usually the sweet pork—he hated the chicken; a pepper or carrot or radish to temper the meat in his mouth; a dozen swigs of ale; and a lousy night's sleep on his woolen blanket that did nothing to shield him from the damned stones and roots that nudged their way into his spine. Sometimes he opted to sleep inside the lord's tent, being permitted, but on the warmer nights he preferred the ironically quieter outdoors. The snoring of four battle lords would find anyone in a red-eyed delirium come sunrise. It was a fair trade-off, though: red eyes for warm feet.

In the early-morning darkness of the day they would mount the Mendips, Christopher heard a voice while huddled on the ground, trying to stay warm outside the tent. It was familiar, and when the words repeated, he sensed they were Orvin's. He raised his head, cocked it around. The ears on his nearby rounsey flinched under the icy breeze. A smoldering cookfire sent thin wisps of nearly undetectable smoke fading into nothingness. The tent stood, no one around it. Three images, no Orvin. There it was again. He sat up, pulled the blanket off his breech-covered legs, then padded toward the voice, which seemed to originate from inside the tent.

He pulled one of the flaps aside and ducked his head into the traveling chamber. Sloan, Condon, and Malcolm were twisted into odd and humorous positions. Arms were pulled across backs and foreheads, legs were crossed at strange angles, and mouths hung open, undamming the saliva within.

But Hasdale slept flat on his back, his arms Xed across his bare chest as if positioned by the living while he was already dead. His face was ashen and his mouth worked. "Let the boy accompany you and watch you die," he said. "Let the boy accompany you and watch you die." Had he not been looking at Hasdale, he would not have believed it was the lord's voice. Indeed, it was Hasdale's throat which produced the sounds, but the tones and articulations were Orvin's. Father and son did sound alike, but this was a perfect match.

Christopher had two choices. He could quickly get out of there and back under his blanket, since he was at once terrified of this ghastly image of his lord, or he could wake Hasdale and dispel the horror.

He left and went back to sleep, long before the voice subsided.

Sunrise found Christopher jarred awake by a spasm of nerves in his neck. Shivering, he looked around. Just another morning in the field. Nothing unusual about it at all. Nothing. He lowered his head, closed his eyes, and as he was about to slip back into the dreamworld, a horn blew.

16

The Mendip hills broke the flatness of their trail and protected the horizon with their mighty ribs. Hasdale and the other battle lords were expressionless as they reached the deep valley that formed a perimeter around the sister slopes. Christopher eyed the hills, wondering if it were really possible to ascend them. It certainly looked impossible.

They moved through the valley as the afternoon dragged on. The sky darkened—not with a setting sun, but with thunderheads: the predicted rain. Christopher flashed a knowing grin Doyle's way as sheet lightning flickered in the white towers above him.

"Tarps on the wagons!" Sloan ordered, and the

order drifted back, carried on the lips of every lieutenant in the line.

Christopher felt a cool drop of rain touch his nose. Then another. And still another. Then nothing for a hundred yards.

Then the sky opened up and hell poured down.

Someone cursed loudly, and the wind spit back a reply. Earth's cold breaths swirled around Christopher, trying to find contact points to chill him. He pulled down on the collar of his tunic, then hunched forward in his saddle, trying to keep the water running down his back and not into his eyes. The effort had only minimal effect.

The ground was softening quickly, and he could already see the hooves of the lord's courser sinking deeper into the grass, and soil below.

Everyone knew they weren't going to stop. The question had certainly entered everyone's mind, just as it had Christopher's, but the lord was there to drive them up these godforsaken hills despite the tempest, and drive out any notions of making camp here—or, by God, turning around.

Christopher's rounsey didn't care much for the rain, rattling its bridle with every shake of its head and neighing frequently. And the horse was extremely agitated by the thunder: its volume, its jolt, its lack of rhythm, its sheer domination of the ear. With every clap, the horse tried to nose out of line and Christopher had to rein the steed back in. Christopher did this easily at first; then, becoming agitated himself, yanked on the reins, shouting, "Come on now! Come on!"

Spearheading the lines didn't seem so bad when you looked back at the poor, wet bastards who were just footing the base of the first slope while you had already reached the muddy crest. But then again, you had already experienced the misery of the climb, and forgotten the chore quickly. Christopher turned his head forward and saw two more slopes ahead, followed by a bunch more that were fuzzy to his eye in the heavy rains. There could have been a million more for all the difference it made.

Water found its way inside his tunic and shirt, and the nipples on his chest were damp and stiff around the gooseflesh that fanned out from them. He tried to contain jitter after jitter, but they kept coming, and soon he gave up.

The squire next to Christopher was Kier. He was a dark-skinned boy two years older than Christopher, a member of Sloan's lance and leader of all junior squires. Kier talked himself through the ordeal. "It's just rain, that's all. A little storm. Nothing that can stop us. We a-a-are the best. We are the finest of this land. It's not so c-c-cold. Not so wet. We . . . we are the best."

We are wet, is what we are.

Christopher almost wished he wore the heavy armor of the battle lords, and the thick woolen tabards and surcoats they pulled around themselves. Certainly the wind wasn't bothering them, but then he considered the weight. Suddenly it wasn't so bad to be in his simple padded tunic.

He tried to picture warm things, any image that would take his mind off the miserable climb. He started with a torch, tried to hypnotize himself with the flames that heated the air. Soon the torch became boring. He thought of any one of a thousand hot days in his old workshop, pounding away at the bench. He imagined the rainwater as sweat cascading off his face. He didn't realize he had opened up a dangerous and painful memory until it was too late. The image of Sanborn smiling over a saddle Christopher had just completed filled his mind. *He wasn't always strict. He did smile. He did love me.*

"The scouts return, lord!" Sloan shouted.

Hoods of leather concealed all but the eyes of the two scouts as they approached. Reining in their horses, the men descended the grade cautiously and reached Hasdale. Christopher noted that the men were barely armed; only scabbarded spathas hung from their saddles. They traveled light and armorless, taking nothing that would slow them down.

Christopher couldn't hear the whole conversation Hasdale had with the scouts, but he did hear the name "Wells." That was unexpected. The knight's betrayal and banishment was well known, and Christopher had wondered what became of the man.

A thousand yards and another slope, and Christopher got his answer.

A seam of lightning opened a jagged hole in the sky and illuminated the dead form of Wells. The knight lay supine, his rotting face exposed through his open bascinet. A javelin sprouted from his breastplate, and a gauntleted hand still clung to the pole. As Christopher got closer, he could see how Wells's skin had melted into his bones. The knight's beard seemed directly attached to his jaw without the aid of flesh to hold it there. With his lips gone, it appeared as if Wells smiled, a kind of twisted toothy grin as odd as anything Christopher had ever seen. Grass had sprung up around the knight, as if nature herself had tried to bury him. Christopher remembered something his father had said, something that stayed close to him and showed itself now: "the spoils of a knight."

Christopher looked over at Kier, who stared at the corpse. "You all right?"

No reply.

Four of the carts near the rear of the lines became stuck in the mud, their wheels nearly half-buried, the packhorses pulling them unable to go on. They should have had mules fronting them, but there just weren't any. This, combined with the horrible morale the storm effected, convinced Hasdale to halt the lines. The order to set up camp was so pleasant to

Christopher's ears, it sent a ripple of chills through him. Or that might have been the cold. The order was good to hear, anyway.

It was a curious stroke of luck, and Christopher almost didn't believe what he heard when the scouts returned from their second expedition. He was assembling the lord's tent with Murdock, and chatting with Doyle, who had never looked so literally blue in the face, when it was reported that Garrett's army was just over the next rise. Surrounded by a shallow valley, the Saxons were stationed on top of one of the largest slopes in the area, some hundred tents jutting up from the mud. The good news was that the scouts had gotten in close and provided a detailed description of three sides of the encampment. The bad news was that Garrett had strengthened his army by a rough estimate of three hundred men. That meant the numbers were about equal.

Christopher and Doyle exchanged looks of concern, while Murdock was unmoved by the suddenly even odds. He continued positioning a tent pole, intent on getting the job done.

"What do you think, Murdock?" Doyle asked, trying to get a journeyman's opinion of the situation.

"I don't think. I simply do my job. As you should."

Doyle snorted at the answer.

"A lot of us are going to die," Christopher said, hoping that would light something within Murdock.

"That's right," the senior squire answered.

"Maybe even you," Doyle challenged.

Murdock dropped the second tent pole he was fitting into place and grabbed Doyle by his collar. "Maybe we all are. But what is important now is doing our jobs—and being with who we belong, *varlet.*"

Doyle got the hint. Christopher shrugged as he watched his friend leave. Murdock, a streak of aggression banding his eyes, got the tent assembled in a few violent pulls and tugs, barely letting Christopher help.

As ironically as the storm had begun, it let up, the timing near-perfect as the last tent was raised. For a brief moment, the penumbra of the sun was seen above one of the lower, western slopes, then it drifted down into the morrow.

17

Cookfires were out of the question. The food was cold, a lot of it damp. Twenty-five men were denied immediate dinner altogether, winnowed out for watch duty. Hasdale's element of surprise would be as carefully guarded as the jewels within the walls of his keep. Night fell, and an even stronger wind than the one which accompanied the storm scourged up the hills, blew the sky clear of clouds, and rattled the tents and the nerves of Christopher.

Inside Hasdale's shelter, planning for the battle commenced. Christopher sat in on the briefing, and spent as much time studying the anxiety on Hasdale's face as listening to the actual particulars of the attack. Hasdale divided the army into the Vaward, Main, and Rearward Battles; he also designated a rear guard, fifty men who would remain here at the camp. The two hundred men of the Rearward Battle would fall back in a position behind the Saxons, while the two other groups of about a hundred and fifty in the Main Battle, and two hundred men in the Vaward Battle would engage in a full frontal attack from the right and left flanks, driving the Saxons back into the Rearward Battle. In the event of impending defeat, the last fifty of the rear guard would advance, with only two targets on their mind: Garrett and Kenneth—if they weren't already dead. Normally, the lord would be a member of the rear guard and direct the battle from the relative safety and distance the group's position afforded. But Hasdale chose to lead the Vaward Battle, putting himself in the thick of the attack.

Junior squires like Christopher weren't going to accompany their lords into actual battle; they would remain with the rear guard. Varlets, however, would. They windlassed crossbows for their masters, kept the cycle of bolts splitting the air. It seemed unfair to Christopher that Doyle got to participate in the attack while he had to sit around like a serf woman washing her clothes at the lake and waiting for her husband to return. It made him feel helpless and worthless. He had tricked himself into thinking the lord would let him ride with Murdock and Collis, but when he asked Hasdale at the end of the meeting, the lord looked at him as if he were drunk. It was out of the question. The only way he would get to partici-pate in the battle was if the last fifty Celts were called in to make the final charge. And if that were the case, it was certainly a one-way trip.

18

The weather had turned against them while they climbed the Mendip hills, and now that they had reached their destination and were about to attack, it had done the same once again. The dome overhead glowed with starlight, and the much greater beams of the waxing gibbous moon. Christopher's hands were filled with heaps of mud that he rubbed all over Hasdale's armor. Every junior squire did the same for every knight. A flash of moonlight off armor caught by the curious eyes of a Saxon watchman would sound off alarms through-out the enemy camp.

"Rain would've been good *now*," Hasdale thought out loud.

Christopher nodded and continued smearing the cold, mushy earth over Hasdale's greaves.

The Rearward Battle had already left, and cantered their way around the slope to their position behind the Saxons. The slope provided good protection for the Saxons, but it also provided good cover for the first wave of Celts.

Christopher saw the remnants of the Rearward Battle vanish behind the slope as he helped Hasdale mount a fresh courser. He checked the broadsword in its scabbard, making sure it was securely fastened to the saddle next to the lord's mace. He examined each hoof of the courser, making sure all shoes were tightly in place. He checked the lord's belt, the dagger sheathed there, and finally handed Hasdale his escutcheon, the rectangular shield much heavier than it looked. There was a precise order to fitting and checking the lord, but Christopher was so nervous he'd forgotten to go by it, studying whatever struck him at that second.

Hasdale joined Collis and Murdock, as well as Sloan, Condon, Malcolm, and their senior squires at the head of the Vaward Battle. The Main Battle was already some three hundred yards away and waiting for the order to advance.

Christopher stood outside the tent, watching this almost magical display of men and horses. Two great masses of force spread out, about to charge up the slope in the far distance and ride over into battle.

He never heard the order to attack, but the spurring of rounseys and coursers, and the loud clatter of the animals' feet told him it had come. He half expected to hear battle cries, but remembered it was a surprise attack. Anxiety-induced screams would have to be stifled.

He wished he had had the time to talk with Doyle before his friend left. He wanted to wish Doyle luck and to tell him that it was, indeed, ten days later and that he was, indeed, nervous. But there wasn't time. And Doyle was somewhere in that wide group of men on the right who bounced forward through the night wind toward the enemy.

"There they go," Kier flatly stated.

Christopher watched, and the more he did, the more depressed he got. "How can we just sit here and wait?" He studied the other squires who stood with them, some dozen boys whose gazes were all locked on the advancing troops.

Behind the squires, the cart drivers were huddled around a recently started cookfire, casually roasting a leveret, the young hare twirling on a small spit. The drivers sucked down jugs of ale and didn't consider for a moment that the good men they served headed off into battle. Christopher turned his attention away from them.

The two lines of Celts rose, twin serpents sidewinding over the crest of the slope, home to Garrett's army. A great roar, a sound the combination of many sounds all happening at once, hit the squires' ears: the *sring!* of spathas pulled from scabbards; the *klang!* of those spathas on shields; the *fwit!* of triggered crossbows; the *thong!* of nocked arrows released from longbows and shortbows; and the *thump!* of misthrown battle-axes burying themselves in the ground. The sounds of horses and men mixed in, added to the roar, made it grow louder, gave it a rhythm that increased and worked its way under the flesh of all the young boys who listened to it.

And then a different kind of roar hit Christopher's ears. A cry from every squire around him—including Kier. He turned, and was shocked to see the boys scramble from their vantage points and mount their nearby rounseys. Some began to charge off toward the great Saxon slope. Others followed suit.

"Wait!" Christopher screamed, running after Kier

as the boy made it to his horse and put his left foot in
its stirrup. "Where is everyone going?"

"Where do you think, Christopher?"

"We're not supposed to attack! It's against the
lord's orders!"

"We know. But we want to. And they need us.
Coming?" With that, Kier snapped his reins and his
rounsey whinnied and jumped forward.

He didn't think about his actions as he climbed onto
his rounsey. All he knew for a sudden second was that
the junior squires were joining the battle and he wasn't
going to be left behind. He wasn't sure whether he
wanted to go. Yes, he was completely disappointed by
Hasdale's refusal earlier, but the cold harsh reality of
riding toward combat brought on serious misgivings.
But he just did it, drove his horse forward, checked
and rechecked his sword as it bounced up and down
off the rounsey's left flank. He caught up to the others,
and they all rode, a line of twelve mounted squires
charging up the hill and wondering what would be the
first image to strike their eyes when they reached the
top. Christopher threw a quick glance over his shoulder and saw they were pursued by six of Hasdale's
men from the rear guard. No matter. They were too far
ahead of the soldiers.

As the grade became steeper, Christopher felt his
mount struggle. He looked left, then right, and saw
the others slowing as well. All heeled their steeds,
and Christopher did likewise as that distinctive battle
thunder seemed to hit him now with the force of a
fist. He sprang onto the crest of the slope and reined
in hard with the others, twin jets of breath firing
from the nostrils of all the rounseys.

For Christopher, it was the tents that stood out
among the horses and men. The whites, the blues, the
reds, all added the only color to the otherwise ocher
mud that covered everything else. He could barely
pick out his own forces. If the enemy were true

Saxons, it would have been easy, but Garrett had turned them into a kind of Saxon/Celt blend, mixing the savagery of the Saxons with the intelligence and armament of the Celts. That was a bloodcurdling mixture and spelled serious trouble for himself and the other boys.

"What are we waiting for?" Kier screamed.

Another howl from the boys and they all galloped forward, splitting up into the battlefield.

Christopher pulled his broadsword out of its sheath and held it tautly in his right hand. He bounced past a tent, reined his rounsey left, and found a Saxon horseman hacking away at the shield of an infantryman. Christopher galloped up behind the Saxon and swung his blade into the back of the barbarian's head. The Saxon lost his balance on the gelding he was astride and fell to the mud. He had barely hurt the Saxon, but dismounting the enemy soldier gave the infantryman an opening he used to bury his spatha in the Saxon's neck. Christopher left as the blood spurted.

Malcolm flailed away with a double-headed battle-ax at three Saxons who surrounded him. Two of the Saxons waved javelins, while the third brandished a mace. In the second it took Malcolm to drive his ax into one of the Saxons' chests, another of the Saxons buried his mace into the forehead of the young knight. Christopher fought back the desire to vomit as he approached. Malcolm fell to the ground. Christopher slashed at the shoulder of the Saxon who had killed Malcolm; the spatha found a crease in the armor and drew blood from the man. The Saxon's eyes spoke his anger. Christopher didn't wait around to see just how much anger that was. He heeled his rounsey away.

The tolling of weapons was everywhere. Shouts, groans, and piercing death screams came from both attacked and attackers. The smell of his own rounsey was dominant, though the musty earth backed it strongly.

No sign of the lord yet.

He dodged engagements as he galloped, nearly ran over a pair of his own infantrymen, turning his horse at the last second. Finally, a face he recognized: Sloan.

Every thrust of blade his helmetless trainer made against the two advancing Saxons carried with it an exhalation of sheer will and sheer anger. A fire of sound spewed from Sloan's lips as he fought: "Ahhhhhh!"—blade crashing on shield—"Ahhhhhh!"—blade impacting on shoulder armor—"Ahhhhhh!"—blade sinking deep into a Saxon heart. "Die, bloody filth! Die!"

The unwary Sloan didn't see the Saxon behind him.

The tall, lean barbarian one-handed a double-edged battle-ax, holding it high over his hairy head.

Christopher heard the Saxon's shoulder armor rumble as his arm brought the ax down toward Sloan's shoulder.

"Lord!" Christopher cried.

Sloan turned his head, and the blade of the Saxon ax shaved off his right ear. The iron continued down into the base of his neck, plying past the top ring of his breastplate and finding link-mail hauberk, then leather gambeson, then linen shirt, then finally skin and the heavy muscle below.

The Saxon tried to yank the weapon free, but it was wedged in Sloan's armor.

With the ax hanging from his neck, Sloan switched sword hands and slashed out madly with his spatha, cutting a deep gash across the face of the towering, beardless man. The slice ran from the Saxon's upper left cheek, across his lower lip, taking part of it off, and ended at his jaw. Blood the color of wine wiped quickly across the Saxon's face as his hands went to the wound. Oddly, he didn't scream.

Sloan turned and smiled mildly at Christopher, who could not return the grin. His eyes were fixed on the ax protruding from his trainer's neck.

"Help me, boy," Sloan barked.

Christopher lifted himself out of his saddle and splashed down into a puddle. He scuffled his way the ten yards toward Sloan.

Without warning, Sloan suddenly fell face forward into the mud, revealing an iron-tipped arrow buried in the back of his head. Christopher recognized the blue dye of the feather fletching; the shot had been wild and had come accidently from a Celt.

He was about to reach down and touch Sloan, compelled to do it, not knowing exactly why, vaguely thinking his trainer might still be alive. But the rumble of hooves only a few yards in front of him stole his attention.

It was Conway, Fiona's father, and three infantry- men who had confiscated Saxon horses and were now mounted. "Boy!" the gray-templed man called, "what are you doing here?"

Fortunately Christopher wouldn't have to answer, for behind him he heard the drumming of many hooves; the sound took Conway's eyes off the squire and on the present danger.

Christopher turned around. As many as ten Saxon horsemen bore down on them. He barely had enough time to remount his rounsey and move off. He was a scant five yards away when Conway's group clashed with the Saxons.

It felt a little strange not being an obvious target. He was a boy, unarmored, with only a broadsword to fight with. He could blend in rather easily with these Saxons, and he noticed that most looked at him oddly, trying to size up whose side he was on. And he didn't feel scared as he watched Conway's men fall under the hacking arms of the enemy. He wasn't ter- rified as the Saxons finally finished Conway himself.

Two of them sliced apart Conway's face with daggers. It was grotesque, yes, but it was as if he were standing over the scene, not a part of it.

"Christopher!" a voice called.

He cocked his head sharply moonwise, and, in the silvery light, saw the form of a man struggling on the ground near a collapsed tent. He yanked on his reins and moved his rounsey toward the injured person.

The bolt from a crossbow whistled by his head and he ducked, spurring his rounsey hard. Another bolt followed, and he arced his horse around the fallen tent, taking advantage of the minimal cover it provided. He dismounted and rushed over to the figure on the ground.

He didn't have to roll the boy over to know it was Kier. He knew Kier's tunic. He had almost recognized his voice. He certainly recognized death when he saw it, this time in the combined form of a spatha stab in the center of Kier's back and the arrow from a longbow stuck in his left shoulder blade. Christopher felt that same desire to touch Kier as he had felt with Sloan. Nothing interrupted him this time as his fingers connected with the back of Kier's head, the short soft hair that grew there. There was something sharply different about the living and the dead—something beyond the obvious. A living, breathing human being was unlike, say, a sword. The complexities of a person exceeded those of a sword by vast numbers, yet when broken, both were disposed of in the same fashion. Thrown away. It was hard to think of a dead person as a broken sword, yet they were both the same, inanimate, useless.

You meant something, Kier. You did.

"Condon's dead!" someone shouted. "Condon and Murdock and Collis, God help us!"

He needed no lesson from Sloan to know they were losing. He had seen the trainer himself die, as well as Conway, Malcolm, and Kier. Now Condon and

Hasdale's two senior squires joined the death ranks. He didn't see many Saxon bodies littering the ground. In fact, there were none in the immediate area. Only Kier. He rose, and saw that the shout had come from one of two mounted archers. Then he recognized the armor on one of the archers, and his red-colored tunic below: it was Varney, Doyle's master.

He ran toward the man, calling, "Varney, do you know where Doyle is?"

"You're supposed to be back at the camp, squire," Varney said in a voice that was far too authoritative for an archer.

For a split second, Christopher felt something warm pass near his neck.

A flaming glaive burrowed into Varncy's chest. The pole was thrown with such a force that Varney's armor did little to protect him. The archer slumped in his saddle, his boots still clamped in their stirrups. His horse trotted away of its own volition.

Thc other archer fumbled to unfasten his crossbow from its saddlestraps. Christopher turned around and saw six Saxons on foot run toward them, five holding flaming spears, the sixth empty-handed and smiling broadly.

Christopher just stood there. He didn't run. He didn't do anything. He imagined the Saxons throwing their spears over his head, missing him completely, and, in fact, some did just that. Behind him, he heard the archer fall from his horse with a blood-choked moan.

Christopher's knees weakened. The Saxons beat closer. Two of them still held their glaives and pulled their arms back, ready to throw.

The fat, hairy one, who appeared to be the leader, indicated with a hand for all to stop, then to the spearmen to hold their fire. He stepped up to Christopher, breathing heavily over him, the smell like something had died a moon ago in the back of the Saxon's throat; it was nearly enough to make Christopher pass out.

You could take a Saxon and put him in armor, but you could never take the Saxon out of a Saxon. He seemed more animal than man to Christopher, and all that hair on his face and head did nothing to wash clean the image. The Saxon fired off a salvo of unrecognizable syllables.

Yes, I agree.

The Saxon leader communicated again, this time louder, gesturing broadly with his hands.

I have to make haste now.

Despite the spearmen, and despite the hulk of a man before him, Christopher knew that if he didn't turn and run, he was either going to be killed now, or going to be killed later. If he was going to die, it would be while trying to escape. He tried to convince himself that that would make it better. But he had seen a great deal of death in a very short time. Nothing was going to make it better. *Run!*

They started shouting as he leapt over Varney's dead partner, whose tunic smoldered from the blazing spear homed there.

He ducked behind a tent some twenty yards away, then heard their approaching footsteps, the clanging of their armor, and their strange voices. He caught his breath a second, then dashed toward a distant confrontation of some hundred men on the far opposite side of the slope.

He saw so many bodies now, picked out by torchlight and the firelight of burning tents. But at least he saw some Saxons among the lifeless Celts. He also saw three familiar faces. Squires. Boys.

It was a good run, a run that seemed to have been stored in his body for a long time, a run from many more things than just the Saxons. A pure, simple run from death. From every face gone to pale stiffness, beginning with Airell and leading right up to Varney and his partner. There had to be a way to escape all of it; had to.

He was too preoccupied with the noises and silhouettes of the battle ahead to hear the single horseman that came up behind him. It was only when the steed was a cart's length away that Christopher turned his head. The nine black fingers of the whip cut across the side of his face with their leather nails, knocked him off-balance, then sent him headlong into a shallow pool.

The cool water instantly stung the cuts across his face. He pulled his head out of the water and blinked hard, the vision in his right eye blurry. He pushed himself up with his hands and sat back on his haunches.

The horseman trotted around, stopped, then swung off his steed. He unsheathed his spatha and walked toward Christopher.

But then he paused, eyeing Christopher with an odd look, as if he recognized the boy. He came closer, lowered his blade, and reached out a hand as if to touch the cuts on Christopher's face. Christopher recoiled. Then the horseman offered his hand to pull Christopher up.

Christopher didn't take the hand; instead he asked, "Who are you?" There was something about this Saxon that looked intelligent.

"I am Garrett," the man answered in a tongue he understood.

His premonition was right. Bitterly right.

Christopher edged slowly away from the Saxon lord. He was a part of the scene now, and was more frightened than he had ever been in his life. Here he was at the mercy of the man who had killed his parents. He should engage the man with his broadsword, as in his dream, but everything was so different, the meeting and the man so utterly real, the blade so utterly gone. Garrett wasn't even the man he imagined. He almost looked kind.

My God, that is *scary.*

"I have never seen junior squires engage in combat, as so many of Hasdale's have this evening. Did he allow you to ride along?"

Here they were in the middle of the battlefield, and the enemy of his black sleep wanted to have a chat?

Christopher would not talk to the man. He made an immediate vow never to address him.

"Which knight do you, or should I say *did you* serve?"

He tensed the muscles in his legs, prepared them to carry him away from this nightmare. He was fast, and he knew if he had a single moment's surprise, he would gain some lead.

Christopher darted, but his boots found no traction in the mire under them. He fell flat on his side.

Garrett shook his head, eyeing Christopher as he would some small, pathetic creature in his path. "Let's go."

19

Hasdale's rear guard never attacked. Christopher didn't know exactly why, but he suspected that word of the deaths of Sloan, Condon, Malcolm, and Conway had reached the camp and had been ample persuasion for retreat. The purpose of the last fifty was to attack in the face of such an event, but no one actually believed it would happen. And when it did, Christopher assumed that the men had run.

Outside Garrett's tent, the Saxons stripped Hasdale and tied him across a pair of his banner poles, making him look very much like a crucified Jesus. He had taken a crossbow bolt in the shoulder, and there was a long, deep slash on his right forearm, bone flashing underneath the flapping skin. The positioning of Hasdale's arms, and the stretching of his shoulder muscles served to increase his suffering.

Beyond Hasdale, small clusters of Saxons put captured men to death, the Celts' horrible last cries rolling into an ugly harmony that fell on deaf, Saxon ears.

Christopher's legs and arms were bound with leather straps, and he sat on the wet grass near Garrett's tent, viewing the horror before him and listening to the horror in the distance. He tried to stand, but could not gather the balance. He could only watch as Hasdale was paraded around in the middle of a circle of Garrett's filthy, hairy men.

One of the Saxons escorting Hasdale put a torch up to the captured lord's face, singeing Hasdale's beard, then let the flames continue to curl most of the blond hairs off. Then the Saxon moved the torch up to Hasdale's head, repeating the process on his hair, the putrid odor making Hasdale cough and nearly choke. Then the torch went to Hasdale's groin.

Garrett came out of the tent and waved the Hasdale parade over toward him.

Christopher was about to close his eyes. He knew they would kill his lord, and it seemed they would drag it out. He wouldn't watch any more of it. But if he closed his eyes . . . what?

There were none of the expected words exchanged between Garrett and Hasdale. Christopher assumed the Saxon would lap up the moment, suck in the pleasure of Hasdale's capture and the lording over his fragile life. But Garrett just stared hard and unblinkingly into Hasdale's eyes.

The lord was in great pain. The burns on his face and head and groin had to be crying out, and the wounds in his arm and shoulder were definitely joining the chorus. Despite all of it, Hasdale mustered enough saliva to spit on his enemy. The glob was

thick and heavy and caught Garrett on the right
cheek.

Garrett wiped Hasdale's spittle off his face, then
licked the hand he used to do it, tasting Hasdale's
phlegm. Christopher felt sick.

There was a diamond flash of steel as Garrett
pulled his dagger and sheathed it in Hasdale's heart,
twisting it around in short, winding motions as the
blood fountained over his hand.

The entire murder took no more than ten seconds,
and when it was done, Garrett turned away and took
in a long breath of the cool night air. He exhaled
hard.

Wiping his hands on a linen rag handed to him by
one of his men, Garrett squatted down in front of
Christopher, leveling his gaze with the squire's. "You
served him, didn't you?" He spoke the fact, not the
question.

Christopher tightened his jaw, caged the rage in his
throat.

"Not anymore," Garrett continued, again speaking
evenly and only of the fact. "I believe most of the
other boys have been killed. And if they haven't, well,
they will be. But you"—Garrett pointed with an index
finger—"you remind me of my brother. Quinn was an
excellent servant of his lord, as I'm sure you were of
yours—even in the face of death. But Quinn could
never learn to serve another. Will you?"

PART THREE

GARRETT AND MALLORY

1

Over four hundred looted bodies were strewn over the green slopes, fleshy tors that drew blue-black rooks and gray pigeons and speckled starlings. The birds pecked happily away at the forms that had once been men, then soared away toward their children, the carrion clenched in their beaks.

There was no wood to kindle the funeral pyres. What little oak and beech the Saxons did possess they kept selfishly to themselves. No Saxon hand would wrap itself around a grave shovel.

Christopher sat where he'd been all night, on the ground outside Garrett's small, tarpaulined hovel. He could barely feel his legs, and rods of stiffness spiked his shoulders. His eyes were heavy with sleep grit and his mouth tasted of something metallic and bitter. The cuts on his face still stung; they were not deep and he hoped they would heal quickly, though he suspected he would be scarred.

He shivered in the morning wind. He shivered as he thought about the utter defeat of last night, and the utter darkness of his future. He shivered as he heard the voice of Garrett come from within the tent, calling out in the Saxon tongue. He shivered as he saw two Saxon soldiers strip another infantryman, pull his breastplate off hard, let the edge of it slam into the dead man's cold face. The rag doll of a Celt felt no pain; Christopher felt it for him, pulling his head back under an imaginary blow. Garrett called out again, and the soldiers stopped their plundering and marched, one behind the other, toward the tent. They rounded Christopher, paying him no heed.

The scent of meat spitted over a nearby cookfire made Christopher's stomach groan. His flesh said eat, but his spirit said no. How could he eat while sitting in the middle of such carnage?

Inwardly, he told his stomach to be quiet. His spirit was right. Somewhere out there among those bodies was Doyle. It seemed unlikely Baines's brother had escaped. He was part of the Vaward Battle, and the odds were overwhelmingly small that he had made it out. And even if he had survived the battlefield engagement, the failure of the last fifty to attack left the surviving Celts vulnerable. Doyle and Bryan were dead. If Christopher could accept that now, perhaps the pain would not burn deeply and dwindle quickly.

But he couldn't trick himself. Accepting it now would not have anything to do with the hurt. The loss was the loss. Now or later. It would always burn.

My lord is dead. Orvin, your son is dead. But there will be no funeral pyres today.

Christopher looked up at the sky. Large rolls of soft, gray-looking clouds floated slowly by, the sun peeking through the thin deck and sending down diffused beams of light. If Orvin was right about those beams, the souls of the dead men were being carried up on them. Christopher wondered if there was enough room in Heaven for the dead Celts. There were so many. . . . There was certainly enough room in Hell for the dead Saxons; their losses were few.

"Since you refuse to speak, and I do not know your name, I will call you Kimball, royally brave, and for you, boy, I think it's appropriate." Garrett wiped bits of meat from the corners of his lips with the back of his index finger, then belched loudly. He knelt on a single knee in front of Christopher, the miasma emanating from him thick and rank on the air. "You truly remind me of my brother."

Do I remind you of a killer? Christopher thought blackly. *Do I remind you of your own killer? Oh, how I would like to carve up your charming face with my sword, you bastard.*

Garrett continued, "I've sent my two oafs to fetch you some pork. And some eggs. You'll find them to your liking. The cooks at Hasdale's castle have produced some fine delights, as I know you're aware."

The pork and eggs might have once been good, but, with Saxon hands on them, were now spoiled.

He forced all emotion from his face as Garrett studied him. He did not want to show this Saxon or Celt or whatever he was that he feared him. It was true that the longer he was around Garrett, the more comfortable the thought of killing him became; it was much stronger than the occasional whitecaps of fright that broke his mind's sea. He could look the Saxon leader in the eye, blank his own face, and remain that way in silent defiance. He could do it for as long as it took. To do what? That was the question. First thought: to escape. He would begin planning immediately. Even in the first hours of his capture.

"I can have your bindings removed if you'll behave." Garrett stood, brushing his right poleyn free of dirt. "Will you?"

Like a good little squire. Just find me my sword.

"I will tolerate your silence only so long." Garrett's voice was tied with loose knots of tension. He turned away from Christopher, then another thought hit him and he turned back. "You'll be home in ten days, if it makes you feel better."

Garrett's smile twisted in Christopher's heart.

2   She volunteered to change the sheets on the trestle beds in the garrison quarters, not because she enjoyed the job or wished to be among the young, brawny men who shifted about the quarters, but because she thought she might hear the first word about Christopher there.

Brenna was right. One of the lieutenants who had returned the previous night from the Mendip hills clanked into the long, narrow room. She did not know his name and felt awkward about asking him the fate of the army. She continued absently to remove the dirty linens and listen as the lieutenant addressed a sergeant who sat on his bed, honing his dagger on a whetstone.

"Is Uryens's garrison on their way?"

"He has loaned us ten lances of men."

"Not enough!"

"Lot has promised another five."

"And what of the other lords?"

"The king has ordered them to spare as many as they can."

"How do we defend without a leader?"

"I don't know."

"I say we abandon the castle."

"No. But we can send our women and children to Uryens's castle."

"Agreed. I'll pass the word. Let a few armorers, the hostlers, and the cooks remain. All else will ride."

The sergeant rose and marched past Brenna. As he left the room, the lieutenant collapsed noisily onto the sergeant's bed. "Do not make this one, maid. I wish to sleep now." His voice reflected his weariness, if not the grave state of affairs that surrounded all of them.

We lost. And the Saxons are coming to attack.

Christopher, where are you? Are you dead? Please be alive. Lord, please let him be alive.

She hid her tears from the lieutenant, even after she heard him begin to snore. She wanted to cry out her pain, to let some of it go. She wanted to fall to her knees and just cry. But she kept her hands busy and swallowed and sniffled back her hurt. If she were alone, she knew she would be hysterical. In a small way, she was glad for the sleeping lieutenant. He wasn't someone she could talk to, but he kept her sorrow in check. She really did not know if Christopher were alive or dead, and until then she had to keep heart and not bemoan him.

Her eyes caught a flicker of green tunic and white hair near the doorway. She looked up from the trestle bed she was stripping and saw Orvin.

"Morning, young raven maid."

"There is nothing good about this morning," she shot back coldly.

Orvin's brow rose. "'Good' did not pass these lips."

Suddenly she felt a little foolish. It was just . . . She changed the subject. "Do your linens need changing? I thought Mavis was sent to your quarters, lord."

"My linens are fresh, my chamber clean."

Orvin stepped toward her and rested one of his flabby, leathery arms around her shoulder. She didn't know exactly why, but the feeling of his arm, the notion that he understood her pain, brought a legion of tears to her face. She couldn't repress the sorrow anymore. She turned and rested her wet cheek against the old man's tunic.

He held her a little tighter as he spoke. "Our young patron saint breathes, believe me. I, on the other hand, have lost my son. There is no preparing for it. His going to battle made me ill, and his death blights me further still." He paused, then, "But you should not grieve. Be sad only for the distance between you. That is all."

Brenna lifted her face from his tunic and craned

her head up, looking directly into his soft, silvery eyes. "How can you be so sure he is alive?"

Orvin shut his eyelids and nodded. She wondered what he saw when he closed those eyes. She wondered why he nodded. Was it some affirmation of Christopher's survival? Nodding didn't exactly make Christopher live. Seeing Christopher standing in the doorway would be perfect proof for Brenna.

She turned away from Orvin to the door. She tried to see Christopher. She saw nothing. Her gaze shifted back to Orvin. "You cannot be sure, can you? It has been nearly a moon. He has still not come back."

Orvin stared beyond Brenna. She turned around and saw him looking through the cross-shaped loophole in the wall that framed a bit of forest supporting a cloudy sky above. "The young doubt so much," he said. "If you would only cling tighter to your faith, you would not be so troubled. Such a simple thing."

"What of your faith?" Brenna asked.

"My faith lies where yours should. With young Christopher."

He had helped her feel better, but now depressed her all over again. Their lord was surely dead. Their castle was about to be attacked with barely enough men to defend it, and now they would have to leave their home. What was Christopher going to do about all of it? Probably nothing. But she loved him, and would love him whatever their state, be it free or in prison, in this life or the next. She felt young, but very sure of one thing. If her happiness had to depend on something, she would let it depend on Christopher. And if he was dead, her sorrow would pull her down to join him.

The lieutenant began to talk in his sleep as they left the room. Brenna carried a tall stack of sheets, while Orvin insisted on helping her with another pile. They exchanged no words. With silence came a fragile inner peace.

3

Kenneth was the only other Saxon besides Garrett who could speak to the cut-faced boy. And Kenneth's squire had been killed when the Celts attacked. It was only natural that the boy became his squire. Only natural to Garrett, however.

Kenneth had argued with his lord that the boy should be put to death, that he represented a living host for the specters of Hasdale and the other battle lords to inhabit. Keeping the boy alive would surely bring treachery into their ranks. But Garrett had said he did not believe in the specters and superstitions that accompanied them. Kenneth continued his argument for most of the journey back to Hasdale's castle. But Garrett would not concede.

The boy wouldn't talk. They unstrapped him and he ran. They had to tie him to a rounsey. What kind of squire was that? Why keep the boy?

Kenneth took a long pull on his jug of ale. He swallowed the strong brew, then exhaled loudly. He looked to his right, saw the boy astride his rounsey, his head hung low, his lips tight, his spirit clearly broken. The winds that accompanied twilight were upon them, but Kenneth saw no indication that the boy was chilled. He seemed devoid of all emotion. Kenneth admired that. He had never seen a boy numb himself as completely. He returned his gaze to the field ahead.

They would be at the castle by noon the next day. The anticipation of battle spun around Kenneth's heart. He knew the castle better than anyone, and, facing only a skeleton garrison of defenders, he expected to be in bed with Fiona by nightfall.

They, of course, had some unfinished business.

He had yet to find another woman who excited him as much as she. He had had most of the serf women in the neighboring towns, rough, heavy

females who bruised him before he had a chance to
kill, then lie with them. Fiona was different; she was
soft, vulnerable, feline. These sudden thoughts made
his groin ache. He forced the fantasies from his mind;
they would drive him wild. He flipped another glance
to the boy.

*You're just waiting for Hasdale to take you. And
then you'll come for us in the night.* He considered
killing the boy in the coming siege. His doing so
could be easily explainable to Garrett. *Done. You die
on the morrow. Sleep well.*

Kenneth grinned in self-satisfaction. He felt a tiny
rush of power course through his veins; it was the
thought that, as he looked at the boy, he knew he
was in control of the squire's fate. And the young
Celt knew nothing of it. The boy was a leveret sniff-
ing in the wind, unaware of the fox poised in the
gorse just behind him.

4

"Every tower is fortified, my lord. The wall-
walks are lined with bowmen. There is even an
infantry banded along the berm. They received help."

Kenneth squinted in the sunlight that fisted down
on himself, Garrett, and the young scout. The bad
news was a mace blow to the head of his lord, inflict-
ing about as much damage.

Garrett's wide eyes would have said it all, but he
added, "I cannot believe the word spread this
quickly. Whose men are these?"

"I don't know, lord," the grave-faced scout said.
"Perhaps Uryens's or Lot's. There are rumors the
king has formed a new union."

"I DON'T CARE ABOUT THE KING OR HIS
NEW UNION!"

The scout was jolted and took a step back from Garrett, sinking his head into his neck. "Sorry, my lord."

Kenneth did not react to the news with anger. He was annoyed at the setback, yes, but his mind raced to find the answers to two questions—how to get back into the castle and be with Fiona, despite the new garrison, and how to murder the boy and make it look accidental.

If they were smart, they would not attack. It would be a long, drawn-out battle, they would lose many men, and even if they did gain control, there might not be enough Saxons left to form a garrison. Thus, another army of Celts would soon come and overthrow them quickly.

That was it. He had to convince Garrett to attack. He might be able to breach the curtain walls himself and find Fiona. He would certainly be able to murder the boy. Victory was an empty purse to Kenneth. It was Garrett's dream to rule a castle, not his. Garrett didn't have any problem following his own agenda, and so neither would he. Rape and murder. The words didn't sound as pleasurable as the acts really were.

Kenneth pounded a fist into an open palm. "If we strike hard and fast this evening, I believe we can win."

Garrett shook his head negatively. "We've tried twice to take this castle, and with smaller garrisons defending it."

"The men are borrowed, lord. They fight not to protect their home, but because they are ordered to. A hard first strike will send many of them running."

The Saxon lieutenants that now crowded around Kenneth murmured their support for his plan. Kenneth waited for Garrett's reply, shooting Garrett as intimidating a look as he could muster.

Garrett thought a moment, gazing through

Kenneth and the rest of the men. "No," he said curtly. Then walked away.

You're very wise, lord. And very foolish.

5

Christopher slept well. He hadn't understood the conversation between Garrett, the scout, and Kenneth, but he understood a worried look, understood a shout of frustration, understood the fact they would not attack. They spent the rest of the day retreating, and the castle was out of sight by the time they set up camp for the night.

Dreams tunneled through his mind, short ones lasting only seconds, quick visions of people and places. Brenna's face flashed many times, as well as the warm, soft smile of his mother, and the harder, more thoughtful look of his father.

Garrett came to him too, not as an ugly, horrible demon, but as a man weeping. He repeatedly called out something in the Saxon tongue. The image was bizarre and made Christopher claw at the pair of saddle cloths which he slept on.

Some time during the night he woke. He didn't open his eyes, but remained still, listening: the embers of a nearby cookfire crackled softly; the snoring of drunken Saxons volleyed overhead; crickets announced tomorrow's heat; and then, the very minute *flip-flap* of approaching sandals.

He was about to keep his eyes closed, feign sleep, but thought better of it. Who would lurk around camp in the middle of the night? A sudden, chilling, though hopeful thought: someone to take him away. He opened his eyes, rocked himself into a sitting position.

In the silver-and-copper light delivered by the haloed moon, he saw Kenneth step over sleeping men and come toward him. Strange. Maybe the Saxon could not sleep. If so, why step so precariously over men when the perimeter field provided open ground for a night walk?

Something shimmered at Kenneth's waist. Christopher squinted, blinked hard, then his sleepy eyes took in the blade sticking from Kenneth's fist.

Reflex overrode thought. He pulled at the leather straps that trapped his arms and ankles, binding him into helplessness. His legs pushed his buttocks six inches back in retreat, then another six. If he just had a weapon. His sword, the one given him by Baines, was lost on the battlefield.

He kept his gaze on Kenneth. The Saxon's near-pretty face was sour, his eyes dull, the lids narrow, his mouth turned down, and the skin on his nose bunched up. Kenneth extended his free arm to pin Christopher, while his other hand would work the dagger.

Another six inches on his butt. Christopher made little progress. A million fears unleashed themselves within him, and at least one found its way to his throat. "No! Kenneth! No!"

Kenneth fell to his knees before Christopher and thrust his hand toward Christopher's throat.

Christopher ignored Kenneth's free hand and used his bound hands as one unit with which to stop Kenneth's dagger as it came down on him. His hands vised around Kenneth's wrist. Saxon muscle struggled against squire muscle, the tip of the blade a forearm's length from Christopher's shirted chest.

Kenneth forced Christopher to fall onto his back, all the while remaining silent, wearing his murder mask perfectly, menacingly.

Christopher wanted to cry out for help, but the struggle gave his mind that second it needed to reason the cry away. He was in a Saxon camp. Who was going to help him?

The blade was now a hand's length away from his chest.

The fingers on Kenneth's free hand dug into his neck; untrimmed nails pierced skin, gouged, burrowed, cut off part of Christopher's air supply.

The muscles in his arms were giving in to the greater mass and strength of Kenneth's. He began to feel light-headed, but it was a different, terrifying feeling—not the one ale produced.

The dagger was a finger's width away from his breast.

His strapped hands vibrated under the force of Kenneth. He began to choke, his air slipping away. Saliva rolled over his lower lip and down his chin; the foamy phlegm seeped onto Kenneth's hand.

Christopher realized he was going to die. He did not want to feel the dagger punch into his chest, but he knew it was inevitable. He was willing to let go now; he just did not want any pain. He closed his eyes.

Let it be over. Quickly. Please.

The hand clamped around Christopher's throat went slack, and he felt Kenneth fall to his left.

Christopher's first breath hurt. His second gave him his life back. On his third breath, Christopher mustered the energy to open his eyes.

He felt soft fingers caress his cheek as his vision focused. The shadowy form of Garrett hovered over him, the Saxon leader's eyes full of concern.

Garrett withdrew his hand. "Just breathe."

Christopher looked over at Kenneth. A dagger of equal size and similar hilt to the one with which Kenneth had tried to murder Christopher was sunk in Kenneth's back, just under his left shoulder blade.

He edged his gaze tentatively to Garrett. Christopher's lungs galloped and his pulse charged alongside. He did not believe what had just happened. Garrett had sacrificed one of his best men for Christopher. Why? Christopher possessed no magic, no unique skills, nothing that he thought was out of the ordinary. He could make saddles, was told he was a fair squire, and that he was royally brave. Scores of other boys shared the same characteristics. And yet, Garrett had saved his life. Was it simply because he reminded Garrett of his brother? Christopher wasn't sure.

But now, not only was he "in the service" of the man—but he owed his life to him.

He owed his life to the same man whose army had slain his parents.

Do I thank him or kill him?

Christopher could justify to himself that Garrett didn't intentionally kill Sanborn and Cornelia, or Baines for that matter, but he felt he would betray himself if he did that. The most he could do now was break his vow of silence and speak to the man. Thanking Garrett wouldn't put him in bed with the man; it would simply acknowledge his act. He would talk to him. But he would never forgive him.

"Thank you," he rasped.

The barest of grins turned on Garrett's lips. "Young Kimball has a voice." Garrett caught him staring down at Kenneth again. "A dagger was destined to be in his back. I warned him. Don't think I did it for you."

Christopher had seen how the Saxon soldiers often sided with Kenneth. Kenneth was the handsome, popular knight, Garrett a great leader but still a Celt. Indeed, Garrett had cleared one problematic rogue out of his path, but in doing so had saved Christopher. That fact remained.

Garrett helped him off his back. The Saxon leader turned and picked up the dagger which had fallen from Kenneth's hand. Garrett cut the leather straps from Christopher, freeing him. "You've run many times. My watchmen have always caught you. Sleep free this night. If you don't try to escape, the bindings stay off."

Christopher rubbed his neck with a free hand, felt the impressions Kenneth's nails had made in his skin. It was nice to be able to do that, to now be able to scratch the itches that came every night and not have to think them away.

He smiled mildly, though reassuringly. "'Til sunrise."

Garrett nodded, then turned to two men who had awakened and stood twenty yards behind them. He fired off a salvo of orders and the Saxons hustled over to Kenneth's body, lifted and carried it away. Garrett watched them a moment, his expression grim, then stepped into his tent.

Christopher was much too exhausted to try to escape that night. He would keep his word. Maybe that was it. Build up a sense of trust in Garrett, make the Saxon leader come to believe he was loyal, relate to the man in a way the Saxons could not: appeal to him as one Celt to another. Talk of God and not ghosts, of love and art and beauty, simple pleasures the Saxons discarded for war. The Saxon thirst for violence was unquenchable, but so was the Celtic thirst for knowledge. The abbot had taught Christopher these simple lessons, a history he thought he would never use. The abbot spoke frequently about the invaders, convincing Christopher how much better Celtic life was than Saxon life. Christopher would pass on the lessons to Garrett. He was only a boy, but he would try. Despite his army, Garrett was a Celt.

He slid under his blankets, closed his eyes, and never remembered falling back to sleep.

Later, the sky still the blue-black color of night, Christopher snapped awake and clutched his throat.

6 Orvin watched Brenna and her family pull out of the outer bailey and slip under the gatehouse. The cart carrying their belongings was pulled by Cara. Orvin wanted the old mule to be as safe as the girl, behind the protective curtain walls of Uryens's castle. The invaders had still not mounted their attack. Fears burned, steady torches that played havoc with his mind.

He was warned not to stray beyond the confines of the castle, but needed one of his walks in the wood down near the practice field; it would settle his stomach, and his head. A few moments after the cart was gone he followed its path, walking in the shallow trails cut in the dusty yard by the wheels. He was accosted by three sentries as he left the gatehouse and descended the slope. He ignored them.

Slipping into the wood was slipping deeper into himself. Moments alone were painful years ago, filled with loss, but he had come to enjoy them, to need them. And he was not really alone. The oaks and the beech trees were all around him, familiar friends whose silence was as much appreciated as the shade they cast on summer days. Within these tall men of bark were the tiny sparrows, lorded over by the dark knight crows. Orvin had watched the larger birds chase the smaller ones from their nests; it seemed unfair, but not any more so than the taking of a castle. The more powerful always wished to dominate—even here.

He let his fingers run across the flowers of the gorse, and the other shrubs that framed and neighbored the narrow path. His steps were irregular, and he stopped, scanning to find a bird who called out, then turned his head toward the rustling of a hare or fox or doe.

A fallen oak, whose life was taken by a lash of lightning, paralleled the path; the trunk provided a natural bench that Orvin had taken advantage of on many occasions. He sat down, taking the weight off his weary legs.

Sunlight mazed through the leaf canopy and picked out shrubs and portions of the path to color yellow. The low drone of insects was all around, and a faint trace of mold scented the air. He let his surroundings take him. He surrendered to the forest, to a place that seemed truly a home.

He no longer felt the trunk under him, no longer felt the stiffness in his legs and neck, no longer experienced the stinging in his gums and the occasional jabs in his chest. He let his mind open.

Do well, boy. I will try to help you.

7

Christopher rode on a black courser, one he sensed was Celtic trained, and shared a loaf with Elgar. Kenneth's funeral pyre dwindled in the distance behind them. A long stretch of lazy brown hills was the path ahead.

Elgar was not unlike Orvin, though far more agreeable to the eye—which was ironic for a Saxon. Elgar's hair was slate gray, and rose thickly off his head in a widow's peak. The elder's eyes were nearly the same color, and his face was split only by a dozen or so lines, not the regiment that marched across Orvin's skin. Christopher could not speak to him, but could sense his loyalty to Garrett and was witness to his consideration for others. He usually shared his portion of food with someone, an archer, a bowman, or even Garrett. His jug was every man's jug, and he seemed to take pleasure from his own generosity.

The Saxons had long since used up the supplies

confiscated from Hasdale's carts, and now their own stores diminished. There was no castle to support their army, no kitchens, armorers, hostlers, maids, or scullery boys to wash their plates. They caught and cooked what food they could as they traveled, mended their own armor and the shoes of their horses, washed their own shirts and breeches in the many brooks that straddled their paths, and abandoned the use of plates altogether. They were self-sufficient, and their only protection was their mobility. The only way to acquire more supplies was to pillage. Christopher knew it was only a matter of time before that terrible fact became a reality.

He turned his attention from the path to Elgar. The old Saxon smiled while chewing his bread. He was the only Saxon Christopher had ever seen smile. Even when they drank their faces held a long, cold look, one that was at once somber, at once fierce. Maybe they viewed smiling as a sign of weakness. Maybe they didn't know how to. Christopher thought about it as he looked at his bread, then took a healthy bite. He knew something brewed in the minds of the Saxons behind him. They were not happy over Kenneth's death; they loved and worshiped the young man. Garrett had told them Kenneth was a traitor, but Christopher doubted that the army believed it.

A wandering column of smoke rose in the sky above the farthest hill. Christopher could see it clearly, as they were on a crest and began to descend. Murmurs that sounded like animal noises grew behind him.

From the rear, four scouts galloped outside the lines of cantering Saxons, passed the entire group, and headed toward the smoke.

Christopher guessed the gray clouds came from a village just like his. He knew they would burn it just like Shores. Only this time he was supposed to help.

He had decided to make Garrett trust him. He had not tried to escape, now rode freely with the army,

and was shielded from the other Saxon squires by
Garrett. The young barbarians eyed Christopher
with contempt, and he was glad Garrett kept him
away from them. He did not need another attempt
on his life. But at the moment, he was confronted
with the inevitable. If he cooperated with the
Saxons, actually helped them in the raid, it would
surely strengthen his position with Garrett, and perhaps the Saxon squires would look at him with different eyes. But how could he participate in the
violence? To stand by and watch it happen was bad
enough, but to join it?

They needed food, fresh horses to replace lame
ones they had abandoned, new carts, for many had
broken down, and whatever armament they could
steal. They didn't need to kill every serf and freeman in their way; they didn't need to rape every
female of age and some not of age; they didn't need
to burn everything in their wake. But they would.
And there was no changing that. Christopher would
either accept and join or create a new plan. A perfect trust in Garrett's heart would allow him a perfect escape. That fact seemed so true that he saw no
other way.

He had already killed. Maybe it would be easier
the next time. He would ride in as a warrior, not a
squire, and show Garrett the violence that lurked in
his heart, a violence he would harness for Garrett.

And he would address Garrett as lord.

They crossed four more hills, then the scouts
returned. They reported seeing a village. And it
waited for all of them.

8 On a patch of ground that was mostly dirt, Christopher and four Saxon lieutenants watched Garrett use his dagger to draw a map of the village.

A main road arrowed straight through the town, with four narrower intersecting paths that curved into a perimeter road linking all the dirtways. Garrett used the tip of the blade to mark attack points, spouting off commands to each of the lieutenants as he did so.

Christopher looked back over his shoulder. Darkness had come, and he saw the flickering candlelight that illuminated the windows of the tofts in the far distance. It was a silly notion, but Christopher thought the light held some kind of innocence—an unsuspecting light that lit the homes of unsuspecting citizens about to be robbed and killed.

When the meeting was over, Christopher mounted his steed. A feeling of regret took root in him.

He watched as three groups of Saxons, each of about forty men, rode ahead of his group. They would circle around to the rear of the village and concentrate on the manor house.

The village did not support a castle as Shores did, but a smaller, much more vulnerable and uncurtained structure, next to which was an even more accessible abbot's tithe barn, from which they could steal the eggs, poultry, fruit, bread, and ale stored there.

Christopher would stay close to Garrett. The Saxon leader's group of one hundred would ride straight into town and do most of the butchering. The rest of Garrett's men would rifle the needed supplies and load the stolen carts. The two hundred inhabitants of the village were outnumbered more than two to one; what resistance the Saxons encountered would be easily suppressed.

Christopher wished he knew the name of the village. For some reason he felt he should have that information, to keep the name in his memory; when they were done with it he knew it would be unrecognizable, as Shores was in the aftermath of Garrett's attack.

"What village is this?" he asked Garrett, as they cantered down the final slope and were about to cross a shallow stream on the outskirts of the town.

"Why do you ask?"

Christopher shrugged. "Curious."

"It belongs to Fitzralph. I do not know what he calls it."

"Thank you."

"I want you close to me, Kimball. I don't want you to do anything."

"Yes, lord." The word left a sour taste in his mouth.

Garrett's eyes were blue suns of surprise. The man studied Christopher, perhaps searching for some physical change in him that accompanied his new attitude.

Christopher turned his attention to the town ahead, the sleeping little village that was about to plunge into a nightmare.

Garrett raised his arm and circled his fist in the air: a silent signal to gallop.

Christopher was jolted by his courser; the animal responded much better than the rounsey he had ridden to the Mendips. He couldn't be sure, but he suspected the horse belonged to Condon or Malcolm, or even the lord for that matter. It had been stripped of its saddle when given to him, so he would never know. All around him Saxons charged, and it was odd to be riding *with* them instead of *against* them. These were supposed to be his brothers-in-arms; that notion would take some getting used to.

As they hit the first dirt of the main road, doors on

houses swung open. Sleepy eyes that were thin slits
widened in the face of the attack.

Behind Christopher, Saxon soldiers launched
quicklimed glaives and arrows into the air; the flaming missiles found the sagging gables of the old tofts
and set them ablaze.

Even now, as the attack began, Christopher hunted
for some means to demonstrate his loyalty to Garrett.
He couldn't just observe, even though that had been
Garrett's order. He sensed the Saxon leader feared
for him. Doing nothing would put him in no better
position with Garrett. He needed to act in order to
gain trust, and that trust would gain him his goal.

But in gaining trust, would he have to kill? It
seemed the ultimate proof to Christopher. *There, I've
killed for you. I'm with you. See?*

What about the victim—some innocent man protecting his land? Wasn't *Christopher* once the victim? Wasn't *he* the one who had ridden into his
village and found it dead? Wasn't *Garrett* the man
responsible?

He could not think about the victim, for if he pondered any more on that subject, he would put a dagger in his own heart. He had to think of it as a game
and play by the rules. But the game was life and
death and someone had forgotten to tell him the
rules. It got painful and confusing and he pushed it
all out of his mind, took in his surroundings, and
thought only of the moment.

Most of the Saxons behind them had dismounted
and entered the first row of houses. Four other soldiers accompanied Christopher and Garrett as they
turned down the first intersecting road. Each side of
the street was lined with tofts, many sharing a common wall that would only aid the fires.

A man with long, silvery hair stepped in front of
his door, wearing only his breeches. He one-handed a
rusting hatchet, apparently his only weapon. The man

pulled his arm back and let the ax fly. The blade tumbled end over end, and its wooden handle connected with the gaskin of a courser behind Christopher. The horse bucked and neighed, kicked up its forelegs, and threw its rider.

Garrett dismounted and ran after the man. The villager fled into his house. Christopher guessed Garrett was more insulted than anything else, and was now bent on killing the man. Rage motivated Garrett, nothing else. Christopher was already off his horse as Garrett entered the home, the Saxon leader's spatha slipping in ahead of him.

Christopher pushed in the door; the setting was painfully familiar: workshop bench, leather pegged to the wall, snippets scattered about the floor, the stench everywhere. The man was a craftsman. His life was in this room, this town. Surviving serfs would be taken care of by Fitzralph if he lived, or sold to a neighboring manor by the abbot. Freemen like this leatherdresser would be left with nothing, and would have to start again. A lifetime of work, of nurturing business relationships and developing a reputation would all end in a single night. Death seemed ironically easier than starting again.

He heard a struggle in the back of the house and moved through the workshop into a cooking area shielded by a partition wall. He arrived in time to see Garrett knife the man in his ale belly; dark blood drenched the craftman's hairy skin and filled up the man's navel. The villager shot Garrett a black look as he fell onto his back.

Christopher heard a woman scream behind him. He turned to see a pale, bone-thin villager, her eyes red and tearing, her face twisted into the growl of a wild dog. She came at him with a scythe held high, the hooked blade used for threshing hay about to thresh his neck.

"Kimball!" Garrett yelled reflexively.

But Christopher didn't need Garrett to tell him he was in trouble; the flash of sharpened iron was a better alarm. The blade touched his neck, and was about to draw blood, but he fastened his fingers around the oak handle of the farming tool. The woman was not strong. Christopher forced her back with a single shove, a motion that was so abrupt that she lost her grip on the scythe and fell back, unarmed.

As the woman slunk back from him, crying and feeling with her hands for the workbench behind her, Christopher pulled the scythe back. He would hit her hard. Bash her across the face with the blade and crack her skull open like a nut. He felt the power to do that surge in his arms.

He pitched a look back at Garrett. The Saxon leader gave no indication of what to do; he only watched.

The woman moaned, "no" as he looked back at her. Then she spun around and ran for the door.

Christopher started after her, but then his heart seized his mind. He stopped. He could pursue and kill this woman, but was gaining Garrett's trust more important than human life? He knew it would come to this, but tried to force the guilt that accompanied murder out of his mind. But it wasn't him. He was not a cold-blooded killer who thought only of his own goals.

The craftsman's wife slipped past the door and vanished into the night air.

Behind him, Christopher heard Garrett say, "Thank you."

Christopher turned, regarded the Saxon leader with a frown. "For what?"

"Had you not been here, she might've hooked me from behind."

But Christopher knew he hadn't saved Garrett; the Saxon leader could easily have turned and gutted the woman with his blade, and done it alone. But Garrett made it easy, almost as if he *wanted* to believe

Christopher would have saved him. "A good squire always lends assistance to his lord." A perfect, Orvin-inspired answer.

"That he does." Garrett sighed, then furrowed his brow. "I sense you want me to trust you, Kimball. I will. But don't cross me." He took a step closer to Christopher, emphasizing the seriousness of his next dialogue with proximity and a pointed index finger. "I want you to know I don't enjoy killing. I don't."

Christopher nodded, remembering how Garrett's murder of Hasdale seemed an ugly, but necessary task to the Saxon leader. "But you'd force yourself to kill me if you had to?"

"And you would do the same, were you in my boots," Garrett said. "In fact, you've probably thought of killing me yourself."

Christopher bit his lower lip, bit back the truth.

"It's all right. Most of England wants me dead. It's no insult." Garrett smiled, then started for the door. "We're finished here."

9

The saddle stared up at her.

A score of moons had passed since Christopher had gone to the Mendip hills. Brenna had long since forgotten the pain of losing him and had abandoned the notions of suicide. She could no longer see the image of his face clearly in her mind. She had not returned from Uryens's castle, but had remained there and had become a respected chambermaid. She was fourteen now, and felt as much a woman as her mother. She was courted by a young varlet and entranced by his advances. Fortunately, the saddle did not bother her as much now as it had when she had been alone, uncourted, still grieving for Christopher.

The saddle was one Christopher had made for Orvin, and it had come along with them, to be used by Orvin to ride Cara when he came to the castle. But Orvin had never come, and the rumors were that he had died. She had kept the saddle under her trestle bed ever since, but now that they were moving their quarters, and the beds were coming too, the dusty seat sat uncovered on the floor.

Brenna reached down and fingered the pommel. Her finger came up dark gray. She frowned and wiped the finger on her apron. She considered throwing the saddle away, or giving it to someone who could use it, or selling it; she could probably get a fair number of silver deniers for it. She could purchase a new shift and a matching tunic.

Brenna wiped the saddle down as best she could and took it to the leatherdressers' hut in the outer bailey.

She immediately stopped breathing through her nose as she entered the workshop. The heads of two journeymen leatherdressers and four apprentices all popped up simultaneously, and she saw right away how inviting smiles came to their lips and their eyes seemed to touch her.

"I wish to sell you this saddle," she said, holding up the heavy seat.

One of the journeymen rose from his bench, rounded the table, and took the saddle from Brenna's hands. He studied the craftsmanship carefully. "Where did you get this?"

"I've had it for a long time. A boy I knew made it."

The journeyman could not take his gaze off the saddle, and Brenna felt a bit ignored, considering the initial reaction everyone had given her. "This is the most detailed and refined work I've ever seen," the leatherdresser said. "The stitching is perfect. And I cannot believe how even the cuts are."

"Do you wish to buy it?" she asked.

"I would not sell it, were I you," the journeyman answered.

"I need to."

"If you must."

They negotiated a price agreeable to Brenna, and she left the shop with more than enough deniers to buy her shift and tunic.

She felt wistful as she entered the keep and climbed the spiral staircase. All physical evidence of him was now gone. She paused on one of the steps, remembered a prison cell, a blanket, and a jug of ale. She smiled.

10

How many chances had he had to escape? He had lost count moons ago. Every night was a chance to run. There were two particular occasions that stood out in Christopher's memory.

The first was after they had pillaged Fitzralph's village. He remembered waking up in the back of a cart filled with armor and smith's tools. It was early morning, and the army had paused some distance from the village they had burned the night before. They were regrouping, reporting their losses and stuffing their bellies with a celebratory breakfast.

His first view was of the black smoke that belched into the sky above the indistinct hill, one massive funeral pyre for the innocent. He recalled how he uttered Orvin's name out loud, told the old man, "Maybe you were right."

He had summed up his situation quickly. No one was within a hundred yards of him. Knots of men surrounded the food carts and cookfires, or sat in their own cliques discussing the battle. Christopher had not seen Garrett.

The team of two packhorses that pulled the armor cart grazed quietly, still tied to the wagon. All he had had to do was untie one of the horses and make a gallop for it. But he didn't.

As he thought about it, moons later, pulling on the fine hairs that had recently sprouted from his upper lip and chin, he reasoned he should have tried to escape. The Saxons had been gorging themselves and would not have reacted as quickly.

The second occasion came only the day before, when Garrett had sent him and Seaver to spy on a small hunting party led by Lord Nolan of the castle of Rain in West Camel. The lord, accompanied by a falconer, a bowman, and a huntsman with two large, gray hounds, was completely unaware of their presence.

Seaver was a dwarf-sized man who suggested they rub mud over most of their bodies to disguise themselves and hide their scent from the hounds. Seaver was an expert scout, and though Christopher had no aspirations in that field, Garrett said he could learn a lot from the Saxon. Christopher's meager Saxon vocabulary limited him to simple conversations, but he needed no words to pick up a few tricks from Seaver: the mud, the way to run silently without pounding one's feet, the way to notice, to keep one's mind focused on sights and sounds, not thoughts.

They had followed the hunting party through the lord's private forest, had taken note of the garrison men posted in the wood for the lord's protection. If Garrett was going to kill Nolan while the lord was on another such hunting trip, the plan had to be well thought out.

Christopher had carried a small dagger sheathed and belted around his waist, and as he had watched

the lord through a veil of leaves, a sudden thought
flashed through his mind: kill Seaver and run to the
lord, ask for mercy, and tell Nolan what had happened to him.

He could have reacted quickly, surprising Seaver
and gaining his freedom. Garrett trusted him enough
to let him go out with only one man watching him.
And a remarkable and ironic feeling had stopped
him. The guilt of betraying Garrett.

And now here he was, riding on another inter-
minable field under a winter sun that didn't stray far
from the horizon, struggling with who he had
become. Was he a Saxon now? Garrett had taught
him many things about fighting, and about living. He
had come to admire the man. He didn't know when
that had happened, but somewhere, sometime, it had.
Garrett was strong, and true to what he believed in.

His plan to appeal to Garrett as one Celt to
another had worked. They had discussed art and God
and things bigger than the world itself. Riding was a
time for discussion, but Christopher had kept silent
this morning, pondering yesterday. *Why didn't I do
it?* He was held against his will—or was he?

"Young Kimball holds his tongue this morning,"
Garrett said, riding next to him. "Why?"

"Lord, if I wished to leave, to go home now, could I?"

Garrett thought a moment while stroking the poll
of his ride. "But on the morrow we lay siege to
Nolan's castle while he hunts. You and Seaver will
lead us through the wood. You want to miss that?"

"No." He was being honest. The expectations and
excitement before an engagement, and the rush of
flirting with death was too much to give up.

"Then why do you ask?" Garrett said.

"I wish to know if the option is there."

"It is."

"I could ride away now and not be stopped?"

Garrett reined his horse next to Christopher's so

that he was close enough to put a hand on Christopher's tabard-covered shoulder. "You have tried hard to prove your loyalty to me. But I've always known that you wish to remain a Celt, and not serve these men or me." He looked over his shoulder, as if to make sure no one was listening when, in fact, no one understood them anyway. "You have been with us for a score of moons. You have done well. I enjoy your company. More so, I admit, because you are a Celt. I do not want you to leave. You are a good squire." He sighed. "But if you wish to go, go."

The guilt that had stopped Christopher from escaping the day before flooded within him. He wondered if it was just guilt. Probably not. In light of the past, he hated to admit that what he felt for the man slipped beyond admiration and into love. An almost father-son relationship, one which he had wished to foster with Hasdale. He would not have believed twenty moons ago he would come to love the man who had caused the death of his parents and friends.

But Garrett wasn't numb to the pain he inflicted on others. He spoke often of his own guilt, the remorse he felt after burning Shores and the eventual killing of Hasdale. He told Christopher it was the way of their world, and he didn't like it, but had to react within it. The Saxons drew strength from the killing, and that was why they made a perfect, though ironically unsuccessful army. Christopher had asked Garrett why he *had* to react within the world, and not try to change it.

Garrett had only sighed resignedly, as he did then.

"Thank you, lord."

"For what?" Garrett asked.

"For making me realize where my home is." Christopher had not expected to say anything of the kind, but it came out, and though the words lacked complete truth, they expressed a feeling within him, a sense of belonging not to the Saxon army, but to Garrett.

"Until we have a castle," Garrett said sadly, "we do not have a home."

"Perhaps our luck will change." He thought a moment, considering whether he should tell Garrett or not, then decided a better time would not come along. "Maybe a little fate will work for us if I tell you something." Garrett craned his neck toward Christopher, his face intent. Christopher went on, "You chose to call me Kimball. But my name is Christopher, and as a friend of mine was fond of calling me, 'the young patron saint.'"

"The patron saint of travelers. Maybe there is a little bit of helpful spirit in you." Garrett reached out his hand; Christopher took it. "It is good to meet you, Christopher. Young patron saint. Protect us on the morrow, will you?" Garrett grinned broadly.

Christopher returned the look. "I'm only a squire."

"No," Garrett said, "you are *my* squire."

They rode on, the wind steady and cold, but not particularly piercing, and Christopher caught Garrett smiling to himself some moments later.

He had decided to stay with Garrett. And he reflected on the consequences of that decision. He was giving up the past, giving up Orvin, and, more painfully, Brenna. He wondered what they were doing, painted mental images of them at the castle.

He wanted to see Brenna praying in the chapel every night for his safe return, but couldn't. He knew it had been too long, and time had distanced their love more than the actual land between them. He forced himself to believe she had forgotten him, and gritted his teeth over the idea, no matter how loud the truth rang.

His last memories of Orvin had been happy ones, but the old man had not seen him off as he mounted up for his first battle. Hasdale had said Orvin had

been too ill to attend, and now that image flickered
to life in Christopher's mind. He saw Orvin lying in
bed, a nurse tending him. She tried to get the old
man to drink some water, but the fluid just poured
over Orvin's wizened chin. Suddenly the image was
whisked away and Christopher felt an intense heat
push across his face. He turned his absent gaze from
the neck of his courser to the sun mounted on the
tableau dead center between the zenith and horizon.
The yellow orb burned much brighter than it should
have, filled his eyes with golden light. There was
nothing but the light and the heat.

"Christopher?"

He turned his head and saw Garrett next to him.
He looked forward. The sun was normal. Christopher
dropped his reins and rubbed his eyes with the heels
of his hands, then looked again. Countryside. Sun.
Sky. Clouds.

"Here." Garrett proffered a horn of ale.

Christopher took the ale, muttered, "Thank you."

His troubled tone was noted by Garrett. "All
right?"

"I'm just tired."

11 Mallory stood in front of the attenuating
flames of a cookfire that kept him and his loyal band
of twelve warm. They were camped in the dense forest below the castle of Rain, sipping ale and chewing
on pork and boiled cabbage plundered from a wool
trader whose path had forked into unlucky territory.

"You men who have chosen to stand with me will be
heavily rewarded!" Mallory's thunderous tone provoked
the men surrounding him. They shouted and growled
their approval, breaths thick and white on the air.

"I, a banner knight, gave up my castle and lands to pay for this quest. We have all made sacrifices. That is what King Arthur fails to understand. He wishes to sit behind the curtains of Uryens's castle, grow fat, and spout off ideals. I say down with King Arthur!"

Swords were banged against shields, and a pair of Mallory's fighters slammed their bascineted heads into each other to produce a *klang* of agreement.

"My Saxon friend tells me that on the morrow an army led by our old friend Garrett is going to lay siege to Lord Nolan's castle—but they will never make it there. Because we're going to stop them. Tonight."

Smiles fell. Talk ceased.

"Yes," Mallory continued, "we thirteen men against Garrett's force."

"They number as many as five hundred, lord," his eldest warrior said, nonplussed. "When we were three hundred strong we could—"

"Do not think in numbers, Fergus." He studied the visible fear that controlled the old man. "We are not an army, but a single spatha thrust at the right moment. Our timing and our speed will prove deadly. Who expects thirteen to ride against five hundred?"

"No one," the men grumbled to each other.

The sheer insanity of the plan tickled Mallory's groin. "It may seem mad to you, but your faith, your devotion, and the memories of your lost ones will power and protect you."

"What is the plan, then, lord?" Fergus asked.

"I know Garrett. I knew him when he was a boy. I knew his brother Quinn. If it were Quinn leading this army, the situation would be grave.

"Garrett has organized his small army into the Vaward, Main, and Rearward Battles. Each of you will murder one of Garrett's lieutenants, rendering each of those groups without a commander. I will kill

Garrett himself. We'll strike quickly while they sleep, create chaos, then flee."

"It cannot be that simple," Dallas said. He was the strongest of Mallory's men, a bearded ox on hind legs, who had never questioned an order before.

"Dallas, you sadden me. As all of you do now. I look around and suddenly I do not see the faces of warriors but the scared faces of squires. We'll go in against five hundred and emerge victorious. Doesn't that excite any of you? Garrett's men are cattle waiting dumbly to be slain."

"Maybe they are not," Dallas said firmly.

Mallory pushed his way out of the circle of men, climbed up on the flatbed of their single cart, and delivered his next words from there. "I believe this is the way to win our battles against the invaders. Attack them first, with small groups such as ours, saving the many numbers for the garrisons. Why must we sit back and defend? Arthur's so-called advance still requires a first attack by the invaders. Let's hit them tonight. Who is with me?"

Fergus stepped out of the group. "I am, lord."

Two more men followed. Then another pair, a trio, then another.

Dallas held his ground. Mallory looked at his best man with utter derision. After a tense moment, Dallas, seeing that he stood alone in his fear, resignedly joined the group.

It was a feeling like no other. What lunacy it was! What joy it brought him. "Prepare yourselves. We ride when the moon sets and early-morning darkness is still upon the land."

The group disbanded and chatted as they sauntered toward their coursers.

Mallory hopped off the wagon, and with anticipation in his step, headed for one of the four tents they had erected. The end one on the left was his, and he moved through the flap and inside.

It was dark, and the breathing of the wind over the tent filled the small hovel with an incessant rattling.

She was under the woolen blankets and squirmed as he moved closer.

She was a caged animal, dangerous and desirous of escape. But her skin was smooth, her breasts large and filled with milk, as she had recently given birth. Her yellow hair was soft and flowed over her shoulders. She was anything but a beast.

She had been taken quickly from her husband and child, and there was something ironic in the small amount of time, only hours, that it had been since that moment and the first time Mallory had slept with her. She had been with him for two days now, and would provide the release he needed before the attack.

It was his ritual. A simple though necessary session before combat. It relaxed him and made him feel complete with the idea that if he did die, at least his moments before were spent in pleasure.

But the intercourse sessions before fighting were a battle themselves.

Mallory yanked the blanket off her naked body, and she cried out. He smiled and shook his head. She would put up a fight. Again.

He fell to his knees, reached down, and grabbed her breast sharply, clawing the soft flesh until a thin trickle of pale milk, barely distinguishable in the dimness, sprang from her dark, erect nipple. He hungrily lapped up the sweet liquid, a soft groan resonating from the back of his throat.

Mallory let go of her breast and stood. He removed his sword belt. The eyes of the woman seemed to be the only thing in the darkness. His hauberk came off, then his shirt and breeches.

He moved toward her, his erection pumping with blood. The night was full of surprises. She lifted her legs in the air and welcomed him into her womb. She was damp and warm and he entered her easily. She moaned softly as he sucked more milk from one of her nipples while thrusting into her. The heels of her feet drove into his buttocks, guided him, pulled him into her.

He felt something like a punch hit him in his right rib cage. The blow was followed by a backdraft of pain.

Mallory tried to pull back from her, but her legs and feet held him close. His hands went to the hot lightning in his side, and he felt her hand around the hilt of a dagger. *Whore!*

His erection fell into softness as blood rivered down his chest and threaded into his pubic hair.

With one swift pull Mallory removed the dagger, then ripped it from her grip. He screamed. The blood rushed freely from the hole in his body.

Tears of pain splattered his cheeks as he turned the blade on the woman and punched it home into her heart. She gasped, stiffened, and then relaxed, dead.

He knelt there, breathing and bleeding for a moment, then got unsteadily to his feet. He made it to the edge of the tent and pushed his head through the flap.

He saw Dallas slip a spatha into the scabbard hanging from his courser's saddle. "Dallas. Come here." Mallory fell through the flap and onto the frozen earth.

He heard Dallas hustle over and felt the man's thick fingers grab his arms and roll him over onto his back. The pain seemed to lessen if he kept his eyes closed. "She got me good this time, Dallas."

"I'll fetch the needle. We'll stitch you up quick." He heard Dallas leave.

It dawned on him then, and the thought was so powerful that it overrode the pain and brought a grin flickering across his lips. The risk was even greater now. He would ride *injured* with his twelve men against an army of five hundred. It was magnificently beyond comprehension. It was a quest that no one in his right mind would follow. It looked, sounded, smelled, felt, and tasted like Mallory. It was gorgeous.

12

Twelve Saxon watchmen fell one after the other, each with an arrow marking a lethal point on his body. Another four men caught the bolts from crossbows with their backs. One interesting soul used his eye to stop a shot from a longbow, and the blue feather fletching quartering the arrow's base kissed his eyebrow. He stood a moment, wondering what had happened, then spun anticlimactically to his demise.

Christopher watched it all happen, thinking it was a dream. Something had troubled his sleep and he sat up. He didn't move, sounded no alarms, just eyed the silent killing with a horrid fascination.

Then, like a knee in the face, he realized it was no dream. First thought: to scream for Garrett. He was about to yell, but reconsidered. He got on all fours and crawled his way from his saddle cloths and into Garrett's tent.

The Saxon leader slept soundly.

"Lord!" he hissed. "Wake up! Someone's killing the watchmen!"

Garrett's eyelids opened and he sat up, disoriented. "What?"

"Outside. Look . . . "

Garrett crawled his way to the edge of the tent and peered stealthily beyond the entrance flap. He yanked his head back in, then rose. "Arms, Christopher. Quickly."

"Shouldn't I find the hornman?"

"Yes . . . wait . . . no. Help me first."

Christopher had never seen his lord as nervous. It made his own hands jitter and his heart flutter.

Garrett climbed clumsily into his shirt and breeches. Christopher found and handed his lord the leather gambeson, helped him into it, then buckled the belts across the sleeveless garment's chest.

He followed with the link-mail hauberk and was about to hand Garrett his breastplate when his lord stopped him with a hand. "No time, Christopher. Where's my sword?"

Christopher scanned the interior of the tent, but deep down he knew the sword wasn't there; he had put it safely away—somewhere.

"I beg forgiveness, lord."

Garrett shook his head in anger, then sliced through the tent flaps. Christopher followed.

Outside, Garrett rushed toward his courser as a pair of horsemen wheeled around and turned toward him. Christopher sprinted off to find the hornman.

He ran past a row of ground beds, the men occupying them stirring, sitting up to have a look at what was going on. He found the hornman, a boy much older than himself. He backhanded the musician awake.

"Sound the alarm!"

Christopher jogged away from the hornman as a loud note split the icy air behind him.

What to do? What to do?

He saw no one attacking as he ran, only the rising forms of Saxons who would probably obscure an advance from his eyes anyway. What he did come across were the victims of the first assault, the watchmen he had seen die through sleepy eyes. They were very real and very dead now. His feet came within a yard of the Saxon who had caught an arrow in his eye. If not for the wound, Christopher would have

thought the man was sleeping, for he had fallen
rather neatly. He picked up something on his periphery, a complete enough image to halt him. He turned
back toward the dead watchman and studied the
arrow, the blue fletching, the Celtic blue fletching. At
least he knew it wasn't the Picts or the Jutes that
attacked—only his own people.

In the distance, he saw Garrett outside the row of
tents. His lord engaged a swordsman whose forehead
was lit by a blue gem mounted on a headband. He
ran toward the scene, but he tripped. The frosty
ground came up and smacked his chest and cheek.
He pushed himself up on his hands and looked over
his shoulder. He had fallen over a dead lieutenant,
the Saxon's face maced into an unrecognizable pulp.
He got to his feet and moved into a sprint.

To Christopher's left, a team of a dozen Saxon
horsemen galloped after a pair of riders who fled the
encampment. To his right, the rest of the army
scrambled for their arms, cried out to each other, and
lit torches to find their way in the moonless night.
The cacophony grew louder as he neared his lord.

Who is this fighter? He must be a Celt, but who?

Garrett parried the Celt's sword with a mace, but
the Celt used his escutcheon to push Garrett back
and unbalance him. Garrett was shieldless, and
Christopher felt his heart drop as he saw how vulnerable his lord was. Garrett needed a shield—and a
sword, and the first ones Christopher could find he
would get into his master's hands.

The old man Elgar came to Garrett's aid, two-
handing a broadsword that he brought down on the
Celt's shoulder. The Celt spun around, his blue gem
flashing, and in that movement he cut the air horizontally and beheaded Elgar. The old man's head
rolled past his legs, and blood jetted from his neck,
speckling Garrett and the attacking Celt. The headless body shook involuntarily, then collapsed.

Christopher kept his gaze off the dead form of Elgar and focused on the sword. He tried to cancel out the grief he felt for the altruistic old Saxon, but experienced it along with the nausea marching up from the back of his throat.

A pair of Saxons stared in horror at the headless corpse as Christopher came upon it. He pried the broadsword from Elgar's fingers and held up the weapon. He felt sick. But then he noticed *it*.

Something had worked in the universe that he had no control over, and if fate was its name, then it was alive and well and had harnessed the power of serendipity for Christopher.

The broadsword in his hand was the very one Baines had given him so long ago.

I thought I had lost this. Elgar, why didn't you tell me you had found it? Why did you keep it from me? But did he even know it was mine?

Christopher ran behind the duel, and shouted to his lord. "Sword!"

Garrett found a moment to turn and Christopher tossed the blade into his lord's hands. Garrett struck back hard with the broadsword, driving the Celt a few steps back, his power seemingly renewed with the blade. But Garrett still lacked an escutcheon. Christopher tore one from the hands of a startled infantryman who watched the fight.

He ducked under one of the sword swipes delivered by the Celt, fed Garrett the shield, then shot out of the melee unscathed.

As he stood panting, watching, it dawned on him how dangerous the maneuver had been: he had weaved himself into the fight, become a part of it for a second, then slipped out of its spokes before being snapped in half. But at the time, it was all reaction. It *felt* right. He hadn't thought about what he had done, he had just acted.

Did you see that, Orvin?

He lifted his attention to the sky. Was it only the clouds and blue wash that told the future, or could stars speak of the morrow as well?

Garrett fell onto his back with a scream, and Christopher twisted his neck sharply at the sound.

"Mallory," Garrett said, "you're still a madman."

Mallory answered the words with a combination of slashes that were followed by: "That is amusing, coming from you. I actually thought us very much alike. Daring. Vengeful. Though you lack the skills of a true leader. You have more men than you can handle."

Garrett crawled a yard back, gave himself enough distance to get back on his feet. "And you have too few." Garrett saw an opening, feinted left, then slammed his blade against Mallory's plated ribs. Mallory flinched, then groaned.

He has a sore spot, lord. Go for that.

Christopher's thoughts did not have to be read by Garrett. His lord complied out of his own experience, concentrating his blows on Mallory's right side, but the Celt was able to deflect each and every one of the strikes.

By now, the pair of Saxons watching had become a throng rooting for Garrett. No one would interfere; the men around Christopher found it much more interesting to let the fight progress to its natural conclusion—their leader's victory.

Mallory flung his shield away and two-handed his spatha. He hammered the blade onto Garrett's sword, and finally Garrett's grip faltered.

Christopher watched his sword fall from his lord's hands.

Mallory thrust his blade forward. Garrett blocked the advance with his shield. Mallory made another attempt, this time jerking his blade around and over Garrett's escutcheon; then he whipped it under, forcing Garrett's shield arm to go away from his side and leave his chest open.

Christopher had logged four types of death in his mind.

There was the sight of death, after the fact, as in his parents or the knight Airell.

There was the causing of a death, as with the Saxon he axed when he was thirteen.

There was the presumption of death, as with Doyle and Bryan.

And then there was the act of death, the killing before his eyes, as with Baines or Hasdale or Sloan or Conway or Varney or Malcolm or Kier. For Christopher, it was the worst kind.

Mallory's blade went flatwise into Garrett's chest, cut past the hauberk and gambeson, parted its way into his skin, and nestled itself in his lung. Garrett coughed, then coughed again; blood mixed with saliva spewed from his mouth and splattered on his chin and neck. Mallory tightened his grip on his blade as Garrett fell back, effectively removing the sword from Garrett's body. Garrett lay on his back, clinging to a final shard of life.

Christopher ran to his master's side, his eyes hurting from the tears he fought back. All he could do was look at Garrett as the man died. No last words. Just a groan. A hush fell over the Saxons. The smell of human feces found its way to Christopher's nose.

As memories do, one struck Christopher out of nowhere, ignited by something he couldn't put his fingers on. Something Orvin had said about balancing heart and mind. He had tried to work it out with Brenna, but it applied here. His heart lay now with Garrett, but his mind was Celt. And though he hated Mallory for slaying his lord, the reason for it was perfectly clear. Garrett was considered a Saxon. Christopher's loyalty to the Saxons died with Garrett.

Reality blurred into a sequence of quick movements. Mallory charged toward a gap between the tents. Christopher picked up his sword and followed. They emerged behind the tents, where Mallory's courser was tied and waiting. Mallory straddled his horse.

Christopher ran beside the steed. "Please, lord," he said, "take me with you. I am a Celt who has been held against my will by these Saxons."

"Your tongue tells me that. Hop on, boy."

Christopher climbed behind Mallory, and the Celt heeled his horse into a gallop.

The Celt's ponytail blew into Christopher's eyes, but it was a minor discomfort in comparison to his mental anguish. He could not help himself. He cried, at once for being among Celts again, at once for Garrett. He had grown to understand Garrett, and even learn more about the Saxons. Their farmlands had been spoiled and they sought new ground to till. Their quest was purely one of survival, but their means were admittedly questionable.

Garrett had taught him a lot. And along had come their world again in the form of another weapon that had taken another life away. Was life that cheap, that trivial? Was there not one fulgent quality of life that would bring warmth and happiness and prevent it from ending as abruptly—as unnaturally? Some said it was love. But where was love now?

He battled his pain, clutched his broadsword, and gazed at the stars as they rode.

13 Morning sunlight coruscated off the thawed lake around which they camped. Christopher squinted, waving a bit of smoke from the cookfire away from his face, then focused again on the water. There was a small family of ducks on its surface, mother, father, and three babies. They all swam in a neat little line that was abruptly broken by javelins

thrown from the shoreline. Mallory's men were poor shots, and though Christopher knew how tasty the birds would be, a part of him was glad the ducks would survive. They paddled farther out into the middle of the lake, making themselves an even more difficult target.

Then Mallory's biggest man picked up a longbow, and *fwit! fwit!* the parents of the ducklings were slain. The burly Celt stripped himself and swam out to retrieve his catch while the others commented on his marksmanship. One of the javelin throwers scoffed at the huge Celt, claiming there was no sport in using a longbow, that the true test of marksmanship would have been with the javelin. The longbow made the kill too easy.

Christopher watched the ducklings swim away from the heavy Celt as the banter continued, then fell back onto the thin, ragged blanket Mallory had given him to sleep on. The night had been bitterly cold, and Christopher had removed the tarpaulin from the supply cart for use as a cover. Two of the other Celts thought this a good idea and had shared the wide fabric shield with him. Those men were up now, replacing the tarpaulin. He heard the thumping of boots on the hard ground behind him and craned his neck; his gaze leveled on Mallory's knees, then rose to the man's face.

"We move shortly, Christopher. Eat something while there is still time."

"I will."

Mallory got down on his haunches. "But before you do that, tell me for a moment about your service to Garrett."

"It was terrible, my lord," he lied, peppering his words with a tone that suggested the unspeakable horror of it. He would not tell Mallory about his relationship with Garrett. He needed to gain Mallory's trust and would not suffer through the same mental rigors he had to win Garrett's. It would be far simpler this time.

"Go on," Mallory urged.

Christopher rolled onto his stomach, then sat up, crossing his legs, one under the other. "They screamed at me with words I didn't know. And they beat me and made me shovel dung."

Mallory grabbed Christopher by his shirt collar, pulling the linen tightly around his neck. "I am curious, then, why you were so quick to supply Garrett with arms when I engaged him."

Christopher struggled to swallow against Mallory's grip. He hated being choked, more so since the night that Kenneth had tried to kill him. Mallory's act brought back the ugly memory. "I was his squire, lord. I had to. He would have killed me."

Mallory relaxed his grip and let go of Christopher's shirt. "Why didn't you try to escape?"

"I tried at least a score of times. But he had too many men. . . . Eventually I obeyed his orders. It was better than being tied."

Mallory sighed. "Perhaps I would have done the same. It just angers me to see a strong young Celt like yourself serve a traitor so quickly and willingly."

"Quickly, for fear of my life. Willingly, never," Christopher answered.

Mallory stood. "Eat then. We must keep moving."

"Lord? I know we are moving south. My home is Shores. I wish to return there."

One of Mallory's eyelids twitched. "That's not possible."

"May I ask why, lord?"

Mallory fingered the blue doublet on his headband for what appeared to be no particular reason. "How long have you been away, boy?"

Christopher thought about it. "Twenty moons, I believe."

"Arthur has given the castle of Shores to the sweet-tongued Lord Devin of Bristol, a man who bears quite a hatred for me." Mallory's face flushed and his eyes went distant. His lips curved into a smile. "My

men and I tried to ambush and murder him. We
failed, but live to tell the sad tale."

"Why did you want to kill him?"

Mallory turned his gaze to the sky. "I don't quite
remember. I never liked the man. Much too tradi-
tional for my tastes. I think he insulted me as well.
No matter, since I am, as you now know, not welcome at Shores."

"May I ride alone then?"

Mallory shook his head, no.

Christopher felt a rope of panic wrap around his
spine. "Lord, I must remind you that I am the son of
a freeman. A leatherdresser. And it is against the law
to hold me against my will."

"Let me tell you something about laws. The laws
are made by men who do not understand this realm,
men who are not out on the land but holed up behind
the walls of their chambers. Those laws are meaning-
less to the man of the land. In his heart, the man of
the land knows what is right and what is wrong, and
that is his guide—that is his law."

Christopher wondered if challenging Mallory further
would put him in an even worse position; it probably
would. So now he was in the hands of a man who had
once been a lord, but had somehow descended into a
reality of his own making, a world where he decided
the law. There was something extremely powerful and
extremely dangerous about that.

"What do you wish of me then, lord?" Christopher
asked, his voice weighted with resignation.

"We are a small band. You will squire us, prepare
meals, scrub blankets, *shovel dung,* and, you say you
were the son of a leatherdresser?"

Christopher nodded.

"Then you know something of the craft?"

There was no use in lying; he nodded again.

"Good. You will repair our saddles as well. You
are quite a find, aren't you?"

Christopher could not believe he sat with Celts, wishing he were back among Saxons. At least they had come to respect him as a human being. Mallory wanted him as squire and slave. He wondered if his life would go on like this, a series of escapes only to be "saved" by another group of captors, traveling from army to army, being treated like an animal, living a long, hard, miserable life. He could run from Mallory, but where would he wind up next? Maybe he could go to the castle, but what kind of a man was Devin? And what now of Orvin and Brenna? Where were they? Moved on, more than likely. He was all alone, with a past he needed to find, but a present he was chained to. Could he learn to like Mallory? He didn't know. Perhaps he would begin by tolerating the man. It was a first, arduous step.

Mallory squatted down and put both hands on Christopher's shoulders, then looked directly into his eyes. "It's not that bad. Soon, I'll take other boys into my service and you will become one of my fighters. I crave the battlefield, as you will. Give me a chance." Mallory stood, turned around, then walked back toward his tent, groaning softly as he rubbed his ribs with a palm.

"Lord?" Christopher called out.

Mallory stopped, looked over his shoulder.

"Who is this Arthur you spoke of?"

Mallory smirked. "He calls himself king of all England."

"By what right?"

"By the right of magic. Pay him no heed. He'll fall like Uther before him. They all do. Uniting this land is only a dream. Protecting it from the invaders is the reality. That is my vision, but the others . . . " Mallory let the discouraging notion trail off. He resumed his course toward the tent.

The big Celt who had shot the ducks ambled up to Christopher holding a couple of pasties filled with fruit and a tankard half-full with ale. "Call me Dallas. Call this food." His voice was boomy and thick, and he smiled, enjoying his own feeble wit. He handed the pasties and ale to Christopher.

"Thank you."

"The duck shall be ready momentarily."

"None for me," Christopher said.

"Why not?" Dallas asked, mildly insulted.

"This is enough."

"But the meat is tender and sweet."

Christopher took a bite of the cake. "The pasties are sweet."

Dallas stepped away, confused. "'The pasties are sweet.'"

Christopher had never seen back muscles as large as Dallas's. He hadn't seen the man in full armor, but guessed that it must be an incredible sight. He was envious for a moment, pictured himself as stocky and tall as Dallas, muscles like plates of armor bulging below his skin.

He sat apart from the group that circled the cook-fire, finishing up the pasties. Mallory's men ate quickly, but far more neatly than the Saxons. He had almost forgotten what a civilized meal looked like. They wiped their mouths and drank without slopping up their faces. It was a little thing, but caught by his eyes. All fighters ate aggressively, but watching a Saxon eat for the first time would surely make you lose your own appetite.

Christopher swallowed the last bit of ale in his tankard, rose, and ambled toward the lake. He doffed his dirty breeches and wrinkled shirt, then tossed them in the water. He dived in next to them.

For a second, he thought the shock of hitting the icy water had stopped his heart. He came above the surface, shook his hair free of water, and let out a shivery cry.

There were no stones with which to scrub his

soiled garments, so he just pulled them under the clear water as he trod back toward shore. *Enough washing for today. Too cold.*

Then he remembered they were leaving shortly. No time for his clothes to dry. *You fool!*

On shore, he called to Dallas and asked if he could borrow a shirt and breeches. Dallas fetched him the clothes, which hung off him like a robe. He balled up his own freezing garments and stowed them on the supply cart.

It was ungratefully colder as Mallory's band mounted their horses, then rode away from the lake.

Christopher sat on the flatbed, and after a few long, bumpy moments down a narrow trail edged on one side by the wood, he felt his clothes. They had frozen into a stiff, hard ball.

A crossbow bolt needled through the air, stuck into Christopher's clothes, pushed the ball away from his hand, then pinned it against the oak lip of the cart.

Another bolt found the nape of the Celt driving the cart, a one-legged man who had not uttered a single word to Christopher. The driver slouched.

Christopher finally set eyes on a pair of Saxon archers; their light horses and sparse armor gave them the flexibility they needed to fire their crossbows. They slipped from the wood as three other pairs of Saxons did likewise in a string ahead.

Mallory and Dallas engaged the first pair, while four more of Mallory's men took on the second and third pairs.

The rear pair galloped toward Christopher, and though their faces were familiar to him, he had never spoken to them.

"Kimball, climb on!" the taller one cried in the Saxon tongue.

Christopher had about twenty yards to decide what to do. It was, if nothing else, an interesting dilemma.

He was captured by the Saxons, then grew to admire and serve them willingly through Garrett. Then he was rescued by Mallory, whom he already despised but who was a Celt. Now he might be rescued again by the very Saxons from whom he had escaped. The words *rescue* and *escape* had lost their meanings over time.

But I can get closer to my home with the Celts.

The Saxons braked their horses next to the stalled cart.

"Climb on!" the taller archer insisted again.

Christopher shook his head, no, made sure he uttered nothing in Saxon for Mallory's men to hear.

The tall archer turned to his heavy partner and gestured for him to dismount.

An arrow caught the heavy archer in his side, just above the waist, and he dismounted much quicker than he had intended.

The tall archer brought his horse around and booted the animal toward the cover of the wood.

Christopher watched Dallas gallop by, nocking an arrow in his shortbow while also holding the reins of his horse. Dallas let the arrow fly, but it struck a beech tree, missing the Saxon by a yard. The archer disappeared down a trail curving into the shadows.

Of the eight Saxons who had attacked them, two had fled and the other six had been killed. Not a very organized or professional attempt, Christopher judged, but the men had probably staged this on their own, without the consent of whoever led them now. Why did these men want him back? He asked himself that as Mallory swung off his horse and walked over to confront him.

"Who were they?" Mallory asked—in the Saxon tongue.

The words made Christopher's heart drop. *He knows Saxon?*

Mallory took another step closer, then reared back a gauntleted hand and smacked Christopher across the face. The hard steel stung like ice. He felt something wet, warm, and salty touch his lips. His nose bled.

"They were your Saxon friends, boy," Mallory went on, "come to rescue you. For a prisoner, you must have been very popular." Mallory sighed deeply, then pushed a metallic thumb toward Christopher.

He thought of flinching as the thumb came toward his head, but he remained stolid. Mallory wiped the blood from the top of Christopher's lip with his thumb, then rubbed the bloody metal thumb together with his index finger. "I don't blame you as much as I blame Garrett. What a persuasive man he was. Getting a single squire to follow him was nothing, you understand. But recruiting an enemy army—*that* was a feat. I will always remember him." Mallory frowned a moment, thinking as the wind picked up. "Now what to do with you, young *Kimball*."

The air moved through his loose-fitting clothes and easily chilled Christopher. He shivered, and knew it wasn't entirely because of the wind.

"You know what I think?" Mallory asked. "I think nothing changes. Onward."

14   Christopher had not been forced to participate in the many robberies that followed in the six moons he had spent thus far with Mallory and his men, but in performing his squirely duties, he knew he had been an accessory to the crimes. He had followed orders without compromise and had been rewarded with heavy meals and pats on the head— which he loathed. He had seen stewards, earls, dukes, and even a poor messenger fall under the hands of Mallory. Soon, Christopher had realized

that Mallory had forgotten who the enemy was and had sought revenge on the very Celts who despised him. In a strange way, he was not unlike Garrett. But Garrett was no criminal.

Mallory's most complex and dangerous crime was yet to come: the abbey at Queen's Camel was to be robbed of its tithe. The village there was larger than Shores and produced an unrelenting flow of goods that serviced the inhabitants and found the trade routes to the markets of West Camel, South Cadbury, and Glastonbury. One-tenth of all the profits from the trading went to the abbot, as was his right.

One hundred percent of that one-tenth would go to Mallory, as was his desire.

Christopher waited at the camp they had made in a clearing along the shoreline of the River Cam. Mallory and Dallas would soon return from their spying on the abbey. Christopher was left under the careful watch of Fergus, who, in the last six moons, had proven his senses were as keen as those of a man half his age. Christopher had found no opportunity to escape. And always the question had burned: if he did get away, where would he go? Was home still *home?*

Mallory and Dallas returned with the knowledge they needed to form a plan.

The abbey, which had been built along the river's edge, consisted of a main cruciform church, which was the largest and tallest building. Behind it was the chapter house, and next to it were the cloisters. The cellarium, refectory, prison block, and the monks' dormitory lay farther behind. A prison block, conversorium, and garderobes stood in the rear. All of these rooms were connected by narrow passages that would afford the robbers easy access to the most important room of all: the abbot's quarters. That was where Mallory guessed the tithe was stored. The quarters were behind the church, and they would have to pass through the main room to get to them.

Following the service of compline in the church, the monks would go back to their dorter and sleep until midnight. Then, a rule of customs bell would knell them back to duty to sing matins and lauds. After the last three psalms and the Lord's Prayer followed, they would return to their room to sleep until the morning bell. But Dallas had noticed that many would remain awake, praying through the night. Everyone, however, slept after the service of compline. It was between eight and midnight that they would strike, rob the tithe, and get out without being spotted. Four hours was a large window for success. No one feared the unarmed monks.

Christopher sat with them around the cookfire and listened carefully. His job was to rouse the abbot, get the man out of his quarters. Mallory did not want the crime to be noticed until at least the following morning, giving them ample time for escape. And so it seemed Christopher's father was dying, and the abbot needed to come right away. Christopher hated the lie, more so because he kept hearing the word *dead* in his head. *My father is* dead *not* dying.

"There are a little over one hundred monks down there," Mallory said between bites of the leveret leg he held between his long fingers, "and eight watchmen, who are relieved at midnight."

"They're not a problem," Dallas added.

"The monks will only be napping while we do our work. Remove your boots or sandals when you get inside. We don't want to disturb them." Mallory grinned sardonically.

Christopher got up from his seat and moved away from the fire. He scuffed over the soft earth onto the already wet grass and found a short oak tree to lean on. He always felt better distanced from the group, knew he would never fit in with them. He could admit to himself that there was something exciting about robbing and getting away with it, something similar to the thrill of the battlefield, but both feelings were fleeting, and always left one wanting more. To cease experiencing them might be better. He saw how Mallory was possessed by each and every scheme, and he wanted to ask the man what they were all going to add up to. Yes, they needed food to survive. Yes, Mallory was more or less banished from Arthur's new union of knights, but that didn't mean the man had to go on robbing. He had enough money already to purchase some land from one of the other lords; he could till himself a reasonable living. Christopher smiled inwardly. Mallory would never stoop that low.

The still-young night had grown old, and perhaps he was a little overtired, Christopher wasn't sure, but he decided to voice his thoughts without care to the consequences; the question had been nocked in his lips and now just arrowed out. "Lord Mallory," he called, using the title though it no longer existed, "for what purpose do we rob the abbey?"

Mallory's men choked on their meat, spit out the ale in their mouths, and broke into laughter.

"He's a jester as well as a squire," Mallory said to Dallas.

"But weren't we all fools at his age," Dallas answered.

Mallory turned to Christopher. "You wonder why we want money when most everything we need we plunder, yes?"

Christopher nodded, feeling sheepish under the gazes of everyone.

"You gave me the idea, boy," Mallory said.

"I don't understand."

"You told me Shores was your home. You said you wished to go back there."

"And you told me that was impossible."

"Yes, because of my little affray with Lord Devin."

"Forgive me, lord. But I still don't understand."

Mallory waved him over. Christopher pushed himself off the tree and halfheartedly returned to the group. Mallory gestured that he take a seat next to him. Christopher retrieved his saddle cloth and lowered himself onto it.

"When we rob the tithe there is going to be a great outcry," Mallory said. "The abbot will hire mercenaries to apprehend the criminals and return his small fortune. The mercenaries will receive a tip from us that the tithe is in the solar of Lord Devin of Shores, and that *his* men robbed the abbey. The mercenaries will find the tithe in Devin's possession and take him back to Queen's Camel, where he'll rot in the abbey's prison block. The trial, if any, will be a mere formality."

"Revenge," Christopher uttered, in a tone that said he didn't like it.

"Not exactly," Mallory corrected. "More of a disciplinary action. It will be quite a thrill to see Devin fall—and to be given his castle by Arthur."

"I thought Arthur was your enemy as well."

"Oh, he is. But I've reconsidered my grand plan. If we're going to defeat the invaders my way, I'm going to need a lot more power. And I'm only going to get that from Arthur. It's taken me this long to realize it—but I cannot stay an outcast forever."

"So he's going to lie to Arthur," Dallas said through a wide grin. "He's going to beg for forgiveness and move into Devin's spot."

"Will it happen that easily?" Christopher asked.

Mallory shook his head. "Of course not. I might have to kill Arthur. We begin with the abbey and ride the plan from there. I think we've all grown tired of the road."

Fergus looked up from his tankard. "Indeed."

15

"Please! I need to see the abbot immediately!"

Christopher stood at the foot of one of the transept entrances to the church, groping for the motivation to tell the bored guard there that his father was dying. He couldn't use the story. He kept seeing an image of his father smiling, then the picture would fracture into one of blackened flesh. The lie would not come.

"I need a blessing right now," he pleaded.

The guard furrowed his heavy brow, then scratched a hairy jowl with long, dirty fingernails. "How did you get within the walls?"

He could tell the guard that he had climbed on top of Dallas's back and had slipped over the wall unnoticed—but that would be insulting the man.

"Please! There is very little time!"

His vague story did not draw any sympathy from the guard. Christopher fingered the hidden dagger on the belt he wore under his baggy tunic.

"I asked you a question, boy," the guard said, his words freighted with anger.

"The other guard passed me through the gate. Now please let me in!"

"He wouldn't do that," the guard said.

Christopher heard an arrow split the air a millisecond before it pierced the cheek of the guard and went straight on through, the tip birthing from the back of the man's head. Christopher was surprised at how quiet the sound of death was. A *fwit!*, nearly no sound as the arrow passed into skin, then the crumple of the man. He looked over his shoulder, saw Dallas duck down behind the wall.

Christopher dragged the body of the guard to a line of shrubs that jogged off to his left, paralleling the building, and placed the corpse under one of the shrubs. For some reason he thought of removing the arrow in the guard's cheek, that the guard looked rather hideous with the thing sticking out of his head; but Christopher's stomach argued against doing so.

He left the man, stepped gingerly back to the door, scanned furtively around, unbolted the door, then moved inside the church.

Christopher had to get the abbot away from his quarters. What was the story going to be? Just a blessing? That could be done anywhere. He needed something else, but what?

In the rafters, clouds of incense from the recent service moved with underwater slowness. The smoke was picked out by rows of candles set on ornate stands in front of a gleaming golden altar. As he took a moment to look around, it was apparent that nothing was too rich or too lavish for the abbot. It seemed he, and the abbots before him, spent most of their tithe decorating this building. From the rich fabric curtains, of a material Christopher had never seen until now, to the finely carved crucifix suspended from the ceiling, the church was as much a thing of beauty as a place of worship. If he had to describe it to someone in the future, he would run out of words.

And the place did something to him; it made him feel miserable. About his life. About everything. His parents had died in a place of worship. A man had just died back there. He was going to lie to an abbot. Would God forgive him for all of it? Could he cross this room, pass through the nave of the church, and still be able to live with himself? He looked back at the entrance door. What would happen if he ran away? What if he was caught by Mallory? What if he told the abbot what was happening? Could the man help him?

Christopher was either going to move forward or back. He could pause no longer. *God, feel my fear.* He ran quietly toward the altar.

Mallory had not been sure where the entrance door

to the abbot's quarters was, but he knew it had to be on the back wall behind the altar; the layout of the abbey told him it could be nowhere else. But when Christopher slipped up the wooden steps and moved along the wall, he could find no door. The physical discomforts that come with panic assailed him. His palms were sticky, his mouth parched. He darted his gaze quickly here and there along the doorless wall. *Why do I have to do this? What is it all for? What am I doing here?*

There was a large painting of a spring scene, a beech tree alive with meadow pipits and starlings under a heavenly sky; it was an arm's length wide and slightly taller than Christopher. The base of the painting was flush with the floor, and something about it caught Christopher's gaze. The way it was framed on the wall, appearing cut out. He looked to the middle right of the painting, and there it was: a door latch. He had expected a door like the one on his old house. He flipped the latch and pulled the painting/door toward him, slipping his nose in behind it.

A narrow passage led off into darkness. He stepped into the shadowy vein and carefully closed the door behind him. He took off his sandals and padded quickly, feeling his way along the wall. Farther on, light wedged from somewhere ahead, and as he drew closer to it, he saw that the light seeped out from under another door. The room beyond it had to be the abbot's quarters.

Should he knock? If candles were still lit, perhaps the abbot was awake. Should he burst in? What was the story again?

Christopher came upon the door, paused there, breathing. His mind would not focus. He didn't realize he had inadvertently pushed the door in until it was too late.

The abbot was asleep, lying supine on his narrow pallet, a rough woolen blanket pulled up to his waist.

A scroll he had been reading was rolled around both his thumbs, connecting the fingers across a linen nightshirt that was tented by his wide belly. The candles on the stand near his bed were only a finger's width high, for the wax had melted down over the lip of the stand and now dripped steadily to the cold, wooden floor. The abbot's snoring, and the dripping, were the only sounds—although Christopher swore if someone else were in the room that person would hear his thundering heartbeat.

His gaze focused on the man, and the rest of the room blurred on his periphery. It was time to do something, and like entering the room, he simply and abruptly dropped his sandals, put a hand on the man's chest, and shook him.

The abbot's head swayed and his eyelids yawned open. He blinked a few times, trying to focus in the candlelight, and when he did, he bolted up in the bed. "What is the—who are you, boy?"

Christopher sensed the abbot had a million more questions tarrying on line in the back of his throat, but Christopher wouldn't answer a single one of them. "Come outside the church. Quickly. You must. You are in great danger."

It wasn't exactly a lie; in fact, it bordered closely on the truth.

The abbot was, in a word, difficult. "I will not! How did you get in here?" The line of questions would not stop coming.

Christopher set his grip around one of the abbot's wrists and yanked the man from his pallet; the abbot screamed.

How was he going to slip the abbot out of the church quietly? Christopher was botching the entire job and, deep down, it didn't bother him a single bit. If the abbot wanted to scream, let him scream. Christopher would be caught and go to prison and maybe that was all right. Maybe he deserved it. The past six moons had made him very depressed, and he might as well sink as low as a man could.

The abbot was much heavier than he looked—and he looked plump. Christopher managed to get him to the doorway of his quarters, but the abbot used his free hand to latch onto the frame and pull his other hand loose. He moved inside the room and slammed the door in Christopher's face. Then Christopher heard a ringing noise, and guessed the abbot banged two metal things together, a homemade alarm.

Reflexively, Christopher fled.

When he slammed by the entrance door to the church and hit the ground outside, he heard the church bell clanging from the overhead tower. Someone shouted in the distance. A dog's bark answered.

Christopher sprinted toward the three yards of wall that shielded the river beyond. The blocks that formed the barrier were laid with painstaking precision, and Christopher's bare toes could find no purchase in their cracks.

"Dallas! Anyone! Throw me the rope!"

The rope came over. He seized the twine and scaled the stone. He reached the top and did not look down as he jumped. His legs quivered as they made impact with the ground, and he bent his knees to absorb the blow. He took a deep breath, then got waveringly to his feet.

It was Fergus who had helped Christopher. The old man stood alone next to his rounsey, his face reflecting none of the danger of the moment. "We go now," he said.

16   Christopher and Fergus were the first ones back at the camp. Fergus had yet to ask how it

had went, but somehow Christopher suspected the old one already knew. Fergus's enthusiasm for the entire plan had never been visible. He agreed with everything Mallory said and usually kept his own opinions to himself. He busied himself with starting a cookfire, one which Christopher thought was a bad idea.

"Won't the monks see the smoke?"

"In the dark?" Fergus retorted.

"What about the light?"

"It could be anyone's light."

"Or it could be ours."

"I like my meat warm, if you don't mind."

It all came into place for Christopher. He and Fergus were very much alike. They had both gone along with Mallory, more out of intimidation than anything else. And perhaps this fire was Fergus's way of letting himself be caught. Christopher had had the same notion back at the abbey, and realized it was truly a cry, to be rescued from Mallory.

Why should he go to prison for Mallory's actions? He certainly wouldn't let Fergus make that decision for him.

Take control of your life.

The old man leaned over the small pit he had dug, emptying kindling from his hands into the hole. Christopher moved behind the man and picked up one of the small logs Fergus would use to build the main fire. He clubbed Fergus across the back of his head. The old Celt fell onto his cookfire ditch.

Time to go. Wait. Wait. Wait. Don't be rash. You need a horse. And don't forget your sword. The old man's got it. And some food. Money? Whatever Fergus has in his riding bag will have to do.

Christopher rushed over to Fergus's rounsey, opened up one of the riding bags, and found a small ration of wrapped meat, a leather purse that was full of deniers, and a pair of simple daggers in leather sheaths. He checked the other bag: empty. He ran over to Fergus, snatched the woolen blanket near the fallen man, rolled and stuffed it into the riding bag. He checked for his sword; it was in one of Fergus's heavy scabbards tied onto the saddle. Next to the broadsword was a spatha in a thinner, lighter sheath.

Good. Two swords. Two daggers. Some food. Money. You're organized. Go!

Christopher put his left foot into the stirrup, hoisted himself up, and slung his right leg over the horse. He cracked the reins and dug his bare heels into the black rounsey's ribs. The animal beat a retreat along the river.

The iron stirrups dug into his feet as he rode. He thought he heard the hooves of another horse in pursuit, and shot quick glances back, but saw only the dim waters half-obscured by mist, the tall grass, and the shrubs, all moving away from him.

Up ahead, a thicket blocked his path. He steered the horse around it, but the rounsey responded too slowly, rounded the corner too closely. Christopher winced as the shrubs scraped over his foot. He looked down to see if he bled, but couldn't tell.

His destination wasn't important; he'd figure that out once he found a place of sanctuary. Anything would do, but it would have to be at least a day's ride away. He would work the horse until it fell.

As he rode, a thought jelled: for the first time in his life he was totally alone. He'd gone from his parents to Hasdale and Orvin, then to Garrett, and finally to Mallory. He answered to no one now. It was unnerving. There had always been someone to regulate his life for him. Now he was in complete control. It was a challenge he would face with a racing heart.

17

By daybreak, Christopher arrived on the perimeter of an expanse of fallow fields that bordered on the village of Falls, a bustling nest two days ride from the remains of its sister village Shores. He had been to Falls once when he was ten, or eleven; he couldn't remember. It was there in the marketplace he hoped to purchase a pair of riding boots. He wished he could buy a new body. His rump was sore, the soles of his feet red and beginning to blister, his left foot scratched and caked with blood.

His rounsey had fallen off into a canter some hours ago, and was now barely able to trot. Christopher took pity on the animal and braked it to a halt. He climbed down, and his feet made painful contact with the dewy grass. Bones in his knees and arms cracked. He walked the rounsey down to the shore-line, and the horse lowered its head immediately to the murky water.

Christopher took off his tunic and threw it over the rounsey's croup. He stretched out his arms, twisted his torso, then bent down, keeping his legs stiff. The night ride had taken half the life out of him.

There would be no serfs with ox and plow tilling this land. Christopher saw that the fields were not sown, this being the year for these grounds to rest. It was a good place for him to rest as well. He opened one of the riding bags and fished out a scrap of roasted pork. He chewed on the meat, savoring its salty sweetness. Then he padded down to the river. He cupped his hands, scooped up and downed a mouthful of water; it was cold and refreshing, if not a bit dirty-tasting. He splashed some over his head and shivered. He raked his hair off his forehead, rubbed his eyes with his fingertips, then put on his tunic. He pulled the woolen blanket out of the other riding bag, spread it out on the ground, and settled himself onto it, resting his head in his palms. He closed his eyes.

Christopher felt the warm sensation of sunlight on his face and flickered his eyelids open. The summer sun climbed toward noonday zenith, the sky clear, the river devoid of mist.

How long have I been sleeping?

He shot upright and stood. His rounsey was there, its ears twitching away flies. The horse whinnied, as if acknowledging Christopher. He cocked his head field-wise. No one. He breathed a small sigh of relief. He pushed his shoulder blades together, feeling the tightness, then he ambled down to the river and, once again, he splashed water over his face.

When the dreamworld was fully gone from his head and eyes, Christopher repacked the blanket and mounted the rounsey. He spurred the horse away from the river and brought it onto a path that had been rooted with wheat the previous year. He followed the strip toward the wood on the horizon and the village beyond.

18

The marketplace of Falls took up both sides of the narrow main road. Each shop was essentially a stall, with a pair of horizontal shutters that opened upward and downward. The upper shutter was supported by two posts, making it an awning. The lower shutter rested on two legs and acted as a display counter.

The first group of stores Christopher trotted past were those of the food purveyors, a dozen or more shoppers scattered in front of the stalls. At one of the counters, a pig was slaughtered on the spot, the blood drying in the sun amid piles of offal and a swarm of flies; at another, geese were tied to the apron of the stall, honking and gabbling; still another was fronted by chickens and ducks, their legs trussed, causing them to flounder like fish on the ground. Christopher saw two housewives, dressed in tunics with sleeves laced from wrist to elbow, pinch some of the fowl. One of the women opened her purse and handed over four deniers to the grizzly shopkeeper for one of the chickens.

Next he came upon a pastry booth with a sign offering three pasties for a denier. In the shop behind, Christopher saw an apprentice taking the cakes from a stone oven with a long-handled wooden shovel. Christopher suddenly realized his pork breakfast was not enough. He reached down into his riding bag and pulled out the leather purse. He pushed the string that bound it open and dumped the coins into his palm. He counted ten deniers. Christopher stopped his rounsey, but remained mounted. He called out to the fair-haired shopkeeper tending the booth. "Three pasties, if you will, sir."

The keeper stacked the pasties on his palm, slipped back into the shop, then emerged through the open doorway next to the stall. He walked up to Christopher, the exchange was made, then the keeper nodded and returned to his booth.

Christopher took a bite out of one of the pasties; it was filled with raspberries. He closed his eyes in ecstasy.

"Fresh-brewed ale. Try some here!"

Christopher opened his eyes and saw an ale crier in the road ahead. The man had been hired by the local tavern owner to draw in customers by giving out free samples of the ale. The crier was a thickly bearded, potbellied man with a lazy gait attributable to the oversampling of his product. He held a tankard and a flagon of wine stoppered with a bit of hemp. "You, boy. Some ale?"

Christopher shook his head, his mouth still full with the pasty. He chewed quickly and forced himself to swallow. He cleared his throat, then asked, "Do you know where the shoemaker's shop is?"

"Turn right at the end of this road. It's just down the way, next to the saddler's shop."

"Thank you, sir."

The crier nodded, then moved on. "Fresh-brewed ale. Try some here!"

Christopher passed the farrier's, then armorer's stalls, helmets, swords, and plates being made by individual specialists, as they were in Shores. He drew closer to the end of the main road and could already smell the stench from the saddle and shoemaker's shops. But it wasn't a stench now. It was familiar, and settling, and it made him feel wistful. He sensed he was a little closer to home.

He dismounted in front of the shoemaker's shop. The counter was filled with rows of sandals and goatskin and cordwain shoes.

A young woman appeared behind the counter. She was plain, her eyes dull from sleep, her hair flattened from a pillow. She yawned. "I've a nice pair there, in the front." Her glance lit upon the cordwain shoes she mentioned.

"I need riding boots."

The woman looked over the counter at Christopher's bare feet. "Indeed, you do!" She waved to him. "Come inside."

The shop was simple enough, not unlike his father's workshop or that poor soul's in Fitzralph's village, with a bench supporting tools, and tanned leathers hung from the walls.

"My husband died four moons ago. This shop is mine now." The edge in her voice told Christopher she was still not used to the idea of being a shopkeeper and widow. "I have a pair of boots in the loft that I think will fit you. Wait here."

She disappeared through a hall, and he listened to her pad up the stairs. He walked absently around as he waited, touched the leathers, examined the stitching on a pair of shoes. She returned with one of the finest pair of riding boots Christopher had ever seen.

"I'm stunned," he said.

"Try them on," she urged.

Christopher sat on the workshop bench, then slid his right foot into one of the boots. He marveled at the softness of the leather and the irony of such a perfect fit. He slid his injured foot into the other boot, careful not to break open the scabs that criss-crossed his skin. He stood, wiggling his toes. "I want them. How much?"

The woman shook her head. "They're yours."

Christopher did not believe her. "Why would you give this excellent pair of boots to a stranger?"

"I have no need for them. And I do not wish to sell them." Her next was delivered in a singsong way. "Now go. Ride away. Savor the comfort of your boots."

"At least let me pay something. If I take them, I feel I will be in debt to you."

"You owe me nothing. You've done me a favor. I am in debt to you."

Christopher shrugged his confusion. "Thank you?"

"Yes. You are welcome."

He turned slowly away, then stepped out of the shop, the new boots spoiling his feet. He climbed on his rounsey, then heeled the horse on. He looked over his shoulder and saw the woman wave good-bye to him from behind her lonely counter.

It was then he realized that the boots had been her husband's.

19

Mallory used his boot to squash the rat in the corner of his cell. The rodent's eyes bulged and had dark gore erupted from its mouth.

"You won't be bothering me anymore, will you? WILL YOU?"

He had spent the entire morning in a rage. Four of his men were locked up five cells down from his, and had repeatedly asked him if he was all right. It must have been his screaming.

His only luck—the word sarcastically humorous to him now—was that Dallas had not been captured. *The boy, the damned boy. He failed to lure the abbot out. And who counted on the monks to be armed with spathas? It was ludicrous! Have they been robbed before?*

He picked up the dead rat and tossed it through the bars of his cell, into the hall. "Dinner is served, watchman!"

It felt good to talk, to release some of the fire inside him. He wanted to kill badly now, to punch a dagger into someone again and again. To taste another's blood, to strangle the life out of someone, to gouge out the eyeballs of the fat old abbot, the bastard. *When I'm free, you die, man of God.*

He attempted to see the thrill in being locked up, but for once Mallory was at a loss. The thrill would only return if he attempted to escape. That was a thought. Get caught robbing the abbey, become imprisoned awaiting trial—then slip out like early-morning fog, damning them all to hell and laughing in their faces. Oh, it was good to be locked up now. To think about how exciting the escape would be, how the monks would remember him for the rest of their sheltered lives. Mallory could already see in his mind's eye himself and his men on horseback, their dusty wake clouding the vision of the abbot's clumsy men. Then they would turn tail and surprise the pursuing guards, slash swiftly and take lives. He rubbed his back against the iron bars of his cage, then grinned.

"You say nothing now, lord," one of his men called. "Are you all right?"

Mallory dropped his smile and sighed disgustedly. "Will you please HOLD YOUR TONGUE?"

20

The night sky shone with a brilliance Christopher could not ignore. As he rode onto the practice field below the castle of Shores, his gaze was stolen by the heavens. Across the white stars came streaks of light that, like glowing embers wafting up from a fire, were there and then gone as quickly. It was a rare night, and he fancied something special was happening, as if the local sky were welcoming him home.

What will be?

Many questions and many fears still lurked within him. But it was good to be out in the balmy air of a summer night, watching stars shoot above the gray curtains of the castle. Absently, he fingered the soft hairs that grew on his cheeks, chin, and under his nose, then reached higher to the scars on his face. He would look different to those who knew him. As different as he felt. He had seen much more than he could have imagined on the day he had left Shores. And now he brought himself and his story back.

What he was going home to, he wasn't sure. But he was going home.

PART FOUR

SQUIRE OF THE BODY

1 Christopher slept in the wood below the ramparts of the castle. It was a black sleep, and in the darkness he traded blows with a faceless enemy who wielded a broadsword much larger than his own. All he could do was lash out, for if he stopped, he felt he would lose his life. He woke, chilled. The din of the night creatures enveloped him. He stared up through the broken leaf cover. The sky had dulled into a gray dome of clouds. He heard a branch crack. Then another. Then the sound of leather soles pressing into the soft, wet earth. He rose and gingerly padded over to his rounsey. He pulled his broadsword silently from its scabbard, then assumed the en garde position.

He had become a light sleeper. Most of the horrors of his life had happened at night. No one would ever attempt to kill him again while he slept. He was alert, not frightened. It had to be a guard or perhaps a pilfering serf. He didn't want to hurt anyone, but it would be hard to see in the shadows. He would have to call out, revealing his location. It was either that or try to render the trespasser defenseless and then identify him or her later. It was dangerous either way.

Christopher heard the footsteps stop. And then a voice. "God, remove this curse from my shoulders and let these old, tired bones have one night's rest. Why can I not sleep? Why do I walk this path every night, and spend my days squinting and even more tired? Let me rest. Bring me peace. I beg of you."

Christopher grinned with recognition. "Sir Orvin?"

"Who calls?" the old man shot back tersely. "Show yourself."

"I will."

"I know . . . I know you," Orvin said.

"Where are you, Orvin?" Christopher felt his pulse thump in his neck.

"Here!"

"Keep calling out!"

He followed the voice, plowing his way through benches of low-lying shrubs and over a carpet of fallen leaves toward the silhouette of Orvin that was framed by a pair of thin beech trees.

When he came upon Orvin, he could not see the old man's face clearly. But he saw enough to know it was his master. And Orvin, too, recognized his form. Christopher felt Orvin's arms wrap tightly around his back and hug him hard. He hugged back, wanting the embrace to mean something, to mean he would never have to be separated from his master again. They broke their embrace.

"Is it chance we meet here?" Christopher asked.

"Is it?" Orvin's question was a challenge. The old man was the believer in magic and mystical portents.

"It does seem destined. How many nights have you walked these woods?"

"For the last two moons."

It did seem coincidental that for the last two moons Christopher had been as close as ever to home—and it had been during that time that Orvin had not been able to sleep.

Orvin studied Christopher. He brought an index finger up to Christopher's face and fingered one of the nine scars that mapped Christopher's cheek with the past.

He was about to explain the scars to Orvin, to tell the man about Garrett, but wasn't sure if Orvin would understand. Garrett was the man that had killed Orvin's son, murdered him in front of Christopher.

Being with Orvin made Christopher feel guilty about his own relationship with Garrett, but it had happened and he would have to accept it. Eventually, he would have to tell the old man. But why not keep this a joyous moment?

"I have so many questions," he told Orvin.

"I can tell you this much, young patron saint. I knew you would live."

"How?"

"I could tell you I saw it in the clouds, but it's best I say I simply knew. You will never die in combat."

Christopher shook his head unbelievingly.

"I speak the truth."

"Then I guess I will no longer be a squire."

"Why do you say that?"

"Because if I remain a squire, the odds are that I will die in combat. What you are telling me is that I will not be a squire in the future. Or even a knight."

"You will always be a squire," Orvin said firmly.

Christopher sighed, though it was through a grin. "It is good to be talking about things that make no sense to me again, Sir Orvin."

"And it is good to be with one who makes me work at my philosophy. One who makes me strain to deliver the truth. My head has lacked that exercise for too long."

Christopher rested his palms on Orvin's shoulders, feeling the rough leather of the old man's tunic. "Tell me about people now. Brenna."

"We feared a siege after the battle with Garrett, and sent many to Uryens's castle. Your raven maid has not returned from there."

"Then I ride to Gore to see her."

"You expect she has been waiting for you?"

The excitement in Christopher's voice ebbed away. "No."

He had told himself it had been too long, over two years, and many other things had obscured his thoughts of her. But now he was home, and he expected to see her. The expectation fostered the hope that there was still something between them. But just seeing her wasn't going to rekindle what they had had. He felt much more mature. If they came together once again, it would be a different kind of relationship.

"She did care a great deal for you," Orvin said.

"So maybe she did wait?"

"Do not beg for alms of love. See her. Greet her. Expect nothing."

Christopher nodded, then other faces came to mind. "What of Lady Fiona?"

"There is a sad story. And I weep when I think of how it ended."

"She's not—"

"By her own hand."

"When?"

"Only a moon after the survivors returned."

"They were the rear guard," Christopher said. "They were supposed to attack. Instead, they ran."

"Is a man a coward if he wishes to preserve his own life? Must he always step into the wake of death and chase it? Can a man decide not to die and live with himself?"

Christopher yawned. "On the morrow we will debate this. Now we sleep."

"You sleep."

"Has Lord Devin given you a chamber?"

"He did—but I refused it."

"Then where do you reside?"

"You have a mount?"

"Yes."

"Fetch it, then. And I'll show you."

2   Leatherdressers' Row was completely barren, save for the three new stone-walled houses on the

right where the road began. In the ocher light of sunrise, Christopher could see that reconstruction had begun, monitored by Lord Devin's steward and financed by whoever the new abbot was. The black timbers that once littered the ground were gone, the earth now leveled in preparation for more tofts. Stone buildings were expensive, and Christopher marveled at the picture he drew in his imagination of a whole town built of the heavy rocks. It did seem that that was Lord Devin's plan. The new Shores would be a strong, heavily peopled village, Christopher hoped.

Orvin rode the rounsey and he walked alongside the horse. He tried to find the location of his old toft, but couldn't be sure. Everything had changed. But the characteristic odor of the air, a blend of gorse and humus cut with the stench of leather, was still present. Or maybe he wanted to smell it. No, it was there.

They turned right at the end of the empty road and walked toward a row of stables. The buildings were under repair; sections of new roof created juxtapositions with older, more weathered timber, and once-wooden walls were now made of stone.

Orvin pointed to the first stable, behind which was a small corral, home for two rounseys. "Here."

Christopher opened the wide door of the stable and pulled his rounsey inside. He helped Orvin down from the horse and then closed the door. The old man flinted a torch to life.

"Mind your flame," Christopher told Orvin, nervous about the torch among the old wood and straw.

"Yes, yes."

A dozen stalls stood below a storage loft that was accessible by a wooden ladder. The place reminded Christopher very much of the old squires' quarters back at the castle. And it struck him as curious that Orvin chose to live in such a place. The old man ascended the ladder.

"You pick a stable over a warm chamber in the castle?"

"I am a curiosity now. The last member of a family that no longer exists."

"I will be your family."

"That is kind of you, young patron saint. But your life will carry you well beyond these stables. You can be my company for now."

Christopher climbed the ladder behind Orvin, reached the top, then crawled onto the floor. When he stood, he hit his head on the ceiling. He rubbed his sore noggin and silently cursed.

"Mind your head," Orvin said.

"Oh, I am, sir. And it hurts!"

In one corner of the loft there was a shabby, thin-mattressed pallet, a pile of scrolls sitting on the floor next to it. The bed was as rickety and uncomfortable-looking as the one Christopher had slept on in the squires' quarters. It seemed unlikely Orvin actually used it for sleeping.

"This is where you retire?" Christopher asked.

"No," Orvin said. "We ride hackneys through here. Of course it is."

"On that bed?"

"What's wrong with it?"

"What of your back?"

Orvin sat down on the bed and slid off one of his sandals. "This bedding has done wonders for my bones."

"You hate this place."

Orvin furrowed his brow. "I do not."

"You live with *horses*, master. Like a farrier apprentice."

"I like horses." He removed his other sandal.

Orvin had changed. Hasdale's death had changed him. And now his master wanted to run away from it, to live here in solitude with the horses and a few hostlers and builders. It was too easy to see. Christopher wondered if the old man knew how transparent a disguise it was; Orvin could not face life in the castle, the eyes that stared at him and the whispers that said, "Poor Orvin. His whole family is gone."

Christopher decided to confront his master. "You cannot face your loss. You hide from it here."

Orvin rubbed his bloodshot eyes. "No. I simply desire to be alone. I do not wish people buzzing about me, tending to me. I live my own life here. I am content."

"You hide."

Orvin yawned. "Later we will debate this. Now we sleep," he said, quoting Christopher.

"I thought you could not?"

Orvin pushed himself back onto the straw-filled mattress, and his head found the pillow. He lay on his side and within seconds began to snore.

Some host. Where do I sleep?

Christopher found a spare woolen blanket under the pallet and spread it out on the wooden timbers of the loft. He sprawled on the wool and eyed the rafters, unfolding an imaginary reunion with Brenna in his mind.

3 Dallas threw the watchman against the pitted bars of Mallory's cell. Mallory watched as Dallas thrust his spatha into the man and saw the blade pop out of the victim's back, a metallic serpent rising from its gambeson hole.

Dallas wrenched his spatha from the guard. The watchman's head thumped over the pair of horizontal bars as he fell to the floor. Dallas relieved the dead man of his keys and fumbled with the cell door lock.

Mallory had an erection. The thrill was present, and he stood in the middle of it, throbbing with its energy. "You had to come the night before my trial. Why not a minute before? It would've been much more daring."

Dallas ignored Mallory and struggled with the lock. Finally, the tumbler dropped and the door screeched open. Mallory yanked the keys out of Dallas's hand and hustled for the cell that held his other men. He freed them, and the group hurried out of the prison block.

As the others rushed through a hall that led to their waiting rounseys in the courtyard, Dallas and Mallory found their way to the sunlit tunnel of the cloisters, and then to the entrance of the church.

Dallas handed Mallory a small dagger, an anlace, then led the way with his own spatha. They banged into the church. The abbot stood, in all his obese glory, at the altar.

Mallory ran straight toward the abbot. The old man cowered, putting his hands up in defense. Mallory let the momentum of his feet carry him up the wooden stairs and into the abbot, knocking the old man onto his back.

Mallory heard the monks behind him scream as he punched the abbot in the heart with his anlace, and damned the man with his eyes. Again. And again. The abbot's surplice became soaked with blood, and the old man's eyes were so wide that they looked ready to burst from their sockets.

Why had he wanted to kill the abbot so much? The humiliation of being incarcerated, he reasoned. Yes, that was it. *Punch. Punch. Punch. Now go!*

As a last moan escaped from the abbot's mouth, Mallory pushed himself to his feet.

"Come on!" Dallas begged.

Mallory looked around. Here he was in the middle of the house of the Lord smeared with the blood of the abbot. There wasn't much more he could do to defy God. He shuddered. God would understand. God knew how he felt. God knew the thrill of it.

Mallory stepped down from the altar as the last of the monks fled the church. Dallas ran toward the transept entrance on the river side of the church. Mallory followed, still dazed by what he had just done. It was a different kind of killing; at least it felt different. Was he cursed now that he had murdered in the house of God? No. *God understands. He does, he does, he does.*

As he passed through the transept door, the anlace, which was slick with blood, fell from his hand and onto the floor. Mallory did not stop for it. Something told him to leave it behind. To leave as much as possible of what had just happened behind him.

Four of his men stood brazenly on top of the perimeter wall, nocking arrows into their shortbows; they sent their missiles into the air toward the monks, who poured out of the dorter doors and brandished their spathas.

Mallory and Dallas roped their way over the walls, then mounted their rounseys. The archers leapt from their perches and joined them.

Now he could feel good. He was away from that place. He loved the feel of his rounsey between his legs as the animal galloped along the river. He loved to be among his men again, free from those iron bars, which had seemed to close in a little tighter as the hours had worn on. He loved the idea of leaving a mental slash across the minds of the monks, an indelible memory that would be whispered among the clergy for many moons to come.

He loved being himself at the moment. Every aspect of it. He peered over his shoulder. The abbot's mounted men pursued them, as he had dreamed they would.

4 It would be some time before all the preparations for the tournament were completed and the actual event could be scheduled. Arthur himself planned to attend, and this shook Lord Devin to the core of his being. Everything *had* to be perfect. But wasn't that the order of his life? Perfection? Lord Devin had never met anyone more fastidious than himself. He constantly reviewed everything he did, as well as the deeds of those around him. Some called him too critical. He paid them no heed. How could anything be less than perfect for the king? It was incomprehensible.

He sat before his breakfast table as his steward voiced a progress report on the reconstruction of Shores, but he ignored the old fool. His mind was focused on one thing: the tournament. He wanted messengers dispatched immediately with the invitations. He wanted to know the date of the event now. He wanted the tents pitched, the grandstand built, the tourney ground cleared, and the bachelor and banner knights ready now. What was the delay?

He interrupted the droning syllables of the rodent-faced steward. "Enough. I want to know about the tournament."

"What is it you wish to know, lord?"

"When will it happen?"

"The preparations have begun."

"That tells me nothing!" He wasn't sure why he was so furious. It had to be the fear of having the king at his castle. He hated criticism and worried that the king would find fault with him. Criticism from the king would kill him.

"Before the next moon, lord. The tournament will commence before the next moon."

"Can you promise that?"

The steward rose. "I will." The man turned and scurried out of the great hall.

Devin had to calm himself. He already knew his tournament would be the most talked about one in all of England. No one would put on a better time of festivities. He might be fussy, but the spoils were worth it.

Marigween stepped gracefully into the hall, and it saddened him to see how radiant she was. Her long, red locks were bound with a colorful linen tie, her cheeks flamed, and her vert eyes caught the sunlight pitched in through the smoke hole in the ceiling. She was beautiful. What a pity. His only daughter would be swept away from him. She would live in the castle, but once married, he would see little of her. How old was she now? Sixteen? There were only scant moments left. The eyes of his battle lords seemed to find her no matter how hard he tried to shelter her. A knight would take her and she would be gone.

"Father. I wish to watch the archers practice, but the sentries will not let me leave the bailey."

He sighed. "They are under orders."

She stepped back from him. "Your orders?"

He frowned, turning his head to the unfinished pork on his plate.

"I thought we spoke of this already," she said. "I thought you agreed to let me go where I wish. Instead I am your prisoner!"

"No. I just don't want you to be hurt."

"By whom?"

"How about a game of chess?"

"Don't change the subject!"

Her torments could no longer be ignored. He stood, his legs pushing the high-backed chair out from under him. "You are my daughter and you will obey me. You may travel anywhere you please within the walls of the castle."

"I repeat—I am your prisoner, *not* your daughter !"
Tears brimmed in her eyes.

"I don't know how to explain it to you."

"What?"

"You . . . you're all I have left."

"Ever since Mother died you have nosed into
everything I do. I cannot breathe!"

"When I die, your husband could become lord of
this castle. Do you know what that means?"

"It means you wish to pick my suitors. You have tried
for too long, Father. I will go to a nunnery if I must!"

"Perhaps that is best."

He had called her bluff and it infuriated her. She
blew out her breath disgustedly, iced up, and
stormed off.

A nunnery was the last place in the realm
Marigween desired to be; she was too consumed by
her friends and her flirting with his men. *Someone
should teach fathers how to manage situations like
this. A lesson in fatherhood, that's what I need. Why
were these things not taught to me earlier? Why was
I not warned of situations like this? They are common, but no one speaks of them. What is a father to
do?*

Devin collapsed into his chair. He tried to turn his
thoughts away from Marigween and onto the tournament, but his mind galloped along a single path. He
massaged his temples with his fingertips. He had to
make sure she did not fall into the wrong arms. He
would give her to the champion of the tournament.
He hated the idea, but it was the only way to ensure
her marriage to nobility. At the moment, she was as
likely to marry a serf as a knight banneret. She had to
be controlled, and, in doing so, he would lose her
after all.

5

What is he cooking?

It was a difficult way to wake up to the smell of something horrible cooking; the fumes were like quicklimed spears in Christopher's nostrils. He sat up, crinkled his nose, then felt his back crack. *I absolutely refuse to sleep on the earth or another wooden floor. I am home now. I need a trestle bed!*

Christopher looked down to the floor of the stable. Orvin had the door open and had built his cookfire just beyond the building. A small iron cauldron hung from a chain fastened to an iron tripod, and a noxious liquid steamed with life over the rim of the pot. "Master? What poison are you brewing?"

Orvin sat on a small bench near the cauldron, stirring the evil brew with a long wooden spoon. He either ignored or did not hear Christopher's question.

Christopher crawled to the ladder, turned, and lowered himself onto one of the rungs. He started down, and in his foggy state missed a step and fell six feet to the hay-dappled floor. He lay on his back as the dust settled around him. His left buttock stung. He tasted dirt, craned his neck, and spit. Then he coughed and rolled up with a groan. He glanced to Orvin. Still, the man was in his own world, stirring his breakfast. Christopher stood, hobbled over to the cookfire while rubbing his rump. By the height of the sun, it already looked to be noon.

Orvin noticed the shadow darken his cauldron and the encompassing ground. He lifted his gaze to Christopher. "Clean up, boy. It's almost ready."

"I fell off the ladder."

"By the looks of you, yes."

"What *is* that?"

"My morning stew. Wait until you taste it. . . ."

Christopher clamped his index finger and thumb around his nose. "It's a little late for morning stew. I'll settle for a loaf, if you have any."

Orvin shook his head negatively. "Try the stew." He pulled the spoon from the pot and offered Christopher a tiny sip of the thick, brown liquid.

Christopher continued to hold his nose, opened his mouth, and let the spoon touch his tongue. He closed his lips over the wooden utensil as Orvin pulled it away. The stew made contact with his taste buds; it was rich and spicy, nothing like it smelled. "How can it taste good and smell bad?"

Orvin shrugged, then rose awkwardly to his feet. "Well, now that it is a new day, I seem to recall a bit of unfinished conversation from last night. Something on the order of an accusation, I believe. Something about me hiding here."

A party of four mounted men rounded the corner of the stables row and galloped toward Christopher and Orvin. Old man and squire turned their heads as the men slowed to a canter, then finally braked in front of them, a dust cloud blowing over the riders. They were archers, armed with longbows, quivers of arrows, and swords and bucklers, the latter a small concave shield that Christopher never thought was effective. They wore gambesons over their bright blue shirts, shin-high riding boots, gauntlets, and iron-framed kettle-hats.

Behind Christopher and Orvin, a pair of hostlers ran up to greet the men. One of the horse handlers, a man of many chins, shouted, "Your rounseys are ready."

Christopher noticed how one of the archers had suddenly turned his head away from him, staring at the wood in the distance. It struck him as odd, but he sloughed off the thought.

"Let me help you down, Doyle," the many-chinned hostler offered the archer.

"Doyle?" The name slipped from Christopher's

lips; he wasn't aware of it, though, only of the notion
that this could be Baines's brother, and his friend
from moons ago, impossibly alive and here before
him. He needed to see the archer's face. "Doyle! Is it
you? It's me, Christopher!"

With that, the shy archer cracked his reins and
heeled his rounsey away from the group, forcing the
animal into a gallop down the dirt road. The other
archers looked on, confused.

It is him. It has to be. But why does he flee?

Christopher frantically scanned his surroundings, and
his gaze came upon the fresh rounseys waiting inside the
open stable next to Orvin's. He darted away from the
archers and ran into the cool shadows of the building.
He opened a stall door and freed one of the animals.
The horse was already saddled, and Christopher quickly
mounted it. A hostler inside the stable tried to stop him,
locking his beefy fingers around Christopher's leg.
Christopher unhooked the quirt from the rounsey's saddle and whipped the hostler in the head. The man fell
back, clutching his bald pate.

Christopher and the rounsey bolted into the sunlight.
He steered the animal toward the dirt road.

The archer pressed forward, traversing Leatherdressers' Row in a matter of minutes. Christopher
kept him in sight. They followed a path which took
them out of Shores, around the castle, and down the
steep incline that emptied into the wood.

The rough arms of the oaks hung low and fettered
Christopher's path. Ahead, the archer ducked, kept
his arms in; the branches brushed harmlessly over his
kettle-hat. Christopher did as the archer, though his
exposed head brushed against many of the limbs.
Finally, they broke out of the forest and onto the flatness of the practice field. Christopher raked the bits of
leaf and twig out of his hair, then cracked the quirt
across his rounsey's croup; the horse responded, giving Christopher the extra speed he demanded.

The archer galloped into a part of the practice field that made riding dangerous: it was the deceptive grass on which Hasdale had trained Christopher. Christopher could not be sure if the archer was aware of the ditches that lay hidden under the green blades. The archer's unweaving course indicated that he was not, but maybe that was his strategy—ride straight and let his rounsey leap over any of the holes.

In his effort to stay on the archer's tail, Christopher decided he had to, like the archer, ignore the ditches. Part of him wanted to stop, but the desire to catch and confront the man was enough to keep him ᴏ.. course. He saw a shadow in the grass ahead and pulled back on his reins. His rounsey slowed, then dodged the ditch. The movement put Christopher a horse's length farther behind the archer. He swore under his breath, then quirted his steed. The noon sun drew beads of sweat from Christopher's forehead and upper lip, and he tasted the salt of his exertion. The archer did not compromise his course, arrowing straight across the grass. It was horrible luck for Christopher that the archer's steed did not hit a single ditch. There were so many of them. How could the animal not hit just one?

As if Christopher had willed it to happen, the archer's horse cried as its right hoof slipped into a ditch. The rounsey's knee caved in and it rolled onto its side, throwing the archer some four yards. His kettle-helmet fell from his head as he hit the ground, and his arrows slid from their quiver on his back, splaying onto the grass.

Christopher veered around the fallen archer, then braked his rounsey. He jumped from his horse before the animal came to a complete stop and rushed to the archer, afraid of the blood he might find, but yearning to know the archer's identity.

The archer lay on his side, his back to Christopher. Christopher put his hand gently on the archer's shoulder and rolled the young man over. The archer's cheek was red and smeared partially with earth. A tiny trickle of blood rivered from his nostril into his mouth. His eyes were red with pain. All of these things did nothing to hide the archer's identity.

Doyle closed his eyes and choked up, blowing short puffs of air through his nose, forcing a little more blood through the one nostril and onto his lip.

"Where is the pain?" Christopher asked.

Doyle covered his heart with a palm. "Why did you have to come after me?"

"Why did you have to run?" Christopher shot back.

"It was easier thinking you were dead."

"You're not glad I'm alive?"

"I am," Doyle confessed.

"Then what are you saying?"

Doyle struggled to bring his body into a sitting position. Christopher gripped his friend's shoulders and helped him up.

Doyle wiped the blood from his lip with an index finger, cleared the dust from his lungs with a loud, hard cough, then continued, his gaze not meeting Christopher's. "I cannot face you after what happened."

"Why? What are you talking about?"

"The attack. It was moons ago, but seeing you now makes it feel like it all happened only yesterday. I ran, Christopher. I ran like I did just now."

Christopher thought about Doyle's words, his friend's admission of cowardice. After seeing the aftermath of the battle—the hundreds of bodies strewn over the slope—could he really hate Doyle for not wanting to join them? Doyle had spoken of his fear before they mounted the Mendips, and that fear had controlled him. Christopher knew the feeling, but was able to blanket it with anger. Doyle was not as lucky—not as cursed. Running from the battlefield seemed immediately a bad thing, but given time to weigh the circumstances, it was not. Christopher was thrilled that Doyle was alive. That

joy was greater than anything else. Life was most important, and thank St. Michael he had his friend back, no
matter how or why. The heroes, Christopher reminded
himself, were still on the slope. . . .

"And I was a fool and joined the junior squires on
the battlefield," Christopher said. "We were ordered
to stay behind, but we did not. All of the lord's great
knights were slain. The attack was a mistake, and you
were *smart* to run."

"I deserted my archer. That's why he's dead."

"No. I saw Varney die. No one could've stopped it.
Don't feel guilty for what you did. I'm glad you're
here. I don't care what happened."

Doyle frowned. Christopher sensed that his friend
wanted to believe the words, but wasn't ready accept
them as the truth.

At last, Doyle brought his gaze to bear on
Christopher. "How is it that you live?" he asked.
"And what happened to your face?"

A chill spidered up Christopher's spine and broke
into a many-taloned ripple across his nape. The chill
was triggered by an overwhelming sense of relief: now
would come the release of his story. Since the day of
Garrett's death, Christopher had wanted to confide in
someone about his relationship with Garrett. He could
not tell Mallory, nor could he tell Orvin—at least not
yet. But Doyle would lend a sympathetic ear, and perhaps in telling the story, Christopher could also cut
through the traceries of guilt that still imprisoned him.
The guilt of being loyal to the very man who had killed
his parents, Baines, Hasdale, and many others. He
needed to make Doyle understand. Even if Doyle
resented him at first, he needed to tell his friend that
underneath Garrett's killing exterior was a man struggling for an identity, a home. He was no different than
any other knight. Garrett was a victim of their world, as
were all of them. Killing was the way, God help them.

Christopher rose, then walked over to Doyle's rounsey. He reached down and gripped the animal's right hoof, then felt his way up the leg, past the pastern and cannon to the forearm. "She's just got a sprain."

Doyle pushed himself off the ground, then brushed off his gambeson and breeches. "You didn't check to see if any of *my* bones were broken," Doyle chided.

"Your screams would have told me. You will walk with pain, though."

Doyle nodded, then reminded, "You have yet to answer my questions." He bent over and gathered his fallen arrows.

"I'll answer them on the way back. Your partners await you, I'm sure."

Doyle looked up, sighed. "Yes. I tell you it is no pleasure serving Lord Devin. Though I'm a paid archer now, the job concerns us more with appearances than with marksmanship. Look at this livery."

Christopher studied Doyle's clothes; they were rather fanciful for an archer. Hasdale's men had worn dull, rough tunics, and some had donned leather or scaled armor. They looked like dirty, rugged fighting men. Doyle's livery was more tournament-worthy than battlefield-practical. The sky-colored shirt under the gambeson seemed to beckon to an enemy, "I'm here! Shoot me!"

"But you are a sight to the ladies, I'm sure," Christopher said, trying to raise a smile from his friend.

"True," Doyle said, blushing slightly.

Christopher handed Doyle his reins, then walked over and snatched up his own rounsey's bridle. They walked their steeds toward the wood below the castle.

"Have you seen your Brenna?" Doyle asked.

"Sir Orvin tells me she fled the castle after the attack on Garrett's army. She's been at Uryens's castle ever since."

Doyle rubbed his shoulder with his free hand. "Oh, this hurts." Then, to Christopher, he added, "Yes, that's right. Most everyone left. My parents are there."

"Have you seen them?" Christopher asked.

Doyle hesitated.

Christopher remembered the awkwardness and pain his friend felt when it came to his mother and father. Christopher hoped that time had scabbed the wounds to the point where Doyle could at least speak with his parents.

The slow clumping of the rounseys was too loud in Christopher's ears. "Sorry," he said, pitching his voice softly, and with regret.

"They, I suspect, do not know I'm alive."

Christopher stopped, turned to face Doyle. "Will you ride with me to Gore? I wish to see Brenna. And you—"

"Should make amends with my parents?" Doyle cocked his head away from Christopher, stared at the ground while huffing. "Why? Because it is the right thing to do? I barely knew them when I was taken. They did not raise me—Weylin did. And he's dead. And I'm here. And that's it."

"You have a family. I don't have anyone. I *wish* I were you. I wish my parents were alive."

Doyle returned his gaze to Christopher. "I had a family and lost it like you. I don't think I have one now."

"You haven't tried. Ride with me and see what happens. Tell your sergeant at arms you need a leave."

"Without pay," Doyle tossed in darkly.

"It may be worth it. Just talk to them."

"I don't . . . I don't know if I can. It feels strange. I could barely utter a word to them when I returned. I was glad to leave Shores."

"Then it's settled," Christopher said, assuming Doyle's company, and in doing so, forcing his friend into the journey. Christopher slid his arm over Doyle's shoulder, and they resumed their walk. "Sir Orvin will help fill our riding bags."

"I always thought he was dead," Doyle said. "Where has he been?"

"Hiding. Mourning his son." Christopher thought a

moment, rolling the words in his head. And then they came out. "I saw Hasdale die."

"By whose hand?" Doyle asked.

"Garrett. But our lord sought revenge. The campaign was wrong."

"Garrett must die," Doyle said through clenched teeth.

"Lord Mallory has already seen to that."

"Mallory? I've heard mention of him. A rogue knight, isn't he?"

Christopher sighed. "I'll say this quickly—and start at the beginning. Please listen. Make no judgments until you've heard everything."

Doyle smiled. "I don't wear a surplice, Christopher. Nor am I as round as most abbots. But let's hear your confession anyway."

"I was taken by Garrett and served him. At first because I was forced to, but then because I was loyal."

Doyle froze; his legs would not carry him another step, and his face clouded over with horror.

"He was a Celt. He was like us, alone and looking for a home. Yes, his men killed my parents, yes, his men killed your brother, yes, his men killed your Weylin. But it's our way. I hate it, but how do we escape it?"

"Not by serving a traitor! He might've been a Celt—once—but he commanded the Saxons. I believe he had the heart of one."

"You're wrong. He missed our ways. I reminded him of them. Don't you think I felt bad giving my loyalty to him? But it wasn't wrong. I tell you it wasn't."

"Why do you tell me any of this?" Doyle asked. "It makes me hate you."

"Perhaps I, too, feel in some way like a deserter."

By the look on Doyle's face, the flush of guilt, Christopher knew he had struck the right chord in his friend.

"When I first saw you," Doyle said, "I hated you. I hated you because you didn't save my brother. Then you made me like you. And now you make me hate you again. But I despise you now because you are too much like me. We both need to mend our lives somehow. What do we do?"

"You have a home here in Shores—but no family. We ride to Gore and see what we can do about that."

"But what about you? You have no family, and no home."

"I have friends. For now, they will be my family."

"That thought makes you feel better, eh?"

"Some food would make me feel better! I rode after you without getting any stew."

"You mean Orvin's foul-smelling cauldron."

"The very same."

"You've spent too much time with the Saxons."

"Not to mention six moons with the rogue knight."

"This story is getting worse," Doyle said.

A field mouse scampered underfoot and disappeared into a tiny burrow; the animal reminded Christopher of someone. "Do you know what happened to Bryan the mouse catcher?"

"I suspect he's dead," Doyle said.

Christopher nodded; he had thought the same.

They reached the edge of the field and stepped into the welcoming shade of the wood. Christopher told the tale of Queen's Camel Abbey. Doyle listened, as intent as he was incredulous.

6

The thick, gray walls blocked out the sun.

Neither Doyle nor Christopher had ever seen a castle as great. As they trotted over the drawbridge toward the gatehouse, they could not help but crane their heads up and stare at Uryens's curtains and towers; Christopher estimated they must be twice the height of those of the castle of Shores. Doyle shouted

a request not to be heralded to one of the gatehouse
sentries. Christopher wanted to surprise Brenna, and
Doyle did not want to call any attention to himself,
still battling with whether he would confront his parents. "Just because I'm coming doesn't mean I have
to talk to them," he had told Christopher.

They came into the outer bailey, where the sun was
visible and bathed the dozens of bustling freemen
and serfs in warmth and light. The bailey was a small
town itself, with a marketplace, craftsman's row, sta-
blehouse, kitchens, brewhouse, piggery, smithy,
chapel, gardens, and dovecote. So many people
swarmed the bailey that Christopher wondered if he
would ever find Brenna among such a multitude.

The journey had been long and uneventful, save for
the one night Doyle had walked sleepily to a nearby
brook for a cool sip and had fallen in, startling the
life out of Christopher. He hated sounds in the night.
Hated them.

Orvin had overstuffed their riding bags with provi-
sions, and had bargained with the hostlers for a fresh
pair of rounseys. Doyle's sergeant at arms had not
been not as helpful. He had given Doyle his leave and
an instant demotion. Doyle would be windlassing
crossbows for a long time, having lost the privilege of
firing the weapons. Doyle was, in a word, upset with
the sergeant.

They dropped off their rounseys at the thatch-roofed
stables. A money-hungry hostler informed them it
would be one denier per day for each of the horses.

"Do you bathe them for that price?" Doyle asked.

Christopher put an index finger to his lips, indicat-
ing for Doyle to argue no further. "That will be fine."

As they turned away from the short, squinting
man, Doyle mumbled, "Quick to give away your
money. I'm losing pay for this."

"It will be worth it," Christopher said.

"False promises create anticipation, and then misery."

"You already feel both," Christopher guessed, "so what's the difference?"

"How do you know what I feel?"

"Come," Christopher urged, getting them away from the stables and the argument.

They walked past the fences of the piggery toward the bakery, its elaborate chimney jutting into the sky and emitting spirals of thin, sweet-smelling smoke. They could have walked to the marketplace and bought a loaf from one of the merchants, but Christopher wanted a loaf fresh from the oven, and Orvin had taught him the way in which to acquire such a treasure.

Christopher and Doyle reached the entranceway to the bakery, and Christopher gestured for Doyle to wait outside.

Christopher's mouth watered as he stepped into the heavenly place. Three brick ovens made up the back wall of the bakery. A long worktable stood before the ovens, and he counted six serfs pulling loaves from the oven with their long-handled, wooden spatulas. Christopher considered what it would be like to work in such a place, wrapped every day in the blissful smell of bread, able to sample as much as you want of the soft, sweet loaves. But he reasoned that if he did work in a bakery, he would not appreciate the bread as much as he did otherwise. That truth was worn on the bored faces of the bakers.

"Good day, sirs. I am the reeve's servant sent for two loaves to be tested."

"The steward was here just yesterday," one of the serfs fired back.

Christopher's mind raced. "Yes, but the loaves were mixed up. We apologize for that, and require two more loaves today. Picked at random, please."

The serf who had spoken frowned, then reached to his left and picked up two warm loaves. He set them in a basket which another serf pulled from a storage shelf, then handed the package to Christopher. "Tell your lord that all of this testing is unsettling the bakers. We have never cheated on quality or weight. His suspicions are unwarranted."

"I will." Christopher ran toward the doorway, but caught himself in time to slow down and walk out casually.

Outside, Doyle's gaze lit on the bread. Christopher handed his friend one of the long, steaming loaves. Doyle bit off a hunk and chewed with a fierce delight.

Christopher nibbled on his own bread, eyeing the bailey. If he were younger, this crowded castle would have scared him. So many people. So many alleys in which to get lost. But he had been through so much. This place was only an obstacle to cross in order to get to Brenna.

The serf who had given Christopher the bread emerged from the doorway. "I should have known!"

Christopher and Doyle bolted away, hearing the serf's booming voice trail off behind them. They threaded their way through people and horses, turned right at the corner of the chapel, then paused behind the building, sucking down air and exchanging smiles.

"You're a criminal," Doyle said playfully.

"I am wanted by the abbot of Queen's Camel. And now by a baker. Call me the rogue squire, I guess."

"What I'm wondering is what your plan is to meet Brenna, young rogue."

"I think I like patron saint better. But yes, you are right. I do need a plan. I want to appear before her, startle her, and see if she still has feelings for me."

"What you're talking about is breaking into the keep, slipping past all the guards, and catching her while she's at work in some chamber."

"That's perfect."

"What did they teach you, Christopher? Or perhaps it was Mallory and not the Saxons. Why do you want to attempt something that risky?"

Doyle had posed an interesting question. Had a little bit of Mallory's thrill-seeking crawled into Christopher's veins? Christopher could not deny that the idea of sneaking into the keep and surprising Brenna excited him. Perhaps before encountering Mallory he would not have entertained such a thought. If he learned to control the feeling and not let it consume him as Mallory had, then it was a good thing. He felt it bolstered his courage and gave him the ability to walk along the edge of a wall and not fall off, the danger spurring on the will to do so. The thrill.

Doyle stared at him. "Well?"

7 When twilight purpled the sky above the keep, and the serfs had gone home to the one-room houses on their tofts, and the craftsmen had set down their tools and filled their hands with warm, sweet meat, Christopher and Doyle hunkered down near the base of a tower that stood near the keep's gatehouse.

"We don't even have a place to sleep," Doyle whispered. "There's an inn in the valley. I think I'm going there. I'll figure out a way to pay the keeper."

"Your brother would've liked this, Doyle. I wish you wouldn't go."

"Sorry. You don't know how you're going to get in there." Doyle started off, and in the shadows did not see the sentry, who had materialized from the corner of the tower.

Doyle bumped into the man.

"Halt!" the sentry yelled, brandishing his javelin. Then he hailed his comrade on the wall-walk above. "Chief of the watch. Two trespassers down here!"

They had refused to answer any questions, and so they had been escorted by the sentry to the prison block. They had been pushed roughly into one of the musty cells, the door slammed behind them. If they would talk, they might be released.

Unfortunately the first question had been their names. If word reached Brenna and Doyle's parents that they were in the prison, everything would be ruined. But, Christopher had argued to himself, if they didn't talk, when would they ever be released?

"I'm telling them who I am," Doyle said. "I'm done walking this path."

"You said we needed a place to sleep. . . . "

"Amusing, Christopher. Perhaps you missed your calling. The lord is looking for more jesters."

"Someone else said I would be a good jester. Anyway, we're inside the keep, aren't we?"

Doyle *tsk*ed loudly for effect. He stepped to the bars, pressing his cheeks against them. "I wish to speak to the chief of the watch."

"Yes," Christopher added. "We're ready to be released."

After a few moments, they heard the jingling of keys, the yawning of a door, and then the chief paraded into view; he stopped before their cell. The head watchman was a broad boar of a man with hard, miss-nothing eyes and a smile that had died many campaigns ago. If he had any emotions, the chief kept them sheathed. "Names?" he asked in his rumbling voice.

"Uh, Doyle and Christopher of Shores," Doyle said. "I'm Doyle."

"Why were you loitering outside the gatehouse?"

"We were waiting for a friend," Christopher answered.

"Who is this friend?"

Doyle shot Christopher a pleading look. "Let's tell him the truth." Then he faced the chief. "I'm here to see my parents, maybe. And he's here to see a friend. Brenna. She's a chambermaid."

"Who are your parents?" the chief asked.

"Lord Heath and Lady Neala."

As if commanded by a silent leader, the chief turned and exited quickly.

"Your father must wear some title around here," Christopher said.

Doyle shrugged.

The chief was gone for what seemed a moon. Christopher did not want to risk conversation with Doyle, for he felt his friend was on the verge of argument; he could see the frustration rimming Doyle's eyes.

When the chief returned, he was not alone. In tow were Doyle's parents. And Brenna.

Christopher was denied view of the initial shock wave that must have passed through Brenna's body upon hearing he was alive. He had wanted to see that very badly, and with her right in front of him, standing just beyond the bars, all he could do was imagine what her reaction had been for a second—and then her voice thrust him into the present.

"Christopher?" She uttered his name—a question— as if not fully recognizing him. Had he changed that much?

Lord Heath tugged nervously on his gray beard. "Get my boy out," he ordered.

"Yes, lord." The chief unlocked the door, then Christopher followed Doyle out of the cell.

"You couldn't have planned this any better," Doyle whispered grimly over his shoulder, then turned toward Lord Heath and Neala.

As a stiff, fragmented conversation between Doyle and his parents began behind him, Christopher found himself lost in by the raven maid's eyes.

Do not look too deeply into her eyes. Let her make you happy. That is all.

She touched his cheek with her index finger. "What happened?" Then she lowered her hand.

Self-consciously, Christopher reached up to his face and ran fingers over the scars. "I got hit." He wasn't concentrating on his words. He felt his fingers trembling on his cheek. He dropped his hand, balled it into a fist to stifle his nerves.

"I can see that," she said.

Everything he had wanted to happen had gone wrong. The surprise meeting, the things he would tell her, the moment they would share. All of it was changed, forgotten. But it didn't matter. The moment was as good as he could have wished. He hadn't realized how much he had wanted to be in her presence until now; he hadn't realized how happy it would make him feel. She did make him happy. Too happy. He didn't want it to end, as he knew it might.

"I wanted to surprise you," he said softly.

"You did."

Behind them, Lord Heath, Neala, and Doyle moved toward the exit at the end of the prison block.

"We're going to eat," Doyle called out. "Meet you up there."

Christopher craned his neck. "Fine." Then he shifted his gaze to hers. "I have a moon's worth of stories to tell you."

"And I have as many questions." The light that he wanted to see in her eyes was there, and the color that flushed her cheeks complemented it perfectly. She turned her head slightly, and he caught sight of the back of her hair, much longer than his memories had painted. It was only now he noticed her dress, a simple wool gown, linen shift, and wool stockings. He remembered her bright-colored clothing, but felt even her present drab attire did not deplete her beauty.

He stepped toward her, extending his arms. They embraced. Time had made him feel awkward about hugging her on first sight, but as he felt the curvature of her back, he felt anything but odd. He felt wanted.

She broke the embrace. "I really thought you were dead. And I—"

Christopher put a finger over her lips. "I'm hungry. Can we eat together?"

She pursed her lips, nodded. "I still have to tell you about—"

"It's all right. I didn't expect you to wait for me. I just wanted to see you. To tell you I'm alive. To tell you I missed you. That's all. As Orvin is fond of saying: expect nothing. And I do."

Brenna smiled knowingly, then her grin faded with another thought. "He's not dead, is he? I've heard rumors."

"Oh, no. He lives. He cooks. He makes his funny noises and wrinkles his forehead in that odd way. And he's still reading the skies." Christopher took Brenna's arm in his. "Show me to the hall."

"We'll be dining with my parents—and with Innis. He's a varlet."

Christopher stopped. "If you don't feel right about this—"

"I'll set you a place at our table," she said firmly.

She might have given some of her feelings to another, but he knew she still had some left for him. She wasn't just being nice, or showing him pity. He found truth in her words, in the way she looked at him.

As they were about to leave the prison block and mount a staircase for the garrison quarters, they both paused, turned, and glanced at the row of cells, then each other.

8 Simple pleasures. Meat that was cooked
well and peppered. Vegetables that were boiled,
not cold and raw. Fresh-brewed ale. The merry
sounds of minstrelsy. The company of people he
liked—Celts—not Saxons or criminals. Christopher
sat at the trestle table with Brenna's parents and
her suitor Innis, breathing in the moment of dining
once again in a great hall. Like so many other
things, routine things, you took them for granted
until they were lost. Now he treasured the moment
and hoped it would once again slip back into his
routine. If he found a lord who would take him, it
would.

Uryens and his nobles sat at his long table on the
dais, and Christopher studied each of the lord's
knights, wondering which he would ask for the
chance to prove himself as a squire. But he also
felt a strong desire to be home, to serve one of
Devin's knights at the castle he knew so well. He
wanted to be close to Orvin, be able to seek his
master's guidance when the need arose. This was a
great place, and Brenna was here, but he felt a
guest. He did not know if he wanted to stay. He
needed to talk to Doyle, to find out how things
were with his friend. He spied Lord Heath and
Neala at the first trestle table closest to the lord.
But strangely, Doyle was nowhere in sight.

A conversation took place between Brenna's
mother, the vociferous Fenella, and Innis. Brenna's
father, Arlen, a fat, dark-faced man who had become
one of Uryens's private armorers, was too busy gob-
bling down his food to pay attention to anyone.
Christopher himself was too lost in thought to listen
to the discussion until he was yanked from introspec-
tion by a question from Innis:

"Christopher. What is your opinion of Arthur's new union?"

Christopher averted his gaze from Lord Heath's table to Innis. He had hated the varlet at first sight, not because the boy was cocky, and not because the boy had insulted him by not looking him directly in the eye when they had first met, but because, he admitted, he was jealous. Simple pleasures were now simple pains. Innis had moved into Brenna's life. Christopher must be mature and accept that, he knew, but just then he wanted to rip the vaunting boy's head off and mount it on a spear. Brenna deserved better than Innis. Christopher wasn't sure he was worthy of her, but this Innis, this in-love-with-himself arrow-shooter was certainly not.

"What was your question?" Christopher asked. *You foul boy.*

"I asked," Innis repeated annoyedly, "what do you think of Arthur's new union?"

Christopher had never given it much thought. Mallory had told him a few things about the new king, but since then, Christopher had only stowed the desire to meet Arthur. He had no opinion of the new union. He guessed it was a good thing. "I'm for it," he answered.

Innis flattened his pretty, pudding basin haircut, then pulled an errant wisp from his eye. "But what do you think of the delegation of power he and Lancelot have established?"

Christopher sensed that Innis was trying to prove him politically inferior, which he knew he was. He had never given any thought to the way their land was governed. He knew the structure like everyone else, and now the new order was changing it. If it worked, that was fine with him. The games nobles and kings played bored Christopher. "I will be glad to serve any knight who is true to the king."

"One with such a small view will not achieve knighthood quickly. I think the king seeks ideas."

"From a varlet? What plans have you to offer him?"

For a second, Christopher looked at Brenna. He saw she was not appreciating their verbal duel; she kept her gaze locked on her plate. But it wasn't his fault. Her new love had struck the first blow.

"I have many. But will not disclose them now."

"Battle plans?" Christopher asked.

"Indeed."

Christopher smirked. He didn't have to listen to this know-it-all anymore. Now they were treading waters Christopher knew a whole lot about. "What do you know of the battlefield? Have you been on a single campaign?"

"No. But I have studied past campaigns on my own. I know enough now—"

"You don't know anything." Christopher tapped his scarred cheek with an index finger.

"I've heard about your Lord Hasdale's failure and death. That I know."

Christopher saw Fenella nudge her husband with her elbow; he continued shoveling beef down his throat.

"Have you ever seen the body of a dead man? Have you ever killed a man yourself?"

Innis stood, then smote the tabletop with a fist. "And how are you going to change the world, squire?"

Brenna pitched Christopher a scornful look. Arlen looked with equal disgust at Innis for banging on the table and disrupting his supper. Fenella scowled at her husband for not intervening.

Christopher knew that if the dispute continued, he and Innis would be outside with daggers. Time to concede, if only for Brenna's sake. "Sit down. It belittles us to argue this way," he told Innis. "You are right and I am wrong."

Innis's anger lapsed into hunger. He sat down and fingered a piece of meat, pushed it into his mouth.

Christopher noticed that the minstrels had stopped playing.

"I hope you will not—" Brenna began, but was cut off.

"The king!" a herald called from his position on the dais. "King Arthur!"

A pair of trumpeters played after the herald's call, the notes echoing off the stone walls and reverberating in Christopher's ears. From a side hall, he saw the king step onto the dais and find a seat in the middle of Uryens's table, a seat normally reserved for Uryens himself. Christopher followed as everyone rose.

Arthur wore no crown, no gold-trimmed tunic or fancy jewelry. He sported the link-mail hauberk and woolen breeches of a common fighting man. In fact, he appeared to have just stepped off the practice field and into the great hall, perhaps having engaged in a little torchlight swordplay. He looked like king of the combatants to Christopher, and that made him feel good about the man. Here was a king who knew something about fighting. Or at least his appearance said so.

After the king sat, everyone else resumed their benches. Christopher did not take his gaze off Arthur. He watched as the king sipped ale from a shiny silver tankard, smacked his lips, then cleared his throat.

"Messengers from Lord Devin's castle bring news of a tournament," the king said.

A cheer lifted in the room.

"Devin offers the champion his daughter Marigween's hand in marriage, and the rank of knight banneret in his army. The pay, I might add, is excellent."

Chuckles erupted from many of the fighting men seated at the table next to Arthur. Christopher didn't quite understand the joke, but suspected it had something to do with the fact that just becoming a banner knight, second only to a lord, was such an accom-

plishment in and of itself, that being paid for the
honor of carrying one's own banner into battle was
only a mild concern.

"As the day for our attack on the invaders draws
near, I trust it will be good for all of us to ease the
tension at a tourney."

Innis stood, a lone boy among the seated. "My
liege, if I may?"

Christopher was astonished by what he witnessed;
how could Innis be that bold?

Arthur squinted to see Innis, as all eyes in the
room found the varlet. "What is it, boy?"

"Now, when battle torches are already lit, is it not
foolish to twiddle?"

A hush blanketed the room. Christopher swallowed, feeling nervous for Innis, but at the same time
hoping Arthur would put the boy in his place once
and for all.

One of the sentries who stood guard at the main
entrance to the hall marched from his post and up
one of the side aisles of the room, pivoted, and stood
before Innis. The sentry gestured with his head for
Innis to leave.

Arthur chuckled, a laugh which put the hearts of
everyone at rest. "No, guard," the king said, "let the
boy stay. He might be bold but he does have a point.
Why should we play when battle is upon us?
Anyone?"

Uryens stood. "As you said, my sovereign, to ease
our fears."

"Exactly," Arthur said. "Every man has his rituals
before combat. Let this tournament be an unwinding
for every fighter. Do you understand now, boy?"

"Yes, my liege," Innis said. "I will listen more carefully in the future." The varlet took his seat.

It wasn't the scolding Christopher had hoped for,
but it was nice to see Innis's eyes glass up and his
color fade in the face of the king.

Arthur sat down to enjoy his meal as the sweet music of the minstrels rose above the clanking of plates and *chink*ing of tankards.

Brenna and Innis exchanged a smile, and for the first time Christopher saw her affection for the varlet. And suddenly he felt that the entire dinner had been a mistake, that even coming to Uryens's castle might have been wrong. She had obviously moved on with her life and why should he put himself through any more torture? It hurt to be with her. He wanted her back, but it didn't feel right. At least not at the moment. Maybe it would never be. Perhaps her eyes only teased him.

Christopher stood. "If you'll excuse me?"

Brenna looked surprised. He quickly turned and left the table. He strode toward the hallway that would take him to the stairwell and out of the great hall. As he walked, he felt his face stiffen and he rubbed his eyes. His fingertips became wet with tears.

9

The inn, constructed of irregular stone courses, stood on a long road that stretched into a field swept in darkness. It was the largest and only two-story building in this, one of the many small villages that circled and supported Uryens's castle.

Torches burned within the inn and illuminated the unglazed windows, adding to the light already droping from the waxing gibbous moon. A shingle hung over the warped front door spelling out simply: inn. On the opposite side of the road, Christopher noted six merchants' carts parked in a line, two covered

with thick tarpaulin; their owners surely enjoyed a
night's rest inside.

As Christopher dismounted, a boy half his age
came quickly from the front door and took the reins
of his rounsey. Before he had a chance to thank the
young servant, the boy escorted his horse around the
side of the inn, toward a stable.

He had ridden this far, and even if Doyle was not
inside, he might as well spend the night. As he
pushed in the front door, he was immediately taken
by the smell of something wonderful.

Glazed, roasted duck and steaming carrots were
being forked off a large tray to a score of chatting
guests at a single, long trestle table by two heavyset
women, the red-faced keepers of the inn. One of the
women turned her attention to Christopher, then
looked to the merchants and knights-errant at the
table. "Slide over," she ordered in her baritone voice.
"Make room for the boy."

"I have eaten already, madam. But thank you."

"The price of a night's stay includes a meal," she
said.

"I'm looking for a friend."

"Ah . . . I'll take you." She set her fork down and
gestured to the other woman who was serving the
carrots to finish dishing out the meat.

Christopher followed the woman through a narrow
hall that turned right and ended in a staircase. The
innkeeper's heavy, sandaled feet *ka-chunk*ed down
on the coughing timbers. Christopher imagined the
steps giving way and the woman plunging with a
bloodcurdling scream into the cellar. He kept a few
steps back in case that happened.

They stepped into another narrow hall. On each side
of them were the doors of the guest rooms, and the
woman led Christopher to the last door on the left. "I'm
sure he's the one you're looking for. Now, one to a room.
If you are staying, it will be five deniers for the night."

Christopher untied Fergus's purse from his belt and emptied into his palm the last six deniers Orvin had given him. He kept one and handed the rest to the woman.

"Your room is right next door," she said. "And if you change your mind about eating, I'll have a plate warm for you."

"Thank you," Christopher said in earnest as the woman left.

Tentatively, Christopher knocked, then pushed the door in; it was unlatched, and furtively, he peered behind it.

Doyle lay supine in a wide trestle bed, an arm slung over his eyes. The door creaked a little as Christopher pushed it fully open and came into the room.

Doyle lowered his arm and sat up, blinking to focus. When he saw it was Christopher, he fell back onto his goose-feather pillow and yawned.

"You never told me you were coming here," Christopher said, realizing his voice bannered more irritation than he actually felt.

"Now *you're* going to play father like he wants to?"

Christopher moved to the edge of the bed and sat down. A small candlestand stood near the bed, and since Doyle was not looking at him, his eyes closed, Christopher gazed at the hypnotic flame of the stick as he spoke. "Tell me what happened."

"I listen to you. And you get me to believe I need them. You make me think how wonderful it is to have a family. But it is not I who will have a family, it is they who will have a son—own a son. Control a son. They do not approve of anything I do. My father wants me to become a steward like himself. It's horrible. I need to get back out and fight!"

Christopher knew exactly what it felt like to be dominated by a father, to be forced into a future that you had no desire for, to be expurgated of your "soiled goals" of becoming a squire, or in Doyle's case, a master archer. It was odd, though, that Baines had not fallen under the same pressure. He had been allowed to become Hasdale's squire, which would certainly lead him to knighthood. But then Christopher considered Baines's death, the effect it must have had on Lord Heath and Lady Neala. They didn't want to lose Doyle, a son already lost and found. They, like so many parents, wanted to protect their boys from the swords of the battlefield. They had given Baines his chance—and had lost him. . . .

But how to ease Doyle's pain?

"I'm an expert saddler," Christopher told his friend, "not because I want to be. But it's good I know the trade. It's helpful. You don't have to be a steward, but maybe you could learn more about your father's duties. That could be of value."

"I don't see how. All he does is inspect everything, make lists and reports. The job bores me!"

"Tell him you don't want to be a steward, but you would like to learn about the duties of one. Give him that much time. He only fears for you. He wants to protect you. He and your mother have already lost one son."

"Yes," Doyle said sardonically, "they don't have much luck with sons, do they? Coming, going, dying . . . "

"I don't want to say this, but I think you know it's true. No matter what happens, they will always be your parents. You'll never escape that, and if you never see them again, deep down there would always be pain. I'll never see mine again. It *hurts.*"

"I'll never see Weylin again. Your bastard friends stuck a sword in his neck."

Christopher rubbed a frustrated hand over his face. "Weylin may have been your father, but he wasn't your blood."

"And there is no way out of bad blood?"

"I don't believe there is. But you're mistaken in

thinking it's bad blood. It's the blood that gave you life. It's noble blood."

"It's the blood that cursed me."

"I don't know how to make you feel better," Christopher said. He had grown more and more disconsolate during the conversation, and was now ready to lay down his mental arms.

"Let me sleep," Doyle said.

Christopher rose from the bed. "I'm next door. We'll ride home at dawn. Maybe coming here was wrong, I don't know." He moved toward the door and exited soundlessly.

He found his own trestle bed much softer than it looked. Cradling his head in his palms, Christopher watched shadows cast by his candle fluctuate ever so slightly off the timbers of the ceiling. Downstairs, he heard the moans and cries of the ale-laden merchants who were engaged in a game of dice.

He wished now he had never left Shores to ride with Hasdale. Then his relationship with Brenna might have continued. The attack on Garrett's men affected everyone he knew in one way or another. Did Hasdale realize how many lives he had disrupted? He had paid the price for it, but his terrible judgment would linger on for many, many more moons. Orvin had changed. Brenna had changed. Doyle had changed. Doyle wanted to get back on the battlefield, and this time not run. His obsession with proving himself could get him killed.

Christopher realized his old life was beyond repair. He would have to go back to Shores and begin again, like every other villager. He would discard the wood of his past and lay new walls of stone. At the same time, he would focus himself, not be baited by lost desires. If he wanted to be a true servant, he needed to find truth, and truth was not at Uryens's castle.

10

Mallory and four of his men hid behind a hedge on the outskirts of the dense wood that stood to their rear. To their right, a young cornfield, nearly waist high, concealed a tilled ground, and the wind carried its muddy scent to the rogue party's nostrils. To their left, three farmers' huts stood on the edge of a lonely, fallow field cornered by marshy grasslands obscuring the Cam. A path was beaten through the planted and unplanted fields, a course now taken by Duke Edward of Somerset and his entourage of two bachelor knights and three squires. As he watched them through claws of leaf and branch, trotting innocently toward Shores, Mallory's pulse quickened.

Ambush. The very word cvoked chills which flared along his spine; every hair on each of his arms stood on end. He'd beaten many an unsuspecting traveler to his knees, nobleman and merchant, serf and freeman alike, but this, this was the first step up a spiraling staircase to the solar in the castle of Shores—a solar which would ultimately be his.

Following his escape from Queen's Camel Abbey, Mallory had done a lot of thinking. And he had discovered that giving up his estate and his lands to finance an army had been great error. Twelve men left, and they truly were not enough to be effective. His dream of running a series of whirlwind night strikes against the Saxons had dwindled. The men had run off as the money had run out. And even these last dozen were discontent. He should have retained his estate and lands, financed an independent army that operated outside Arthur's rule. But could that have happened? He was not sure. The past was a ball of confusion now, but the future seemed clear. His plan was simple, and he would not back out of it.

Mallory rubbed his thumb over his unsheathed spatha, tightening his grip on the smooth, brass hilt. The duke rode closer.

Dallas, crouched next to Mallory, edged forward, startling a rook, which flitted from its perch in the hedge.

Mallory put his free hand on his best man's shoulder. "Easy. Let him come closer."

Dallas, eager for the confrontation, nodded impatiently.

While Mallory and Dallas were armed with spathas, the rest of the rogues bore halberds. A quick unhorsing of the duke and his men would render them vulnerable. The bachelor knights and squires would be killed at leisure, and Mallory felt a whisper of guilt at the back of his ears as he stared into the too-young eyes of the approaching squires. He shook the feeling away. *Unlucky boys.*

The duke's party passed the first farmer's toft. Mallory curled his thumb and index finger, touched them together into an O, then put them to his opened mouth; a piercing note came from his lips, and the duke's party braked their steeds.

Rear doors on the second and third farmers' huts banged open and two groups of four of Mallory's men rushed from their hiding places onto the path. They jabbed their halberds forward and charged toward the duke and his men.

Mallory and Dallas pushed through the hedge in unison, and, having donned thin gambesons and light bascinets, were able to jog the fifty yards toward their prey.

Fergus, who had hidden in one of the huts, hooked his halberd around a bachelor knight's neck; the halberd *klang*ed off the knight's metal gorget. Had it not been for the knight's neck protection, Fergus might have killed the man with the force of his pull. The brass-plated bachelor clutched the halberd with gauntleted hands, but the attempt to pull the weapon away was futile. Fergus dragged the man off his courser and he crashed loudly to the groumd. As the man rolled over, Fergus dug the swordlike tip of his pole arm into the bachelor knight's exposed forehead. The knight let out a horrible cry that became a gurgle as he drowned in his own blood.

Two of Mallory's men worked on the other bachelor knight, who was already on the ground but had managed to unsheath his spatha. The knight hacked away at the advancing halberds, but unsuspectingly backed into Dallas. Before the bachelor knight had a chance to turn around, Dallas yanked off the man's bascinet and made a downward strike with his spatha. Dallas had cracked open a skull before, and judged the force of this blow correctly; the entire width of his blade passed into the knight's head. He had trouble removing his blade from the crumpling man's skull, but on the second pull it came.

One of the three squires kicked his horse and attempted to flee. Four of Mallory's men teamed up on the boy, using their halberds to catch each of the legs of the squire's ride; the horse went down hard, throwing the squire into unconsciousness. The boy never felt the halberds impale his chest.

The other two squires were braver, and gave Mallory's men a tougher time. Smaller and more agile than the bachelor knights, and not constrained by heavy armor, the boys ducked under the halberd strikes and wheeled their horses around as they *sringed!* out their spathas. They fought their attackers with hard, determined blows, but the numbers were against them. While the squires were busy fighting off attackers in front of them, two of Mallory's men slid up behind the squires, hooked them off their steeds, and ran the boys through. The faint cries of the squires were lost in the clattering of hooves and gleeful screams of Mallory's men.

Gradually, all fell silent. The duke, still mounted, was alone and a ring of rogues now locked around him. Mallory, the jewel of the ring, stood in front of Edward, looking into the man's enraged eyes.

"Kill him, lord!" someone shouted.

Mallory lowered his gaze to the ground, saw the duke's banner lying near one of the dead squires. He stepped away from the group and picked up the lance which held the banner. He let the gold flag hang down so that he could see the device: a red phoenix— the proud arms of the duke. He resumed his position in front of Edward. "Dismount," he ordered.

Edward remained in his saddle, his face as hard and cold as his plating.

"DISMOUNT, I SAID!"

Fergus and Dallas pulled Edward's sabatoned feet from his stirrups, then grabbed the duke's arms and dragged him backward, out of the saddle and over the rump of the horse. Pained by the awkward dismount, the steed neighed, then bolted through the ring of men. Edward jerked his arms free of Fergus and Dallas, then marched up to Mallory. "Arthur was right about you."

A trace of a grin flicked over Mallory's lips as he shifted his gaze from Edward to the banner in his own hands. "There will be no pyre for you, Edward. No ash for you to rise from." With that, Mallory nodded a silent order to Dallas.

Held by two other men, Edward was stripped by Dallas of his armor, then his shirt and breeches. Finally, he stood naked before the rogues. "You cannot humiliate me, Mallory. I'll die cursing you—not fearing you."

Mallory sighed. "I don't really care how you die as long as you do." Dallas moved in front of Edward and handed Mallory the duke's great helm. The large tournament helmet which Edward had stowed in a riding bag slid easily over Mallory's head. "I think it fits," he said. His men erupted in laughter.

"You're going to the tournament," Edward said, the horror darkening his face as it all, Mallory guessed, flowered in his mind.

"I'm glad you see better than you fight," Mallory said as he removed the helm. "The duke of Somerset will hold the lists for many days."

"If you're going to don my armor, God, spare me that sight. Kill me and let it be over with."

"You're going to marry Marigween," Mallory informed him through a broad, though sardonic smile. "I'll carry your banner with pride." Mallory held up the flag and waved it.

Edward sprang toward Mallory, arms raised, fingers tensed and ready to vise around the rogue leader's throat.

Dallas moved behind Edward and slung an arm around the duke's throat. This, however, did not stop the duke, and Dallas had to leap on Edward's back and attempt to drive the man to the ground by the force of his own weight. The duke carried Dallas four steps before he shrank to his knees and gasped for air. Dallas released his hold on the duke, and, out of breath, unsteadily withdrew.

Mallory dipped the banner over Edward's head, let the flag drape over the kneeling duke. "I'd choke you with this if I didn't need it so badly."

But Mallory had already grown bored. He could toy with the duke for only so long. He had originally considered dragging the duke along to watch, tormenting the man, a minor thrill along the way to reacquiring a domain. But that would've been sloppy. Better to have no loose ends.

Mallory dropped the banner, then gestured for Dallas to haul Edward to his feet. As Edward rose under Mallory's will, Mallory unsheathed a small anlace from his belt. The dagger had a horn hilt carved with the picture of a boar; Mallory found himself staring at it. He admired the artist who had designed the

hilt, for Mallory's own artwork was too often on
human flesh, and always sloppily rendered. There was
painstaking detail on this hilt, and for a brief second
he wished he had the patience to accomplish such a
task, to paint, carve, play an instrument. But that was
not his fate—nor the order of this moment.

He rushed up to Edward, gripped the head of the
duke's penis with his thumb and forefinger, extended
the organ, and sliced it off. Edward's scream echoed
off the distant hills. Mallory dropped the soft organ.

He could have lingered, taken the thrill of seeing
the duke grow fearful with the notion that his man-
hood was about to be cut off, but Mallory had been
merciful. He had done it quickly. But, he reasoned,
there was still a respectable thrill in it.

The duke's groin bled, a river of red rushing to the
earth. As Mallory turned away from Edward, he
heard the sounds of his men unsheathing their
spathas and daggers. He studied the hilt of his anlace
once more.

The duke let out a cry, but it was immediately
strangled.

11

Christopher had not gone to Uryens's castle and bid his farewell to Brenna. He had not wanted
to see her again, knowing she was with Innis. He had
resigned himself to the situation and had folded in on
his own love. He had tried to convince himself that
he had had a good learning experience, that next time
he would guard his feelings more carefully. Whether
it had been a learning experience or not, it still had
made him feel miserable, had made him want to bury
his head under a pillow. He had battled his emotions.

And had lost.

Both he and Doyle had consoled each other on the ride back to Shores, each having failed to make the other feel better.

On the last night of their journey, in the faint light of their small cookfire, Christopher and Doyle sat, Doyle with a small, thin blade in his hand.

The blood oath had been the archer's idea. A promise between Christopher and Doyle that no matter what came between them, they would always remain friends.

"Can't we just make the promise without blood?" Christopher shifted nervously on his saddle cloth.

"Our blood seals the oath."

"My word is as strong as my blood."

Doyle smiled as he fingered the blade. "You're scared?"

"No," Christopher lied.

"It's just a little cut."

Christopher touched his cheek, remembered the pain. *Any* cut hurt. "I think my loyalty to you—to our friendship—has already been proven."

"In what way?" Doyle asked.

"I have sincerely tried to help you reestablish your family. And when you were hungry, I, at great personal risk, fed you."

"You also got me locked up. You also forced me into a confrontation with parents who want to own me like a serf." Doyle handed Christopher the blade. "Do it."

Christopher would not have thought twice about making a blood oath with Baines. Was it really the sight of blood that held him back—or something else? Was he afraid to get too close to Doyle, for fear of one day losing his friend. That possibility would always loom on the horizon. They both had to realize that, and not let it hinder their friendship. Up until the past two years, death never seemed real; it had happened to someone else, never to someone close.

But Christopher had lost so many people he cared
for, maybe his feelings were burning out. He couldn't
let that happen. He would make the blood oath with
Doyle, but he didn't feel comfortable with it. It felt as
though he was unshielding his emotions for anyone
to stab. He was attaching himself to someone who
could die like all the rest. But he loved his friendship
with Doyle, admired the way Doyle handled the
crossbow and longbow, and held precious the way
they could talk to each other honestly and openly. He
never wanted any of it to end, and maybe Doyle was
right. Maybe blood would bond them, and protect
him from being hurt, as he was with Brenna.

The blade was cold, the hilt warm. Reflected
flames danced on its shiny surface. Christopher
turned the knife over and over, as if picking the right
edge on which to cut himself.

"Do it," Doyle repeated. "Or you're not my friend."

"You mean that?" Christopher asked.

Doyle nodded; his face gave no indication that he
jested.

"Why is this so important to you?"

"You were right," Doyle answered.

"What do you mean?"

"I need a family—and you're it," Doyle explained.
"You said your friends will be your family. So I'll be
yours. You'll be mine."

"I'm not sure if two friends make a family."

"Two brothers do."

"Brothers?"

"Blood brothers."

Christopher returned his gaze to the blade. He
stopped rolling it in his hand. He put the tip of the
knife to his wrist, saw three bluish veins waiting
innocently there. He moved the blade a little higher,
closer to the heel of his hand, then flicked the knife
across his skin. A thin slice appeared, but no blood
came out of it.

"Let me see," Doyle said.

Christopher refused to show Doyle his hand.

"You're probably not even bleeding. Come on. Give me the blade and I'll show you."

Reluctantly, feeling embarrassed, Christopher handed over the knife.

Doyle took the blade in his hands and sliced open a long, thin line that paralleled his veins. The cut bled well, more than enough to mix with Christopher's own blood. "See." Doyle showed his wrist, then returned the knife to Christopher.

Christopher closed his eyes and put the blade to his wrist, pressed the tip into his skin, then flicked it. A quick needle of pain followed, then he opened his eyes. Blood from a deep fingernail's-length cut oozed onto Christopher's wrist. He pushed the skin together with the fingers of his other hand, forcing more blood to the surface. He held his wrist up for Doyle's inspection.

Doyle pushed himself across his saddle cloth and moved as close to the cookfire as he could. He raised his arm over the flames. "Press your wrist against mine."

Christopher edged forward and extended his arm. His wrist met Doyle's, and they pressed their bloody skin together. It felt warm and slippery. Christopher coughed as he inhaled a little smoke from the fire.

It seemed the longer they could hold their wrists together, the stronger the bond would be. Finally, his arm too heavy, Christopher broke the connection.

"Blood brothers," Doyle said, wiping his wrist on his saddle cloth. "How does it feel?"

Christopher coughed again, the smoke still tickling his throat. "It feels the same," he managed. "Is it supposed to feel different?"

Doyle shrugged. "I don't know."

"How does it feel to you?"

"Somehow I feel safer. It's odd. It's as if I'm protected as long as I'm with you."

"But my fighting skills are not as good as yours."

"Have you really put them to the test?"

"I think so."

"Perhaps not. Maybe there'll be a contest for squires at the tournament. You should enter."

Christopher wiped his bloody wrist on his shirt-sleeve, then spit on the wound and rubbed the saliva in to cleanse it. "I have to find a knight to serve. That's my first priority." Christopher yawned. "Let's sleep. And dream of the tournament."

"That we will," Doyle said.

12

"Another lesson for one who believes he has learned them all," Orvin said, his voice soft and carrying the warm notes of a fine wooden instrument. They stood outside the stable the old man called home. "Close your eyes and face the sun."

Christopher complied, turning his face toward the orange globe that had just cleared the castle. He experienced the heat, and though his eyes were closed, the blackness was somehow full of light.

"Now," Orvin sang, "if you were to open your eyes, you would be blinded, yes?"

"Yes."

"And wouldn't you consider it possible during combat to be blinded by the sun?"

"I would."

"Then what is one to do during that completely vulnerable time when one is blinded and one's opponent is about to strike?"

"Pray," Christopher joked.

"If one is smart, one is praying during the entire engagement."

Christopher bit his lower lip, imagined an enemy knight in front of him, about to bring his battle-ax down. He saw the sun just over the man's head, and the rays fired blinding dazzles into his eyes. *I can't see his weapon. How do I block it?*

"Some say duck and move. Which is commonly effective. But some opponents are quicker than you, and as you duck, they take off your head."

"Which in that case you don't even know you lost."

"Ah, for a split second you do," Orvin said.

"Well, you could try to avoid the situation in the first place."

"Now we're learning. Simple rule: in daylight, always fight with the sun at your back. Turn and put it there. Make it your ally. But its loyalty often wanes, and thus you're faced again with the dilemma."

"If the sun's in your eyes, and your opponent's about to strike and you can't duck or move, then all you can do is attempt to block him without seeing him."

"Are you thinking about what to do—or feeling it?"

Just act. "Sorry." Christopher felt Orvin push his broadsword into his hands.

"Do you remember Sloan's lesson in arms identification? Finding them in the darkness?"

"All too well."

"Is it possible that one could fight by sound?"

"One could try. And probably die."

"Open your eyes."

Christopher craned his head away from the sun and opened his eyelids; he squinted at the old man.

"We'll finish this another day. I've invited someone to meet you." Orvin pointed over Christopher's shoulder.

Christopher turned around and saw a fully armored bachelor knight cantering toward them on his black destrier.

"He's looking for a squire?" Christopher asked, his voice buffed with excitement.

Orvin winked. It was a wonderful wink.

The bachelor knight looked like a king. His armor was ebony black, trimmed in gold, and his mount wore a matching set: champfrain on its head, crinière on its neck, poitrel on its chest, and croupiere on its rump. Horse and man were foreboding. And beautiful.

The knight's great helm was under his arm, and he held the reins with his free hand. His face was round, his cheeks shadowed by the fine hairs of a three-day beard, and his eyebrows connected into a single line of hair. His too-soft eyes made him look like a younger version of the Saxon Elgar. Christopher had liked that generous Saxon, and at first sight, Christopher guessed the knight might share the same altruism simply because he *looked* the part. It was a speculation Christopher hoped was right.

His breath tripped as the knight neared him. He remembered the day he had first spoken to Hasdale, how his mouth had become instantly dry and the words had not come. He recalled his first encounter with Brenna and how a similar set of plagues had fallen upon him. And time had not changed him that much.

"Good morning, Sir Orvin," the knight said. His voice was deep, and Christopher could tell right away that when he wanted to, the man commanded respect. He had a knight's voice. But it was a friendly voice now. The knight turned his attention to Christopher. "And you, boy, are the squire Orvin tells me so much about."

Christopher looked to Orvin. "Good things, I hope." He had to calm down. He had to sound intelligent, not the jittering boy he was. He felt one of his eyelids twitch.

"Nothing but," the knight said. "I am York, and I serve knight banneret Lord Woodward, who serves Lord Devin." He levered himself out of his saddle.

Christopher rushed over to help the knight down; York accepted his hand, and the man slung one heavy leg over his destrier and hopped to the ground. Christopher stepped back from the knight. "I'm Christopher."

York stood a full head taller than him, and with his armor on seemed twice as wide. "You served Hasdale." York frowned. "I knew him very well. I shared a great meal with him at Uryens's castle. That was the last time I saw him." York's expression stiffened with sudden intent. "Tell me. Did you . . . *see it?*"

Christopher shifted his gaze away from York and let it fall on Orvin. At the mention of his dead son, Orvin could not lift his head; he eyed the ground, and Christopher could tell that time had not eroded the old man's pain. Orvin had tried to hide it from him, but Christopher saw it now.

He faced York once more. "My lord fought with valor and dignity and died a knight's death." Christopher uttered the words to protect Hasdale's memory, but he didn't believe them. Hasdale was butchered; it was an act as despicable and grotesque as the murder of Baines.

A knight's death had two meanings: dying heroically on the battlefield, which was what you told the poor man's relatives and passed on over the years, and the truth—that he died over something that should have been solved with words instead of weapons, something like revenge, or greed.

"So you didn't see it," York said.

Better to let the knight think that than get into a telling of the grisly tale. "You—you're looking for a squire?"

York breathed deeply through his nose. "Ah, yes. Why I'm here. Enough gossiping, eh? I've no time to put you to the test. I intend to joust today. Are you ready to meet the challenge?"

"That I am, sir."

York shooed Christopher away with his hand. "Then go on, boy. Prepare yourself!"

Christopher spun away from the knight, but before he would race into the stable, climb the loft, and don his gambeson and riding boots, he paused before Orvin, grabbed one of the old man's hands with both of his, and mouthed silently, "Thank you."

Orvin covered Christopher's hands with his free palm, and returned a genuine, if not exceedingly wrinkled, grin. "I'll come to watch you."

"Please do," Christopher said. He broke away and arrowed toward the stable.

13

It was the Feast of the Assumption of the Virgin Mary, and the tournament would commence immediately after matins and mass were heard. Christopher rode next to York on a black-and-brown rounsey that York promised he would replace. Christopher was glad for that; the other squires would either have coursers or destriers.

They followed the path that swept around the castle, ribboned through the wood, and led to the practice field. As they reached the ramparts of the castle, Christopher was able to look down and take in the spectacle in one magnificent breath.

The sun-drenched practice field had been converted into the tourney ground, and at least five score of tents were pitched in rows on the north and south sides of the field. White splashes of color dotted the brown field, and the tiny forms of people and horses bustled among them.

In the center of the field, a long, rectangular

stretch of land served as the jousting ground. Arms racks stood on the east and west ends. Many of the racked lances bore the banners and pennons of the first knights who would joust.

The main tent, which Christopher guessed shaded Devin, Uryens, and King Arthur, was centered on the north side; its great dimensions and bright blue fabric made it easily distinguishable. To the right and left of the main tent were the hastily erected grandstands, long wooden daises covered with rows of benches borrowed from the great hall. The stands were beginning to fill with excited tourneygoers.

"I've never entered a tournament this grand," York said. "So many competitors. I wonder how long I'll last."

They descended the ramparts, traveled slowly through the wood, and came into the swarming throng of the practice field.

Their first stop was the herald's tent, where York was placed on the list of knights to joust. The heralds, donning the blue livery of Lord Devin, would not tell him who his competitor was; he would find out when they called him onto the field. They did say his turn would come late in the afternoon.

As they exited the tent, York said, "We've a lot of time. We'll inspect arms in my tent, and then get something to eat. I'm going to fetch your mount now. I'll meet you." York reined his courser to the left and trotted off.

Christopher heeled his rounsey in the opposite direction. He passed an open stretch of grass where two knights made practice tilts at a shield mounted on a counterbalance. The first knight's lance pushed the shield around while the second one missed, and he swore loudly. Then Christopher traversed a narrow path between a long row of tents. He searched for York's pennon—an argent flag deviced with a sable falcon—flying from one of the tent tops. He came to the end of the path and saw it opened into a clearing on the left, more tents on the right.

The clearing was a target field, and it was here the archers would hold their own competition. A hundred yards away, a dozen straw-filled butts rose knee high, spaced some three yards from each other. Christopher sensed the real games had not begun; the atmosphere was light. Crossbowmen and longbowmen joked with each other, took quick aim, and fired random shots at the butts, warming their fingers and stretching out their strings. A food merchant's cart was parked nearby, and tankards of ale were filled and handed out to a group of bowmen. Christopher spotted Doyle among the drinkers. He directed his rounsey toward the group.

Doyle caught Christopher's approach on the periphery and turned his head. "Where have you been?"

Christopher climbed down from his mount as Doyle left the group and joined him. "I told you I would find a knight to serve—with a little help from Orvin."

"Who is he?"

"Lord York."

"I've heard of him. He serves Lord Woodward. You've done well."

"Thank you." Christopher glanced at the target field. "Have you entered this competition?"

Doyle nodded. "I'm hoping to win at least one day's laurels."

"You will," Christopher said. "But don't let the ale sway your aim."

Doyle smirked, then took a rebellious sip from his tankard. "I've asked a few, and unfortunately there is no competition for squires. But I think you will be competing in a different game today." Doyle craned his neck southward and gestured with his head toward a tent, its flaps pulled open.

Inside the shelter, Christopher made out the form of a dark-haired girl sitting with a bowman on a short bench. He squinted, and saw it was Brenna and Innis.

"He's boastful, that one," Doyle said.

"Can you beat him?" Christopher asked with all seriousness.

"Probably."

Christopher grabbed Doyle by his tunic collar. "No, you have to beat him."

Doyle smiled. "The trick is to make him beat himself. That I can do."

Christopher's heart suddenly said hello to his stomach as he saw Brenna and Innis get up from the bench and duck out of their tent. They started toward him.

"You exchange the bitter pleasantries and leave the rest to me." Doyle licked his lips, as if preparing his mouth for the verbal clash.

"Good day, Christopher," Brenna said, as she and Innis stopped before them.

Christopher smiled his hello. It pained him so much to see Brenna with Innis that he knew his voice would betray his feelings. He would remain silent. His jealousy would not flatter him.

"Serving a knight today, are you?" Innis asked.

Christopher nodded.

"What's the matter, lost your voice?" Innis begged to be beaten.

"Quiet reserve is a skill many cannot master," Doyle said.

"You're Doyle, aren't you?"

"Yes, *varlet.*" Doyle made sure the boy knew who outranked whom.

"I guess it was nice of your sergeant to let you compete today. I heard you lost your bow privileges. Something to do with time off to come to our castle?" Innis looked to Brenna, expecting her to enjoy the reproof as much as he did, but Brenna was not smiling; in fact, her eyes had not left Christopher since she and Innis had stepped from the tent.

Christopher had trouble meeting Brenna's gaze, but in the flashes that he did, he sensed there was something there. He had assumed she wanted to be with Innis, and had not questioned her feelings back at Uryens's castle. But now her expression was lit with her longing, and it renewed his passion and his pain.

"It was good of him," Doyle agreed, "so that I could teach a few boys here. Many of you have not refined your skills."

"We'll see how much you know," Innis challenged.

"I can offer you this advice. Shoot hard. Shoot with anger, for that is the way of the battlefield."

"Thanks," Innis told Doyle. "Perhaps I will." He turned his gaze on Christopher. "Good luck to you and your knight." Innis was polite, not sincere.

Christopher tipped his head forward as Innis pulled Brenna away, back to their bench inside the tent.

Brenna looked over her shoulder at him, and he wanted to see the pleading in her eyes so much that he wasn't sure if it was really there. She was melancholy; there was no imagining that. He had to talk to her alone, but Innis kept her chained to his arm.

"I have to talk to Brenna," Christopher said tersely.

"You'll get your chance," Doyle answered. "Innis will try much too hard today. His rage will unbalance him. He will become obsessed with winning. And his mind will be fixed on that."

"So when do I see her? I've a knight to serve, remember?" Christopher's hopes tore at the seams.

"I'll fetch you when the time is right. We'll make it work. Where is your tent?" Doyle's determined face consoled Christopher.

"I'm still looking for it," he said. "An argent pennon with a sable falcon."

"I think I know where it is. Come on."

Christopher grabbed the reins of his rounsey and

followed Doyle away from the archers' field toward a cluster of tents on the perimeter of the north side of the practice field. As they walked, they passed a pair of jugglers who practiced their routine, anlaces tumbling in the air over each of their heads.

A short squire Christopher dimly recognized fitted a gold-and-red horse trapping over a destrier that stood behind a blue-striped tent. The animal bucked as the squire pulled the hood over the horse's head, then settled down as its eyes and ears were centered in and through the hood's holes. The squire gave Doyle and Christopher a passing nod, then shouted "Wait!" as they were about to move on. "You're Christopher!"

Christopher eyed the squire once more; a name still evaded him. "Yes."

The boy ran over to them, and Christopher could not take his gaze off the boy's ears; they protruded from his head like the small wings of a starling in flight. "I'm Leslie. I trained with you. I trained with you both. I had heard you'd come back, Doyle. But Christopher. I thought you were dead."

"I will be if I don't meet my knight now," Christopher said playfully. "I'm mad at myself for not remembering you. How could I have forgotten those ears!"

Leslie grinned, tugging on his left ear self-consciously. "Well, good luck. Perhaps this evening we can talk?"

"Perhaps. St. George be with you today, Leslie."

Christopher and Doyle smiled, then moved on.

They found York's tent, and, upon seeing that York had already arrived, Doyle smartly exited. "Remember, I'll come for you."

Before going inside the tent, Christopher paused to examine the black destrier tied to the left tent pole next to York's. The horse was slightly smaller than the knight's, making it a perfect match for Christopher. He patted the animal's head and the mount whinnied softly. Then he moved along the side of the horse and scrutinized the saddle. March and Torrey were alive and well and still producing seats of marginal quality. Christopher almost laughed out loud when he saw the careless stitching and wrong-sized pommel. He tied his rounsey next to the destriers, parted one of the tent flaps, and moved out of the scorching sun to join York.

"I saw you with your friends," York said. He had stripped down to his breeches, shirt, and gambeson, and did not look up from the silver greave he was inspecting. "Perhaps you and the archer could exchange skills."

"I'll have him teach me, though you should not expect much."

"Your modesty does you credit. Like your new mount?"

"Very much so."

"She's only borrowed—so be easy on her." York set the greave down among the other pieces of his armor. "We're off to the king's tent."

14

They found the high-backed chairs of the main tent comfortable, and Christopher and York spent most of the day sitting, eating, and watching the tournament. Christopher felt uneasy with the idea that behind him were the king, Lord Uryens, and Lord Devin. Once, he looked over his shoulder, simply out of curiosity, and the king's eyes met his. Shaken, he looked away, and concentrated on the games.

The jousting matches went as follows:

> Sir Woodward versus Sir Carney: Sir Carney unhorsed.
> Sir Jarvis versus Sir Gauter: Sir Gauter unhorsed.

Sir Ector versus Sir Bryan: both lances broken.
Sir Richard versus Sir Bors: Sir Bors unhorsed.
Sir Cardew versus Sir Allan: both unhorsed.

When the sun touched the banner that flew from the top of the keep, York and Christopher left the main tent and returned to York's.

Christopher helped his lord into the link-mail hauberk, then fitted and buckled the knight's breast-plate around him. Next came the upper and lower vambraces that protected his arms, then the couters over his elbows. York slipped his hands into his gauntlets while Christopher finished adjusting the pauldrons that covered York's shoulders. A steel tasset shielded the knight's upper hips, then Christopher fetched and dressed York with a pair of cuisses for the lower hips. The poleyns that hid the knight's knees gave Christopher a little trouble as the bindings were worn. He reinforced them with extra strips of leather he cut from the tie of a riding bag. The greaves went on quickly and the sabatons, recently purchased by the knight, fit over York's riding boots perfectly.

York gave Christopher a surcoat which bore his coat of arms. The livery fit well, and Christopher felt awed to be displaying the sable falcon across his chest. York donned a similar surcoat over his breastplate.

Outside, York helped Christopher fit the trapper over the armored destrier; it too bore York's coat of arms. The white fabric draped down to the destrier's beige cannons.

Christopher slipped a saddle cloth over the horse, then heaved up the saddle. "If I may," Christopher said, regarding the seat, "the workmanship here is not what you deserve."

"Orvin told me you were a leatherdresser's son."

"The next time you commission a saddle, take me with you."

"I will."

Christopher helped York onto the destrier. It took three tries, but finally the knight was able to swing his weighted leg over the horse. "I suspect I will not get up if I'm unhorsed," he told Christopher.

"Do try, lord."

"Ha! Of course I will."

Christopher fetched York's lance and leaned it against his mount. This was only an ornamental pole, used to fly York's pennon, and would not be used in competition. The knight's shield was a long, rectangular heater, and it, too, bore York's arms in paint. Christopher picked up the escutcheon, then slipped his arms under the guige, effectively suspending the shield around his back, archer style.

Stifling a groan under the weight, Christopher mounted his destrier. Knight and squire trotted slowly down the path toward the jousting field. The heads of other knights and squires preparing armor and arms outside their tents turned, and some shouted their wishes of good fortune. If there was anything good about being a knight, this was it. To be treated with high respect and to feel important, loved, and admired. To don colorful livery and look larger than life.

The ride to the jousting field was too short, for in the fleeting moments that passed, Christopher savored his duty as squire. Yes, he was on parade in front of peers who might carp at him, but all the while he found himself smiling.

They were met at the west end of the jousting field by a young herald. The herald nodded to the four trumpeters who stood centered on the north side. The men put their horns to their mouths and sounded three short notes, followed by a higher, longer fourth one.

When the trumpeting had echoed away into the hills, the herald announced: "York of Shores." And then came the blazon, a description of York's coat of arms for the audience. "Argent. With sable falcon."

Another herald, some two hundred yards to the east, signaled to the trumpeters, and again, the notes resounded. The herald announced York's competitor: "Duke Edward of Somerset." Then the duke's blazon: "Or. With gules phoenix."

"See you on the other end," York said with a wink. He untucked his great helm from under his arm, removed the bascinet from inside it, slipped the close-fitting caplike helmet on first, then topped it with the helm.

"You will," Christopher said. He lifted a fresh lance from the pole arms rack, checked it for cracks, then handed it to York. As his lord steadied the lance, resting the butt of the pole on the hook attached to his right breastplate, Christopher kicked his destrier into a trot toward the east end of the field. Duke Edward's squire came toward him, and Christopher was surprised to see Leslie.

"Well this is fate," Leslie said. "At least we're not at each other's throats like most of the others."

The two boys passed, and Christopher shouted over his shoulder, "I still wish your lord luck."

"And luck to yours!" Leslie returned.

Christopher neared the duke of Somerset. He would take up his position behind the duke, standing ready with a fresh lance for York.

The duke's helm concealed his face. If Christopher were able to see Edward, he might be able to find some flaw there, some sign of weakness on the duke's face that would ease the tension in him and make him more confident in York's abilities. As it was, he knew York was a great fighter, but the duke appeared equally adept. Christopher noted the small movements Edward made, the way he rolled his lance, checking it himself for cracks and finding the perfect grip on the pole. As he passed the duke, he saw the man crane his helmeted head up to regard him. The duke's head jerked back for a second, and his destrier shook its head and neighed as Edward had accidentally tugged left on his reins.

Christopher knew he couldn't have startled the man, but for some reason the duke had acted so. "Sorry to disrupt you, lord."

The duke looked over his shoulder at Christopher, but did not answer. Edward's gaze then switched to the tourney ground ahead.

Two abbots came from the side of the field, each one blessing a jouster. Christopher could tell by the way Edward's abbot fired off his Latin that the man had been doing it all day, and there was something missing in the words: emotion.

As the abbots left the field, York raised his lance to signal he was ready. The duke did the same, then all eyes fell upon King Arthur, who rose from his seat in the center of the main tent and walked to the edge of the dais. He thrust his fist in the air. Christopher swallowed. The fist came down. Both knights kicked their mounts, and the horses galloped toward each other.

There was no dividing wall on this field, which made the competition all the more dangerous. A collision of horses would prove deadly.

But York and Edward were expert riders, and tilted toward each other unwaveringly. The sharpened tips of their lances flashed a moment in the sunlight before the knights connected.

Klang!

From his angle, Christopher could not see where York's lance had struck the duke's body, but he could see that the duke's lance first touched York's shield, then slid over it to stab York in his pauldron-covered shoulder. York fell back off his destrier and hit the ground, head and shoulder first. A cheer erupted from the audience as the still-mounted duke circled around his fallen opponent.

Christopher heeled his steed into a gallop. As he drew closer to York, he saw that his lord lay flat on his back, unmoving. Everything that was Christopher trembled as he jumped down from his destrier and fell on his knees before York. Gently, he lifted his lord's head and pulled off the helm.

York's face was ashen, his eyes closed. Christopher put his ear to his lord's mouth, but someone pulled him away by the shoulders.

Lord Woodward assumed Christopher's position over York. "Not you. Not you, York." Woodward's voice was weighted with anguish, his clean-shaven face wan and creased with grief.

Christopher stood, his eyes stinging with tears. *It must be my fault. Maybe I'm cursed. Hasdale, Garrett, and now York. God, help me to understand this.*

Christopher saw Duke Edward at the herald's tent, making sure his victory was properly recorded and his next match scheduled. Then Edward rode off toward the first row of tents with Leslie in tow. Leslie turned sympathetic eyes on Christopher and mouthed the words, "I'm sorry," before disappearing with his master.

The tournament was halted for the day. It was late anyway, some argued, but even if it were early, Christopher thought it should have stopped—out of respect for York.

Stiff with sorrow, Christopher rode slowly back toward Orvin's stable. He could not think of anything; his mind was folded in darkness. He carried York's lance, the pennon fluttering in the wind. For a moment, he looked up at it, at the falcon.

15

For the next four days, Duke Edward of Somerset took the laurels, defeating a grand total of thirty-nine opponents. There were many injuries along the way, but the only fatality was York. York's death seemed more than an accident to Christopher, and he fell grew more somber as the tourney progressed. It didn't help matters that the man who defeated York kept winning.

"You're not a curse, young patron saint," Orvin told him as they sat in the grandstand and watched the opening joust of the sixth and final day of the games. "You accuse me of running away from my son's death. But look who runs now. Doyle has come for you twice, and yet you refuse to see him. He tells me he's trying to bring you and Brenna together. But here you sit, wallowing, blaming yourself for things you could not have changed."

"But isn't that the point," Christopher said, staring at his sandals. "Why can't we change them?"

"What is life without death? What is good without evil? There must be something to oppose the other; otherwise, I believe, neither exists."

Christopher shrugged. "So what does your sky say about me now?" He tilted his head back and eyed the passing puffs of white with cynicism.

Orvin was about to speak, but the charging of horses on the jousting field thieved the old man's attention.

Duke Edward and Sir Jarvis tilted at each other, and when their lances crashed into each other's shields, both men were unhorsed.

The audience went to its feet. It was the first time during the tourney that Duke Edward had been taken down. Christopher and Orvin jockeyed for a better look.

Jarvis got to his feet first, took a mace from his

squire, then circled right around his opponent. Edward rose with the aid of Leslie, and was handed his mace. Jarvis ripped off his great helm, bore his clenched teeth, then lunged forward.

Edward ducked away from the blow and brought his mace around Jarvis's back in repartee; sharp spikes connected with Jarvis's gorget. Jarvis stumbled forward but did not fall. He pivoted and faced Edward once more.

As if powered by the force of a hundred charging men, Edward ran toward Jarvis, feinted right, then hooked his mace onto Jarvis's and tugged it from Jarvis's grip. The weapon flew a short distance then fell to the ground. The audience wowed. With his opponent unarmed, Edward advanced. Jarvis's squire attempted to slip between the knights and feed Jarvis a broadsword, but Edward turned and put himself in the squire's way. In the second that Jarvis flicked his gaze upon his squire, Edward brought down his mace. The spiked ball swiped past Jarvis's cheek, and the man fell onto his back, bleeding profusely.

Edward stepped up to Jarvis and put one of his sabatoned feet on the man's chest. He lifted his mace over his head, about to finish his opponent.

"I concede," Jarvis yelled. "I concede."

Shouts and guffaws came from the audience. Edward lowered his weapon.

Orvin turned to Christopher, shaking his head. "I tell you that knight is unbeatable. I wish Arthur's Lancelot were jousting. Only he would defeat the duke, it seems."

Christopher started to leave. Orvin snatched his shirtsleeve.

"Where are you going?" the old man asked.

"I've been thinking. Maybe I should talk to Doyle. And Brenna."

"Grieve, yes. But live your life." Orvin's advice and compassion were welcome now.

"I once swore to myself I wouldn't rebuild the past. But she keeps haunting me."

"As she should. But don't look—"

"Too deeply. I know all about it," Christopher said.

He shouldered and elbowed his way out of the grandstand and started down a row between tents that he guessed would take him near the archers' field. The shields of victorious knights hung from spathas stuck in the ground outside the colorful shelters. No taps of challenge would be made on the shields now. All competitors had met once, and the final jousts would take place before sundown. Christopher had once been excited about the tournament, but now it only soured him. It was good to focus on something else. The past four days had been miserable. York's funeral pyre had prompted Christopher to tell Orvin about the many others, and how horrible and ugly the world was and how everything amounted to nothing, to death. He lingered on his guilt and nothing else, and Orvin's many words of wisdom reverberated in unhearing ears.

He turned down another row of tents, and saw the archery field at the end. Christopher's step increased. He wasn't sure if the timing would be right, but he marched with determination. If Innis was there, he would tell the varlet he wished to speak with Brenna alone—and if the varlet objected, well, he would leave it up to Brenna. She might be a serf, but she had the right to decide to whom she wanted to talk. Still, there was the fear that she did not want to talk to him. But he remembered her eyes, the way she looked back at him the last time. His confidence level rose.

Four lines of archers took turns shooting arrows with longbows at the butts. Two sergeants standing on the immediate right and left of the field shouted scores to a herald borrowed from the jousting tournament. The herald sat on a bench behind the shooters, scribbling with a feather pen.

Christopher saw Doyle on the end of the far left line. Hoping the sergeants did not notice him, he sneaked behind Doyle. "Where is she, Doyle?"

Doyle recognized Christopher's voice and did not look back. "She went to fetch Innis his lucky quiver in their tent. Can you believe that? A lucky quiver?"

"Are you beating him?"

"Yes, but not by much."

Christopher searched the lines to his right and saw Innis standing behind two archers, three more waiting to his rear. The varlet had not seen him yet. "Thanks." Christopher turned away.

"Hey," Doyle called, then turned to face him. "I'm sorry about York."

Christopher nodded solemnly.

"YOUR TURN, DOYLE! WHAT ARE YOU WAITING FOR?"

Startled, Doyle faced his target, nocked an arrow under the near-demonic gaze of the sergeant, then pulled back one hundred pounds of draw.

Christopher paused to watch Doyle's shot. The arrow arced in the air and touched the ring of the bull's-eye, but was a finger's length off-center. The sergeant called off the score as Doyle turned away, his face registering nothing.

"Was that good?" Christopher asked.

"All right. Maybe enough to keep me ahead of the varlet." Doyle gestured with his head toward Innis's tent. Christopher directed his attention there: Brenna was coming out. "Better hurry," Doyle urged.

Christopher hustled away from Doyle and double-timed toward Brenna. She stopped when she noticed him, and the color flushing her cheeks said she was glad to see him. She carried Innis's lucky quiver, a gaudy, bejeweled pouch which, by the way she held it, must be heavy. Christopher took the quiver out of her hands; indeed it was weighty. "Will you talk to me?"

"Innis needs his quiver." Her tone implied she wasn't trying to get rid of him, only obeying a wish of the varlet's.

"Can it wait?"

She nodded. "Come on." She led him back into their tent, and once inside, closed the flaps. "Sit."

It was private and comfortable, and the bench had a thin, straw-filled pillow over it. She offered him a bowl of fruit, but Christopher was not hungry. She took a seat on a bench opposite his and shifted her gaze from him to the tent floor, then back again. He knew she was nervous, but she couldn't be more wool-mouthed than he was.

"What did you want to talk about?" she asked coyly.

"I guess, first, I wanted to apologize for not saying good-bye when I left the castle."

"Accepted."

He could not think of the next thing to say. She accepted his apology too quickly. If she had argued with him, blamed him for something, then their arguing would have kept them talking. But she made it too easy—and too hard. What did he want to tell her? That he still loved her? That he wished to court her once more? That she haunted his mind? That he kept running away, yet kept coming back to her?

Yes. But how could he articulate those notions without sounding like a poor, lost boy begging for love?

"What else did you want to talk about?" He sensed her prodding, but needed it.

"I—this is difficult. I wanted to know if there's any chance, well, you know, if we—" Christopher sighed; he hated the sound of his voice.

I'm sorry, Christopher. But I love Innis, he heard her answer in his mind.

Brenna's eyes were glassy and reflective. "Remember that saddle you made for Orvin's mule? I kept it for a long time after you were gone. Finally, I sold it. But you came back."

"I'm sorry."

She rose, moved across the tent, and sat on the bench next to him. "No, don't be." She palmed his cheek, pulled his lips toward hers. She closed her eyes and kissed him softly, then pulled back. "I can't forget what I felt for you."

"What of Innis? Do you love him?"

She exhaled with frustration. "I don't know."

"Brenna! My turn came and went. Where is my . . ." Innis's voice trailed off as he entered the tent and saw them. "What is this?"

Christopher and Brenna sprang to their feet as Innis marched up to Christopher and came nose-to-nose with him.

Christopher stood before a fork in the road. He could go left, initiating an argument with Innis, which by all accounts would evolve into a challenge. Or he could go right, bite his tongue, remain calm, and let Innis do the shouting. That path would make him appear more attractive to Brenna. Innis would be the screaming monster, he the innocent boy.

He went right and pursed his lips.

"Christopher wanted to talk to me," Brenna said.

"*Inside* our tent with the flaps *closed?*" Innis's cheeks were crimson, his eyes brimming with jealousy.

"He's been through a lot," she argued.

Innis tried to stare Christopher down, but Christopher knew how to turn himself off at such times. He remembered the way Garrett and Mallory had first looked at him. He had not let their eyes, nor would he let Innis's, bother him. He stared back and his deadpan enraged Innis even more.

"I do not believe a word I'm hearing," Innis cried. He looked to Brenna. "You've been seeing him ever since he returned—haven't you?" His words were definite, packing more accusation than question.

"No!" Brenna shot back.

Innis took a step closer to her. "Yes you have!"

Brenna shook her head, no. She bit her lower lip nervously.

In a flash, Innis backhanded Brenna across her face.

And in another, Christopher bounded for the left path and unleashed his anger.

I'm sorry, Brenna. I'm going to look ugly. But I won't let him hurt you anymore.

Christopher vised both hands around Innis's throat. Innis tried to face Christopher, but the force of Christopher's grip was too much.

The varlet gasped.

Christopher pushed Innis forward, and the varlet tugged on Christopher's hands, trying to pry them off his neck. Christopher pushed a little harder and Innis stumbled into one of the benches. Both he and the varlet fell over the wooden seat and slammed onto the tent floor. Brenna screamed her futile protest.

Christopher lost his grip on Innis's throat. Innis kicked himself away from Christopher, backed up, and got to his feet. Christopher rolled over and stood.

Innis looked to the dagger sheathed and attached to a thick leather belt on the floor near his spare bow. Christopher noted the weapons and moved to put himself between them and Innis.

The varlet's back was to the tent entrance, and as Christopher edged left, closer to the weapons, he saw Doyle slip through the tent flaps and put a finger over his lips. Doyle slipped up behind Innis, wrapped his left arm around Innis's throat, then used his free hand to snag Innis's right arm and pull it behind the varlet's back. "Enough," Doyle said.

Christopher relaxed his fists, then took a deep breath. He gazed at Brenna, who stood, wringing her hands. The soft skin of her left cheek was cherrying with the imprint of Innis's hand.

"Let me go!" Innis shouted. "Damn you, Doyle, let me go!"

"He needs a bit of water to cool him off." Doyle dragged Innis outside the tent. The varlet's wailing continued.

"I don't want to stay here now," Brenna said.

Christopher wiped perspiration from his head. "Come on."

16

They returned to Orvin, who still sat in the grandstand watching the tourney. The old man was delighted to see Brenna. "Once again I am blessed with a vision of beauty. You, raven maid, are indeed a sight for sore, weathered eyes."

Brenna blushed. Christopher shook his head and rolled his eyes.

"Sit down," Orvin said. "You're in time for the final joust. Lord Woodward is the last knight to go against the duke."

Duke Edward and Lord Woodward were announced by the trumpeters, blazoned by the heralds, then blessed by the abbots. Lord Devin stepped down from the dais under the main tent and walked out to the center of the jousting field. He faced the audience. "This joust will decide the champion!"

The crowd responded to Devin's excited words with their own cheers.

Behind him, Christopher could hear the wagering. Though forbidden, the betting on combatants occurred at every tourney. "If I had a few deniers to bet," Christopher said, "I'd put them on Lord Woodward."

"He does have a personal stake in this contest," Orvin observed. "I pray he does not foster revenge in his heart, for surely that will break him."

Hasdale's death was a testament to that truth, Christopher knew.

Devin continued, "The victor will take my daughter Marigween's hand in marriage. God bless the fighters!" Devin marched off the field.

"Everyone already knows the champion gets Marigween," Christopher said.

"Lord Devin is about to lose his daughter," Orvin said. "He wants all the fathers here to share his pain."

Lord Devin stood on the edge of the dais, his arm raised, his gaze flicking from Woodward to Edward. His arm dropped.

Hooves sank in the churned quagmire of the field as each knight leaned into his lance and searched for an opening in his opponent's defenses. Conditions had worsened on the field, and Christopher saw how slowly the knights tilted at each other. In effect, it made the contest more interesting; it would be easier to unhorse an opponent since each knight had more time to hook his lance.

The impact sounded: a short, single *ka-ching!*

Duke Edward landed on his back, sinking deeply into the mud; his cutlet, backplate, and the link-mail fauld covering his rump became encased in the thick, brown ooze. The duke sat up, shaking his helmed head clear of the blow.

Lord Woodward fell on his right side, his arm still hooked under his lance. From the way his arm had twisted, Christopher knew Woodward must have broken a bone. Woodward rolled over onto his rump and sat up. He tugged off his great helm with his left hand, then remained on the ground, cradling his right arm.

The knights had decided on broadswords if both were unhorsed, and Leslie rushed over to the duke and handed Edward his weapon. The duke stood, heaving up his sword with both hands.

Woodward's squire, a worried blond boy, had trouble getting Woodward to his feet. He reached under the knight's pauldrons and tried to pick him up, but the effort was to no avail. The squire heaved again as the duke advanced.

The sight of Edward coming toward him with his broadsword raised must have overridden Woodward's pain, Christopher suspected, for Woodward wrapped his left arm over his squire's neck and fought his way up. Once standing, he one-handed the heavy broadsword delivered by his squire and balanced himself, ready to defend.

Edward struck the first blow, a slow horizontal swipe that Woodward parried at the last possible second. Christopher saw Woodward grimace.

The tension inside Christopher reached a breaking point. He had to get down onto the field. Woodward's squire was inept.

Without warning, Christopher walked in front of Brenna and Orvin and hopped down from the grandstand. He heard them call after him, but the voices seemed part of a distant reality. What was real right now was getting near the battle. He threaded through more spectators and found a position next to the trumpeters, who were lined up a mere six yards from the combatants. No one noticed Christopher's approach. All eyes were trained on the field.

Woodward, still nursing his right arm, lunged forward in a weak riposte. His sword was blocked by Edward's, but continued on, slipping over the duke's blade; the weapon came crashing down on the breaths of Edward's helm.

But as Woodward withdrew his sword, the duke made his own riposte, an abrupt, upward thrust. Blade met blade, and Woodward's broadsword was flung out of his grip.

"Mace!" Christopher shouted to Woodward's nervous squire. The straw-haired boy's gaze darted over the weapons lined up on the small rack near him. The squire panicked.

Christopher ran to the rack, scooped up the mace, then hurried onto the field. Woodward regarded him curiously for a second, but then offered his hand. Christopher tossed the knight the weapon.

Woodward dropped the mace. He attempted to pick it up, but the duke reached it first and kicked it away. The duke stormed after the unarmed Woodward, his broadsword drawn up over his shoulder.

Christopher reacted again, sprinting behind the duke and retrieving Woodward's lost sword. Christopher circled around the men and found his way to a position behind Woodward. As the knight continued to recoil from the duke, he reached Christopher, who handed him his broadsword. For a moment, Woodward's eyes thanked him. Christopher jogged to the side of the field.

The knights attacked each other again, this time much more aggressively. The duke made a flurry of lunges, each countered by Woodward's sword. Woodward backed away with every slash but fought with stiff, unyielding determination. Christopher sensed, however, that Woodward was tiring.

It was the show of shows for the audience. There were so many shouts behind Christopher that his ears rang into numbness. He shot a glance up to the main tent and saw lords Devin and Uryens on their feet, and next to them, the king. All three men were wide-eyed, and Devin beat a fist into his palm.

"You don't belong here," Christopher heard someone yell in his ear. He gazed over his shoulder and saw Woodward's squire.

"No matter," Christopher answered. "You'd best stand ready—so I don't have to help you again!"

The squire shot Christopher a dark look then and returned to his position near the weapons rack.

By now, Woodward could only defend. Duke

Edward gave him no time to strike. The duke's
lunges came from high, low, left, and right, and were
pounding, rhythmic, seemingly endless. It was clearly
an attempt to wear Woodward down, and it was
working.

In the middle of the melee, with Edward still hammering away with his broadsword, Woodward, pale
and at his end, lowered his weapon and shouted, "I
concede." He stepped back from the duke, in time to
miss a final high-to-low, left-to-right slash from his
opponent.

Duke Edward pivoted to the audience and raised
his broadsword in the air; the blade dazzled menacingly in the sunlight.

Christopher lowered his head dejectedly and
turned to walk off the field. He bumped squarely into
another knight. The knight's surcoat bore the coat of
arms of the duke, and Christopher assumed he was
one of Edward's bachelor knights. He looked up at
the man's head, saw only a great helm. The knight
tilted up his visor, and with horrid recognition,
Christopher stared into the roundness of Dallas's
face.

"Fergus is very upset with you, Christopher," the
rogue said through an ugly, gap-toothed smile. "And
Mallory, well, it is enough to say you are dead."

Christopher looked down and saw Dallas's hand
resting on the hilt of an anlace sheathed and belted at
his side. But there were too many people here. Dallas
wouldn't kill him now—would he?

Repressing his fear, Christopher sprang right, but
felt one of Dallas's thick-fingered hands wrap like a
manacle around his wrist. "No, no, Christopher. You
stay with me. We're going to watch." Dallas gestured
with his head toward the main tent.

Duke Edward stood on the field before the dais,
gazing up at Lord Devin, Lord Uryens, and King
Arthur. Lord Devin spoke: "Duke Edward of

Somerset. I declare you champion of the tourney of Shores, and, as is your right, bequeath my daughter Marigween to you."

"I accept the honor." And though the voice was muffled by the helm, it was familiar to Christopher.

His suspicions were answered as the duke removed his helmet, and a hush fell over those in the main tent.

Mallory smiled. The blue doublet centered on his headband twinkled.

The name began to drift among those who knew him: Mallory, Mallory, Mallory. Mutters, shouts, whispers, rumbles, cries; they all echoed the name with surprise and utter hatred.

Lord Devin turned to Arthur. "It cannot be! He cannot marry Marigween!"

Mallory started toward the wooden steps that would take him up to the dais.

"Stop right there, Mallory," Arthur ordered.

Mallory ignored the king. "I'm getting the crown of laurels put on my head whether you like it or not, Arthur." He faced the audience. "Who can deny my victory? Is there anyone who did not hear Woodward concede?"

Devin turned around and pulled Uryens's spatha out of his sheath. "You come up here and I'll strike you to hell!"

Mallory mounted the steps.

Christopher felt Dallas's grip tighten on his wrist. He looked to the audience, trying to pick out Orvin and Brenna. Scores of faces, none recognizable. No comfort there. He had to do something.

Both he and Dallas had free hands, but Dallas's readied an anlace. What could Christopher do with his? He tapped his foot nervously, thinking, thinking, thinking. He could pull up Dallas's hand and bite the grip off, but that might give the rogue time to work his anlace.

Wait a minute. I'm thinking. Wrong. Just act.

Christopher closed his eyes and let his body feel the way out. Though Dallas's grip seemed permanent, Christopher took a long, deep breath, rolled his wrist toward Dallas, and as he rolled he pulled away. When he felt his arm spring toward him, Christopher opened his eyes and ran.

He didn't look back to see if Dallas was pursuing; logic said he was. He bolted straight for the stairs leading to the dais.

As he charged forward, a question tugged on Christopher's mind: where were the rest of Mallory's men?

He got his answer as he mounted the stairs. Above, Mallory's band ambushed the nobles from three sides. The tent was a hurricane of arms and swords and shouts and confusion.

As he set foot on the dais, he saw Mallory and Devin trading sword strikes. Uryens fought off Fergus, blocking blows from Fergus's spatha with a helm he used as a shield.

Two more of Mallory's men fought Arthur, and for the first time Christopher set eyes on the legendary sword Excalibur. The blade sang its sweet, deadly song as it penetrated the link-mail of one of the rogues; the man fell away, freeing the blade. Arthur feinted right, then spun around and beheaded the other man.

At the rear of the tent, the wives of the great knights cowered, but Marigween found a spatha, rushed up behind Mallory, then hacked at the rogue's plated back as he engaged her father. Mallory took a swipe over his shoulder with his sword, cutting a deep gash in Marigween's arm. She dropped the spatha and screamed.

Christopher bolted for the fallen weapon. He picked it up, then turned and helped Marigween over to a nearby bench. "Get under here!"

Marigween complied, squeezing her small, lithe

frame under the wood. She clutched her wound, and blood stained her fingers.

Dallas reached the top of the stairs, his anlace drawn. His gaze met Christopher's.

Christopher told himself that all that was now happening was nothing. Nothing compared to that night on the Mendips, when he had been surrounded by the Saxons. But all around Christopher were the same sights and sounds: blades flashed in the air; metal *pang*ed on metal; men gasped and howled; and then, always, the blood. He hated all of it, was scared by it, would not accept it—but knew he had to act within it.

He was going to kill. But this time it would be Celtic blood that he shed. If not, he wouldn't have to worry about anything ever again.

Christopher remained on the defensive, dodging each of the bulky rogue's swipes with sharp, agile movements. It was anlace against broadsword, and Dallas would have to get close to kill him. That was Christopher's advantage. But Dallas was as handy with a blade as he was with a longbow; he would try something else.

A pair of men locked in combat fell over the benches behind Christopher, and a bloodcurdling scream followed the cacophony of armor and wood. Distracted by the sounds, Christopher saw Dallas's blade only on the periphery. As he adjusted his full attention to the rogue, he saw Dallas finger the blade end of the anlace with his thumb and index finger. He cocked his arm and let the blade fly toward Christopher.

His spatha went up to deflect the tumbling anlace— but Christopher missed. He felt a lightning bolt of searing pain strike his shoulder. He saw the anlace, like a horrible growth, protruding from a point just below his collarbone. He reached up, about to pull the blade out. But he looked to Dallas, whose elated expression woke as much strength as was in Christopher. He rushed forward, aiming the tip of his spatha at the crease he knew rendered every suit of armor vulnerable. The spatha slipped vertically under Dallas's pauldron, cut through link-mail and gambeson. Then Christopher heard the terrible pop of cracking ribs and felt a shudder rise up the spatha to his hand. The blade would not go in any more, but Christopher pushed harder; he scraped past Dallas's broken ribs and found the man's heart. Blood gushed over armor, and Dallas crumpled onto his back, his face twisted in agony.

Christopher's expression mirrored Dallas's as he pulled the anlace from his shoulder. The pain was so strong that he saw the world darken around the edges and suspected he was about to pass out. The flash of blackness passed, and Christopher looked down to see that the wound had not bled that badly; the blade had pierced mostly muscle.

As Christopher turned, in pain but still heady with his victory over Dallas, he saw Mallory pin Lord Devin to the floor. Devin squirmed for escape, but found none. Christopher stomped over the fallen benches and dead men, coming to Devin's aid.

Mallory placed his broadsword under Devin's chin.

Christopher dropped his spatha as his leg became caught on a bench leg. He recovered the blade and looked up.

Mallory rammed his sword into Devin's neck, then worked the blade up into Devin's head as the man gargled his last breath.

"Arthur!" Uryens yelled, having seen Devin's death while still battling Fergus. "Arthur!"

But Christopher saw that Arthur was busy with another pair of Mallory's men. Mallory had made sure that no less than two men at a time would engage the king.

Mallory turned away from the dead man under him and raised his malevolent gaze to Christopher. "I spent time in a cell because of you, boy! But at least you're here to pay for your sins."

When he had first broken away from Dallas and had run toward Mallory, Christopher had known then that a confrontation was what he wanted. He hated admitting it now because he feared he acted out of revenge. Many nights had passed during the time he had spent with Mallory, nights Christopher had plotted Mallory's murder and his own escape. He was free now, but the desire to see Mallory dead was still unrewarded, and still present. But he had to know why. Why did he want Mallory dead? To make the man pay for all his transgressions? Wasn't that revenge?

Or was it justice? Justice for the frightened girl who huddled under the bench, and for her father who lay dead. Justice for the other people Mallory had robbed and killed. Justice for Garrett.

Christopher had to make the distinction. He would fight for what was right, not to make Mallory pay for the deaths. He would detach his emotions and act. Not feel or think. Just act.

Mallory continued to taunt him verbally, but Christopher did not hear the words. He concentrated on his breathing, on letting his body do the work. The heavy spatha felt a part of his arm. His shoulder throbbed, but the pain gave way to numbness. The sweat on his upper lip and forehead cooled him, and the wetness under his arms only made them glide more gracefully. All the discomforts were friends as he let his mind go to his form. No pressure. No fear.

The sun shone into the tent from the front opening, and Christopher felt its warmth on his back. A friend watching over him; he would keep the sun there.

Mallory stood and wrenched his sword from Devin. He wiped both sides of the bloody blade across the cuisse shielding his right hip, as if he needed a clean blade to draw more blood.

Christopher let Mallory do all the preparing he
wanted. As with Dallas, he would let Mallory attack.
With several engagements still going on behind and
around them, Mallory made his first move; he feinted
right, then swiped horizontally left. Christopher coun-
terswiped, feeling the power contained in Mallory's
arms. Again, Mallory moved, hammering his blade in
a deadly downward arc that was stopped short by
Christopher's spatha. Their blades touched and seemingly stuck to each other; Mallory barreled down
while Christopher strained to hold his own.

It was a trick of Mallory's, and Christopher did not
realize it until it was too late. With their blades
locked, Mallory circled around and put the sun in
Christopher's eyes.

*Did you know, Orvin? Did you know this might
happen?*

Christopher attempted the same move, but Mallory
pulled his sword away and lashed out horizontally
once more; the broadsword's tip nicked a tiny hole
on the breast of Christopher's leather gambeson. He
assumed the en garde position, waiting for Mallory's
next strike. The rogue shifted his heavy sword from
one hand to the other, boasting his strength.

The sun's own blades of light struck over Mallory's
shoulder, cutting Christopher's vision to shreds. He
squinted, saw Mallory a moment, then whiteness,
then Mallory.

The time had come to fight by sound. Christopher
had never done it, nor believed he could. He could
surrender to the natural current of his body, acting
and reacting without thinking, but to lose a vital
sense . . . it seemed impossible.

Christopher heard the wind created by Mallory's
blade. For a moment he saw the broadsword come
out of the blinding light and razor toward his left eye.
He lifted his spatha and countered the stroke, then
fought back the desire to riposte. He had to let

Mallory beat himself. His heart kept telling him to kill the monster, but he had given control over to his body, and his body knew what to do.

He shifted his position slightly. He could see Mallory's armored feet, his greaved and cuissed legs and part of his breastplate, but higher than that—nothing. He wanted to move right or left, put the sun to his side, but fallen benches blocked both paths. Mallory knew exactly what he was doing.

The whiz of steel through air, and Christopher forced his squinting eyes fully open; all he saw were flashes of orange and yellow and white.

I'm helpless!

He gripped his spatha as tightly as he could and tipped it toward the noise, then *klang!* Mallory's blade connected with his. He'd countered the stroke without seeing it.

Another attack from Mallory, and Christopher saw the blade swiping left as Mallory's head blocked the sun. Christopher parried the lash, then used the second of shadow to finally, though nervously, riposte. He flicked his spatha over Mallory's before the rogue had time to cut it up and away. The tip of Christopher's blade cut across Mallory's forehead, tore through the rogue's bejeweled headband, then came away at the hairline. The headband fell over Mallory's back. The cut was only minor, and if Mallory felt any pain, he buried it.

The sun thrust its fiery fingers back into Christopher's eyes. And now he heard a shout behind him: "Help the boy! Sire, can you get to him?"

A clatter of swords answered. Below him, the rumble of approaching horses rose among the sword fights. He listened again, though it was hard to drown out the background noise and the sound of his own panting to focus on Mallory's blade. He stiffened, grimacing in the harsh glare.

Wishhh! Klang! He successfully countered.

Wishhh! Wishhh! Klang! Another good block.

Something about that last stroke put Christopher's body in motion. He hadn't *thought* about making an offensive blow, since he had still been in the sunlight. But that had been why his body moved. He hadn't been making futile strokes at Mallory, but accurate, measured ones. He lunged forward, felt Mallory's parry, knew the position of the rogue's blade, heard Mallory bring it around and sensed where the opening was. With his blade flatwise, he made a short stroke right, slicing horizontally through the air. He felt the blade connect with flesh. And he heard Mallory scream. The rogue fell backward onto the tent floor, and Christopher saw the damage he had done.

Mallory clutched a deep gash that curved from his earlobe to the point where his gorget protected his collarbone. Christopher's spatha had severed a large vein in Mallory's neck, and the man's lifeblood fountained through his fingers in a grotesque spray that blossomed with each beat of his heart. Christopher flinched, then turned his head away.

Semiarmored garrison men poured onto the dais from all sides, brushing past a stunned Christopher. The last three survivors of Mallory's band surrendered, but Christopher couldn't have cared. Killing made him feel bleak, and in a sense, evil. It would never get easier. He felt the desert in his mouth and tried to swallow; it hurt. Then he heard Marigween crying. He lifted his absent gaze from the tent floor, and spotted her kneeling over her father's bloody corpse. He dropped his spatha, then rushed through men and benches to be next to her.

Even through her red eyes and tearstained cheeks, Christopher could see her beauty. For one selfish moment he let it take his breath away.

She barely noticed him as he hunkered down near her. As she looked at Devin, he looked at her. And maybe it wasn't completely selfish of him to focus on her; looking at Devin would only make him sicker.

He felt a hand come to rest on his shoulder and turned to see who it was.

Arthur's eyes, green as the slopes of the Mendips, stared back. The king nodded his approval. Then he looked past Christopher. His face paled with sorrow and his eyes washed over with tears.

Christopher could not take his gaze off the man. He tracked a drop that fell from Arthur's right eye and darted for cover in the king's beard.

All the emotions Christopher had repressed during the fighting woke, and now it was all right to free them. He choked up, not only over the sight of Devin's body, but over the entire moment. Sorrow mixed with the guilt of killing and images of the happier times with Mallory. There weren't many, but the few moments he and the rogue had chuckled together were enough to make him feel horrible. But he had done the right thing. He kept telling himself that.

17

He would be *Sir* Christopher.

The great hall was set for a massive feast which would follow the ceremony. Already, the trestle tables buckled with food, and the older serfs and freemen who occupied them waited impatiently for the whole thing to be over so they could eat. The knights and nobles who sat at the front tables or up on the long dais table were more tolerant. They remembered the day they had become knights, or the times those they loved had knelt before the blade.

Christopher sensed the sympathy and restlessness of the crowd as he stood at the rear of the hall, waiting for the trumpets to announce him. Arthur had

had Christopher fitted with a suit of armor for the
knighting, and Orvin and Doyle had helped him don
it. He wasn't sure if he would make it to the other
end of the hall. The armor weighed in at nearly sev-
enty pounds, and the hauberk underneath tugged at
his bandaged shoulder, sending occasional pinpricks
of pain shooting up and down his arm. It was a magnificent suit, though, all silvery and radiant. At his
side, the broadsword Baines had given him rested in
a bejeweled sheath that was a gift from Arthur. All of
the glitter, like the parading before a joust, was the
better part of being a squire. No, *knight,* he corrected
himself.

He saw Brenna wave from a trestle table on the
right. Her family had let her stay for the ceremony,
but she would return to Gore the day after.
Christopher was not sure where he would be. The
uncertainty of his future bothered him more than it
ever had, and the confusion was sparked by something Orvin had said after helping dress him. The old
man had whispered: "Never be afraid of the truth.
Even in the face of a king!"

Never be afraid of the truth. He rubbed his sweaty
palms together, listening to more words in his mind:
*"In the name of God, of St. Michael and St. George, I
make you a knight."* How long had he dreamed of
becoming a knight? Ever since the days of living on
Leatherdressers' Row, when he had worried about
telling his parents what he wanted to do.

His father's voice came to him now, a stern warning which echoed from the past and darkened his
spirit: *"The spoils of a knight."*

He'd seen the spoils: a knight who had died a
painful and lonely death on the floor of his old house;
a lord he had been proud to serve burned and then
murdered; an enemy he had grown to understand cut
down by a man of his own blood who had truly been
the evil one. There were many more faces that would

haunt him: his father, mother, Baines. . . . The death masks fell on into darkness. The only truth in all of it was the pain.

The trumpets blew, jolting Christopher to attention. A herald announced his name: "Christopher of Shores! Step forward and become a knight!"

His armor rattled as he trudged toward Arthur, who stood below the dais in his red velvet robes, gripping the hilt of Excalibur with both hands. Moonlight shone down through the smoke hole and painted the hall silver. He glanced left and saw Doyle sitting with a group of other archers. His friend shook a fist of pride in the air. Christopher trembled.

He walked a little farther and saw Orvin seated at the end of a table. The old man touched the skin of the roasted duck plated there, then licked his finger. At the sound of his approach, Orvin turned, then raised and lowered his eyebrows; the skin on his forehead did its dance. Christopher tried to smile, but his lips would not curl.

Over two hundred people in the hall, and the only sound was his armor. He was twice relieved as he stopped before the king, once for the burden of keeping the suit moving, once for the noise it made. But those were physical dilemmas now gone. The mental burdens he carried were about to break him.

"Young man. Kneel," Arthur said curtly.

Christopher was about to say something but found himself moving to his knees, helped by the weight of his armor.

Arthur raised Excalibur over Christopher's head. "In the name of God," he began, about to touch Christopher's left shoulder with Excalibur's tip, "of St. Michael—"

Christopher's left arm sprang up and his gauntleted hand locked around the blade of Excalibur before it touched his shoulder.

A wave of murmurs rolled toward the back of the

hall and broke at the rear entrance. Christopher knew everyone in the hall was shocked. Everyone except Orvin.

"Christopher," Arthur gasped, "what's wrong?"

Christopher released his grip on the sword. Arthur withdrew. "If I may stand, my liege?"

Arthur nodded, appearing confused and more than a tinge insulted. Christopher brought one leg up, but found himself losing his balance. Doyle's father raced from his table and helped Christopher to his feet, then, like a leveret, scampered back to his seat before he was noticed by those in the rear.

"I mean you no insult, Your Majesty, but knighthood is not my true place."

Arthur frowned. "Young man, do not be modest. Perhaps you think fifteen is too young. That was the age I became king." Arthur addressed the crowd. "Was I too young?"

"NO!" was shouted back by everyone.

"Thank you." He stared at Christopher. "Do not tell me you're too young or that you think you're not worthy."

"No," Christopher said confidently, "I *am* worthy. I do not *want* to become a knight."

That last brought on another flood of talk behind Christopher.

There was no mistaking Arthur's anger. "You refuse my generosity? Dare you insult your liege in such fashion?"

Christopher trembled. How could he make Arthur understand his decision? "Forgive me, sire. I believe I have found my place in this world, have acted to the best of my ability and employed my true talents." The words were once Orvin's, but were now his.

"And what talents are those? Squiring?" Arthur asked sarcastically.

"Every man is a servant, sire. He is a servant to his heart, his mind, and to God. And each must serve as he serves best. For me, that means being a squire. There is no shame in that."

Arthur held Excalibur in one hand and stroked his beard with the other. A long moment passed before he spoke again, but when he did, his voice was softer, calmer. "At once you confuse and anger me, but now utter truths we all need to learn." Arthur put his hand on Christopher's pauldron. "If you are going to serve, then serve me. Will you be my squire, squire of the body?"

Christopher grinned. "I will."

Arthur looked up to his subjects. "Well, we have here not a knight, but the most loyal squire I'll ever find." Good-natured laughter erupted from many. Arthur raised his sword. Christopher cowered. "No fear. I can do this and still not make you knight." Christopher dropped to his knees, then raised his head, ready to accept the sword taps on his shoulders. "In the name of God, of St. Michael and St. George, I make you squire of the body of all of England."

The tension in the air snapped as the crowd applauded. Uryens stood from his seat on the long table and raised his tankard. "A toast to the squire."

Arthur leaned over and whispered in Christopher's ear, "You should face the people."

Christopher whispered back, "Can you help me?"

Arthur helped him up, and he turned to gaze upon the smiling faces and the sea of tankards held under them.

Uryens shouted behind him: "To young squire Christopher. May he serve his heart, his mind, and God to the best of his ability."

Christopher looked over his shoulder to spy Uryens; the toastmaster winked.

As he stood awash in the clanking of tankards, he found his attention wandering to the faces he knew, to his blood brother Doyle, who once again shook his fist of pride; to Orvin, who nodded knowingly, then made Christopher smile broadly with his forehead skin dance; to Brenna, whose hair caught the torch-light and moonlight just right, and whose eyes spoke an assured love. And then he saw Marigween's radiant image behind the first trestle table. Her smile brought undeniable heat to his face. He hoped Brenna had not seen him blush, and he looked to the raven maid.

No, she hadn't.

EPILOGUE

Christopher and Brenna bored holes in two pairs of shinbones given to them by an amiable hostler, then tied the bones to their boots with leather laces. Alone, they skated on the frozen pond outside March and Torrey's hut. Darkness would come soon, and most inhabitants of the castle of Shores were inside at Lord Woodward's dinner party, bathing in the warmth of cookfires, for it was the day of Christ's birth. Christopher was invited to attend, but had declined. There was something very important he had to do, and when he explained it to Woodward, the new lord of the castle understood.

Brenna's cheeks and nose were red, and the woolen coif wrapped around her head did not shield her earlobes, for they, too, were crimson.

The air was clean and fresh-smelling, and Christopher took a deep breath of it, then let the steam blow from his nose. He skated to the edge of the pond and pivoted to face Brenna. The more he looked at her, the more he hated leaving.

Her visits to the castle during the past four moons

had strengthened their bond and been the heaven in an otherwise worldly training and formation period. But now Arthur's armies were ready, and the king's campaign against the Saxons would commence on the morrow. Christopher would ride to Gore with the men-at-arms hired from Shores. Brenna would canter with them on her way home, but Christopher would not have the privacy for a proper good-bye during the journey, nor the time once they reached the castle. He suggested skating, was fond of it as a boy, and knew it was too cold for anyone else save the sentries to be out.

"Watch this," Brenna said, then glided to the middle of the pond and twirled on one bone, gesturing extravagantly with her mittened hands.

Christopher applauded, then skated up to her, balancing himself with palms on her shoulders. Then he kissed her, and felt her icy nose on his cheek. He drifted back. "You're cold!"

"I'm freezing! *You* wanted to come out here!" She shivered visibly.

It was time to tell her why. He searched for the right words, but all he came up with was a summation of the obvious: "We're back to where we started."

Brenna nodded. "This is where we first met."

Christopher surveyed the bailey. "You're right."

"Why is it that only women remember those things?"

"I remember," he lied. "That's why I wanted to—"

Her look of disbelief cut him off, but then she grinned. "I know why we're out here."

Christopher grew serious. "It's not going to stop—at least not right away. I'll come back, then have to leave again. But maybe one day I can help it end. War is so easy and peace so hard. It's going to take a lot of work."

"I know," she began, then sniffled from another chill. "But I'll be here."

"You don't have to," he urged. He knew visions of the raven maid would always rattle his heart—but he didn't want to sentence her to the loneliness, the waiting. Christopher would take the pain for both of them.

"I know what to expect," she argued. "I know how to wait, and this time I really will. And I know how to love." She shrugged. "At least I think I do."

"You do," Christopher said softly.

She looked past him, focusing far away. "I loved seeing you in front of the king that day. And your words . . . they made me so proud." Her gaze came home to his, and she touched his cheek with one of her mittens. "You're blushing," she teased.

"It's the cold," he said coyly. "Let's go inside."

They skated awkwardly arm in arm toward the lip of the pond and gingerly mounted the frozen shoreline. They sat on the hard ground and untied the bones from their boots. Once standing, they rejoined arms and started for shelter. It took a score of steps before both were used to walking again.

A north wind lashed down from the graying sky, and Brenna urged him onto the drawbridge before the keep. Chains clanked as the bridge was lifted behind them. He felt Brenna's arm shiver in his, then she tugged him as she broke into a sprint up the forebuilding's steps. They both arrived at the door, out of breath.

A blast of warm air hugged them as they rushed inside, and Christopher shuddered through a long sigh. He had to reacquaint himself with the temper of winter, as a drafty tent would be his home well into spring. But for the moment, it was good to be out of the cold.

Here is an excerpt from

SQUIRE'S BLOOD
Book Two of *The Squire Trilogy*

PROLOGUE

Christopher of Shores fell on his rump before the Saxon, his broadsword wrenched from his grip by a mighty horizontal swipe from the ax-wielding soldier. The young squire watched as the Saxon, his face streaked with blood, narrowed his eyes and hoisted his weapon over his shoulder.

For a second, Christopher saw the outline of the Saxon against the dull iron sky above the Mendip hills, saw that the barbarian wasn't much older than his own fifteen years. He wished the Saxon was much older, his reflexes slower. But most of all, he longed at this moment to be back at the stable in Shores, to have a warm, sweet loaf of bread to his lips, and have his ears filled with the amusing tales of old Orvin.

Christopher cocked his head and reached out futilely for his broadsword; the weapon lay just over an arm's length away. Every sinew in his arm tensed, and in his mind's eye Christopher saw his arm extend to the sword and his gloved fingers clench around the bejeweled hilt. With his other hand he urged his armored body toward the sword, but on the periphery of his vision, he caught a flash of metal he knew was the Saxon's battle-ax, cleaving the air. Immediately, he abandoned the idea of his weapon and thrust his body forward with both hands. The armor that Arthur had given him, the armor that was supposed to protect the squire of the body, now permitted him to move dooming inches instead of hopeful yards. He looked back at the Saxon with eyes acknowledging deep terror.

Strangely, as the Saxon's ax dropped, his body followed it. He collapsed onto his stomach and his head bounced once off the frozen winter ground. An arrow broke the flat wool landscape of the Saxon's back; the shaft's blue feather fletching marked it as Celt.

Some twenty yards away, on a hillock that put him six feet above Christopher, Doyle lowered his longbow. With casual grace, he reached down and unfastened a leather flagon from his belt, pulled out the hemp stoppering it, then tossed his head back and drank. The clatter of hooves behind him caused Doyle to choke and expel what Christopher knew was ale. He hustled down the slope while refastening his flagon.

At once Christopher was ashamed for needing help and thankful for the presence of his blood brother. But Doyle belonged with the rest of the archers in the Vaward Battle group led by Sir Lancelot. What was he doing here?

"One of the king's squires alone? Why aren't you at Arthur's side?" Doyle asked, his eyes never leaving the slopes around them. The battle roared just over the eastern rise, and threatened to move closer.

Christopher pushed himself to a sitting position, tried to rock his body forward to stand, but found it impossible.

"Get up," Doyle said curtly.

Christopher reached out a gauntleted hand. "Help."

Doyle's gaze lowered to Christopher's. He frowned. "The archers in my group still think you're mad to have turned down knighthood, but looking at you now, I can see why you wish to remain a squire." Doyle took Christopher's hand and pulled him up.

Christopher's armor rustled loudly and slid out of place. He adjusted the metal fauld digging into his waist, then the couters covering his elbows. "Every squire has his misfortunes."

"Misfortunes—"

"—put you on your shield, I know," Christopher finished. "Why aren't you with the rest of the Vaward?"

"Answer my question first," Doyle said.

"We were surrounded by a Saxon cavalry and I was separated from Arthur. Someone unhorsed me, and this man"—Christopher pointed to the dead Saxon—"pursued me here."

"He chased you?"

"He would not engage anyone else."

"Maybe he knew you," Doyle said. Then, much darker, "You did spend a year with them."

"Not *them*. I served a *Celt* who led Saxons. Besides, I don't think Garrett's army still exists. At least not intact. Most of them probably went home across the narrow sea."

"Maybe some stayed. Maybe he was one of them," Doyle argued. "Maybe he holds some anger for you. Who knows?"

Christopher moved to the dead Saxon, bent down, rolled the body onto its side, then stared into the enemy soldier's face. He shook his head. "I'm sure I've never seen this man before."

"Look," Doyle said, pointing to a small leather pouch which had detached itself from the dead Saxon's belt. Doyle hunkered down, picked up the pouch, opened it, and dumped its contents into his hands: a half dozen shillings. "This is a lot of money for a Saxon—especially when he has no use for it." Doyle untied the man's leather gambeson and checked the shirt below. There was a silvery neck ring around the man's throat. "He's wearing a torc."

"So he's carrying our money and wearing our jewelry. He stole it. He likes it," Christopher suggested.

"Maybe," Doyle said, then stood. "Or maybe he's not who we think he is. Perhaps he really *is* a Celt."

Christopher was about to snicker at Doyle, but the five mounted Saxons, who rose over the patchy brown hogback one hundred yards to the north, made him change his mind.

PART ONE

AT SWORD'S POINT

1   Christopher picked up his broadsword, then darted for the dead Saxon's battle-ax. He fetched the ax, then assumed a position next to Doyle. Was he ready? He made a split-second inspection of himself. His throat was dry and tight, and his hands, though weighted down with the weapons, shook. Time would never diminish these discomforts; they were as much a part of the battlefield as blood.

Doyle went reflexively into his quiver, withdrew an arrow, and nocked it deftly into his longbow. If he, too, was afraid, he concealed the emotion with the discipline of an abbot.

They stood and faced the horsemen galloping toward them. The Saxons probably thought they looked pathetic, an easy kill, Christopher thought.

He watched Doyle sight the lead Saxon and let his arrow fly.

But his friend had adjusted the arc wrong and the arrow fell short of its target.

"How did you miss?" Christopher asked.

"Hold your tongue!"

Christopher visualized a battle plan in his head. He decided which Saxon he would take first, then calculated where the others would wind up once he made his move.

Doyle nocked another arrow and pulled back ninety pounds of draw. "Now," he whispered to himself. The arrow pierced the air, made a gentle arc, then came down where Doyle wanted it: in the lead

Saxon's neck. The man fell right, and the reins of his charging rounsey slipped from his grip. Startled and unguided, the animal bucked and cut right, crashed into the Saxon horseman next to it. As the Saxon with the arrow in his neck careened onto the hard earth, he was followed by the other Saxon horseman, who slammed to the slope still astride his mount. The third Saxon, who was behind the first two, was not able to steer his rounsey clear of the fallen men and downed horse. Both rider and animal wailed as they made impact with their comrades.

Doyle winked at Christopher. The odds were even. The last two Saxons reined around the pileup and forged toward them.

Christopher reversed the weapons in his hands, put the broadsword in his left and the battle-ax in his right. He raised the ax, taking aim at one of the Saxons. "I have the right one!" he announced to Doyle.

In the corner of his eye, Christopher could see Doyle doing something, but he wasn't sure what. "Are you ready?"

Doyle's reply was a low grumble.

He fired a glance at Doyle. The archer was on his knees before the dead Saxon, trying to pull the arrow from the corpse's back. Doyle's empty quiver bobbed at his side.

Christopher felt the panic shudder up to his lips. "They're not going to wait for you."

Doyle looked up, his face creased with exertion. He groaned as he heaved, then fell back onto the short grass with the freed arrow in his grip.

Christopher returned his gaze to the Saxon on the right, drew in a deep breath, then let the battle-ax fly. The enemy soldier attempted to rein his rounsey away. The blade end of the ax found a home in the horse's neck. Christopher grimaced as the rounsey shrieked, then fell, throwing the Saxon. He heard the *fwit!* of Doyle's longbow, saw the remaining Saxon horseman clutch an arrow stuck in his leathered breast, then fall back off his ride.

The Saxon whose horse Christopher had struck got to his feet and unsheathed the spatha strapped to his belt. The man's beard stuck out in three distinct directions, inverted spikes that gave him a crazed look. His belly protruded from below his too-small gambeson, and his arms seemed to contain more fat than muscle; in either case, they were large. "Fight me, boy!" the man yelled in Saxon. He waved Christopher toward him with his sword.

"Throw your weapon down, otherwise my friend will put an arrow in your belly." Somewhere behind him, Christopher heard Doyle struggle to withdraw another arrow from another grounded horseman. "Do not make a liar of me, Doyle," he said over his shoulder.

"What are you talking about?" Doyle asked.

Instead of trying to translate for his friend, Christopher directed his attention to the Saxon. He noticed the man's surprise over hearing the Saxon language come out of a Celt. "You speak words I understand. How?"

"I once served a man who led Saxons. His name was Garrett."

"You must be Kenneth, his second-in-command," the Saxon guessed. "But why do you fight with Celts?"

Doyle arrived at Christopher's side with a bloody arrow nocked in his longbow. "Let's finish him and move on." Doyle drew back his bowstring.

Christopher reached out, seized the arrow. "No."

Resignedly, Doyle lowered his longbow as Christopher released his grip. "Why let him go? So he can join another army and fight us again?"

"Run!" Christopher told the Saxon.

"What are you saying?" Doyle asked.

The Saxon's actions answered Doyle's question.

The soldier turned and bolted toward the summit of the nearest mound. Doyle raised his bow and fired his arrow. The iron barb found the soft flesh of the Saxon's thigh beneath his breeches. The man wailed as honed metal penetrated his leg.

Christopher glared at Doyle.

Doyle returned a smirk. "Now at least he'll be our prisoner."

"I told you no!" Christopher felt a heat flush his cheeks.

"You might be squire of the body, but you don't have any say about what I, an archer, do."

"I asked you not to do it as a friend," Christopher said.

"You had no trouble killing Mallory at the tournament. And now you have no stomach for war? I worry about you, Christopher."

"You don't know what I think," Christopher shot back.

"Then tell me."

Beyond the injured Saxon, a blue banner, deviced with the Virgin Mary in white, rose above the highest slope. The king's mounted party of five appeared under the banner and descended the slope toward Doyle and Christopher. A hornsman, banner bearer, and Leslie and Teague, the junior squires, all accompanied the bronze-armored Arthur. After a moment, he came to a halt in front of the young men.

Arthur twisted off his dragon-crested helm, handed it to Leslie, then dismounted. On the ground, he drew Excalibur from its steel sheath at his side, turned, and marched toward the fallen Saxon. The invader stood and hobbled away from Arthur. The king ran up behind the Saxon, grabbed the injured man by his shoulder, and yanked him around. As Christopher flinched, Arthur gutted the man's heart with a swift, life-taking lunge. The king withdrew the crimson blade and handed it to Teague, who waited behind him with a rag. Arthur doffed his gauntlets and tucked them under an arm. He walked up to Christopher and stood a long moment, eyeing him stoically. Then he smacked Christopher across the face.

Though his cheek stung, Christopher was thankful Arthur had removed his gloves. He kept his gaze focused on the poleyns shielding the king's knees.

"My senior squire, squire of the body of all of England, leaves me alone on the battlefield." The king shook his head in disappointment.

"I beg your forgiveness, lord."

Christopher knew there would be a lot of explaining. He hoped he could make Arthur understand. He worried more about what Doyle would say. Why had his friend left the Vaward Battle group and become a rogue on the field?

Arthur turned his gaze on Doyle. "And what are you doing here, archer? Don't you belong in the Vaward?"

Christopher glanced over his shoulder. Doyle's gaze was lowered in shame, his lips fastened tightly. Christopher returned his attention to Arthur, saw the king nod to himself, as if he had already considered their fate and now agreed with his own decision. It was the most fearsome nod Christopher had ever seen.

The Best in Science Fiction and Fantasy

A FISHERMAN OF THE INLAND SEA by Ursula K. Le Guin. The National Book Award-winning author's first new collection in thirteen years has all the majesty and appeal of her major works. Here we have starships that sail, literally, on wings of song... musical instruments to be played at funerals only...*ansibles* for faster-than-light communication...orbiting arks designed to save a doomed humanity. Astonishing in their diversity and power, Le Guin's new stories exhibit both the artistry of a major writer at the height of her powers, and the humanity of a mature artist confronting the world with her gift of wonder still intact.

Hardcover, 0-06-105200-0 — $19.99

L OVE IN VEIN: TWENTY ORIGINAL TALES OF VAMPIRIC EROTICA, edited by Poppy Z. Brite. An all-original anthology that celebrates the unspeakable intimacies of vampirism, edited by the hottest new dark fantasy writer in contemporary literature. *LOVE IN VEIN* goes beyond our deepest fears and delves into our darkest hungers—the ones even our lovers are forbidden to share. This erotic vampire tribute is not for everyone. But then, neither is the night....

Trade paperback, 0-06-105312-0 — $11.99

A NTI-ICE by Stephen Baxter. From the bestselling author of the award-winning *RAFT* comes a hard-hitting SF thriller that highlights Baxter's unique blend of time travel and interstellar combat. *ANTI-ICE* gets back to SF fundamentals in a tale of discovery and challenge, and a race to success.

0-06-105421-6 — $5.50

Today . . .

☐HarperPrism

SMALL GODS by Terry Pratchett.
International bestseller Terry Pratchett brings
magic to life in his latest romp through Discworld, a
land where the unexpected always happens—usually to the
nicest people, like Brutha, former melon farmer, now The
Chosen One. His only question: Why?

0-06-109217-7 — $4.99

MAGIC: THE GATHERING™—ARENA
by William R. Forstchen. Based on the
wildly bestselling trading-card game, the first novel
in the *MAGIC: THE GATHERING™* novel series features wiz-
ards and warriors clashing in deadly battles. The book also
includes an offer for two free, unique MAGIC cards.

0-06-105424-0 — $4.99

SEAROAD:Chronicles of Klatsand by
Ursula K. Le Guin. Here is the culmination
of Le Guin's lifelong fascination with small island cul-
tures. In a sense, the Klatsand of these stories is a modern
day successor to her bestselling *ALWAYS COMING HOME*. A
world apart from our own, but part of it as well.

0-06-105400-3 -— $4.99

CALIBAN'S HOUR by Tad Williams. The
bestselling author of *TO GREEN ANGEL TOWER*
brings to life a rich and incandescent fantasy tale of
passion, betrayal, and death. The beast Caliban has been
searching for decades for Miranda, the woman he loved—the
woman who was taken from him by her father Prospero. Now
that Caliban has found her, he has an hour to tell his tale of
unrequited love and dark vengeance. And when the hour is
over, Miranda must die.... Tad Williams has reached a new
level of magic and emotion with this breathtaking tapestry in
which yearning and passion are entwined.

Hardcover, 0-06-105204-3 — $14.99

and Tomorrow

WRATH OF GOD by Robert Gleason. An apocalyptic novel of a future America about to fall under the rule of a murderous savage. Only a small group of survivors are left to fight — but they are joined by powerful forces from history when they learn how to open a hole in time. Three legendary heroes answer the call to the ultimate battle: George S. Patton, Amelia Earhart, and Stonewall Jackson. Add to that lineup a killer dinosaur and you have the most sweeping battle since *THE STAND*.
Trade paperback, 0-06-105311-2 — $14.99

THE X-FILES™ by Charles L. Grant. America's hottest new TV series launches as a book series with FBI agents Mulder and Scully investigating the cases no one else will touch — the cases in the file marked X. There is one thing they know: The truth is out there.
0-06-105414-3 — $4.99

THE WORLD OF DARKNESS™: VAMPIRE—DARK PRINCE by Keith Herber. The groundbreaking White Wolf role-playing game Vampire: The Masquerade is now featured in a chilling dark fantasy novel of a man trying to control the Beast within.
0-06-105422-4 — $4.99

THE UNAUTHORIZED TREKKERS' GUIDE TO *THE NEXT GENERATION* AND *DEEP SPACE NINE* by James Van Hise. This two-in-one guidebook contains all the information on the shows, the characters, the creators, the stories behind the episodes, and the voyages that landed on the cutting room floor.
0-06-105417-8 — $5.99

HarperPrism
An Imprint of HarperPaperbacks

PR-001

HarperPrism

MAGIC: THE GATHERING™ IS HOT!
Read all the books in the series!

MAGIC: The Gathering™ #1
Arena
by William R. Forstchen

Who is Garth One-eye? Where did he get his powerful spells? What is his interest in the fifth House? Why is the Grand Master of the Arena so afraid of what Garth might do? The answer may bring about the fall of the four houses—or Garth's death.

MAGIC: The Gathering™ #2
Whispering Woods
by Clayton Emery

Gull should have known better than to take the job as Wizard's Assistant. Between the brawls, the magical battles, and taking care of that strange *artifact* that turned up, a guy could barely find time to catch his breath!

And the novel adventures continue throughout 1995 with:

#3 *Shattered Chains*
by Clayton Emery

#4 *Final Sacrifice*
by Clayton Emery (May 1995)

**ORDER DIRECT FROM
HARPERPRISM AND BRING
THE MAGIC HOME!**